A Friendly Game of Murder

Other Books in the
Algonquin Round Table Mystery Series
by J. J. Murphy

Murder Your Darlings
You Might As Well Die

A Friendly Game of Murder

An Algonquin Round Table Mystery

J. J. Murphy

AN OBSIDIAN MYSTERY

OBSIDIAN
Published by New American Library, a division of
Penguin Group (USA) Inc., 375 Hudson Street,
New York, New York 10014, USA
Penguin Group (Canada), 90 Eglinton Avenue East, Suite 700, Toronto,
Ontario M4P 2Y3, Canada (a division of Pearson Penguin Canada Inc.)
Penguin Books Ltd., 80 Strand, London WC2R 0RL, England
Penguin Ireland, 25 St. Stephen's Green, Dublin 2,
Ireland (a division of Penguin Books Ltd.)
Penguin Group (Australia), 250 Camberwell Road, Camberwell, Victoria 3124,
Australia (a division of Pearson Australia Group Pty. Ltd.)
Penguin Books India Pvt. Ltd., 11 Community Centre, Panchsheel Park,
New Delhi - 110 017, India
Penguin Group (NZ), 67 Apollo Drive, Rosedale, Auckland 0632,
New Zealand (a division of Pearson New Zealand Ltd.)
Penguin Books (South Africa) (Pty.) Ltd., 24 Sturdee Avenue,
Rosebank, Johannesburg 2196, South Africa

Penguin Books Ltd., Registered Offices:
80 Strand, London WC2R 0RL, England

First published by Obsidian, an imprint of New American Library,
a division of Penguin Group (USA) Inc.

PUBLISHER'S NOTE
This is a work of fiction. Names, characters, places, and incidents either are the
product of the author's imagination or are used fictitiously, and any resemblance
to actual persons, living or dead, business establishments, events, or locales is
entirely coincidental.
　　The publisher does not have any control over and does not assume any respon-
sibility for author or third-party Web sites or their content.

ISBN: 978-1-62490-045-7

To Mom and Pop

Violence does, in truth, recoil upon the violent, and the schemer falls into the pit which he digs for another.

—Sherlock Holmes in "The Adventure of the Speckled Band," by Sir Arthur Conan Doyle

Author's Note

Dorothy Parker reportedly said, "I don't care what is written about me so long as it isn't true." Following her advice, this book is almost entirely a work of fiction, even though it is populated with many real people. The members of the Algonquin Round Table never seemed to let the truth get in the way of telling a good story—and I hope you won't let it get in the way of enjoying this one.

PREFACE

In the 1920s, there was no Internet, no wireless phones, no satellite TV. Even radio wasn't commonplace until the later twenties. Instead of writing text messages and e-mail, people sent telegrams or employed messenger boys. For music at home, they listened to a Victrola or sang around a piano.

For entertainment, New Yorkers had dozens of theaters in which to see plays and a number of movie palaces where they could see silent films. ("Talkies" didn't arrive until the later twenties.)

For information, New Yorkers lacked twenty-four-hour cable news networks. But they did have a dozen daily newspapers to choose from. Presses ran day and night, and printed morning editions, afternoon editions and special editions ("Extra! Extra! Read all about it!").

At this time, the people who wrote the news also became the news. An upstart class of writers, editors and critics emerged. A loose-knit group of ten—and their assorted friends—gathered around a large table for lunch at the Algonquin Hotel. They went to the Algonquin because it welcomed artists and writers—and because it was convenient and inexpensive. Their daily lunch gatherings were known more for wisecracks and witticisms than for the food they ate. But they buoyed one another with merriment and camaraderie. They thought the fun would never end.

Chapter 1

"Mrs. Parker," said Alexander Woollcott, "how about a friendly little game of Murder?"

Dorothy Parker pretended she didn't hear him. Woollcott was a fellow member of the Algonquin Round Table and the drama critic for the *New York Times*. He was also a pompous, paunchy pain in the neck sometimes.

Dorothy was preoccupied anyway. She and Woollcott stood at one end of the crowded lobby of the Algonquin Hotel. Her eyes turned again to the massive grandfather clock to check the time. Normally the lobby wasn't quite so busy and boisterous at eight o'clock on a Saturday night — but this wasn't an ordinary Saturday night. The crowd was elbow to elbow. The tinkling laughter of elegant ladies in glittering gowns mingled with the low chuckles of dapper men in their crisp white shirts, black ties and tails. The air was rich with the intoxicating scents of cigarette smoke and expensive perfume. Most of these people were here for the big party.

Now, where is that hound Robert Benchley? Dorothy wondered for the umpteenth time.

"Please, Mrs. Parker, I beseech you," Woollcott said, like a fly buzzing in her ear. "Murder would simply be no fun without you."

1

Mildly alarmed at this, a tall, burly man who stood just a few feet from Dorothy turned toward them. Dorothy returned his glance to reassure him all was fine. He was an older gentleman, in his sixties, with a bushy walrus mustache and sagging, intelligent eyes. He looked vaguely familiar to Dorothy, but she knew she had never met him.

"Mrs. Parker, please!" Woollcott commanded. "One little murder is all I'm asking—"

"Fine," she said, cocking her fingers at him like a pistol. "Bang, you're dead. Game over. Have a nice night."

Woollcott sighed, exasperated. "It's not just any old night, dear Dottie," he said. "It's New Year's Eve. Where is your sense of fun?"

"It was beaten to death by my sense of taste. And I find your detective game to be distasteful. I'd rather play something else. Russian roulette comes to mind at the moment."

Through his round, owl-like spectacles, Woollcott's dark beady eyes examined her. "What's got your knickers in a pinch?"

She glanced at the grandfather clock again. It was now just after eight. *Benchley should have arrived half an hour ago. He'd better not stand me up.*

"Well?" Woollcott said, and repeated his question about her knickers.

"My knickers are perfectly fine, thank you. It's you and everyone else who's in a twist," she said, as much to herself as to him. "Why is it that everyone insists on making such a big deal out of New Year's Eve? Everyone's in such a lather to have so much fun that the evening ceases to be enjoyable and starts to become one long, tedious chore."

Irked, Woollcott turned on his heel and stormed away; he nearly collided with the large gent with the walrus mustache.

Dorothy checked the clock again, but the minute hand hadn't moved. *Would Benchley stay at home in the suburbs with his wife and family? Or would he come into the city, as*

2

he said he would, for the party? Dorothy had bought a new dress, even though she didn't have the money to pay for it. Its forest-green velvet complimented her deep brown eyes. She toyed with the long strand of faux pearls around her neck.

What's the point? she wondered morosely. Even if Benchley did show up, he wouldn't notice.

A gaunt, white-haired man with gold-framed glasses had joined the big man with the walrus mustache. The two old men shook hands as if they hadn't seen one another in years—decades, maybe.

Out of the crowd appeared the hotel's suave manager, Frank Case. He gave Dorothy a wink and then approached the two distinguished-looking men. Dorothy noticed a yellow telegram envelope in Case's hand.

"Forgive my intrusion, gentlemen," Case said, and turned to the thin, white-haired man. "Dr. Hurst, thank you again for taking the time to examine that family, even though you're here as a guest. So, may I inquire about your diagnosis?"

The white-haired man—Dr. Hurst—spoke with an arrogant authority. "Chicken pox. Keep them confined to their room for the time being." He had a gruff, clipped British accent that reminded Dorothy of military drill instructors or stern schoolmasters.

Case smiled deferentially. "Thank you for relieving our concerns, Doctor." Case turned to the burly man with the walrus mustache. "I feared it might be smallpox. That is, it looked like smallpox to my untrained eye."

"Smallpox?" said the man. He spoke with a soft Scottish accent. "An unfortunate way to enter the new year. I wish them a rapid recovery."

"I will pass your concerns to the aggrieved family, Sir Arthur," Case said to the big man. "I hope you enjoy your evening with us. Nice to finally meet you."

Sir Arthur? Dorothy wondered.

3

"Very kind of you, but I'm only here for a quick cigar with my old colleague," said Sir Arthur, as he heartily slapped Dr. Hurst's bony shoulder. "Haven't seen each other in ages."

Case smiled genially and turned back to Dr. Hurst. "A telegram arrived for you while you were attending to the family with chicken pox." He handed Dr. Hurst the envelope with a polite little bow and excused himself.

Her tiny feet scampering to catch up, Dorothy followed after him.

"Frank!" she said when they were out of earshot of the two older men.

Case turned around. "Good evening, Mrs. Parker! How are you this wonderful New Year's Eve?"

"Annoyed, thank you very much," she said. "Who was that you were just talking to?"

Case raised his eyebrows. "Ah, that's Dr. Quentin Hurst. Not much of a bedside manner, apparently, but highly respected in the medical field. He's in town for a medical conference."

"No, not that old coot," she said. "The big fellow next to him. He looks so familiar."

"That 'big fellow,'" Case said, "is none other than Sir Arthur Conan Doyle, creator of Sherlock Holmes."

Dorothy let out a low whistle. She turned to have another look. Sir Arthur Conan Doyle was saying something; his walrus mustache fluttered as he spoke. But Dr. Hurst didn't appear to be listening. He had turned slightly away from Doyle, and his eyes were fixed on the telegram. His pale complexion had turned even paler. His hands were clenched on the paper as if he might suddenly tear it to pieces.

Doyle stopped speaking. He laid a concerned hand on Dr. Hurst's arm and appeared to ask whether everything was all right.

Dr. Hurst shrugged off Doyle's hand. He looked up from

4

the telegram and eyed the crowded room. He spotted Frank Case and hurried over with a determined look in his keen old eyes.

"Mr. Case, I was just consulting with my medical colleague Dr. Doyle, and I may have been too hasty in my diagnosis," Dr. Hurst said. "Upon further reflection, I do think that family has smallpox, not chicken pox."

"Smallpox? You can't be serious," Dorothy said. She turned to Case. "You'd have to close down the whole hotel!"

Case leaned toward her and spoke under his breath. "Not quite so loud, please, Mrs. Parker."

Dr. Hurst nodded his old head. "The young lady is right, Mr. Case. You will have to institute a quarantine immediately for the entire hotel."

By this time, Doyle had sauntered over and joined them. "Quarantine? A moment ago you said chicken pox, old boy."

"I've revised my diagnosis," Dr. Hurst said with that air of arrogance. "Better safe than sorry."

Why don't they agree? Dorothy wondered. She cast an eye at the telegram. When she looked up, she found that she had met Doyle's gaze. They had both been looking at the telegram.

Doyle quickly collected himself and turned to Case. "I mean no offense, sir, but I would rather not be required to stay here for the next two or three days. My wife is lodged at the Biltmore, and I wish to rejoin her as soon as possible."

Dorothy sympathized with Doyle—because she was thinking of having to spend the entire evening without Benchley. "Not all the guests have arrived for Doug Fairbanks' party, Frank," she said. "Fairbanks will be crushed."

Case, unruffled, glanced from one person to the next.

Dr. Hurst stepped forward and stood nose to nose with him. "I insist that you shut that door immediately, Mr. Case."

Doyle smiled amiably, trying to keep the peace. "Now, now, Quentin, old boy. Let's not be too hasty."

Dr. Hurst ignored these protests and stared threateningly at Case. "I'll call the police and the Ministry of Health myself, if I must."

Dorothy could see that Case was not about to argue the point. "That's not necessary, Dr. Hurst," Case said calmly. He moved toward the hotel's entryway. Dr. Hurst followed him.

Case raised his voice above the din. "I have an announcement to make, everyone!" The noise in the crowded lobby decreased from uproarious clamor to murmurous chatter. Dr. Hurst's somber presence next to him conferred a sense of solemnity. "The Algonquin has just been quarantined. From this moment no one will enter and no one will leave the hotel."

The mood of the crowd transformed from merry to malevolent. Dorothy was dejected. Suddenly Woollcott was again by her side and gripping her elbow.

"What's going on?" he asked.

She turned to him. "Count me in for your game of Murder. If I have to face this night without Mr. Benchley, I'm going to kill somebody."

Frank Case raised his hands in an attempt to quiet the crowd. "As required, I shall inform the Department of Health, and they will insist—and Dr. Hurst here agrees—that in the interest of safety we must quarantine the hotel." A fresh wave of moans and jeers answered this. Case glanced toward Doyle. "Now, fear not, we will make your stay—whether or not you intended to be our guests tonight—as enjoyable and comfortable as possible. But for the time being these doors will remain closed."

As Case was saying this, the doors opened and a stunning young woman strolled in. She was wrapped in furs, with a matching fur hat. A long feather bobbed from the hat as she walked. She stopped just inside the lobby, because everyone's eyes were on her. She seemed to revel in this attention. She flung off the furs and revealed a short, skimpy flapper's dress barely covering her tall, shapely figure.

"Bibi's here!" the woman announced with a dazzling smile and her arms raised over her head. "Let the party begin!"

Several men cheered.

Dorothy, like Woollcott and the others, recognized the flashy young woman. She was Bibi Bibelot, currently the most popular young starlet on Broadway.

Case tried to raise his voice over the cheers. "Miss, you cannot come in. We're in quarantine."

"I don't care if you're in quicksand," Bibi chuckled. "I'm here for Doug Fairbanks' New Year's Eve bash!" And, dragging her furs behind, she pranced on high heels into the midst of the crowd. Woollcott, almost literally riding on her coattails, followed after her.

Case shrugged. Not much could disrupt his cool demeanor. "As I was saying, from henceforth no one shall be admitted in or out—"

Then Robert Benchley came through the doors. He shook the snow off his hat and dusted it from the shoulders of his coat. Then he looked up to see the entire crowd in the lobby staring at him.

"Hello there," he said to the crowd as his mirthful eyes creased. "Did someone call for a plumber?"

Dr. Hurst grabbed Frank Case's arm and shouted in his ear, "Lock those doors!"

Dorothy rushed up to Benchley. She was so happy to see him, she could just hug him. But she stopped herself. Maybe she'd simply give him a peck on the cheek—at midnight.

"Hello, Mrs. Parker," he said. "What fresh hell is this?"

"That's my line!" She smiled and gently squeezed his arm. "But I'll lend it to you for now, because I certainly am glad to see you."

"The feeling is mutual, my dear Mrs. Parker," he said, and smiled in return.

The feeling is mutual? she thought. *If he only knew!*

"So, what's the hullabaloo?" he asked, taking off his coat.

She nodded toward the white-haired man. "That venerable doctor recently examined a family of tourists staying here. He determined they have smallpox. So Frank Case has just declared a quarantine of the whole hotel."

Case and Dr. Hurst rushed past them, followed by Alfred, the uniformed employee who manned the front desk. Alfred had a ring of keys. He selected one key without looking, slid it smoothly into the keyhole and locked the doors with a decisive clack.

Case turned to Dr. Hurst. "The Health Department will be here soon with an official notice and a seal for the door. Is that satisfactory?"

Dr. Hurst tested the door himself. It didn't budge. "Yes, fine, fine," he said dismissively. "By the way, do you have a safe in which guests may keep valuables?"

For the first time, Case looked put out. "Yes, but it's broken. I entrust our valuables to Oscar."

"Who the devil is Oscar?" Dr. Hurst fumed.

"Our doorman. A large and eminently trustworthy fellow."

"Fine, fine." Dr. Hurst dug into his jacket pocket and brought out a silver locket. "This item is extremely important. Please give it to him immediately."

"I can't."

"Why ever not?"

"We've just locked him outside," Case said simply.

Dr. Hurst shoved the locket back into his pocket, turned and charged off in a huff. He muttered over his shoulder to Doyle, "Come on. You can telephone your wife from my room."

Dorothy stood on tiptoes to whisper in Benchley's ear. "That's Arthur Conan Doyle—*Sir Arthur* to peasants like you and me. Let's go pull his whiskers."

8

She and Benchley followed Dr. Hurst and Doyle to the small elevator. Bibi Bibelot was already inside, as was Maurice, the greasy old elevator operator.

Bibi twisted in the tight space and turned her beautiful body and her big bright eyes on Dr. Hurst. "How long will the quarantine last?" she asked him breathlessly. Dorothy wondered how Bibi could make a question about smallpox sound sexy, but somehow she did.

Dr. Hurst appeared immune to Bibi's allure. He stared straight ahead at nothing. "Could be forty-eight hours. Could be two weeks."

"Well, that's okay, then," Bibi cooed. "Fairbanks' New Year's Eve party could very well last that long!"

Dr. Hurst didn't answer. Bibi eyed him up and down. Dorothy knew that expression—it was the look of an unabashed gold digger.

Maurice closed the elevator door, threw a switch and pulled a control lever. The elevator lurched slowly upward.

Dorothy stood behind Benchley's elbow and in front of Doyle's barrel chest. Doyle cleared his throat and broke the awkward silence to address Dorothy.

"Forgive my curiosity, miss, but did I hear you and a colleague discussing a murder?"

Miss! She liked Doyle right away. She would have stepped on his foot if he had said *madam*.

"Not a real murder," Dorothy said to Doyle. "It's a silly party game. We put slips of paper into a hat. One slip is for the detective, one is for the murderer. Everyone else is a potential victim. The person who pulls out the murderer slip pretends to kill someone. The detective, and everyone else, has to solve the murder. If anyone would enjoy such a game, you would."

"Me?" Doyle asked. "Why me?"

Dorothy was momentarily taken aback. "Because you wrote all those Sherlock Holmes stories, of course."

"Hell's bells!" Bibi cried. "You wrote Sherlock Holmes?"

9

"Not in years," Doyle said sullenly. "I've grown weary of that name."

Bibi took no notice of Doyle's sour change in mood. "When we were kids, my brother could not stop reading your silly little detective stories. You must be rich and famous."

"I too am quite an admirer of Holmes," Benchley said sincerely.

But at the mention of the name *Sherlock Holmes*, Conan Doyle's eyes had clouded over. He didn't answer.

Dr. Hurst snorted. He turned and spoke to Doyle as though they were alone. "I've a new attendant. He can pour us some sherries while you make your phone call."

Cripes, thought Dorothy, *one little mention of Sherlock Holmes and they get their noses out of joint?*

She and Benchley exchanged a look. Now Benchley cleared his throat. "So, how do you two gents know each other?"

Dr. Hurst responded curtly, never looking at Benchley. "Medical school. University of Edinburgh."

"Ah, medical school," Benchley said thoughtfully, and turned to Dorothy. "And what school did you attend, Mrs. Parker?"

Benchley knew full well she hadn't even graduated from high school.

"Elementary, my dear Benchley," she said with a wry grin. "Elementary."

Chapter 2

Doyle looked at Dorothy and raised a bushy eyebrow.

The elevator stopped. "Ninth floor," croaked Maurice the elevator operator, and he pulled back the accordion gate and opened the door.

Dr. Hurst hurried out. Doyle followed with another curious glance over his shoulder at Dorothy. Maurice shut the door after the two men. The elevator moved upward.

Bibi turned to Dorothy with a salacious wink of her eye. "Did you hear that? A doctor! He must be loaded."

"Which one?" Dorothy replied. "They're both doctors."

"Either one," Bibi said with a devilish smile. "But I like the look of the old white-haired one. He probably has one foot in the grave already. And he wasn't wearing a wedding ring. The Sherlock Holmes fella was."

"You have amazing powers of observation," Dorothy said dryly.

Bibi nodded in agreement and with a hint of superiority. "I didn't make it to Broadway without brains."

Or a nice pair of knockers, Dorothy thought.

The elevator stopped again, at the top floor this time. "Twelfth floor. Penthouse suites," Maurice said, pulling open the gate. They heard laughter and chatter from the other end of the hall.

"Which way to the Fairbanks' suite?" Bibi asked Maurice condescendingly. "I'm attending their exclusive party."

Maurice looked down the short hallway. At the opposite end were wide-open double doors, and inside was a crowd of people having a party.

"Right there, lady," Maurice said, pointing a crooked finger.

Bibi gave a half glance over her shoulder at Benchley. "Tip him a nickel, would you? That's a good boy." And she sauntered toward the open doors.

Benchley shrugged, fished a coin out of his pocket and handed it to Maurice. Then he and Dorothy followed Bibi toward the Fairbanks' apartment.

Dorothy linked her arm through Benchley's. She was just happy to have him here. She didn't give a tinker's damn about snotty dopes like Bibi Bibelot. As frequent theatergoers, Dorothy and Benchley had seen Bibi on stage not long ago. Bibi had indeed made quite a sensation as the star of a hit comedy written by their friends and fellow Round Table–mates Marc Connelly and George Kaufman.

But despite the promising start to Bibi's career, a new starlet like her appeared on Broadway every fall. *They're like annual flowers, these girls,* Dorothy thought. By the end of spring, her glamour and luster would fade like petals, and she'd be swept aside when a newer, prettier one came along the next year.

Bibi paused at the suite's threshold and raised her arms in the air. "Bibi's here!" she announced as she had in the lobby. "Let the party begin!"

But unlike the cheering welcome she'd received in the lobby, the small gathering of people inside the suite generally ignored her. After a moment she dropped her arms in disappointment. "Where's the booze?" she asked no one in particular, and wandered in.

Dorothy and Benchley strolled in after her and immediately picked out the hosts, Douglas Fairbanks and his wife, Mary Pickford. They stood in the center of the suite's large parlor.

Now these are real stars, Dorothy thought.

Fairbanks was the most famous actor on Broadway as well as a box office smash in Hollywood. He was more fit than an Olympic athlete and more handsome than an Olympic god. But his success was also due to his magnetic charm, his boundless energy—and his relentless ambition to succeed.

Mary Pickford, known in the press as "America's Sweetheart," looked like a teenager, with a cherubic face and long blond curls streaming over her shoulders. Yet, Dorothy knew, she and Mary were about the same age. Indeed, Mary had been Hollywood's most popular and highest-paid actress for a full decade—back when Dorothy was still playing the piano at a dance school to eke out a living.

"Mrs. Parker! Mr. Benchley!" Fairbanks cried, grabbing Benchley's hand and shaking it like a maraca, then giving Dorothy a chaste smooch on the cheek. His neatly trimmed mustache tickled her skin. "How's tricks, kids?"

Despite their riches and fame, Fairbanks and Pickford were as down-to-earth as anyone she knew. Fairbanks was always ready to do a handstand or some acrobatic trick just for a laugh, and Mary was similarly quick to lend a sympathetic ear or a helping hand.

"We have good news and bad news," Benchley said.

Fairbanks and Pickford looked puzzled.

Dorothy said, "The good news is that your party may indeed last for days. The bad news is that it's because the hotel has been quarantined. So the people who are here now are all who are coming."

It took only another minute to explain the situation about the quarantine and the family with smallpox.

Fairbanks looked around at the sparse crowd in his living room. He was downcast, but only for a moment.

13

"Well," he said, his dazzling smile and optimism quickly reappearing, "that just means there's all the more fun for us!"

As he spoke, Case arrived and joined them. Case apologized to Fairbanks and Pickford for stifling their party. Dorothy was well aware that Case and Fairbanks had known each other a long time—years ago, Fairbanks might as well have been sleeping in Central Park if it hadn't been for the generosity of Frank Case. Nowadays Fairbanks could practically afford to buy Central Park.

"No problem, Frank," Fairbanks said. "Put the word out. Anyone and everyone in the hotel is welcome up to our party."

Mary nodded her agreement.

"That's extremely generous of you," Case said. "I'm sure many of our guests will be thrilled to hear it. I'll have the bellhops knock on every door."

"Mi casa es su casa," Fairbanks said cheerfully.

Case smiled politely. "Actually, the whole hotel is *mi casa*, but your point is understood. Now, I don't mean to hinder your party yet again, but you do know there is a Prohibition on," he said pointedly, looking at the half-full martini glass in Fairbanks' hand. "You have no liquor up here, right?"

Fairbanks quickly raised the glass to his lips and drained it dry.

"Nope, no liquor," he said. "Not a drop."

Within an hour, the suite had filled up with hotel guests from every floor. They were summoned to the party by Douglas Fairbanks' generous—and indiscriminate—invitation. *Every guest in the hotel must have come to this party*, Dorothy thought. She recognized hardly anyone. A few were longtime residents like her who made the hotel their home. But most of the partygoers were strangers—out-of-towners who were staying at the Algonquin for the holidays. There were loud, middle-aged men with louder

14

ties and cheap suits. Frivolous, overly excited women flocked together in tight clumps. In one corner, two nuns eyed the room warily and whispered only to each other. *What are they doing here?* Dorothy wondered. *Is this the clientele the hotel always attracts for the holidays?*

Few of the partygoers were the urbane characters — famous composers and musicians, clever newspapermen and magazine editors, amusing artists and illustrators — that Dorothy was used to seeing at these types of gatherings.

"It's like a convention of insurance adjusters and tax accountants," Alexander Woollcott complained.

But Dorothy didn't really care. She and Benchley and a few other members of the Algonquin Round Table were gathered in a close group. They had circled their wagons as though defending against a horde of attacking savages. The group included Woollcott and his close friend Harpo Marx. Also with them was Jane Grant, wife of Harold Ross. (Grant and Ross were desperately trying to get a new magazine, *The New Yorker*, off the ground.) The other member of their group was Ruth Hale, a "radical" feminist and wife to sportswriter Heywood Broun. Ross and Broun had both intended to join their wives for the party, but they had failed to arrive before Frank Case closed the hotel for the quarantine.

It was getting warm in the extremely crowded room. Jane Grant fanned herself with a magazine and sipped a gin and tonic. "How long do you suppose this lousy quarantine will last?" she asked.

Dorothy cast an eye sideways toward Dr. Hurst, who stood with Douglas Fairbanks just inside the door of his darkened bedroom. "Consult the venerable doctor himself. He's right over there, talking to Doug."

Jane glanced at the pair and then looked away. "Oh, never mind. I'm a free woman tonight. I should enjoy it, right?"

Dorothy didn't answer. Something about Dr. Hurst and

Fairbanks held her attention. They were conversing so secretively, and they stood so close that their heads were almost touching. Then Dr. Hurst pulled something out of his pocket. It glittered. Dorothy recognized it as the silver locket that Dr. Hurst had asked Frank Case to put into the hotel safe. Dr. Hurst carefully handed the locket to Fairbanks, who clasped it tightly and nodded his assurance.

Dorothy looked around the packed room. Had she been the only one to see this exchange? But, in surveying the crowd, Dorothy locked eyes with Bibi Bibelot, who winked at Dorothy. Bibi had seen the same thing. Bibi tilted her head toward Dr. Hurst and mouthed the word, *"Loaded!"* And then she winked again. Dorothy quickly turned her attention back to her friends.

Woollcott was saying, "Come on, my inveterate and not-yet-inebriated compatriots. Midnight is a full three hours away. Let us begin the game of Murder!"

Dorothy rolled her eyes, and in doing so, she noticed that Arthur Conan Doyle—Sir Arthur—was standing nearby. He looked as though he didn't know what to do with himself.

"Dr. Doyle!" she called to him. "Don't stand there all by yourself, alone and bored stiff. Come on over here and be bored stiff with us."

Woollcott puffed out his chest. "Bored stiff, are you, Mrs. Parker? Once we begin the game of Murder, you shan't be bored. Perhaps you'll be—murdered!"

"One can only hope," she said. By this point Doyle had joined their group. "Everybody, this is my pal Arthur. Arthur, this is everybody."

She didn't mention he was Sir Arthur Conan Doyle. And, curiously, Doyle didn't correct her.

"Woollcott insists we play a game of Murder," she said. "I mentioned it to you in the elevator."

"Quite so," Doyle said. "I confess I've not heard of this game."

"Save your confessions for St. Peter," Woollcott sneered, bringing forth an upturned top hat. "You may be meeting him before long," he added portentously.

Dorothy leaned toward Doyle. "Don't worry. This is Aleck's latest fad. He picks out a new one every few months. We often find that it's easier to just play along." She turned to Woollcott. "Aleck, perhaps you could explain the game of Murder to Arthur?"

"Most certainly," Woollcott said. "The game is devilishly simple—"

But before Woollcott could say more, the theatrical voice of Douglas Fairbanks filled the room. "Happy New Year's Eve, my dear friends—and my new friends!"

Everyone turned to look. Fairbanks stood at the center of the room with his arms extended like the ringmaster of a circus. Next to him was an attractive, well-dressed woman whom Dorothy recognized.

Fairbanks continued, using his voice with the power of a loudspeaker. "Allow me to introduce our favored guest—a woman who needs no introduction. The first lady of the Broadway stage and our lady of the evening . . . Lydia Trumbull!"

The woman next to Fairbanks made a theatrical curtsy.

"If she's a lady of the evening," Harpo Marx said under his breath, "then I'd demand a refund."

Lydia Trumbull may have been a young beauty at one point—perhaps a decade ago. And she was beautiful still, but now the actress was more likely to play Lady Macbeth than Juliet Capulet. Yet Lydia Trumbull—with her sleek black hair and frost-blue eyes—was probably no more than thirty (or at least not much more than thirty, Dorothy thought). But in addition to her timeless beauty, Lydia's age conferred a sense of accomplishment and hard-won wisdom. Then again, Lydia's flinty glamour also seemed somehow fragile, Dorothy thought, like a pillar of hard black granite that might very easily crack and break under sharp pressure.

Lydia opened her mouth to speak, but before she could say a word, a voice from the other side of the apartment shouted, "Hey, everybody! Let's get this party cooking!"

All eyes turned toward this interloper, and a collective gasp went up from the room. There, at the entrance to Fairbanks' bedroom, was Bibi Bibelot, naked as the day she was born.

"Now, *that's* a lady of the evening!" Harpo gasped.

Bibi Bibelot—nude and proud as a peacock—strutted forth. Now no one smirked. No one tittered or chuckled. And no one ignored her. Every eye was on Bibi.

Dorothy realized that the gorgeous young woman wasn't entirely naked. Bibi wore the high-heeled shoes she had arrived in. Also, she wore a brilliant, saucy smile to go with her bright blond bobbed hair.

A crash and a splash came from the front doors. Dorothy saw a young deliveryman standing there in his overalls. His eyes and his mouth were wide-open in amazement. His slack arms held an empty metal washtub. In front of the deliveryman's feet was a knee-high pile of ice cubes. Bibi gave the deliveryman a wicked wink. The crowd parted as she strolled across the room.

Dorothy couldn't help but evaluate the young woman's naked body—and she found little to criticize. She scrutinized Bibi's round and high breasts, her flat stomach and especially her long, long legs. Dorothy, a pretty but petite woman, couldn't staunch a pang of envy.

At her side, Benchley spoke, "Well, would you look at that. The curtains match the carpet."

Ready to snap at him for being so vulgar, Dorothy whirled on him.

But Benchley, ever the gentleman, had discreetly looked away from the naked form of Bibi, and was genteelly admiring the wall-to-wall carpeting and matching drapes.

Turning back to the center of the room, Dorothy watched

Bibi stroll right past Fairbanks and Lydia Trumbull. Lydia stared daggers at Bibi.

Then Dorothy saw Dr. Hurst stepping forward from a far corner of the room. His face had turned as white as his hair. His eyes bulged in dismay.

Dorothy followed Dr. Hurst's gaze, and as Bibi came closer, Dorothy saw something she somehow hadn't noticed before. Around her long, elegant neck, Bibi wore the sparkling silver locket that Dr. Hurst had so recently entrusted to Douglas Fairbanks.

Chapter 3

Bibi strolled slowly, tantalizingly, across the crowded parlor and toward the bathroom. Dorothy watched Bibi's pert backside amble away.

"What an ass," said Jane Grant, standing next to Dorothy.

"How do you mean that exactly?" Dorothy asked.

"I'd like to kick that cute little backside," Jane said sourly.

Jane Grant and her friend Ruth Hale were both members of the Lucy Stone League, a women's rights group that defended a wife's right to retain her maiden surname as her legal last name. Their husbands—Harold Ross and Heywood Broun—supported them. Or at least they didn't argue about it in public.

"That brainless girl," Ruth said. "What is she trying to pull? Who is she kidding?"

"Oh, I don't know," Dorothy said. "If I had a body like that, I'd strut it around for everyone to see. Why not? This is a party, after all—a New Year's Eve party at Doug Fairbanks' penthouse suite. Maybe someone like Bibi *should* prance around naked at such an occasion."

And if nothing else, Dorothy reasoned, *it'll make a good story to tell to the other members of the Round Table who didn't arrive before the quarantine.*

Jane shook her head. "Can you believe I helped create that Frankenstein's monster?"

Dorothy was surprised. "No, I can't believe it. How so?"

"I had to write an article about her a few months ago."

Jane Grant was the first and only woman reporter in the *New York Times'* city room. She eagerly sought and was usually assigned articles about important women's issues. But in return for that privilege, she sometimes had to write about far less important topics, Dorothy knew.

"Typical puff piece," Jane continued with a shrug. "Small-town girl makes it in the big city. Conquers Broadway with her siren's voice and one swipe of her glossy red fingernails. That kind of thing."

"Ah, and look at what you've done."

"Well, I can't take too much credit," Jane said defensively. "I was just the town crier spreading the news. Bibi had already done all the monster building. She was like that when I found her. She hatched out of the egg that way."

Ruth Hale clucked her tongue. "She had a stage mother pushing her, no doubt?"

"Actually, no," Jane said. "She had a brother or something somewhere, but no mother behind her. She did make a big deal about 'a rich benefactor,' as she called him."

"Rich benefactor?" Dorothy asked. "Who is it?"

"No idea," Jane said. "Bibi made a big deal about that, too. Had to keep him a secret, or every new Broadway starlet would be after him, she said. Her 'guardian angel,' she called him."

"Angel, ha!" Ruth clucked her tongue again. "Probably some drooling old sugar daddy."

They watched as a parade of people followed Bibi to the bathroom. Dorothy could just barely see through the crowd to make out what was going on. Bibi kicked off her high heels, which skittered across the polished tile floor.

"Where's that sinful case of champagne I saw somewhere?" Bibi asked in a sultry voice. She pointed a slender finger at a fat, middle-aged man. "You, baby boy, go get that bubbly. Fill up this tub." She touched her toe against the elegant, bone-white claw-foot bathtub. The man turned and ran, leaving behind his flabbergasted wife.

Bibi then pointed her finger at a tall young man. "You, sugar, get a ladle from the kitchen. A big one." She barely finished speaking before the man turned and scrambled through the crowd.

The fat man returned with a wooden case of champagne, which held a dozen bottles. He was followed by three more men, each carrying a similar case. In moments, he and the other men had opened the bottles and dumped the champagne into the tub. The tall man returned from the kitchen and handed Bibi a large metal soup ladle.

She raised it over her head like a naked queen making a royal proclamation. With a wild, wicked smile, she cried, "Everyone, drinks are on me!"

Then she stepped into the tub and slid into the glistening bath of effervescent wine. The onlookers—mostly men but some women, too—cheered and clapped.

Bibi luxuriated in the bathtub. She lifted handfuls of the champagne and cascaded it over her naked body. Then she held up the ladle, full to the brim with the sparkling liquid.

"So, who wants a wee little drink?" Bibi shouted. The partygoers roared, and the crowd surged forward. Dorothy momentarily lost her view.

Benchley turned to Dorothy. "I think instead I'll sample what the bar—now unoccupied—has to offer. Would you care for a refill, Mrs. Parker?"

Dorothy handed him her highball glass, and Benchley moved through the crowd to the sideboard, which was in use as a bar. But it wasn't completely unoccupied, as Benchley had said. Dr. Hurst stood there. The old man angrily grabbed the nearest bottle and splashed whiskey into a shot glass. He slammed down the bottle, snatched up the shot glass and gulped the drink back with a vengeance.

Then two large figures dressed all in black brushed by Dorothy and nearly knocked her aside.

Dorothy turned to look and was surprised to see two heavyset nuns hurrying toward the bathroom with the backs of their black habits and veils flapping behind them. Dorothy couldn't see their faces, but she could hear their voices.

"Pardon us, please!" the first one said gruffly, shouldering through the crowd.

"Heavens above, excuse us!" the second one added.

The nuns created a stir as they reached the jam-packed door to the bathroom.

"Oh no, Bibi," one leering man jeered. "You're in big trouble now!"

"You've angered the Man Upstairs," laughed another.

Dorothy heard Bibi answer in a condescending tone, "This is the penthouse, dummy. Don't you know what a penthouse is? There is no man upstairs."

Dorothy shook her head in dismay. But still her curiosity took over, so she moved closer to the bathroom to get a better look.

"Young lady!" The first nun squeezed into the bathroom and waved a nervous hand at Bibi. "Step out of that infernal bathtub right this very moment."

"Bless you, child," the second nun pleaded. "But please get out and cover up your shame."

Dorothy couldn't resist. Before she could stop herself, she called out, "Don't worry yourselves, sisters. That girl has no shame."

Angry eyes—including the nuns'—turned in Dorothy's direction. Dorothy didn't like the nuns looking at her like that—judging her, disdaining her. She was about to let another insult fly at them, but they turned away at the sound of Dr. Hurst's angry voice.

"Stop there!" Dr. Hurst charged forward. "Young lady, this is intolerable! Get out of there this instant."

A leering man stood in Dr. Hurst's way. "Come on, gramps. Don't ruin the party for the rest of us."

Dr. Hurst gave him a superior look. "I'm a doctor." Then to Bibi he called out, "Get out of that bathtub immediately, I insist."

Another man now blocked Dr. Hurst's way. "Leave the gal alone, old-timer. We just want to have a good time here. What's the matter with that?"

Dr. Hurst sputtered, trying in his outrage to form a coherent sentence. "It's—it's unsanitary, that's what." He grabbed the man's drink and threw it to the ground. The glass shattered at the man's feet.

"Why, you—!" the man growled, ready to throw a punch.

The second nun grabbed the man's arm. "Stop this, please. The doctor is right. And it's not only unsanitary, it's sinful. You should all be ashamed."

The crowd in and around the bathroom was stirring into a mob scene, ready to break out into a riot, Dorothy thought.

And where the hell is Benchley with my drink? she wondered, looking around the room.

From the center of the parlor, Doug Fairbanks squared his shoulders and prepared to intervene. Next to him, Lydia Trumbull seemed on the verge of tears as well as rage. She had clearly been humiliated that Bibi—a younger, "hotter" actress—had stolen her spotlight. This was supposed to have been Lydia's night, after all.

Several paces behind Lydia stood Mary. She too had a troubled look, anxiety mixed with despair, on her cherubic face. Could this be simply the hostess' reaction to a party going quickly out of control? Dorothy didn't think so. Something else was worrying Mary.

Bibi shouted from the tub, "Okay, you gorillas, you can stop all that monkey business! Let the sweet old boy in. I'll lend him an ear—and anything else he wants."

24

Dorothy couldn't imagine anyone thinking of Dr. Hurst as a "sweet old boy." But then she remembered what that conniving Bibi had said about him: *He must be loaded!*

Like snarling guard dogs pulled by their leashes, the two men at the door begrudgingly stepped back and let Dr. Hurst enter the bathroom. The nuns moved aside as well.

"Well, hello there," Bibi trilled playfully. "Remember me from the elevator?" Then her voice dropped into a naughty tone. "Are you here to give me an examination, Doctor? Or perhaps I'm due for a shot?" Then she held up the liquor-filled ladle. "Or maybe *you'd* like a shot? How about I make it a double?"

Dr. Hurst turned to the few onlookers standing in the bathroom. "Get out," he growled, barely looking at them. "Now."

The partygoers grumbled and filed out of the room. The nuns, however, wouldn't leave so easily. They insisted they should stay in the room as chaperones for the sake of Bibi's modesty and personal safety.

"You leave the modesty to me, sisters," Bibi said, happily waving them out. Dr. Hurst put his narrow shoulder against the door and used it to push the stout nuns back into the parlor. The nuns stood looking at the closed door.

Benchley finally returned and handed Dorothy a half-full glass of scotch.

"Whatever is he doing in there?" he asked, indicating the bathroom door.

"Joining her in a drink, perhaps," she said, clinking glasses with Benchley and taking a sip of her scotch.

In a few moments, though, shouting could be heard from inside the bathroom. The words were indistinct, but the tones were clear. It was Dr. Hurst's voice yelling some kind of order or demand, followed by Bibi's petulant, derisive refusal.

The first nun hurried back to the door and grabbed the knob. "It's locked. Somebody call the manager!"

Doug Fairbanks sauntered over to the older nun. "There's no need to get upset, my dear sister. We have a key around here somewhere. Just give me a moment to find it." He called across the crowded room to his wife. "Mary, darling, do you know where the bathroom key is?"

Mary muttered something about a kitchen drawer, then turned and stormed into her bedroom. Fairbanks followed after her with a puzzled look on his face.

"Somebody should do something," Dorothy said, mostly to herself. She scanned the room for Arthur Conan Doyle. Eventually she spotted him—cornered by old Mrs. Volney, who was probably needling him with medical questions and likely informing him in detail of her many complaints. Mrs. Volney lived down the hall from Dorothy, and Dorothy studiously avoided the prickly old spinster.

"Just in time," she said to Benchley. "The poor dear is being hounded—hounded by old Lady Baskerville."

Dorothy met Doyle's eyes and beckoned him over. Doyle quickly excused himself from Mrs. Volney and made his way to Dorothy and Benchley.

"Ah," Doyle said politely, though he was clearly relieved to be rid of the lady. "What tenacity your fellow Americans have, even the older Americans. Such determination. It's almost enough to try a man's patience."

Dorothy nodded. She understood perfectly. "There's something else we'd like you to try instead."

"At your service, miss." Doyle nodded and made a courtly, old-fashioned little bow. "You know, we never were properly introduced."

Miss! What a terrific old man. She hated to correct him.

"It's *Mrs.*, actually," she said. "Mrs. Parker. And this is Mr. Benchley, if we want to put a label on everything."

"Lovely to make your acquaintance properly, Mrs. Parker and Mr. Benchley. Now, what is it that I can do for you?"

"Do you hear that yelling and screaming coming from

26

yonder bathroom?" she asked. "That's your pal Dr. Hurst. Do you think you might be able to settle him down and open up that door before he bursts a blood vessel—or bursts that naked girl's noggin?"

"Oh dear, now I hear it," Doyle said, his gregarious expression falling. "I'm a little hard of hearing in this ear. But never mind that. I'll go and have a sharp word with my old friend Quentin. He knows I won't stand for such unmanly behavior. That's no way to talk to a lady."

"Don't worry," Dorothy muttered. "That gal's no lady."

Doyle didn't seem to hear her. He had already lowered his brow and stalked off toward the bathroom. But before he reached the door, it suddenly swung open, and Dr. Hurst came hurrying out with one hand shoved inside his jacket pocket. He darted right past Doyle, who spun around after him.

"Quentin, old boy!" Doyle exclaimed. "What's the meaning of this?"

Dr. Hurst ignored him and made a straight line to the bar, where he again grabbed the whiskey bottle. Dorothy thought she saw a fierce, triumphant smirk on the old man's face.

What was that all about? Dorothy glanced toward the bathroom. She could see that Bibi was still in the tub and kicking up a little sparkling splash with one long, lovely leg.

"All's well, everybody," Bibi trilled, waving the ladle. "Anyone thinkie you need a little drinkie?"

The nearby partygoers jumped at this suggestion. They swarmed back into the bathroom and clamored for another sip poured from Bibi's ladle. Meanwhile, the two nuns tried to enter the crowded room and continued to urge Bibi to get out of the tub.

"Don't worry, sisters," Bibi said to them with an impish laugh. "I'm just having a little good clean fun."

Everyone seemed to ignore the nuns after this.

Dorothy glanced at the bar. Doyle was talking to Dr.

27

Hurst and questioning him. But Dr. Hurst ignored Doyle and focused instead on a glass of whiskey.

From the other side of the parlor, Mary Pickford, followed by her husband, came out of the bedroom. Fairbanks seemed to be pleading with her about something. Mary stormed right past Dorothy, who could see the tears in Mary's eyes.

Dorothy grabbed Fairbanks' arm. "What's wrong with Mary?" she asked gently.

Fairbanks stopped. His wife continued on to the kitchen, shoved open the swinging door and disappeared inside.

"Aw, she thinks I had something to do with that girl in there." Fairbanks waved a hand at the bathroom.

Dorothy leaned toward him. "*Did* you have something to do with that girl in there?"

"Heck, no." Fairbanks frowned. "I told Mary that, but she won't listen. She just got more steamed."

"Lot of that going around." Dorothy nodded in the direction of Lydia Trumbull, who stood where Fairbanks had left her. And Lydia still stared angrily at Bibi in the bathtub. "Leave Mary alone for now. In the meantime, why don't you go see what you can do for Lydia? I'll talk to Mary in a little while, once she settles down. Okay?"

Fairbanks nodded and strolled over to Lydia.

Benchley, who had been standing nearby the whole time, took a step closer to Dorothy. "What was all that about?"

She didn't answer him directly. "Have you noticed that if you put a naked woman into a crowded room, the men go crazy—"

"But the women go crazier?" he said, finishing her thought. She nodded and patted his arm.

Fairbanks made an announcement. "All right, folks. Let's liven this party up. How about a song from Lydia? What do you say?"

There was a smattering of applause. Fairbanks walked Lydia over to an upright piano—a player piano. He fiddled with it a moment and soon the piano started playing a loud, jaunty tune.

Lydia sang along in a clear, lilting voice, *"In the morning . . . in the evening . . . ain't we got fun. . . ."*

"Not yet, we don't," groused Woollcott, suddenly standing by Dorothy. "Come gather 'round, children. It's time for Murder."

Chapter 4

W oollcott shepherded them toward an empty corner of the room and away from the music.

"Follow me, little lambs," he said. "The carnage will commence shortly."

Dorothy and Benchley followed. After them came Harpo, Jane and Ruth.

Woollcott looked everyone over. "A pitiful shame that many of the usual members of our group couldn't join us here tonight. Well, that's their loss."

Dorothy thought the same thing. Then she spotted Doyle standing by himself again, looking isolated and irritated. Just a few paces away stood Dr. Hurst at the bar; he was getting angrily and progressively drunk. Doyle appeared to be distancing himself from his old friend.

"I'll be right back," Dorothy said to Woollcott.

She went over to Doyle and grabbed him by the sleeve. "Come on, Artie. If your old pal wants nothing to do with you, then come have fun with some new pals."

Doyle went along with her. He smiled gamely. "So I shall. And gladly."

They rejoined the group. Woollcott eyed Doyle. "Ah, another lamb for the slaughter. Welcome again, Arnold."

Dorothy chuckled. "His name is Arthur." She winked at Doyle and wondered to herself, *Now, how is Aleck going to react when someone lets him know that this old gent is perhaps the most famous author in the world?* She couldn't wait to find out. But now was not yet the time to tell Woollcott.

"Yes, well, *Arthur*," Woollcott continued, "you may need instruction on this devilish little game of ours. You'll be pleased to know that it is actually quite simple. There is a murderer and there is a detective. Everyone else is a potential victim or a suspect."

Doyle nodded. "And, as Mrs. Parker informed me, the murderer and detective are chosen by pulling slips of paper out of a hat?"

"Precisely." Woollcott snatched his top hat off the head of Harpo Marx, who had somehow put it on. "I'll take that now, my moronic friend." Then he dipped his chubby hand in his jacket pocket and withdrew a wad of paper slips. He dropped these into the upturned top hat. "We all draw from the hat. Whoever selects the detective slip announces it to the group." He looked sidelong from one person to the other. "But whoever draws the murderer slip must keep it secret."

Doyle asked, "How exactly does the murderer … commit murder?"

"A worthy question, my portly friend," Woollcott said, drumming his fingers on his own big belly. "After we draw the slips, we disperse to our previous diversions and discussions, resuming our frivolity in the party as though this game is not even taking place."

"But of course it is?" Doyle said, more a statement than a question.

"Most certainly it is, Arthur, old boy." Woollcott smiled deviously. "While we interlocute and imbibe with the other party guests, we also surreptitiously play the game, always on the lookout for the murderer."

31

"And what is he doing in the meanwhile?" Doyle asked.

"He or *she*—we do not discriminate in the gender of our murderers on this side of the Atlantic, old duck," Woollcott scolded. "The object of our murderer is to secure one of us alone and point to that victim and declare: 'You are dead.'"

Doyle raised his bushy eyebrows. "So it's an elaborate game of tag, is it?"

Woollcott sighed. "Isn't it all an elaborate game? Isn't this fancy party just a gathering of whelps in a schoolyard? Isn't the New York Stock Exchange just an elaborate form of bartering wampum? Isn't the U.S. presidency just an elaborate form of king of the hill? I put it to you, dear Arthur, that we are always nothing but children playing schoolyard games."

Doyle's hackles rose at this. "My good sir, you go too far—"

Dorothy intervened. "Going too far—that's the story of Woollcott's life, Artie." She turned to Woollcott. "Enough woolgathering, Aleck. Just get back to explaining the game."

"Quite right, Mrs. Parker," Woollcott said. "Where was I? Oh yes. At some point the murderer must be alone with his or her intended victim, tell the victim that he or she has been murdered, and then—vamoose! This leaves the deceased victim exactly where the murderer encountered this unfortunate person. And there the victim must stay until found."

"So much for the unfortunate victim," Doyle said. "What of the detective?"

Woollcott's eyes gleamed. "Ah, this is the detective's shining hour, although I daresay I've solved many a case in well under an hour. Some in mere minutes. In any event, once the murder victim is found, the detective then questions each player—each suspect—in turn, interrogating them and determining their exact whereabouts—"

"And *when*abouts," Dorothy added.

"Mrs. Parker, as always, hits the nail on the head," Woollcott said with a little bow to her. "By gathering the wheres and whens of each suspect, the detective deduces, as they say, who done it. Let's say, for example, that Harpo here is our victim, found in the hallway. And our Mrs. Parker was with him—and no one else—between nine thirty and nine forty-five in the hallway. So in this simplistic example I easily point the finger at Mrs. Parker as our murderer. And it's another case closed for Detective Woollcott. Do you follow?"

"Painstakingly, yes, I do," Doyle said.

"And now are you game to join us in a little Murder?" Woollcott's beady eyes twinkled.

Harpo Marx crept up behind Doyle and slung his arm around the big man's neck.

"As intriguing as it sounds, I thank you, but no, I shan't play your game," Doyle said, peeling Harpo's arm from around his shoulders. "Perhaps you'll permit me to merely be a bystander, an observer."

Woollcott's face was pink. "After asking me to explain the entire game in detail, you choose not to play?" he huffed. "My dear sir, you put yourself at risk of being a victim of hot-blooded murder, game or no game!"

Doyle puffed out his big bear chest, ruffling his walrus mustache, and smiled. "That's a risk I'm willing to take, Mr. Woollcott. But don't let me delay you any further. Please, get the game afoot."

Woollcott, obviously a little physically intimidated, nodded and turned away from Doyle. "So we shall. Okay, boys and girls, pick your poison." He held up the top hat and offered it to Dorothy.

"No, please, Aleck," she said, pointing to him. "Ladies first. You start."

Woollcott glowered, but all the same he reached into the hat and drew out a slip. His frown changed to a wicked grin as he looked one by one at the other players. "Oh ho, little lambs, I am the detective!" He held up the slip so they could see it. "You'd better be crafty, my fair murderer. Little Acky has never lost a case!"

Harpo was the next to pick from the hat. True to form, he gave himself away—he stuck out his tongue as though eating something disgusting. He was merely a suspect, Dorothy knew. If he had picked the *murderer* slip, he would have smiled ear to ear.

The hat was handed around the circle. When it came to Benchley, he didn't take a slip. Instead he offered the hat to Dorothy.

"Robert, please!" Woollcott admonished.

"I'd rather play dead," Benchley said with a smile, "than play one of your parlor games."

"Pick the right slip," Dorothy said, "and you could play both."

But Benchley just shook his head, passed the hat to Dorothy and took a step back next to Doyle. This didn't surprise her, although she couldn't help but be a little disappointed. Too bad he didn't want to play. If she "murdered" him, she could have him alone for hours.

But Benchley never played these games, and she understood. In the same way that she didn't like how New Year's Eve had become an occasion of compulsory fun, Benchley didn't enjoy the orchestrated amusement of parlor games at any time of the year.

Dorothy debated with herself for a moment. If Benchley wasn't going to play, why should she? But then she considered that the game really wouldn't take much time away from Benchley, especially if she was merely a suspect. She poked her hand into the hat and pulled out a slip. She unfolded it.

MURDERER, it read. She felt a thrill of power in seeing that word.

To her own amazement, she managed to suppress a smile. She even kept herself from glancing at Woollcott, which would have told him that she had picked the murderer slip. Instead she merely folded up the little piece of paper, clutched it in her hand and passed the hat back to Woollcott.

She would get him, though. Woollcott would be her victim! Then how would he go about solving his own murder? She grinned inwardly at the delicious, malicious thought of it. Little Acky had never lost a case? He was sure to lose this one.

Suddenly the sound of breaking glass startled Dorothy from her thoughts. The music and singing stopped. Dorothy spun around. At the bar Dr. Hurst was arguing with Douglas Fairbanks.

"Had enough to drink, have I?" Dr. Hurst was shouting. "No impudent Yank is going to tell me to hold my liquor!"

Fairbanks put his hand on Dr. Hurst's arm. Fairbanks smiled warily, as though he were trying to calm a bucking horse. "Easy now, Doctor. Maybe we should get you back to your room—"

"Unhand me!" Dr. Hurst said, pulling his spindly arm away. Scotch spilled from the bottle in his hand. "You have some cheek, Mr. Fairbanks! First I entrusted you with a very valuable item, which then quickly appeared around the neck of that naked harlot in your bathtub! How irresponsible and disgraceful of you! And now you have the audacity to prohibit me from your self-proclaimed hospitality? You Hollywood fraud!"

Fairbanks, though usually genial and generous, had clearly had enough. He would not be called a "Hollywood fraud" in his own apartment in front of his friends. He grabbed the old man by the back of his jacket and nearly hoisted him off his feet.

"You," Fairbanks called to Doyle. "You came in with

him. You take him out." As an afterthought, he added, "Please."

Without waiting for Doyle, Fairbanks pulled Dr. Hurst toward the front door.

"I say—" Doyle muttered, and rushed after them. "You Americans. It's almost enough to try a man's patience."

Chapter 5

Dorothy watched as Fairbanks practically shoved Dr. Hurst out the double doors.

Doyle rushed toward Fairbanks. "That'll do, sir!" he said angrily, his big hands balled into fists. "Must you treat him so roughly? The man is nearly seventy years old."

"Then he's old enough to know better," Fairbanks said furiously, but quickly regained his composure. "I'm sorry, sir. But I won't have angry drunks in my home, no matter how old they are. Now please take him down to his room and see him to bed. He's had more than enough."

Doyle went into the hallway to tend to Dr. Hurst. Fairbanks threw the doors closed and slapped his hands as though to dust them off.

Bibi's laughter trilled from the tub. "Oh no, Douglas. You didn't toss out my rich old British doctor? I was saving him for later!"

Fairbanks raised a hand to his forehead. "Another one to deal with," he muttered to himself. Then, louder, "You'd better get out of that tub soon, Bibi. You'll turn into a pickled prune."

She called out, "And you've turned into a pickled prude!"

Bibi and the crowd in the bathroom laughed and jeered.

Fairbanks shook his head resignedly and went back to the bar to oversee his butler cleaning up the broken glass and spilled scotch.

Dorothy felt something tugging at her hand. She turned to find Benchley pulling the slip of paper out of her grasp. He unfolded it with a mischievous twinkle in his eye and read it.

"Ah, Mrs. Parker," he whispered. "It's the role you were born to play."

"Who, me? A femme fatale?" she whispered back. "Only if your name is Woollcott."

"So he's your target?"

She nodded. "Such a large target will be hard to miss."

"And how do you plan to kill Little Acky—and the rest of the evening?"

She shrugged. "Somehow I must get him alone. Perhaps you could help me with that." She smiled. "As for killing the rest of the evening, perhaps you could help me with that, too."

They clinked glasses and had a cheerful sip as warmth and contentment settled through them. But as Dorothy lowered her glass, she spotted Mary Pickford, who had returned from the kitchen and was talking animatedly with Lydia Trumbull.

"Hold that thought," Dorothy said to Benchley. "I promised Fairbanks I'd talk to Mary for him. Some kind of lovers' spat. Be back in a minute." She patted his arm and went across the room to the two women.

Mary Pickford and Lydia Trumbull saw her coming and stopped talking.

"Good evening, ladies," Dorothy said. "Don't stop chatting on my account."

They smiled politely but didn't answer. She had seen them stealing glances toward Bibi, who was still in the bathtub. "So, is anyone else in for a swim?" Dorothy asked brightly.

"Don't make me think about it." Mary shuddered. Her girlish face was stormy. Her mascara had smeared from her tears and darkened her lovely eyes. "I can't even think about using that tub after *she's* been in it. My very own bathtub!"

Dorothy looked to Lydia for her response.

"I haven't a word to say about that terrible girl," Lydia said, although she undoubtedly had many words to say about Bibi, Dorothy thought.

Dorothy spoke sweetly. "Well, you know what I always say: If you have nothing nice to say about someone, come sit down next to me!"

She grabbed both their hands and led Mary and Lydia toward a cluster of empty chairs near the kitchen door. She sat the women down and leaned in close. "Now, what exactly is going on between you and Douglas and that Bibi in there? Tell Dottie all about it."

Mary sniffled. Lydia patted her on the shoulder.

"I think Douglas is having an affair with that little tramp," Mary said, anger and sorrow in her voice. "She's certainly made herself quite at home, hasn't she?"

"There, there . . ." Lydia said.

Dorothy would have sympathized with Mary, but she knew Mary was wrong. "I refuse to believe it, Mary. I can't believe it," she said. "Why would Doug ever cheat on you? You're not only beautiful and talented, but you're Hollywood royalty. And you're one of the nicest and most charming people I have the pleasure to know. And Doug is certainly not so stupid that he can't see through the glossy veneer of that vapid vamp in there."

Mary shook her head. "If it wasn't for the proof, I might say you're right, Dottie. But now I know different."

Lydia nodded her head sadly.

"Proof?" Dorothy asked. "What proof?"

"That necklace!" Mary said, her voice husky with choked emotion. "That silver necklace. I saw it on my dresser earlier in the evening. I naturally figured it was a gift that Douglas intended to give to me. But then Bibi stepped out of my own bedroom stark naked except for that necklace! Can you believe that—my own husband making a present to his little slut on New Year's Eve, in my own apartment? How dumb does he think I am?"

Dorothy stifled a knowing chuckle. She opened her mouth to explain that the necklace wasn't from Fairbanks. It was from Dr. Hurst. And furthermore it wasn't a gift. Bibi must have taken it—

But Mary kept talking, "And look at her in there living it up. She doesn't think that I know something's going on? How dumb does *she* think I am?"

Dorothy began again to explain, but now Lydia spoke up.

"Not as dumb as I feel," she said ruefully. "Bibi's been upstaging me for months now. At first I figured it was simply a matter of her taking any opportunity she could get. She's young and hungry and ruthless. But as of tonight I know she's been trying to upstage me on purpose."

"On purpose?" Dorothy asked doubtfully.

Lydia spoke bitterly; her pale blue eyes were as hard and cold as ice. "Didn't you notice how she waited until just the moment that Doug introduced me, and then she burst forth like the great whore of Babylon? Not only does she want to take my place on Broadway, but she wants to take my place in society—and humiliate me in the bargain!"

Before Dorothy could answer, Woollcott sauntered past them and pushed open the door to the kitchen. This was her chance to get him alone! Murdering Woollcott in the kitchen would be perfect.

Dorothy rose and spoke quickly. "Mary, don't do anything rash. I know full well that Douglas is not cheating on you with that woman. But wait here, and I'll explain it all. I just have to kill Alexander Woollcott, and I'll be right back."

She left them with stunned expressions on their faces and pushed open the door to the kitchen. Woollcott stood in front of the wide-open wooden door of the icebox. He was dipping his fingers into a bowl of pink cake frosting. He turned as she entered. He had a pink frosting mustache above his thin upper lip.

"Ah, there you are!" she said. "I want to have a couple words with you—"

The next two words from her mouth should have been *you're dead*. But a sharp, loud crack made her turn her head. On the other side of the small kitchen stood a man in dark blue overalls. The man faced the sink; his back was to her. He raised his arm—it held an ice pick—and jabbed it into the sink with another loud crack, followed by a clinking sound.

Dorothy stepped forward to get a better look. There was a large block of ice in the sink, and the man had broken smaller chunks from it. Dorothy recognized him as the workman who had spilled the entire container of ice when Bibi had made her grand appearance. Now he clearly had to make more ice to replace the large amount he'd spilled— no wonder he seemed to be doing it so resentfully.

The iceman, sensing someone behind him, turned angrily toward Dorothy. He held the ice pick up high; its sharp metal tip glistened right in front of her eyes. She raised her hands in surrender.

"Okay, I get the point," she said. "You want to be left alone."

The man had a rough young face with a thin, upturned nose. He sneered at Dorothy and spun back around to chip more ice from the block.

At the icebox, Woollcott looked expectantly at Dorothy as he sucked the last of the frosting from his fingers. "You had something to say to me?"

Drop dead, she wanted to say.

She had been thwarted. She couldn't "murder" Woollcott with a witness in the room. She spoke through gritted teeth. "You have frosting on your lip, fat boy."

41

Woollcott smiled devilishly, licking his lips. "Not quite the cutting remark I expected of you, Mrs. Parker. Better luck next time." He shut the icebox door and brushed past her; the kitchen door swung behind him.

Damn! She blew it. Surely now he knew that she was the murderer. Even worse, she had put him on the defensive because now he certainly knew that she was gunning for him. She had completely lost the element of surprise. She stomped her foot in frustration.

The iceman turned, anger on his dirty face, the ice pick in his hand.

Indifferent now, she waved at him as though he was a gnat. "Oh, shove it up your ass."

Back in the parlor, Dorothy faced the cluster of chairs, but Mary Pickford and Lydia Trumbull were gone. She glanced around the noisy, crowded room but didn't see them anywhere.

Benchley ambled up to her. "There you are, Mrs. Parker. You said you'd be back in a minute. That was a while ago."

"Forgive me, Fred," she said, truly sorry. She had so wanted to spend the evening with him, and she was doing everything but that. "Let's get a drink and settle in."

They threaded their way to the bar, only to find that most of the booze was gone—casualties of the fracas between Dr. Hurst and Doug Fairbanks and of the other partygoers' heavy drinking.

"Now what do we do?" Dorothy asked.

Together they slowly turned their heads toward the bathroom.

"The tub," Benchley said, "is full of champagne."

They could see that Bibi was still ladling it out to the hangers-on, while the nuns continued their vigil and observed her disapprovingly.

Dorothy asked, "Dare we dabble in the devil's brew?"

Benchley glanced into his empty glass. "Let's see, prohibition or perdition? We're damned if we do, damned if we don't."

"Then what the hell," she said, linking his arm in hers. "Let's go."

It was hot inside the crowded little bathroom. Dorothy noticed beads of sweat on the nuns' heavy brows. As Benchley slowly approached the bath, he leaned momentarily against the radiator beneath the frosted-glass window. He nearly jumped at the heat of it. The only person who didn't seem bothered by the temperature was the naked girl in the tub.

Before Dorothy and Benchley even asked, Bibi had filled their glasses. "Two more satisfied customers," she said merrily. Then Bibi eyed Benchley with that devious look she had first given to Dr. Hurst. "What do you do for a living, sweetie?"

Benchley smiled genially. "As little as possible."

Dorothy had to hand it to him: Benchley was still trying to avoid looking directly at Bibi.

But Dorothy wasn't shy about looking at her and evaluating her perfect body, her flawless skin and her pixie nose. Then Dorothy noticed something else about Bibi. . . . She was still wearing the silver locket—the one Mary Pickford was so upset about. Without having thought about it until now, Dorothy had assumed that Dr. Hurst had demanded the locket back when he'd had Bibi alone, yet here it was still around her pretty neck.

Why would Dr. Hurst be so adamant about Fairbanks protecting his locket, she wondered, *yet leave it with this girl when he had the chance to take it back?*

"Excuse me," Bibi said to Dorothy. "My eyes are up here."

"So they are." Dorothy looked up at her. "But who really cares about your eyes?"

Chapter 6

"All right, everybody!" Douglas Fairbanks announced to the crowd of partygoers in his apartment. "It's eleven thirty. Time to go down to the lobby for the countdown to midnight!"

Dorothy straightened up in her armchair. *Eleven thirty already? How had the time slipped by so quickly?* One minute she and Benchley were enjoying a quiet drink together—then another drink, and then another—and the next minute it was only half an hour until midnight.

She had not talked things out with Mary Pickford, as she had told Fairbanks she would do. And she had not cornered Woollcott alone for the game of Murder either.

The only thing she had done was to waste time with Benchley. For this, she was happy.

But she wasn't done with Benchley yet—she wanted to be beside him at the stroke of midnight to plant a New Year's kiss on him. *What might happen next?* she wondered. They were quarantined in this hotel for the foreseeable future. *Who knows?*

Benchley stood up. "Shall we go down to the lobby?"

Dorothy jumped to her feet. "Certainly."

In a moment they had crowded into the small elevator

with a handful of other guests, including Lydia Trumbull. Dorothy looked around, hoping Mary Pickford might also be aboard, but she wasn't. Maurice, the elevator operator, strained to close the doors. It was so crowded that he had trouble pulling the lever to make the elevator descend.

Some of the people on the elevator were grumbling about being kicked out of the Fairbanks' party all at once.

"That was the bum's rush," said one man—an insurance salesman type, Dorothy thought.

"Never saw a party end so fast," said the woman with him.

Benchley, good-natured as he was, turned to explain. "Don't hold it against the Fairbankses. It's the Algonquin tradition. On New Year's Eve, everyone gathers in the lobby to watch the big grandfather clock count down to the stroke of midnight. People stand on chairs and literally jump into the new year for good luck. The waitstaff parades around and bangs on pots and pans to scare away evil spirits from entering the new year."

"Speaking of spirits," the man said, "are there any drinks available in the lobby?"

Benchley thought about this. "Did you bring any with you?"

"No."

"Then you might want to make a resolution to do so next year," Benchley said as pleasantly as possible.

The man frowned and muttered to the woman. "The Hotel Astor, it ain't. That's where we'll stay next time."

And thank goodness for that, Dorothy thought.

The elevator stopped, and Maurice struggled to open the doors. The passengers on the elevator spilled out into the lobby, where a party was just getting in full swing. Loud jazz music was coming from somewhere—Dorothy was too short to see through the crowd whether there was a real band or a phonograph. In the center of the lobby, the armchairs and coffee tables had been moved away and the carpet rolled up.

Young men and women began spinning and bopping to the latest dance craze, the "Black Bottom Stomp."

Benchley bent to Dorothy's ear and yelled to be heard above the din. "That wonderful gent on the elevator needn't have worried." He pointed to a number of liquor bottles being passed around the crowd. "The waitstaff—and Frank Case—have their work cut out for them to chase all these spirits away."

Dorothy and Benchley weaved their way through the bustling crowd toward the dining room. As they did so, Dorothy managed to grab a bottle. Dinner service was long over, but the dining room was still nearly as crowded as the lobby. Dorothy plucked two empty glasses from the Round Table, poured some booze into them and handed one to Benchley. They clinked glasses and sipped.

She spotted Arthur Conan Doyle, followed by a young man, entering the room. They must have just arrived downstairs, Dorothy thought, because Doyle seemed to be wandering around, looking for a friendly face. She waved them over.

"Ah, Mrs. Parker, Mr. Benchley, is your game over?" Doyle shouted genially.

"Not quite," Dorothy said, reminded again that she had to somehow get Woollcott alone. Then she looked at the handsome young man with Doyle—but perhaps he was not quite as young as he seemed from across the room. He appeared to be in his thirties. He had bright eyes, a square jaw and a suntanned face. "Who's this?" she asked.

Doyle turned as though he had forgotten. "Oh, I beg your pardon. This is Quentin's new attendant, Mr. Jordan."

Dorothy shook his hand. He had a firm, dry grip. "Just Jordan?"

"First name's Benedict. Everybody just calls me Jordan," he said with a wry smile—and an American accent. Dorothy had expected that because Dr. Hurst was British, his attendant would be as well. But he was handsome, she thought, no matter what his nationality was.

"Nice to meet you, Jordan," Benchley said, stepping forward to shake the man's hand, nearly shoving Dorothy out of the way. "Here, have a drink."

Benchley took two more glasses from the Round Table, poured a healthy splash from the bottle into each one and handed them to the two men.

They raised their glasses in a toast.

"To auld lang syne," Doyle said in his soft Scottish burr.

"To better luck next year," Dorothy said.

"Two's company, three's a crowd," Benchley said.

Dorothy gave him a quick, inquisitive look, but he avoided her eyes.

They clinked glasses and drank.

"So, where is the good doctor, Arthur?" Benchley asked.

Doyle knitted his bushy brows in frustration. "Good and drunk, that's where he is. He threw us out of his room. Wanted to be alone, he said. Quentin always did get into a state when he overdid it on the bottle. I had forgotten. I've never seen him like this before, though." He glanced at Jordan. "We'll give him a little while to settle down, then perhaps we'll go up and check on him."

Jordan didn't answer this. He merely nodded his head stoically. He was either too new or too polite to say a harsh word against his current employer—though he likely had a few choice words to say, Dorothy presumed. Dr. Hurst didn't seem like the sweetest person to work for even when sober, she thought.

"Where are you from, Mr. Jordan?" Benchley asked. "From your sunny complexion, I'd say you recently arrived from down south?"

Jordan opened his mouth to answer, but Dorothy interrupted. "Not so fast. Let us guess! What do you say, Artie? How about bringing Sherlock Holmes' powers of observation to bear on Mr. Jordan? Let's see if we can figure out everything about him."

Doyle rolled his eyes and sighed. "Can you imagine how

47

many times I've been asked to do that? If I had a shilling for every such request—"

"Oh, you're full of shillings," she said. "I thought you might get in the spirit of it if we all pooled our thoughts. Never mind. Mr. Benchley and I will give it a try ourselves. Then you be the judge. What do you say?"

Doyle rubbed his big hand on his chin. "Very well, I won't be such a spoilsport to prevent you from trying. If Mr. Jordan is willing . . . ?"

"Sure," Jordan said, evidently amused to be the center of attention. "Knock yourselves out."

Dorothy eyed him from head to foot, taking in every detail. Next to her, Benchley fidgeted. She didn't look at him.

Could he be jealous? she wondered. *Jeez, I hope so.*

After a moment of examining the handsome man, she said, "I have it. You're a former cowhand, recently back from the range. But you weren't born out there. You were raised here on the East Coast. You went to Princeton, I think. But now you've returned because you were injured roping cattle or whatever it is cowhands do. You don't dance, and your favorite food is chili."

"Amazing!" Jordan said. "How did you come to those conclusions?"

Benchley was angry—a rare emotion for him. "Please don't tell me she's right!"

Jordan laughed. "Not even close."

Dorothy frowned. "Fine, Fred. You play Sherlock."

"Very well," Benchley said, smiling warmly again. He rubbed his hands together. "My turn. You were a lifeguard on the beaches of sunny Florida. But you left to join the military during the Great War, where you saw action and were permanently injured. So you returned to Florida as a lifeguard. But having seen action on the front, you bored quickly of the quiet, sunny seaside. So you recently moved to New York to try your hand at acting. But with no experience and no luck, you were forced to take a job as the man-servant to Dr. Hurst. You love pimentos, and your family is Scandinavian. Case closed."

"Brilliant," Jordan said, laughing.

Now Dorothy felt her face flush with envy. "Don't tell me *he's* right?"

"Not by a mile," Jordan said, laughing even harder. "But how did you get those wild ideas?"

Dorothy and Benchley looked at each other. Dorothy spoke first. "First, your foot. I couldn't help but notice—and I gather Mr. Benchley did, too—that you limped when you came this way, and anyone can see you're wearing an over-sized orthopedic shoe on your left foot. So I suppose each of us concluded you'd been injured not long ago. Not so recently as to require you to wear a cast, but recent enough that you're still suffering from the injury."

"Nope," Jordan said. "What else?"

She bit her lip, and said, "You don't have a particularly noticeable accent or manner of speech, so I assumed that you're not from, say, Chicago or Boston. Or Albuquerque or Alabama, for that matter. And I figured if you did have an accent before, you lost it at college, because you speak like an educated man. From the ornate ring on your finger, I guessed your alma mater was Princeton."

"Nope," Jordan said.

"My turn," Benchley said. "You have the suntan and sort of flashy looks of an actor, so I assumed you wanted to try your luck on Broadway. But, seeing as you're employed with Dr. Hurst, I gathered it had not worked out."

"You gathered wrong," Jordan said. "But what about my favorite foods? Wherever did you get those?"

Dorothy leaned close to him. "You have a little fleck of red on your bottom lip. I assumed it was chili, since you came from out west—or so I thought."

"I assumed pimento, because it looks red like pimento," Benchley said. "Maybe from a cocktail olive?"

49

Jordan shook his head.

"Red herring, perhaps?" Benchley asked sourly.

Jordan laughed. "And my family being Scandinavian?"

"Well," Benchley said weakly. "You have blue eyes, like the Swedes often do. . . ."

Doyle frowned and clucked his tongue.

"Fine," Dorothy grumbled at Doyle. "If you're so clever, you figure him out, Sir Arthur Conan Holmes."

Doyle sighed. "He was born and raised in Philadelphia. He never worked as a cowboy or went to war, because he has a clubfoot, which he was born with. But despite his physical impairment, he became proficient as a golfer as a young man—even becoming a private tutor to well-to-do clients. That explains his rather permanent suntanned complexion and his gentlemanly manner of speech. But golfing can be an expensive pursuit, one that he could not pursue without additional assistance from time to time. So he recently used his connections among the wealthy to secure a well-paid but short-term position with Dr. Quentin Hurst, who is traveling for a few weeks in the States. Meanwhile, Mr. Jordan hopes to visit as many golf courses as possible, weather permitting. And he won the ring in a tournament."

Dorothy and Benchley were momentarily dumbstruck. Then Dorothy asked, "But what's his favorite food?"

"Lobster," Doyle said wearily.

They looked to Jordan. "Don't tell us he's right?" Benchley asked.

The handsome man nodded. "Every word. Nailed it exactly."

"You *can* do it. You *can* read a person like a book!" Dorothy said to Doyle. "You are Sherlock Holmes!"

"Oh, nonsense!" Doyle said, exasperated. His walrus mustache fluttered. "He told me his entire life story upstairs while Quentin took a short doze. The only thing I observed was the clubfoot."

"Even the lobster?" Benchley asked.

"Dr. Doyle and I ordered it from room service," Jordan explained.

"I don't believe it," Dorothy gasped.

"It's true," Jordan said. "That's my life to a tee."

"No, not that!" she said gruffly. "Since when does the Algonquin serve lobster?"

"It was the special tonight. Ask one of the staff yourself." Jordan pointed to a short line of waiters emerging from the kitchen doors. They carried various pots and pans, along with metal and wooden spoons and utensils. As they gathered into a group, a quickly moving figure caught Dorothy's eye. She turned and saw Alexander Woollcott bustling through the dining room toward the lobby.

"What time is it?" she asked.

Doyle fished a gold pocket watch out of his vest, and popped it open with one hand. "Quarter to midnight."

She glanced at Benchley. Would she have enough time to follow Woollcott, "murder" him and get back soon enough to kiss Benchley at midnight?

She looked back toward Woollcott. He walked out of the dining room and disappeared into the crowd in the lobby.

She set her glass down on the table and turned to Benchley. "I need to bump off to dash off Woollcott—no, vice versa, I mean! Dash off to bump off Woollcott. So I'll be right back. Don't go anywhere." She gave his arm a squeeze and reluctantly went after Woollcott.

Chapter 7

Dorothy had two goals in the next fifteen minutes—to kill Woollcott and kiss Benchley—and she'd better not get them mixed up.

She entered the jam-packed Algonquin lobby and looked at the crowd. She didn't see Woollcott anywhere. How could she trap him alone in this mob scene?

Suddenly Mary Pickford emerged from the mass of people. She had cleaned up her mascara-streaked eyes and looked entirely better. She greeted Dorothy.

Dorothy responded, "So you've set things straight with Douglas? All's well and understood?"

Mary shook her head. "No, I've been avoiding him the whole evening. If he wants to play his childish games with that little slut, let him play."

Dorothy was surprised by this. "But I told you that necklace wasn't his in the first place—"

"Time I took matters in my own hands," Mary interrupted, her face set with purpose. "As far as I know, that tramp is still up in my bathtub—she was in there when I left just a moment ago. And who knows if Douglas is now with her? It's a good time to find out."

Before Dorothy could respond, Mary brushed past her

and toward the elevator. But it gave Dorothy an idea.... She just had to find Woollcott.

She looked around and spotted two waiters she recognized, Luigi and Pietro. They were setting up chairs and getting ready for anyone foolhardy enough to jump off them "into" the new year at midnight. She rushed over to them, clapped a hand on Luigi's shoulder and quickly hoisted herself up to stand on the seat of one of the chairs.

"Mrs. Parker!" Luigi shouted. "It ain't midnight yet!"

"I want to get a head start," she said. Then she gazed over the heads of the crowd and finally spotted Woollcott's top hat. She jumped down and weaved in his direction through the well-dressed partygoers. She found Woollcott chatting with Harpo Marx, as usual.

She shoved herself between them. "Aleck, I need your help quickly!"

He looked at her skeptically. Dorothy continued, "Mary Pickford and Doug Fairbanks are in a pickle. Bibi Bibelot is in a pickle, too—she's perfectly pickled, as a matter of fact. Being in that tub all night has made her completely smashed. Mary says they can't get her out of the tub. They need your help."

"And why me? Why must I help?" Woollcott asked.

"Please, Aleck. No time for questions. She'll drown in there."

"Impossible," he sneered. "Bibi couldn't drown in a bathtub half filled with champagne."

Harpo smiled. "Did you see her chest? She's so buoyant, she couldn't drown in the middle of the Atlantic."

"Well, fine, then," she said angrily. "Douglas and Mary asked for your help specifically, because you're so discreet and tactful in these embarrassing matters. But if Little Acky can't be bothered to help the world's most wonderful celebrity couple, then I suppose—"

"I never said that I wouldn't help!" Woollcott cried. "Of course I can help Douglas and Mary."

53

He turned on his heel and strode through the mob; his prodigious belly parted people like a snowplow. Now she had him—well, almost. She'd find a way to corner him up in the Fairbanks' apartment. She'd "murder" him quickly, then hurry back down to grab Benchley for a smooch at midnight. What a lovely way to enter the New Year!

Dorothy followed in Woollcott's wake as he moved toward the elevators. Mary Pickford was nowhere in sight, and Dorothy presumed she'd already gone up to her penthouse suite. But if the penthouse was not empty, perhaps Dorothy could "murder" Woollcott in the elevator? Woollcott stopped to press the elevator button, and Dorothy paused right behind him. The elevator door opened and disgorged a small crowd. Waiting inside was Maurice the elevator operator. No, that idea wouldn't work. She had to get Woollcott alone.

She quickly came up with another idea. She could get up to Fairbanks' penthouse *before* Woollcott! She turned away from the elevator and rounded a corner. She pushed through a swinging door to an empty service passage. Bare light bulbs hung overhead—even so, the corridor seemed dark and shadowy. She moved quickly to the end of the passage, where a door led to a serving pantry and dark stairs descended to the basement. But there was also a door to a service elevator that the waiters used for delivering room service and the housemaids used for moving their cleaning carts from floor to floor.

Having lived in the Algonquin for a few years now, Dorothy knew of this service elevator, although she had never used it before. She pressed the call button and heard the deep rumble of gears turning somewhere.

She had an eerie feeling and glanced over her shoulder. No one was there.

The elevator arrived, and she quickly pulled open the door. It was not manned by an elevator operator. She'd have to work it herself. She closed the door and threw the lever, and the elevator car began its ascent—she could see its progress through a small window in the door. She took a step backward and sighed, leaning against the rear wall as if she had escaped something fearful, although there was nothing to be scared of.

Suddenly her feet went out from under her. She landed on the dirty elevator floor in a heap with the wind knocked out of her. Groaning, she put the palm of her hand down to push herself up. But when she did, she felt something very cold. Shocked, she pulled her hand off the floor and examined it. Attached to her palm were two chunks of white ice. She flicked them off with the fingernail of her other hand. The ice chunks had left two painful red marks on her palm.

She finally stood up and rubbed her hands together. Some New Year's Eve this was turning out to be!

Dorothy stopped the service elevator at the top floor. She quietly opened the door and listened. No one seemed to be around. The only thing she could hear was the vague and distant murmur of voices coming from the lobby.

She tiptoed down the hall toward the Fairbanks' suite. Woollcott was nowhere in sight. The service elevator had arrived before the guest elevator, which probably had to make a stop or two. But where was Mary Pickford? And where were Douglas Fairbanks and Bibi Bibelot, for that matter?

Dorothy peeked into the open double doors of the suite. The place was empty but a real mess. Bottles and glasses were on every surface. Ashtrays full of cigarette and cigar butts were on every table, and a foggy haze of smoke still filled the room.

The door to the bathroom was closed.

She moved silently into the suite, looking left and right. She moved toward the darkened bedroom. No one there.

She crossed back through the parlor and went through the open door to the kitchen. The room was empty.

It was getting close to midnight, she knew. Woollcott would be here any moment.

She backed out of the kitchen and then moved stealthily toward the bathroom door. She put her ear to it. Nothing.

She knocked lightly.

No one answered.

She drew in her breath and whispered, "Anyone in there?"

Still no answer. She turned the knob and pressed the door.

It wouldn't move. She turned the knob the other way and pressed the door harder.

Locked.

Now what fresh hell is this?

She remembered that during the party Fairbanks had asked Mary for a key to the bathroom. Mary had said something about a kitchen drawer. Dorothy tiptoed back to the kitchen and searched through one drawer, then another. She finally found the one drawer that every kitchen has—the one full of junk. Inside it were a few pencils, some rubber bands, scissors, spare change, bobby pins, a thimble, thumbtacks—and a ring of keys.

Dorothy grabbed the key ring and hurried back to the bathroom door.

She heard the ding of the elevator bell from the hallway. *Woollcott!* He'd be here any second!

Sure, she could catch him alone in the parlor—but it would be far better if he opened the bathroom door expecting to find a naked Bibi and instead discovered Dorothy there to "murder" him! That would show him. He always thought he was so smart.

She tried one key, then the next, in the lock. Neither of them fit. Moving frantically, she tried a third. It gave a satisfying click in the lock, and she turned it. She spun the knob and pushed the door. But something gently slowed the door from opening. Something was on the floor right behind the door. She looked down. *A towel. Why would someone leave a towel . . . ?*

Then Dorothy looked at the bathtub. She gasped.

Bibi—naked, white, silent and motionless—still lay in the tub. Her head lolled to the side. Her eyes were open, gazing at nothing.

Dorothy rushed to the tub. Kneeling beside it, she placed her hand on the woman's shoulder, then on her cheek. Bibi's skin was ice-cold.

Suddenly Dorothy felt a wave of panic flood into her. She couldn't seem to breathe. She stood up, and the room swam around her. She steadied herself and lurched toward the window. Below the window was an ice bucket and a champagne glass resting on the radiator. She knocked them out of the way with a shatter and a clang on the tiled floor. She grabbed at the window with rising panic—was it stuck shut? No, but it was closed tight. She flung up the sash, had a momentary glimpse of the snowy city nightscape and then she gulped in cold night air.

After a moment, the icy air—and not looking at Bibi—seemed to clear her head.

From the lobby below, and outside in apartments and gatherings everywhere in the city, she could hear a rising clamor. *"Five . . . four . . . three . . . two . . . one . . ."*

"Happy New Year?"

She turned. Woollcott, his eyebrows raised above his round eyeglasses, stood in the doorway.

Dorothy pointed to Bibi's body. "Not for her, it ain't."

Chapter 8

It was twelve midnight. Cheering erupted from the lobby and the city streets. This happy roar was accompanied by the clangs of pots and pans, the wails of horns and sirens, and the blares of noisemakers.

Dorothy momentarily forgot about the cold, dead body in the bathtub next to her. She even forgot about Alexander Woollcott, who stood directly in front of her with a puzzled look on his chubby face.

For the moment her mind was occupied only by the frustrating realization that she had missed her perfect opportunity of planting a kiss on Benchley at midnight.

"Mrs. Parker?" Woollcott was saying softly. "What, pray tell, is going on here?"

"Bibi's dead," Dorothy said.

"Dead?"

She looked down at the pale, lifeless body. "If she's not dead, then she's a much better actress than any of us gave her credit for."

"What—?" Woollcott hesitated. "What should we do?"

"What do you think? Call down to Frank Case, of course. He's the manager. He'll know what to do."

Woollcott turned to find the phone. Dorothy wanted to

leave the bathroom, too, but she found a morbid fascination in staring at the beautiful young girl.

Something's wrong with this picture. . . .

Dorothy bent closer. All around Bibi's mouth and chin, the skin was pink and blotchy, like a stain or a rash. Almost like a burn. *That's odd.*

But that wasn't the strangest thing. . . . Bibi, as a corpse, didn't have the vivaciousness and audaciousness of the living girl. She was not just naked but bare. Raw. Vulnerable. Stripped of life, in every sense of the word.

Poor Bibi. Is this what you get for having fun? For being brash and silly?

Dorothy found her mind wandering. She stared at the ice bucket and the shards of shattered glass on the tile floor. A steamy wisp of vapor crept out of the metal bucket as the last pieces of ice slowly melted. *Like the soul leaving the body.* Dorothy shivered again and told herself it was because the bathroom was so chilly.

Woollcott hurried back in, looked again at Bibi and then at Dorothy. "Let's shut this window. You'll catch your death of a cold." He flung the sash down quickly.

They stood silently for a minute, both looking at the body. Then Woollcott said, "Our magnificent hotel proprietor will be up momentarily."

"Perhaps he'll have housekeeping clean up this mess."

Woollcott ignored her stab at humor. "What do you think happened to her?"

Dorothy didn't answer. She was wondering the exact same thing.

He said, "I can't stand to see her lying there wet as a clam. Should we drain the tub?" He reached for the chain attached to the tub plug.

She stopped him. "Don't. You're liable to throw out the Bibi with the bathwater."

He turned, a quizzical look on his face. "She's not going to go down the drain."

"Leave her be. She went out of this world the way she came into it—naked and wet. Let's let Frank Case decide what to do."

A moment later they heard the ding of the elevator. Frank Case entered the apartment, with Douglas Fairbanks and Robert Benchley in tow.

"Oh, dear," Case said.

"Oh, Bibi . . ." Fairbanks slapped his forehead. "Someone remind me to never throw another party."

Benchley spoke under his breath. "Never throw another party, Douglas."

Case looked to Dorothy and Woollcott. "How did it happen?"

"No idea," Dorothy said. "This is how I found her."

Case put a hand to his chin. "I'd call the ambulance, but we're quarantined. And, well, it's apparently not an emergency at this point anyway. I know, I'll get Dr. Hurst. He helped me earlier."

"Very little a doctor can do for her now," Dorothy said, moving next to Benchley for comfort.

Benchley sighed in agreement. "She needs an undertaker, not a doctor."

"Besides," Fairbanks added, "that Dr. Hurst was dastardly drunk when I threw him out of here an hour ago. He should be sleeping it off in his room by now."

Dorothy asked, "What about Dr. Doyle?"

"Who is Dr. Doyle?" Woollcott asked.

"Artie," she said. "The one who wouldn't play your game of Murder."

Woollcott looked skeptical. "That old bear? He's a practicing physician?"

She considered this. "Nope, I guess he's not. Not practicing anymore, at any rate. But he's caring—and smart."

"I'll bring them both," Case said, walking quickly out the door. "Perhaps two inadequate doctors will add up to one good one."

After he left, Fairbanks smiled ruefully, rubbing his hands. "Well, isn't this a lovely kettle of fish! Mary's going to just treasure this—" He paused, dismayed. "Say, where is Mary?"

Benchley looked around as if Mary Pickford would suddenly pop up from behind the sink.

Dorothy said, "I saw Mary down in the lobby just before midnight. She told me she was coming up here to pry Bibi out of the tub."

"She did?" Fairbanks' handsome face looked worried. "So where is she?"

Dorothy shrugged. "We haven't seen her."

Without a word, Fairbanks left the bathroom and called out in the apartment, "Mary! Darling, are you here?"

It took Fairbanks only a minute to walk through the entire apartment. When he didn't find his wife, he went out the front door without a word to the trio in the bathroom.

"So," Benchley said, "what brought you two up here at midnight on New Year's? Funny place to celebrate."

Dorothy glanced again at Bibi's dead body. "Yes, absolutely hilarious place to celebrate the New Year."

But had she detected a note of disappointment in Benchley's voice? Did his lightheartedness actually mask a wish for her to be by him at the stroke of midnight?

Woollcott appeared irritated. "Mrs. Parker, you told me that Douglas and Mary needed my discreet help. Clearly that was a lie. What do you mean by sending me up here?"

She leveled her eyes at him. "To murder you, of course."

"Aha! I knew it! In the kitchen, you—"

"Shut up, Little Acky. We have bigger fish to fry. The game's over."

Woollcott raised an eyebrow as he eyed Bibi's body. "And perhaps another has begun."

Benchley ignored this. "Then what happened? Woollcott took the elevator up here, and you followed?"

"On the contrary," Woollcott said, turning to Dorothy. "How *did* you arrive here before me?"

"Took the service elevator," she said. "When I arrived on this floor, the suite was wide-open. But the bathroom door was locked. I had heard Mary say there was a key in a kitchen drawer—" She held up the key ring, which was still in her hand.

"Just a moment," Woollcott said. "The bathroom door was locked?"

"Yes, I just said that."

He turned and closed the door. There was no keyhole on the inside of the door, just a standard doorknob and a handle to lock the deadbolt. "So it would appear the door was locked from the inside?"

"Who knows?" she said.

"Whoever locked this door, that's who knows!" Woollcott replied. "So if the door was locked from the inside, that means Bibi got up from the tub, locked it, then got back in the tub and died?"

"I doubt it," Dorothy said. "The floor is dry, and it was dry when I got here. If Bibi had gotten out of the tub, she'd have left wet footprints all over the floor, or at least quite a few drops behind."

They examined the floor, especially right in front of the tub. It was bone dry.

Woollcott took the keys from Dorothy's hand. "So you found this in a kitchen drawer?"

"Yes, that's right," Dorothy said. "What are you implying?"

"I imply nothing. I merely state the facts—that someone locked this door to prevent or delay the discovery of Bibi's dead or dying body. Isn't that how you see it?"

They stood looking at the door when it suddenly swung open. Frank Case, Dr. Hurst and Arthur Conan Doyle entered.

Dr. Hurst's white hair was disheveled, his high collar was undone and his necktie was loosened. He looked pale and sick. When he saw the body of Bibi, he looked even sicker.

62

"Get her out of there!" he croaked, pointing at the body but looking away. "Carry her to the bed. Cover her up."

Woollcott opened his mouth to protest, but when no one moved, Dr. Hurst spoke even more loudly. "Get her out of that tub this instant, I said!"

Instinctively Doyle and Case grabbed Bibi's arms. Benchley reluctantly reached in the tub and held one of her ankles. He shivered at the strange feeling of it. Woollcott, unhurried, took off his tuxedo jacket, rolled up his white sleeves and carefully reached into the tub for the other ankle. By some unspoken understanding, they simultaneously hoisted the body out of the tub, and the champagne cascaded from it. The sweet, crisp smell filled Dorothy's nose, and she winced. Then she watched as a small circle of liquid pooled around Bibi's navel and then drained away as they moved the body. Dorothy moved quickly to cover Bibi with a bath towel—it somehow seemed necessary to lend this undignified girl some dignity, as though the propriety she lacked in life could be bestowed on her in death. The only things left in the tub were the ladle and a washcloth.

They maneuvered Bibi's body through the doorway and carried her to the bedroom, where they laid her carefully on the bed. Dorothy couldn't help but rearrange the towel to neatly cover the girl's body.

Dr. Hurst followed them into the room. He staggered toward the bed and dropped his leather doctor's bag onto the floor. Dorothy was compelled to move out of the way. Dr. Hurst held one of Bibi's wrists for a moment while he felt for a pulse. He let go of the arm and then applied two fingers to her neck.

He stood and turned to them. "She's dead."

"Of course she's dead!" Dorothy said impatiently. "The question is, what killed her?"

Dr. Hurst's mouth tightened. "I can't say."

Frank Case said, "Some sort of accident, undoubtedly."

"An unusual sort of accident," Woollcott said.

"People slip and hurt themselves in the bathroom all the time, unfortunately," Case said. "Most dangerous room in the house."

Doyle cleared his throat and carefully looked at Bibi's face. "What's that strange redness around her mouth?" He moved forward for a closer look, then turned quizzically to Dr. Hurst. But Dr. Hurst didn't answer. He even took a step back to allow Doyle more room to examine the body.

"Perhaps she drowned?" Benchley offered. "We've all heard the old wives' tale of people drowning in three inches of water."

"No," Doyle said, carefully turning Bibi's head. "Her hair is completely dry."

"Maybe alcohol poisoning?" Case asked. "People can go blind or even die from bad moonshine."

"We drank a couple," Benchley said, indicating himself and Dorothy. "We weren't poisoned. Fairbanks wouldn't throw a party with rotgut booze."

Woollcott stuck out his tongue. "You drank champagne that a woman was bathing in? I'd expect that from the thirsty rabble, but from you two—?"

"The alcohol kills the germs, doesn't it?" Benchley said gamely. "Besides, nothing else was available."

"It wasn't so bad," Dorothy said regretfully, pointing to Bibi and unable to stop herself from joking when things looked so gloomy. "Unmistakable flavor of tart."

Case frowned at her and addressed Doyle. "If not alcohol poisoning, then perhaps an alcohol overdose? Could she have absorbed it somehow?"

"Through her skin, do you mean?" Doyle said. "Not likely. I'd wager the skin absorbs only trace amounts of alcohol. However, inhalation is another matter."

"Drunk by inhalation?" Dorothy muttered dismally. "Now that's a gas."

Doyle nodded. "During the war, the armies of the world experimented with all manner of poisonous gases for debilitating and destroying their enemies on the battlefield. I studied it extensively for the British government. Vapors inhaled through the lungs absorb into the bloodstream much more quickly than through the skin."

"Enough to kill her?" Case asked.

Doyle considered this. "In the same manner in which a drunkard will become poisoned by excessive drink, she'd become progressively intoxicated by inhalation. Was she extremely drunk?"

They looked at each other. No one knew.

Dorothy said, "She appeared pretty happy with herself when we last saw her, sometime before midnight. But then again she was full of beans even when she arrived at the hotel earlier."

"Sometime before midnight?" Doyle repeated. "So who was the last to see her alive?"

Dorothy shrugged and wondered again about Mary Pickford.

Case folded his arms and turned to Dr. Hurst as the final authority. "So what did kill her? A slip in the tub and a rough knock to her head?"

Dr. Hurst looked down demandingly at Doyle. "Well?"

Doyle was bent over Bibi and carefully feeling her head. "Her skull appears intact. No lacerations or abrasions. No palpable contusions or swelling." He stepped back, hands on his hips, and shook his head.

"Then how *did* she die?" Dorothy asked.

Suddenly Woollcott pointed at the body and yelled, "Murder!"

Dr. Hurst visibly jumped. He clutched at his chest. "You gave me a start, sir!" he croaked.

"Has no one else noticed?" Woollcott cried. "The locket is missing! She was wearing it all night, but now it's gone. And if it was left in the bathroom, we would have seen it. It was stolen! This was murder. Murder for that locket!"

Dorothy turned to Dr. Hurst. "Wasn't that your locket?"

Dr. Hurst was still breathing heavily. "How did you know that?"

"I saw you with it earlier. In the lobby and again when you arrived for Fairbanks' party."

"No, no," Dr. Hurst said with a dismissive wave of his hand. "It was just a trinket. Nothing more."

Mary Pickford, followed by Douglas Fairbanks, stormed into the room. "Just a trinket? Hardly! I saw that locket around Bibi's neck." She turned and faced Fairbanks. "It's the kind of jewelry exchanged between lovers!"

Fairbanks looked at her wearily. "Now, dearest, I've already told you—"

"Aha!" Woollcott said, pointing a fat finger in the air. "So there is more to this than meets the eye. It's murder, I tell you. And I shall investigate! I've never failed to solve a case, and I won't fail this one. The game is afoot!"

Just then Dr. Hurst groaned. His face twisted in pain and, clutching one hand to his head, he sank to his knees. Then he collapsed to the floor with a thud.

Chapter 9

"Step aside," yelled Doyle. Dorothy and the others moved back. Doyle kneeled by the prone body of Dr. Hurst and carefully rolled him over.

"What's the matter with him?" Fairbanks asked. "He's not—"

Doyle pressed his ear to Dr. Hurst's narrow chest. "He's alive, but his breathing is quite shallow. Let's lift him to the other side of the bed."

"Oh dear," Mary said, biting her lip. She nervously twisted one of her long blond curls with her forefinger as she watched her husband and Doyle lift Dr. Hurst onto the bed and alongside Bibi's dead body. "Oh dear, oh dear."

Doyle resumed his examination of Dr. Hurst, checking his pulse and his breathing.

"You shouldn't have wound him up," Dorothy muttered to Woollcott. "You broke his watch spring."

Frank Case leaned forward. "Is it a heart attack?"

"I don't think so." Doyle lifted one of Dr. Hurst's eyelids, then the other. He muttered to himself, "Hmm, one pupil is dilated." Then he pronounced, "My working diagnosis is apoplexy—a stroke."

Mary couldn't hold her emotions any longer. She

clutched at her husband's arm. "Oh, Douglas! First a dead woman and now a dying man in our bed—*our bed*! I can't bear it. We'll have to burn the sheets. No, we'll have to burn the whole bed and buy a new one!"

"You might want to remove the bodies before you burn it," Dorothy said to her.

Doyle spoke forcefully to Mary. "I never said he was dying! The apoplexy has affected only one side of his body. He has every chance of eventual recovery."

But Mary wasn't listening. She had turned to leave the room.

Woollcott called after her, "Don't go far, Mary. You're our first suspect!"

She stopped and turned slowly. "Suspect? *Me?* What are you talking about, Aleck?"

Dorothy muttered to him, "Not sure this is the time, Detective Woollcott."

"This is precisely the time," Woollcott said to her, then turned again to Mary. "Were you not the last to see the deceased alive?"

Mary put a hand to her chest. "The *deceased*?"

"Yes, the deceased." He pointed to the dead body in the bed. "Bibi Bibelot! Mrs. Parker said she encountered you in the lobby just before midnight, and you were on your way up here to have it out with Bibi."

"Quiet, please," Doyle said. "Or remove yourselves from the room. This man—my friend—is in a most serious condition." He bent to search through Dr. Hurst's medical bag and removed a blood pressure cuff and a stethoscope. He put the ends of the stethoscope into his ears. He glanced at Benchley. "Would you be so kind as to go down to Quentin's room and fetch Mr. Jordan? He may be of the utmost assistance in this matter."

Benchley nodded agreeably and moved toward the door.

Dorothy turned to follow. "Mind if I join you, Mr. Benchley?"

"No, thank you, Mrs. Parker," he said with a smile. "I can manage." He walked out of the bedroom and then quickly left the apartment.

"No, thank you"? She stopped in her tracks. *What now? Is he jealous of Mr. Jordan? Or is he somehow mad at me for not being by his side at midnight? Or . . . what?*

Meanwhile Woollcott, Fairbanks and Mary had moved out into the living room to continue their argument. Dorothy, too, left the bedroom to join them.

Woollcott said to Mary, "I saw you casting daggers with your eyes at Bibi all night. You hated that she was the center of attention at your party. And were you not the last person to leave this apartment before midnight?"

Dorothy interrupted, her voice sharper than she intended. "Enough, Aleck! This is life and death, not one of your little parlor games."

Woollcott faced her with a confident look. "Indeed you're right, Mrs. Parker! No one understands that as well as I. This is most certainly a matter of life and death, and I am dealing with it accordingly. Now, didn't you say Mary was the last one to leave this penthouse before midnight?"

Dorothy didn't respond. She looked to Mary and expected her to profess her innocence.

Instead Mary's husband spoke up. "I was the last one to see Bibi alive. I tried to persuade her to get out of the tub, but she wouldn't," Fairbanks said.

Woollcott frowned. "Hogwash. Don't try to cover for your wife, Douglas. I saw you down in the lobby after you shooed everyone out of the party."

Fairbanks hesitated. "This was before you saw me in the lobby."

"Nonsense, Douglas," Woollcott said, and turned to Fairbanks' wife. "Come clean, Mary. Did you or did you not say to Mrs. Parker that you were coming up to this penthouse to deal with Bibi?"

Mary began twisting another lock of her blond hair. "Well, yes, I did say that—"

"Aha!" Woollcott cried.

Mary spoke more loudly. "Yes, I did say that to Dottie. But I never made it up here. I encountered Lydia Trumbull in the elevator. She was in an emotional state, so I went with her to her room on the second floor to talk."

Woollcott frowned again. This didn't fit in his theory. "Talk? Talk about what?"

Mary bit her lip.

"Aha! You're keeping secrets!" Woollcott said, jabbing his fat index finger into the air.

Dorothy put a hand to her head. "Aleck, stop saying 'Aha!'"

Woollcott looked pleased. "But now we have another suspect. Lydia Trumbull—who was in an emotional state! Where had she come from when you encountered her in the elevator?"

"I don't know exactly," Mary said. "Her room, I suppose."

"Was the elevator going up or going down?"

"Well, down, of course," she said. "Lydia was on it when it arrived in the lobby."

"So she had come down," Woollcott said slowly and dramatically. "As in, she came down from her room—or perhaps she had come down from this very penthouse after murdering Bibi!"

Dorothy folded her arms. "Hang on there, *Detective* Woollcott. Exactly who is it that you suspect? Mary or Lydia?"

He turned to her. "I suspect everyone! You included, Dottie. Were you not alone with Bibi's body when I found you?"

"Oh, good gravy," Dorothy moaned.

"There's more of grave than of gravy in this," he said, his eyes narrowing.

70

"Aleck, stop it," she said. "You're being morbid. I'm not one to surrender to scruple, but the dead woman is in the next room. She's barely even cold."

"She's as cold as the grave, Dottie," Woollcott said. "Silent as the grave, as well. Who will speak for her? The hotel is quarantined. No policeman can enter the building. Someone must figure out what happened, and I'm just the one to do it. Little Acky has never lost a case!"

"Maybe not," she said. "But Little Acky has lost his marbles."

Chapter 10

"You can drop your investigation," Dorothy said to Woollcott. "I'm calling the police."

He made a slight bow. "Be my guest. I welcome their involvement."

An elaborate pearl-handled telephone sat on the end table by the sofa. Dorothy went toward it.

"Dottie," Fairbanks said with a sort of impatient bluster, "is that absolutely necessary? Why bother them with this now? As Aleck says, no one can even enter the building."

"Why *bother* them?" she asked. "You have a dead body in your bed, Douglas. I don't think they'll mind a quick phone call."

She picked up the handset and tapped the switch hook. "Operator?" There was silence on the other end. "Operator?"

She tapped the switch hook again and more vigorously now.

A woman's weary, hoarse voice answered. "Operator speaking."

"Mavis?" Dorothy asked. "Is that you? You sound like a sick kitten."

"I am a sick kitten, Mrs. Parker," the woman's throaty

voice answered. "Been on this switchboard all night. My voice is kaput. So, what can I do for you?"

"Put me through to the police, please," Dorothy said.

"I'm sorry, Mrs. Parker. I'm having trouble making outside calls. There's something wrong with this lousy old thing. Or maybe all the snow affected the lines. You'll have to come down here and place the call directly from the switchboard, using the emergency line."

Dorothy thanked her and hung up.

"Well?" Woollcott said. "Are they coming?"

She ignored him and went back to the bedroom, where Case was conferring with Doyle.

"What can be done for a stroke, Dr. Doyle?" the hotel manager asked. "What's the treatment?"

"Well, I'm not precisely sure." Doyle ran a hand over his chin. "It's been decades since I've been in actual medical practice."

"Maybe raise his head?"

"Of course," Doyle said confidently, but then he looked uncertain. "Or is it perhaps his feet?"

Dorothy interrupted. "I'm going down to the switchboard to call the police. Shall I also call for an ambulance?"

Doyle sighed in relief. "That would be most welcome, Mrs. Parker. Thank you. Bring them at once."

Now Case spoke uncertainly. "I'm not sure if they'll be able to enter the building with the quarantine—"

"Everyone keeps saying that," she said.

Case studied the pale, thin face of Dr. Hurst. "But it's certainly worth a try."

She shook her head and left. Woollcott followed right behind her. He turned to Douglas and Mary. "Don't go anywhere, you two. We shall talk further."

"Where would we go?" Fairbanks asked. "This is our apartment."

Dorothy stopped and faced Woollcott, who nearly collided with her. "Must you come with me?"

73

Woollcott puffed out his chest. "I want to speak with the authorities myself. I want their official permission to investigate this case."

"You're the only case around here. A nutcase."

She went into the hallway toward the elevator and reached for the call button. But before she could press it, the elevator door opened. Benchley and Jordan stepped out.

"Oh, Fred, there you are!" she said. "Please come with me."

Benchley smiled—but it wasn't his usual warm lovely-to-see-you smile. It was more like a don't-bother-me-right-now smile.

"Go with you?" he asked.

"I'm going down to the lobby to call the police."

He made that smile again. "I'm certain you can handle a phone call on your own, Mrs. Parker. Artie and Mr. Jordan might need my help with Dr. Hurst." The smile still on his face, he walked past her. Then he called over his shoulder, "And please stop calling me Fred."

She stood and watched him go.

In a huff, she turned and stomped onto the elevator. *Is he trying to punish me? That's certainly not like Benchley. And punish me for what? For merely giving handsome Mr. Jordan a fleeting glance earlier? The punishment doesn't fit the crime!*

"Where to?" said Maurice, the elevator operator, after Woollcott stepped in, too.

"Where to?" she snapped. "Twice around the park and take the scenic route."

"You want to pick a floor?" Maurice asked impatiently in his creaky old voice. "Or you want me to pick?"

"Lobby," she said gruffly. "And step on it."

"Hmm," Woollcott said. "Is there trouble in Lovey-Dovey Land?"

She gritted her teeth.

When she didn't answer, he spoke again. "No caustic remark? No vicious retort?"

"Sometimes the best reply to an insult isn't another insult," she said, "but a quick knee to the groin. Do you still want my reply?"

They stood in silence as Woollcott cast nervous glances at her.

Before they reached the lobby, a light flashed and a bell sounded on the operator's controls. Maurice stopped the elevator on the second floor. He opened the door, and there stood Lydia Trumbull. Her eyes were wet from tears.

"Aha!" Woollcott cried, pointing his finger at her.

Lydia was taken aback. "Going up?" she asked nervously.

"Not by a long shot, lady," Woollcott said. "You're going down."

"What? *Down?*"

"Down to the jailhouse. You're a suspect in the murder of Bibi Bibelot!"

Lydia's pale eyes widened. Then her eyelashes fluttered, her head tilted back and she crumpled into a heap on the floor in a dead faint.

Dorothy and Woollcott lifted the unconscious Lydia off the floor.

"Wonderful investigative skills, detective." Dorothy spoke in gasps to him. "You nearly frightened the poor woman to death."

With the actress' arms over their shoulders, they struggled to carry her—dragging her feet on the carpeted hallway—back to her room.

"Frightened her, did I?" Woollcott wheezed. "Where there's fear, there's guilt. And guilt flees from Alexander Woollcott!"

"So does common sense," Dorothy said as they reached Lydia's room. "Now, hold her up while I unlock the door."

Lydia had held a room key in her hand when they encountered her. After she fainted, Dorothy had picked it up from the floor. Dorothy shifted the weight of Lydia's body toward Woollcott, who groaned. Dorothy slid the key in the lock, opened the door and flicked on the lights.

Then they struggled to maneuver Lydia through the door. Although the actress was petite, neither Dorothy nor Woollcott was strong, and it took effort not to simply let Lydia drop into a heap on the bed. Instead they did their best to slide her gently onto the bedspread.

"Whew," Woollcott said breathlessly. "Someone should alert the Michelin Guide. Guests are dropping like flies in this hotel."

Dorothy stared at him. "*You* did this to her. This is your fault. Now go back upstairs. Dr. Hurst probably has smelling salts in that medical bag of his. Go get them."

Woollcott snorted. "Why should we offer succor to the accused?"

"Why should I not sock you in the eye? You made her faint, so you wake her up."

He frowned but eventually turned and left. Dorothy breathed a sigh of relief. That little errand would get him out of her hair for a few minutes at least. She wanted to talk to Lydia without Aleck frightening her again.

She looked around the room. What could she use to wake Lydia up while he was gone?

There were a number of medicine bottles on the bedside table. Dorothy picked up a few and scrutinized their labels. A couple were liquids, and the rest were pills or powders. Most she recognized as sleep medicines or tranquilizers— laudanum, Veronal, hydroxycodone, even morphine. But nothing that appeared to be a stimulant.

Dorothy looked down at the inert actress' troubled face and thought for a moment. She had read somewhere that the main ingredient of smelling salts was not salt but ammonia. She went to the bathroom, but of course there was no ammonia. The Algonquin was a residence hotel and had two types of rooms—regular hotel rooms booked by the night, and suites for rent for residents such as herself. Lydia's room was a guest room, of course, not a rental suite. As such, it had no cleaning supplies.

Dorothy went back into the bedroom, and then opened the door and looked up and down the corridor. Dorothy herself lived in a very small rental suite down the hall. She had no ammonia in her apartment, though, because she never cleaned. But across the hall lived old Mrs. Volney. . . .

Dorothy stared at the door. Even at this hour, she could hear the cats mewing inside. But cats were nocturnal creatures, of course. And, for that matter, so was Mrs. Volney. Day or night, the meddlesome old woman would poke her head out of her door at the slightest disturbance, and then she'd grin with her gray teeth and her thin lips when she saw that someone had stumbled and dropped a carton of eggs, or had twisted an ankle on a fold in the carpet.

"Oh, dear me!" she'd always say with a smirk of pleasure. "Someone should *do* something about that!"

But for Dorothy there was more to her dislike of Mrs. Volney than just the old woman's nosiness. In Dorothy's heart of hearts, one of her greatest fears was that she'd someday end up like Mrs. Volney. A wrinkled, doddering busybody who had nothing in her life other than tending her unruly cats and feeding like a parasite off of others' daily misfortunes. Dorothy swore to herself to never become like that. She strode across the hall and knocked on the door as if to spite fate. Mrs. Volney opened it almost immediately.

The old woman's wispy hair was the color of pewter. It lay flattened on her head and rolled in curlers by her ears. She wore an ivory-colored robe that had once been elegant but was now yellowed and shabby. She had a dowager's hump and always held her hands up in front of her frail, narrow body—she looked like a praying mantis, Dorothy thought. Or perhaps a *preying* mantis.

"Well, hello to you, Miss Parker," she said in her shrill,

creaking voice, like a rusty old machine that was missing a few pieces. "My, but it's late for social calls, isn't it?"

"It's *Mrs*. Parker, if you please. And this isn't a social call—"

"Oh yes, *Mrs*. Parker. Where is that darling husband of yours? Tell me once more what happened to him? I forget. . . ."

Like hell you forget!

Dorothy spoke matter-of-factly. "He fell down an elevator shaft and was never heard from again." She would be damned if she satisfied this old biddy's thirst for scandal and hardship—ammonia or no ammonia!

The truth was, her husband had gone off to the Great War in Europe, had seen too much horror, and had come home a shell of a man, hooked on morphine. Dorothy and Edwin Parker had parted ways with sadness and great regret. Dorothy kept his last name—it was the best thing he ever gave her.

But by no means was Dorothy going to repeat the story to this elderly vulture, who had already heard it at least once from her and probably several more times from others.

"Elevator, you say? My mind must be failing me in my old age. I really thought he became addicted to dope. For some women it can be so hard to keep a good man or even a mediocre one, don't you agree?"

Dorothy struggled to hold her tongue.

Mrs. Volney continued, "Now, I've never had that problem. My dear Donald, may he rest in peace—"

"May we all," Dorothy said hastily. "But, as I was saying, this is not a social call. I'm in dire need of a bottle of ammonia. Do you have one?"

"Why, certainly. I keep my little home spick and span. With four cats, cleanliness is a must. Next to godliness, as they say." Mrs. Volney turned and shuffled off to her kitchenette, opened the cabinet under the sink and took out a glass bottle of ammonia. Dorothy looked around the woman's tidy little apartment.

It was the same size as hers, she knew, but it seemed just a little bit larger because every item in the room was smaller: two small armchairs; a small, uncomfortable-looking couch; a small side table; a small knitting basket beside it; a small teacup with a small saucer on top. It was as though everything had been miniaturized just slightly, just enough to fit little Mrs. Volney perfectly.

Was this what old age was all about? Dorothy wondered. *When you're young, the world seems so immense all around you. But as you get older, your world gets smaller and smaller, reducing little by little until your modest apartment is your entire world.* Dorothy involuntarily shivered with the thought.

Mrs. Volney shuffled back to Dorothy with the bottle of ammonia in her hand. "You don't mind if I pry, do you?"

Never stopped you before, Dorothy thought. "Pry away," she said.

"What can you possibly need ammonia for at this hour?"

You think I'm up to something sordid and scandalous, do you?

"Some fellas were lion hunting in my room," Dorothy said with a straight face. "The lion put up a hell of a fight. But we got him in the end. Actually not in the end—we got him in between the eyes. Blood went everywhere. So, thank you."

Dorothy grabbed the bottle from the woman's spindly hands. Mrs. Volney stood there with her mouth open. Dorothy turned to go.

No, that won't do. I can't leave the old hag thinking I'm crackers. That would just give her more reasons for gossiping—especially about me.

Dorothy resolutely turned back around and pasted a friendly smile on her face. "Just kidding, Mrs. Volney. Actually, a friend fainted, and I need the scent of ammonia to revive her. She's an actress. Very dramatic, you know. Always swooning and such. She's a typical thespian."

"She's a . . . a what?"

Dorothy paused. "A thespian."

"Oh, she's one of *those*, is she?" Mrs. Volney's expression was a mix of primness and salacious curiosity. "Well, this is the modern age, and a person's . . . well, a person's romantic proclivities are their own. One mustn't be too judgmental, Mrs. Parker," she said with a decidedly judgmental tone. "No, one mustn't."

Dorothy did not correct the old woman's mistake. Instead she decided to have some fun with it. "Oh yes, Mrs. Volney. My friend is a card-carrying thespian. Quite public about it, too. I've seen her act 'that way' in public in front of hundreds of people."

"Oh, dear me."

"On the Broadway stage, even."

"Heaven forbid!" Mrs. Volney gasped, shocked and thrilled at the same time. "These people should keep such things private! And the theaters these days are dens of iniquity. I'd never attend such a horrid spectacle, much less pay for a ticket. And the prices they charge these days, they're just as obscene! And what . . . what was the name of this show—just so I know to avoid it?"

"It's called *Peter Pan*. Very immoral. Thank you for the ammonia."

Dorothy turned and went out the door, then closed it behind her.

She crossed the hall and unscrewed the bottle cap as she returned to Lydia's room. The sharp, pungent smell of the ammonia made her eyes water. She propped up Lydia's head and held the bottle under her nose. Nothing happened at first. Then Lydia winced. Her eyes flew open. She coughed suddenly and shoved the bottle away.

"Welcome back, Lydia dear," Dorothy said. She put the cap back on the ammonia and set the bottle on the crowded bedside table. She took a quick inventory of the medicine bottles again. "Tell me you have some brandy here among these nostrums and remedies. We could both use a good snort. Though you've just had one, clearly."

Lydia shook her head. "What happened?"

"You fainted when Woollcott literally pointed the finger at you." Dorothy sat down on the edge of Lydia's bed. "Tell me quick, before that gasbag returns: Did you have something to do with Bibi's death?"

Lydia hid her face in her hands.

Dorothy clucked her tongue. "Don't do that, Lydia dear. Makes you look guilty."

"I'm not guilty!" she moaned, dropping her hands. Her eyes were pink with tears. "I was a nurse in the war. I wouldn't hurt a soul. I was trained to help people, not hurt them. I would never, never, *never* willfully harm another person. Not even that bitch Bibi!"

The way Lydia denied it told Dorothy that Lydia was sincere about not having killed Bibi—but it was also obvious to Dorothy that Lydia had certainly done *something* that she felt guilty about.

Dorothy looked up and saw Woollcott standing in the doorway. He clapped his hands once. "A convincing performance, Lydia. Worthy of a first-rate actress such as yourself," he said, stepping forward. "Now drop the act, and tell us the truth!"

Chapter 11

Dorothy shoved Woollcott through the door and followed him into the hallway. Before closing the door behind her, she turned to Lydia, lying in bed. "Pull yourself together. We'll be back in a minute."

In the hallway Woollcott folded his arms across his fat belly. "You can't shelter her all night, Dorothy dear. I'll cross-examine her, mark my words. She's guilty. Anyone can see that!"

Mrs. Volney's door opened a crack.

Dorothy grabbed Woollcott by the lapels. *"Shh!"* Then she dragged him along the corridor to the stairs.

She thought it over as they descended the steps to the lobby. *What* would *make Lydia faint like that? Did she kill Bibi? So the whole fainting bit was just an act, and she had me fooled? Jeez, maybe everyone's playing a game with me. First Woollcott with his game of Murder, then Benchley with his emotional shenanigans, and now Lydia with her act of innocence?*

Dorothy felt adrift, especially without Benchley at her side. She was having a hard time getting along without him tonight. She had realized it early in the evening, when she merely hoped he would show up for the party. But now she felt angry, wounded and confused without him. She needed someone's help. Someone who knew what to do. And in any case this situation called for the police.

Dorothy led the way across the lobby. The lights were turned low. The party had mostly broken up. A few small groups of stragglers leaned against the columns or against each other, swaying to and fro. Other partygoers were slouched or collapsed in the lobby's plush armchairs; their cardboard party hats were askew on their heads. Several were waiting by the elevator to go up to bed.

Dorothy rounded the corner of the reception desk and opened an office door marked OPERATOR. In the tiny room, a tired-looking middle-aged woman sat in front of a telephone switchboard. She coughed as they came in.

"Happy New Year, Mavis," Dorothy said.

"Happy? Tell it to my throat. And my back." Mavis twisted in her chair to stretch. She wore an earphone headset, as well as a heavy-looking hornlike microphone around her neck. She pulled this apparatus off her head and dropped it onto the switchboard with a clatter.

Dorothy made a sympathetic noise. "Long, busy night?"

"Long, busy *day*!" Mavis said in her usual craggy smoker's voice. She also had a thick Noo Yawk accent. "I've been on duty since noon. Alice was supposed to relieve me at eight o'clock for the night shift. But on account of this lousy quarantine, she couldn't get in. I don't know how Mr. Case expects me to make it through the night. This had better count as overtime, that's for sure."

"Oh, you poor dear—" Dorothy began.

Woollcott shoved his way into the room. "Enough griping, you chatterboxes. We need to talk to the police at once. Now, what's the matter with this thing? Why couldn't you place the call from Mr. Fairbanks' suite?"

Mavis' face soured. "Most of the lines are down because

of the snow, sir. There's one emergency line available, but it only goes through this switchboard. I can't connect you through a room telephone."

"Then connect us here, you obtuse operator," Woollcott said in his most pompous tone. "Do you think we came all the way down from the penthouse for nothing? Go ahead, place the call."

Dorothy wondered (and not for the first time), *Why do some people think they'll be helped faster if they act like first-rate arrogant bastards?*

She patted the operator on the shoulder. "Just show me how to do it, Mavis. And then you go take a five-minute break."

For a woman who seemed so tired, Mavis jumped up from her chair surprisingly quickly.

"It's easy peasy! Just put this on," she said, grabbing the headset, and shoving it onto Dorothy's head.

She sat Dorothy down in the swivel chair and turned her to the switchboard. Dorothy faced a wall-like panel full of holes and little unlit lights. Below this, on a desk-like board at her fingertips, was an array of switches, more little unlit bulbs and the upright tips of many cords.

Mavis pointed to the end of a metal-pronged cord. "You pull that out and plug it in that red-rimmed socket up there. That connects you to the emergency operator."

Dorothy did so.

Mavis continued, "When you're ready, pull back your switch there. That'll signal her on her end, and the light above the plug will go on. The light goes off when she answers. Flick the switch back to the middle position, and then ask her for the police. When you're done talking, just unplug the cord. It'll snap back into place on its own, so watch your fingernails. Easy as that."

While she was saying this, she had taken off her thick sweater and adjusted her skirt. She puffed up her hair where the headset had been, and now she put on lipstick.

Dorothy said, "You're coming back in five minutes, right?"

"Certainly, Mrs. Parker! The party in the lobby isn't over yet, is it?"

"Not just yet," Dorothy conceded. "There are still drinks to be had and men to accost. But wait a minute, Mavis. What if somebody in the hotel wants to place a call while we're here?"

She waved her hand and laughed. "Ignore it. What's so important at twelve thirty on New Year's night?" But then she seemed to realize that she wasn't being quite helpful. She spoke less flippantly. "Oh, just tell them the truth—the lines are down and no outside calls can be made."

She closed her purse with a snap and disappeared out the door.

Dorothy faced the large switchboard with its neat lines of wires, rows of plugs, columns of switches and array of darkened lights.

"Well, what are you waiting for?" Woollcott asked. "Place the call, woman."

Dorothy imitated Mavis' throaty and imperturbable operator's voice. "Just a moment, sir." Then she plugged the cord into the emergency line and flipped the switch as Mavis had instructed. A red light went on and then off again as a man's gruff voice spoke in her ear.

"New York Emergency. What's your call?"

"The police, please," Dorothy said in her usual quiet voice.

"Police? Which precinct, Operator?"

"Oh, whichever is available at the moment."

"Whichever is available? Who is this?"

Dorothy became a little nervous. "Which precinct is closest to the Algonquin Hotel?"

The man on the other end snorted. "Hold on. I'll connect you."

The little red light went on again. *Oops, did I do some-*

thing wrong? Then there was a click, and it went off again by itself.

Another man's voice came through the headphones. "Sixteenth Precinct. What's your emergency, Operator?"

"Can I speak to Detective O'Rannigan, please?"

"O'Rannigan's off duty. I'll put you through to the night desk instead."

"Not so fast." Dorothy spoke quickly. She didn't want that little light to go on again. "Is Captain Church there?"

"When is he *not* here? Hold on, I'll put you through."

The line went quiet, but the light remained off. Next to Dorothy, Woollcott crossed and uncrossed his arms impatiently.

There was a click, then a stony voice. "This is Church."

"Good evening, Captain. Or should I say *good morning*? It's Dorothy Parker. You remember me, don't you?"

There was a long, weary sigh at the other end. "I am afraid I do. Mrs. Parker, this is an emergency line—"

"I have an emergency. I'm at the Algonquin Hotel. One of the guests has died. A prominent guest—Bibi Bibelot, the Broadway starlet."

She heard the scratching of a pencil on the other end.

"Bibelot ..." Captain Church repeated. "What happened to her? How did she die?"

"We don't know exactly."

Woollcott leaned toward the microphone horn around Dorothy's neck. "She was murdered!"

"Who is that?" Church asked.

"Alexander Woollcott," she said. "Do you remember him, too?"

"I'm afraid so," Church said.

"Bibi Bibelot was murdered!" Woollcott nearly screamed. "In cold blood!"

In response to his outbursts, Dorothy tried to sound as calm and rational as she could. "It wasn't in cold blood, Captain. It was in a cold bathtub, actually."

Church made that long, weary sigh again. "Mrs. Parker, if this is some kind of prank—"

"It's no prank. Bibi was found dead in Douglas Fairbanks' bathtub just a little while ago."

"Fairbanks..." he said evenly. The pencil scratched again. Any other person would have screamed the famous name. "Why did Mr. Woollcott say she was murdered? Who found her?"

"Well—" Dorothy hesitated. "I suppose I found her."

"You suppose? Is there some doubt?"

"No, Captain. I found her."

"And was she murdcred?"

"I can't say. I'm not a detective—and neither is Aleck Woollcott!" She gave him a reproachful look.

"I am sending over a squad car. Do not do a single thing. Do not even touch the body."

Dorothy decided that now was not the time to tell Church that they had not only touched the body but had already moved Bibi from the tub to the bed. Then she remembered something else. "Oh, and we need an ambulance, too. An elderly man has had an apoplectic stroke."

She heard the rustle of papers on the other end.

"Just a moment," Church said. "You said the Algonquin Hotel, did you not?"

"Yes, we're—"

"Under quarantine. That changes things. A squad car is out of the question."

"What?" she said, dismayed. "Why?"

Woollcott leaned close, trying to hear from the outside of her headphones. "What? What is it?"

Dorothy swatted him away. She focused on getting answers from Church. "You mean your officers can't break the quarantine?"

"Not without permission from the Health Department."

"Not even in a life-or-death situation? Because that's what we have here, Captain. Life or death."

"The earliest we could expect to obtain permission from the Health Department is in the morning. And that is an optimistic estimation."

"Bibi's dead body is lying in Douglas Fairbanks' bed, and his wife, Mary Pickford, is none too happy about it. Wouldn't you call that a health violation? Don't you think the health commissioner would make an exception?"

Church's voice was sharp. "The dead body is in Fairbanks' bed? I thought you said Bibi died in a bathtub?"

"Uh, what I meant is that the *man with the stroke* is in the bed," she said without further elaboration. "So what about the ambulance? That could certainly break the quarantine, right? The ambulance boys could take away Bibi's body while they're here to see Dr. Hurst."

"To be perfectly frank, I doubt it. Not at this hour. The wheels of bureaucracy turn slowly in this city—and that much slower in the early hours of New Year's Day during a snowstorm."

She was becoming impatient. "How about not being perfectly frank? How about you try being imperfectly frank? Would that change your answer?"

"Fear not!" Woollcott shouted into the microphone. "I'm on the case, oh, Captain, my captain! Your boys in blue may take their sweet time, because I'll have this murder mystery wrapped up *tout de suite*."

Church spoke sternly. "Tell him he is not to interfere with a police investigation."

Dorothy turned to Woollcott. "The captain says if you get in the way, he'll arrest you *tout de suite*."

Woollcott grinned. "Ha! I'll clear the way, not get in the way."

Church's voice was threatening. "Please repeat that he is *not* to interfere with this investigation."

Dorothy said to Woollcott, "The captain says he'll lock you in the Tombs and throw away the key."

"Poppycock!" Woollcott sneered. "He'll award me the key to the city. Mark my words."

She ignored Woollcott and spoke again to Church. "If you can't send over a squad car or an ambulance, how about a delivery boy with some Chinese food? We're starving here."

"Please hold the line, Mrs. Parker. Let me see what can be done."

"About the Chinese food?"

Church sighed wearily again. "About the dead body. And the elderly man with the stroke."

The line clicked and went silent, and she was relieved to see that the light remained off, which meant the line was still connected.

Suddenly Woollcott was like a fly buzzing in her face. "Did he hang up on you? He hung up on you! Some public servant! He should be tarred and feathered."

She clucked her tongue at him. "He's just on another line, you ninny. And, as a matter of fact, he *is* quite a public servant. He's on the job in the middle of the night while everybody else is out whooping it up."

Well, almost everybody, she thought glumly to herself. *Whoop-de-do . . .*

"Ha! He's on the job, is he?" Woollcott shook his melon-like head. "Well, I'm the only one in this hotel on the job! And, to that end, I shan't stand around here blowing hot air—"

"Too late."

"I'll resume my investigation posthaste!" He turned to leave.

Church came back on the line. "Mrs. Parker?"

"Yes, I'm still here, Captain."

Hearing this, Woollcott paused in the doorway. He cocked his ear toward her.

Church continued, "I was just on the other line with Dr.

Norris at the Office of the Chief Medical Examiner. Do you remember meeting him?"

"Do I ever. We once went on a date. Let's see . . . cold heart, warm hands—hands he wouldn't keep to himself," she said, but with only slight irritation. "Now, speaking of cold hearts, what do we do with Bibi?"

Church was matter-of-fact. "Dr. Norris said it is important to keep the body at a low temperature to preserve it. Since you are in a hotel, there is certainly an ample supply of ice there. Surround the body with the ice."

"Ice?" *Ice in Fairbanks' bed? Oh well, Mary was going to toss it out anyhow.*

Church replied, "Dr. Norris said that because the body is already in a bathtub, it will be a simple matter to easily add a large quantity of ice. That should be sufficient until we can obtain permission from the Department of Health to enter the premises."

"How long will it take to get permission?"

"Perhaps by morning, as I said before. Or perhaps later in the day. The city government is officially closed on New Year's Day, so it could even be the day after."

"Of course we wouldn't want to disturb anyone's day off, would we?" Dorothy said sarcastically. *Then again,* she thought, *Bibi's not going anywhere.* "But what about the elderly man with apoplexy? Will you send an ambulance for him?"

"No," Church said simply. "Dr. Norris said to keep him stable. Very little else can be done for him right now, no matter whether he is in a hospital bed or in a movie star's bed."

"Eh, between you and me, very little could be done for him even before the stroke. I guess doing nothing will have to do for now."

Church hastily ended the conversation. "Thank you for reporting this matter, Mrs. Parker. I will call the hotel if I have any news. I trust you will do the same for me."

"I'll shout it from the rooftops."

The line went dead, and the tiny red light went on. Dorothy unplugged the cord, as Mavis had told her to do. The light went off.

"Well?" Woollcott stood at the door impatiently.

"He told me to keep Bibi's body cold. To surround her in a bed of ice."

"But what about me?" Woollcott asked petulantly. "What did he want me to do?"

"Go jump in a lake."

Chapter 12

"Put her on ice?" Frank Case asked, incredulous. Dorothy and Case stood in the parlor in Fairbanks' penthouse.

"That's what the police captain said. It'll preserve her until the Health Department says the police are allowed into the hotel."

"Forget it," Fairbanks called from the bedroom doorway. "There's no ice in the whole hotel. We ran out even before the party was over."

"Oh dear. Perhaps you're right," Case said. "Chef Jacques told me we were running low earlier in the evening ... and with all the drinking that's been going on tonight ..."

"Maybe we can borrow a block from someone's icebox?" Benchley asked. He was in the bedroom helping Doyle and Jordan lift Dr. Hurst into a rickety old wooden wheelchair.

Case eyed the wheelchair. "I have a better idea."

"This is a terrible idea," Benchley said sourly.

What had gotten into him? Dorothy decided to take an approach she rarely took with Benchley. The direct approach. "What has gotten into you? You were so lovely earlier. What has made you so cross now?"

"Well, Mrs. Parker"—his voice was artificially merry—"we've been dragooned into pushing a dead, naked woman in a wheelchair to take her to the walk-in freezer in the hotel's spooky cellar in the middle of the night. What could I possibly find objectionable about that?"

With a wave of his hand, he took in the grim little service elevator and Bibi's dead body in the wobbly wooden wheelchair in front of them.

Dorothy sighed to herself. This errand was her fault. When the idea had popped into Frank Case's mind, he turned to Dorothy and asked her to do it. His reasoning was simple. It was too sensitive a task to request an employee to handle, and furthermore Dorothy owed at least two months' rent, a repeated habit to which Case always turned a blind eye. And when he subtly reminded her about it, she couldn't help but agree to his plan.

But was that what Benchley was really angry about? Was he indeed jealous, as she had wondered earlier? Did he treasure her so much that it would throw him into such an unusual fit? That actually made her feel good—that he would be so emotional about her, so jealous for her time and attention.

Then she thought of something else. Perhaps it had nothing to do with her at all. Benchley had a wife and children at home in the suburbs. Maybe he wanted to be home with them, not trapped in this hotel with her? And if so, was he now taking out his anger on her?

She had begged him to be sure to come to the party, and look what she had gotten him into. After feeling so cherished just a moment before, she now felt low, lower than low. Nearly worthless.

She looked at the woman's body covered in a bedsheet. Well, at least she wasn't dead like Bibi. She could be thankful for that.

But realizing this didn't make her feel any better. It actually made her feel worse. *Is that what my life has come to? To be relieved simply for not being a trampy dead starlet who's about to be shoved into a hotel freezer? Is that the best I can hope for?*

The elevator stopped at the subbasement level. She reached over the body and opened the elevator door. "Come on. Let's just put this gal on ice and be done with it."

Compared to the hotel above, the subbasement was like another world. Somewhere up there right now, Woollcott was probably pestering Lydia for answers. Down here it was airless and dark, lit by bare lightbulbs spaced far apart, with gaps of darkness in between. The floor was poorly patched concrete, dingy and dusty, causing the wheelchair to veer off unexpectedly. Wires and pipes ran overhead, creaking and clanging with steam. Narrow, dark corridors twisted off into even darker tunnels leading to who knew where.

Neither Dorothy nor Benchley had ever been in the subbasement before. Frank Case had given them directions, so they were unlikely to get lost—at least she hoped not. At the end of this corridor, they were to turn left. They did so, and as predicted, there was the thick metal door to the freezer room. The heavy door was dull metal, battered and scratched, but solid with no window.

Benchley parked the wheelchair, and Bibi's body rocked to a stop. He moved forward and grabbed the long handle to unlatch the door. It pulled open with a shrill metallic shriek.

"Ouch," Benchley said, wincing. "That was noisy enough to wake the dead."

They both turned around to look at the body in the sheet. It did not move.

The freezer room was about the size of a walk-in closet, and was nearly full with boxes and crates of food. Icicles the size of daggers hung from the ceiling.

He sighed. "We'll have to move and stack up some boxes to fit Bibi and the wheelchair inside."

Leaving the body in the corridor, Dorothy and Benchley silently entered the freezer. Even in a long-sleeved velvet dress, Dorothy felt uncomfortably chilly. She picked up a big cylindrical carton marked *Pistachio Ice Cream* and lifted it against the wall on top of another box, but her hands nearly stuck to it when she tried to let go.

"Ouch," she said, and breathed on her palms to warm them. Her breath came out in puffs of vapor, as though she was blowing smoke.

"Here." Benchley took off his suit jacket. "This will keep you from freezing to death. Put your hands inside the sleeves so you can use them like mittens."

Gratefully, she took his jacket. She could still feel the warmth of his body as she put it on. But, regrettably, the warm feeling quickly went away. She nodded her thanks and picked up another box.

How poetic, she thought. *And how prosaic. The feelings between us keep changing from chilly to warm, then hot to icy. It's a wonder I don't catch a cold from all the ups and downs.*

Working together, they managed to move a number of boxes out of the way. Soon they had cleared an area large enough to fit Bibi and the wheelchair.

"That's enough," Dorothy said. "Let's roll her in and be done with it."

Just as they turned to leave the freezer, the sound of screeching metal startled them and stopped them where they stood. Just as surprising, the door quickly swung closed. They jumped forward, racing toward the shrinking gap of light. But the door slammed tight, leaving them in icy, absolute darkness. Dorothy pounded on the cold metal door with her fists.

There was a handle somewhere on the inside; Dorothy had seen it. She searched for it with her hands in the sleeves of Benchley's jacket and found it. As she did, a loud, violent clang came from the other side of the door, and the handle vibrated painfully in her grip. Reflexively, she pulled her hand away—but the handle came with it. A small circle of light shone through where the handle had just been. Had someone just broken apart the door handle from the out-side? She threw the useless piece of metal to the hard floor. She bent down and peeked through the hole.

There was movement. Rough, dark fabric. A pair of trou-sers! Then nothing. She could see the stone wall opposite, and just a sliver of the bedsheet that covered Bibi. Then the bedsheet disappeared, and Dorothy heard the creak of the wheelchair as it moved away.

"Oh brother," she said, her heart in her throat. "Some guy locked us in here. And now he's taking Bibi with him!"

"That's funny," Benchley said. "Bibi's supposed to be the one in cold storage, but now she's making a hot getaway."

Well, Dorothy thought, *at least Benchley has recovered his sense of humor.*

Chapter 13

"We have to get out of here," Dorothy heard herself saying. "We'll freeze to death!"

She was stating the obvious. It was extremely cold and dark, and she felt a shudder of panic begin to creep up her spine.

"Do you have any matches?" Benchley asked. "Maybe we could light a fire on one of these cartons."

"No, I don't have any matches. I expect a man to light my cigarettes. Do you?"

"No, I usually just light my own cigarettes—or my pipe, as the case may be."

"I meant," she said patiently, "do you have any matches?"

"Why, yes! Look in my jacket pocket."

She searched through the pockets of his jacket, pulled out a matchbox and handed it to him. "You do it."

He struck a match, and his amiable face was visible in the seemingly warm glow of the flame. He brought the match to the edge of a cardboard carton. It soon went out before it could catch fire.

"Well, so much for that," he said. "Must be too icy in here."

"Reach up and break off one of those icicles, would you please?"

She heard him make a small grunt, and then she heard the crack of breaking ice.

"Here you are, one icicle. That'll be twenty-five cents, please, miss."

"Put it on my tab," she said.

"Mrs. Parker, what do you intend to do with that sharp, slender icicle, if I may inquire?"

"You may. I intend to stick it into the latch hole. Perhaps I can use it to somehow pry open the latch or even the door itself."

Aiming at the small circle of light, she thrust the point of the icicle into it. Taking care not to break the icicle, she tried to turn it as though turning a doorknob. But it was too slippery. She tried to push it forward, perhaps to pressure open the latch mechanism. But the icicle didn't seem to affect the mechanism at all. Finally she tried to put sideways pressure on it, as if to free the door from whatever hasp that locked it. But the icicle only snapped apart in her hands.

"Well, you tried," Benchley said. "It's the thought that counts."

"I think I'm f-freezing." She clutched her arms around herself. "Oh, and now I'm st-stuttering!"

Then she felt him reach out to her, wrap his arms around her and hold her close to his body. She knew he was doing it to keep them both warm, and, not caring why, she burrowed herself against him.

They held each other tightly for what seemed like a long time. She knew they couldn't last inside the freezer much longer. They'd either have to get out soon—or die frozen in each other's arms.

"Want to know something funny?" she finally asked him.

"Yes, I'd love to hear s-s-something funny."

"I feel like you've been giving me the cold shoulder all night. And now you actually are."

"Oh yes?" he asked. "Here I was under the impression I had done something to make you hot under the collar."

"Just that you've been avoiding me."

"Avoiding you? Well, I suppose I have been. But only because you've been peeved with me. So I thought I'd just, you know, s-s-stay out of your way."

"Peeved with you?" She held him more tightly. "I've been nothing of the sort, you silly old fool. And even if I were, why would that cause you to avoid me?"

"I thought perhaps you were fed up with me," he said. "You know, stuffy old Benchley, always making the same jokes, never playing Woollcott's games. An old s-s-stick in the mud, that's me. I thought you'd had quite enough of me. And, well, frankly that made me ill-tempered with you."

"Had enough of you? Whatever would give you that idea?"

Could he be serious? Before he had arrived at the Algonquin, she had been waiting like a puppy for its master. She would have jumped into his arms when he arrived, if she could have.

"Well," he explained, "I thought we were having a grand old time at the party up in Chez Fairbanks, just joking and drinking, as usual. But the first opportunity you had to get away, you took it. Something about talking with Mary Pickford, and then you were after Woollcott. And then I didn't see you for a while. 'That's it, old boy,' I thought to myself. 'You're yesterday's news. Stale as a week-old loaf of bread.' No wonder you're sick and tired of me. I'm as exciting as a warm bowl of tapioca."

She nestled her head against him and squeezed her arms around him. If she hadn't been freezing cold, she could just about die happy right now—and there seemed to be every chance that she might.

Still, he wasn't jealous after all. How could she even think he'd be so petty? That wasn't like Benchley in the least. And he wasn't avoiding her because he was missing his wife and children. . . . *Well, maybe he is or maybe he isn't, but in any case he's not taking the loss out on me. How could I have been so silly?*

"Mr. Benchley . . . ?"

"Call me Fred."

"Fred . . ."

She turned her face up to his. *Kiss me, you fool,* she wanted to say, and chuckled to herself at the sappy thought of it.

"What's so funny?" he asked.

"I d-don't know. Just that it required a c-cold room for you to warm up to me."

"N-n-nonsense, Mrs. Parker. I've always—"

There was a sharp bang on the door.

Wait, she thought. *Always? Always—what? What was he about to say?*

There was another bang on the door. "Is someone in there?"

"Go away!" Dorothy shouted.

"Who's in there? Mrs. Parker?" It was Woollcott's voice.

"Aleck, is that you?" Benchley called out.

"Benchley, damn you!" Woollcott responded angrily. "My word, the lengths to which some people will go to avoid playing one of my famous games. What the devil are you two doing in there? Come out of there this moment." They heard him mutter to himself, "Where is the damn doorknob?"

"Some villain broke it off," Benchley answered. "Get Frank Case. We're going to die of hypothermia."

They heard Woollcott puttering around. "Just a moment. Here's something."

There was a clink of metal on metal, and then the clack of the latch. All of a sudden the door opened with a screech. They had to blink because the light was so bright, even though it was merely the few lights of the dim basement. Woollcott's chubby hands reached in and pulled them out into the cellar corridor. He slammed the door closed behind them.

The subbasement's heat was delightful. Dorothy sucked

in gasps of the stuffy air just to warm up her lungs. She leaned against the stone wall to absorb its heat. Benchley did the same.

"You see?" Woollcott said. "Sometimes I'm fairly handy to have around. Wouldn't you say?"

"C-c-can't say a thing. Really shivering now," she said.

"Now, tell me, whatever were you two doing in there?"

They slyly glanced at each other a little guiltily, as though they had been schoolchildren caught necking in the classroom coat closet.

"Nothing!" they both said at the same time.

Chapter 14

"I shall make some of my famous Café Alexander for you," Woollcott said as he led them up the stairs. "That'll heat you up lickety-split."

They shook and shivered as they climbed up one concrete stairway and then another, which eventually brought them into the hotel's kitchen. Soon Woollcott was banging around with pots and pans while Dorothy and Benchley, still frozen stiff, stood motionless with their backs against the hot radiator.

Woollcott couldn't find a kettle or a percolator. So he filled a small pan half-full with water, lit one of the burners on the stove and set the pan down over the bright blue flame.

He waved a hand at Dorothy. "Mrs. Parker, hand me that large can of coffee, if you please."

She turned around and pulled down from a shelf a five-pound can of Horn & Hardart coffee beans, and handed it to him. With the can in his hand, Woollcott searched for a coffee mill. His face lit up when he noticed a small sausage grinder mounted to the countertop.

"Mr. Benchley, your assistance please," Woollcott said as he spilled a handful of the beans into the upturned mouth

102

of the sausage grinder. "Turn that crank, if you would. The exertion will warm you up."

Benchley turned the handle. The grinder made loud, angry crunching sounds as it crushed the beans. Woollcott grabbed the pan of boiling water from the burner to catch the coffee grounds.

"There we are." He set the pan of coffee and water back on the burner. "Now, while we wait for it to steep, tell me what you were doing in that walk-in freezer."

Dorothy told him everything exactly as it happened. Woollcott stopped her only once. "So you saw a man's pants through the latch hole, and that man apparently wheeled Bibi away?"

She agreed that was what she had seen. She didn't, however, go into detail about what she and Benchley were talking about when Woollcott banged on the door. Or how tightly they had held each other.

"So," she asked, "what brought you to our rescue? How did you know we were trapped in there?"

"I didn't." He glanced at his pocket watch and checked the pan of boiling coffee. He snatched up a large spaghetti strainer, dropped in a piece of cheesecloth and placed it over a pie plate. Then he picked up the coffee pan and poured the steaming liquid into the strainer. He set aside the strainer, now lined with coffee grounds, and carefully poured the coffee from the pie plate into two coffee cups, which he had ready.

Fascinated, she watched his every move. "If you didn't know that we were trapped in there, how did you come to find us?"

"After I left you in the switchboard room, I went back up to see Lydia to interrogate her thoroughly, as you did not allow me to do so in the first place," Woollcott said. "But Lydia was a bundle of nerves, and I couldn't get a straight word out of her. I'm not too proud to say that this hardened investigator realized he needed a woman's conniving, feminine wiles to elicit answers from her. So I went looking for you."

"Aleck, you're not a hardened investigator, you're a drama critic," she said. "And if anyone I know has a woman's conniving, feminine wiles, it's you."

"Well, that's a fine thing to say to the person who saved your life," he said without a trace of real anger. He was preoccupied with looking into drawers. "Mrs. Parker, you ungrateful wretch, would you please check the sink for two coffee spoons?"

She went to the sink, but it was empty. Next to the sink was an enormous barrel-like enamel contraption. It was filled with dirty silverware and ball bearings immersed in a blue liquid. "What is this?"

Woollcott didn't even look up. "Is it a hopper of ball bearings and silverware immersed in a blue liquid?"

She looked inside the enamel barrel. "Yes, that's exactly what it is."

"It's for cleaning and burnishing the silverware. The kitchen staff soaks the silverware overnight in that toxic concoction, and they swirl it around in the ball bearings, which loosens the bits of food from the cutlery. Then, in the morning, they rinse it off easily."

She turned to him. "How do you know so much about the hotel's kitchen?"

But he was busy reaching up into a high cabinet. He pulled down an amber bottle of cognac.

"Ah, here we are. Chef Jacques' secret stash." He turned to Parker and Benchley. "I make it my business to know." He held up the bottle as though it were evidence of this fact. "You live here. You should do the same. The spoons, please? Careful, that liquid will burn your skin. Rinse it off immediately."

She plucked two spoons out of the mouth of the big enamel barrel. Woollcott was right. The blue liquid began to sting right away. She turned on the cold-water faucet and washed it off her hands and the spoons. She dried the spoons on a dish towel and handed them to Woollcott.

He splashed a healthy amount of the brandy into each cup. Then he found a canister of sugar and measured out two heaping spoonfuls for each. He opened the icebox (a "warm box" now, as the block of ice had been removed—probably for cocktails) and took out a bottle of cream. He poured a large dose of the cream into each cup and stirred. He had already found a couple of nutmeg seeds, which he now dropped into the sausage grinder. He held each cup under the grinder for a quick sprinkle of the nutmeg.

"Café Alexander!" he announced, proudly handing the cups to Dorothy and Benchley. "Good for what ails you. Drink up."

The warm kitchen had already removed most of the chill from her body, but she nevertheless accepted the cup gratefully.

Benchley raised his mug with that familiar merry twinkle in his eye. "Cheers to you, Mrs. Parker," he said warmly. "Happy New Year."

"Cheers to you, Fred," she said, almost in a whisper. "Happy New Year."

They clinked cups. And just like that, things were right again between them. Benchley was with her, and he would be by her side through this night, she knew, no matter what it brought. Certainly he would—wouldn't he?

She smiled to herself and took a sip of the coffee. The hot, sweet liquid warmed her to her toes.

"Magnificent," she said—and immediately regretted it. She hated to give Woollcott more stuffing for his overstuffed ego. Woollcott grinned with satisfaction.

"Oh, don't look so smug," she said to him. "A hot cup of that silverware liquid would taste good to me now."

"If you say so," he said, smirking. "But where were we? Ah yes, first the naked girl's necklace goes missing. And then she is found in a room that is locked from the inside!

Then, to top it off, the naked girl herself goes missing. Who would have taken her, and where did he take her? For we now can conclude, by the sight of the trousers, that the person you saw was indeed a man."

"And why did he take her?" Benchley asked. "And why shove us into the freezer in the bargain?"

"No doubt he trapped you in there to make a clean getaway with Bibi's body."

"How inconsiderate," Benchley said. "He could have simply asked us for the body. We would have gladly handed her over. No need to freeze us to death for it."

Woollcott folded his arms over his big belly. "Then we can assume it was someone who didn't want you to see him. He has a secret agenda. First he murders Bibi. Then he steals her body."

Dorothy didn't bother to argue now about whether Bibi was indeed murdered. She had come to that certain conclusion while she was inside the freezer. Someone wanted her and Benchley dead—or at least didn't care if they remained alive or not—so it was only logical to believe that this same person had killed Bibi.

"As preposterous as that sounds, I'm afraid I agree with you, Aleck," she said. "But who? And why?"

"If we find out the who, we shall quickly determine the why. Let us consider...." A wicked look stole over Woollcott's face. "Oh, that devious pair! What cunning! What boldness! What effrontery!"

"What—are you talking about?" Benchley asked.

"You mean, *who* am I talking about? None other than Hollywood's sweethearts, Mary Pickford and Douglas Fairbanks!"

Dorothy sighed and drained her cup. "Aleck, just when I start to take you seriously, you jump right off the deep end. Are you still at a loss for your marbles?"

Woollcott raised a finger in the air. "Ah, but that's the beauty of their plan. On the surface it does seem crazy. But take a closer look, and it's devilishly clever. Think about it. Who was probably the last to see Bibi alive? Mary Pickford, correct?"

"Well, that may be true—"

"Of course it's true," he snapped. "Mary somehow killed Bibi in the bathtub, but then you and I appeared before she could get rid of the body. So what does Mary do? She enlists the help of her husband, who follows you down to the cellar, locks you in the cold storage closet and absconds with the body of his wife's rival. You see? Mary and Douglas worked together. She did the killing, and he did the disposing. And then they can cover each other's tracks. Devilishly clever!"

"It's nuts, is what it is," Dorothy said. "Why on earth would Fairbanks steal Bibi's body? What would he need it for? He and his wife are the most successful couple on Broadway and in Hollywood. Why in heaven's name would they waste their time—as well as jeopardize their reputations—on murdering Bibi in the first place?"

"Mrs. Parker has a point," Benchley said.

Woollcott opened his mouth to speak, but Dorothy continued, "And why murder her in their own bathtub in the midst of their own party? No woman in her right mind would agree to sully her own home in such a way."

"Ah, there's the rub," Woollcott said archly. "Perhaps she's not in her right mind."

Benchley nodded. "Aleck has a point. Mary was rather upset with Bibi. You told me so yourself."

Woollcott stepped closer. "And didn't she accuse Fairbanks of some kind of extramarital shenanigans, even bestowing that necklace on the young tartlet? Ahem, I mean starlet."

Dorothy shook her head. "Aleck, you came looking for me because you thought Lydia was the guilty party. Now you have your sights set on Mary and Douglas? Whom will you accuse next?"

"Don't get too comfy, Mrs. Parker," he said, graciously taking her empty coffee cup from her. "I have only your word that you saw a man wheel Bibi away. And I have only your word that you had found Bibi already dead. You could be lying on both counts, for all I know."

"All that you know could fill up this coffee spoon," she said, handing him the utensil. "And there'd be room to spare."

"Room to spare?" His smile hardened. "Speaking of rooms, what do you say we go up to Fairbanks' penthouse and question its occupants? Then you'll see how much I know."

Chapter 15

They rode in the service elevator. It was darker and noisier than the passenger elevator, but it was also right next to the kitchen. So it was too handy to pass up.

"Aleck, this is preposterous," Dorothy said. "Why would Doug Fairbanks and Mary Pickford allow Bibi to sit naked in their bathtub all night, then kill her by some mysterious means but allow her body to be placed in their bed, then demand that it be removed, and then steal the body back? It makes no sense."

Woollcott gazed at her over the rims of his eyeglasses. "Do you have a better theory? I'm all ears."

"You're all wet," she mumbled.

She didn't have a better theory—although she had a different one. *What if Lydia Trumbull murdered Bibi?* Lydia's whereabouts were unknown at the time of the murder. She was apparently one of the last to see Bibi alive. And she most certainly had an axe to grind against Bibi. Also, Dorothy thought, that fainting spell did not seem like the reaction an innocent woman might have to an accusation—even for an actress.

"Benchley, you're painfully silent," Woollcott said. "Something on your mind?"

Benchley shot a guilty glance at Dorothy.

Woollcott became impatient. "Come on. Out with it. What—or *who*—is on your mind?"

Dorothy held her breath. Was it *she* who was on his mind?

"Go on," Woollcott urged. "Tell us who it is."

"Dr. Hurst," Benchley finally said.

Dorothy silently exhaled.

Woollcott raised his eyebrows. "You have my attention. Please speak, Robert. Expatiate. Proclamate. Divulge. Tattle. Spill the beans!"

Benchley took a deep breath. "Well, Dr. Hurst certainly seemed rather displeased with Bibi. Remember how he entered the bathroom during the party, shut the door and then emerged soon afterward? What if he did something to her at that time, something that later killed her?"

Woollcott frowned, although he was clearly intrigued. "Go on."

"Immediately after, Dr. Hurst became drunk and argumentative. Fairbanks asked him to leave, and Doyle escorted him down to his room, where he fell asleep under the watchful eye of his valet. A perfect alibi. But if I'm right, he had already meted out Bibi's death sentence well before she actually died. Perhaps he employed a poison that only a doctor might have."

Dorothy looked up at him with admiration. *What a clever fellow my dear Fred is!*

"Mr. Benchley," she said, "no one would ever guess it from your angelic appearance, but you have quite a devilish mind to come to such a devious conclusion."

The elevator arrived at the top floor. Woollcott didn't make a move to open the door. He seemed displeased— displeased with a reasonable alternative to his theory against Fairbanks and Pickford. "But if it was Dr. Hurst, why would he seem so alarmed when he was brought up to examine the body?"

Benchley shrugged. "Lousy bedside manner?"

Dorothy spoke up. "You were the one who cried murder, Aleck. And that was right after you noticed that Bibi's locket was missing. That was Dr. Hurst's locket. So, it's no wonder that he was alarmed. Don't you find that significant?"

Woollcott held up a hand. "Ah, but Dr. Hurst then said the necklace was worthless. And he evidently had entrusted its care to Fairbanks. Don't *you* find it significant that said locket then wound up around Bibi's neck, and then subsequently disappeared while Dr. Hurst was no longer in the penthouse but down in his room? It directs the blame toward Fairbanks, not Dr. Hurst. And, last but not least, the door was locked—from the inside! And there's no reason to believe that Dr. Hurst or Lydia Trumbull had a key."

"Well . . ." Dorothy felt as though Woollcott had somehow turned her words against her. And she was about to argue that although Dr. Hurst *said* the locket was worthless, perhaps it really wasn't. Perhaps it had sentimental value, or some other value. Perhaps Dr. Hurst said it was worthless just to keep himself from looking guilty. But Woollcott didn't give her the chance to speak.

"Enough of this gibberish!" he said, flinging open the elevator door. "Let's talk to Douglas and Mary, and get to the bottom of this."

But when they entered the penthouse, the place was empty. They looked in every room, but there was no sign of Fairbanks or his wife.

"Now what?" Dorothy asked.

Woollcott hesitated, then thoughtfully moved toward the bathroom. "As they say in the detective novels, let us reconstruct the scene of the crime. Mrs. Parker, show us exactly how you entered this room in the first place, and then every step afterward. Leave out nothing."

"But, Aleck, you were here when I found her—"

"No, I most certainly wasn't. When I arrived, you were

standing over the bath. What did you do just before that? Show us step-by-step. Leave nothing out."

"Oh, well, if I must." She closed the bathroom door. "When I arrived, the penthouse was empty. The bathroom door was closed. If you'll recall, Aleck, I had told you that Mary had wanted your help to pry Bibi out of the bathtub. So I thought it'd be a hoot if you opened the bathroom door and instead of finding Bibi, you found me."

"And then you'd 'murder' me, per the rules of the game."

"That was my idea, yes. So when I found the bathroom door locked, I recalled that Fairbanks had said that there was a key in a kitchen drawer."

She proceeded to show them the drawer where she had found the key, although the key was no longer there. They went back to the bathroom door, and she pointed to the key in the lock, right where she had left it. She opened the door. "There was a towel on the floor against the inside of the door—"

"On the inside?" Woollcott asked. "That's very strange, don't you think?"

"More than strange," she said. "How did the murderer place a towel on the inside of the door—and why?"

"It's impossible," Benchley said. "If there was a towel against the door *inside* the bathroom, that means the murderer either left the room by other means—or didn't leave at all."

They all looked at the tub where Bibi had been, and thought the same thing. *Had Bibi left the tub at some point, put a towel down against the door and then gotten back into the tub?*

"It makes no sense!" Woollcott said.

"Then Bibi's *murderer* must have done it somehow," Benchley said.

"But if so," Woollcott asked, "how did he get out the door, yet leave the towel against it?"

"He *or* she," Dorothy said.

"Whoever!" Woollcott said. "Someone murdered Bibi, then disappeared like a ghost. I don't like it."

They looked all around the room. The only doorway in or out was the one in which they were standing. There was no skylight or air shaft in the ceiling. The only window was four feet off the floor and barely large enough for Dorothy to fit through—and there was a twelve-story drop on the outside.

Woollcott pursed his lips. "For the time being, let's not concern ourselves with how the murderer left the room. Let's get back to reconstructing the scene of the crime. Mrs. Parker, that's your cue."

Dorothy said, "As I told you before, I opened the door, which pushed aside the towel, and then I saw Bibi in the tub—"

"Show, don't tell," Woollcott said. "What kind of writer are you?"

She approached the tub with much less urgency than when she had originally found Bibi's body. "I went over, knelt down and, let's see, I felt her cheek. She was ice-cold. Her skin was white."

"And the room?"

"The room?"

"Was it cold? It was roasting during the party."

Dorothy stood up. "You know, it *was* cold. Well, it was cold after I opened the window, at least."

"So *you* opened the window?" Woollcott asked. "I remember closing it."

"Yes, I—" She was ashamed to admit she had panicked. "I needed some fresh air. So I opened the window." She reached toward it.

"Stop," Woollcott commanded. "That ice bucket on the floor and that broken glass. Were they there when you found Bibi?"

Dorothy hesitated.

Woollcott yanked his silk handkerchief from his breast

113

pocket and used it to pick up a shard of glass. "Perhaps Bibi was poisoned!"

"Poisoned?"

"She took a drink, felt the poison at work in her body, then dropped the glass on the floor in her agony. As her life shattered, so did this glass," he said dramatically.

"No, that wasn't it," Dorothy said. "Both the glass and the ice bucket were on the radiator. I knocked them over in my hurry to open the window. That's all."

"Was the glass empty?"

"I don't know. I think so."

"Well, Bibi may still have been poisoned. But now that the glass is broken, it's doubtful we shall ever know," he said disdainfully. "And the ice bucket, was it empty, too?"

"No, there was some ice in it. That I remember. It had spilled out when the bucket tumbled over."

"That's strange, because the floor is dry now. Must not have been much ice." Woollcott nodded thoughtfully, though she knew he made nothing of this information. "So you carelessly knocked over the champagne glass and ice bucket—"

"Aleck, really," Benchley said. "She had just discovered a dead body. Give her some latitude."

"Not attitude," Dorothy said.

Woollcott continued, "Then you stood up and threw open the sash."

She nodded and opened the window as she had earlier. Looking outside, she saw that the city was snowbound and quiet. It had been loud before, as crowds throughout New York were counting down to midnight.

Behind her, Woollcott asked, "And then what did you do?"

"I took in some fresh air."

"Mrs. Parker, you don't have to tell us every breath you took."

"You said to tell you step-by-step, leaving nothing out."

"Very well," he sighed. "And then?"

114

"Then I turned around, and you were standing there."
She pointed.

Woollcott moved backward to the bathroom doorway.
"And I said, 'Happy—'"

"Footprints!" Benchley shouted, almost in her ear.

"What?" Woollcott asked.

"Look, footprints." Benchley pointed out the window.
"Footprints in the snow, on the roof! What do you make of
that?"

"Someone took the road less traveled by?" she said.

Chapter 16

A FRIENDLY GAME OF MURDER
"When I turned around, and you were standing there,"

D orothy, Benchley and Woollcott crowded together at the tiny window.

Benchley was right. Dorothy hadn't noticed it before: On the outside windowsill, the snow had been pushed aside. She leaned forward. Now with her head slightly out the window, she could see that there was a portion of flat roof — like a very wide ledge or balcony — a few feet below the window. A trail of footprints, now obscured slightly with fresh snow, led away from beneath the window, went off to the right along the roof and turned the corner at the edge of the building.

"Someone came in or went out this window!" Woollcott cried.

"Went out, undoubtedly," Dorothy said. "There'd be snow or at least water on the floor if he had come in."

"Aha! So our killer somehow murdered Bibi, locked the door from the inside, put a towel at the bottom of the door for some reason, climbed out the window and made his escape across the roof."

"Or her escape," she said. "But to where?"

"Is there another way back into the hotel? A roof hatch or some such thing?"

They both looked at Dorothy.

"How should I know?" She narrowed her eyes at Woollcott. "You're the one who makes it his business to know all about the hotel."

He ignored this. "Someone needs to go through this window and follow those tracks."

"You do it, Sherlock," Benchley said to him. "Maybe you'll find Professor Moriarty out there."

"Heh heh," he chuckled, and patted his prodigious paunch. "I'm afraid that window is not my size. Perhaps you'd like to give it a go, Mr. Benchley?"

"I'm allergic to footprints. And snow. Sorry."

"Mrs. Parker?"

"I'm like the cleaning staff here. I don't do windows."

"Tut tut, you want to clear Fairbanks' name, do you not?"

She didn't answer.

Woollcott continued. "Who else could have performed such an acrobatic feat? Not only did he climb out the window, he also must have reached back in and replaced the champagne glass and ice bucket on the radiator, and then closed the sash from the outside. Then he scampered pitter-pat across the rooftop like a cat. Doesn't this answer to the acrobatic derring-do of Douglas Fairbanks, the man who does a backflip or walks on his hands at the drop of a hat?"

"Then let's get Fairbanks in here, and he can give it a try. Not me. I backflip for no man."

"Then how about a woman, as you keep insisting?"

"A woman?"

"Mary Pickford. The lady of the house."

"Mary wouldn't climb out her own bathroom window. Not when she had a key. For that matter, why would Fairbanks do it if the key was in his own kitchen drawer?"

"To throw off suspicion? To be mysterious?" Woollcott said. "Of course Fairbanks would not have expected you to open the window in the first place. By the time daylight arrived, the additional snow would have obscured his foot-prints altogether, and they wouldn't even be noticeable from the window. But you just helped us out with that clue, did you not? So, thank you for helping to incriminate him."

"How do you figure?" she asked.

"If you hadn't opened the window just now, we could never have seen Fairbanks' footprints," he said.

"But they're not—" She gritted her teeth. "How do you know they're Fairbanks' footprints?"

"Why don't you just go out the window and follow them, to find out for sure?"

Woollcott—and her own misplaced sense of guilt—eventually wore her down. Soon she again had Benchley's tuxedo jacket on, and he and Woollcott helped her climb up the hot radiator and scrabble out onto the window ledge.

She paused with her knees on the snowy stone sill. She felt awkward with her rear end to them, but her dress was long enough to cover her small rear end and most of her legs. But her dress and Benchley's jacket weren't thick enough to shield her from the winter chill.

She looked down at the small strip of flat roof, which was only about four feet wide. Even though the cornice of the building was high enough to keep her from slipping off the roof's edge, it was low enough that she could easily look over it. This was the back of the hotel, so she looked down into darkness—whether it was a dark alley or courtyard or what, she didn't know.

"Well, go on," Woollcott said impatiently. "Out you go."

She took a deep breath of frigid air and carefully slith-ered one knee out from under her. She pivoted on the nar-row sill and lowered her leg. She pivoted again and lowered her other leg, and now she could sit on the sill. She felt the cold, wet snow on her backside. The roof was only two feet below her two feet. With a cautious little push, she hopped off the sill. She slipped when she landed, and skidded to-ward the cornice. She couldn't stop. She was heading toward the edge. Her knees slipped out from under her, and she collapsed hard against the concrete cornice. The wind was knocked out of her—and the stuffing was scared out of her—as she found herself peering down into the inky darkness of the alley twelve stories below.

"Dottie, dear, are you all right?" Benchley shouted, halfway out the window. "I should never have let you go out there on your own."

His voice sounded so panicked that it did her heart good to hear it. She calmed down right away.

"Never fear, Mr. Benchley. This isn't the first time I've been out on a ledge." She looked again into the dimness below. "Metaphorically speaking, that is."

Chapter 17

A FRIENDLY GAME OF MURDER

Dorothy got to her feet, brushed the snow from her legs and then followed the half-hidden footprints. She noticed that the shoes that had made them were larger than her shoes—but almost anyone's shoes were larger than hers. She also realized that whoever made them had a longer stride than she did. When the footprints turned at the corner of the building, so did she.

Now she faced a large expanse of flat roof. (In the summertime it would be big enough to allow a rooftop garden. She'd have to make that suggestion to Frank Case.) But the cold wind was more severe on this side of the building. It hit her like a slap in the face. She hugged Benchley's coat around her and shivered. She searched the snow for the footprints and could only just discern them. They were merely shallow depressions in the deepening, windblown snow.

She followed them to a brick wall, where they stopped. As she approached the wall, she realized there was an iron ladder built into it. Whoever had made the footprints had obviously climbed the ladder. She didn't want to climb the ladder, but she didn't want to stay out on this freezing roof any longer either. She used the sleeves of Benchley's jacket as mittens and started climbing.

She was just as cold now as she had been in the basement freezer, only Benchley wasn't here to keep her company. So she vowed that Woollcott would have to make her another one of those hot coffee drinks just as soon as she got back inside the hotel—no matter how she got back inside the hotel.

At the top of the ladder, a gust of wind blew an icy chill up her dress. It was so cold that she could barely catch her breath. Oh, Woollcott would owe her a lifetime of coffee drinks for persuading her to do this! She stepped off the ladder onto this upper roof and saw that the shallow footprints ended a few paces away at a square hatchway. She hurried over to the closed lid, which was covered in thick snow. She clutched her frozen fingers underneath the edge of it and tried to heave it open, but it barely budged.

Oh damn! Is it locked? She tried again and was able to lift it an inch or two. But the hatch itself, combined with the snow on top, made it simply too heavy for her thin arms to lift.

She used the sleeves of Benchley's jacket to brush off the snow. The hatch was wide—about four feet square—so it took her awhile to get all the snow off. By the time she had removed it all, she was dead tired and absolutely freezing cold. *Curse that Woollcott! And curse that Fairbanks and Pickford, too! They're innocent, of course, so why would I brave the elements to try to prove it to that ninny Woollcott? Curse me, while I'm at it.*

She tried to lift the hatch again. Although it was lighter now, she was too exhausted to raise it more than a few inches. She saw a sliver of light shine out, but then she had to drop the lid. Oh, to come so close and to fail. . . . To come out on this roof on a silly whim only to freeze to death. . . . It was poetic in its banality. The story of her life.

Don't be your usual pessimistic, self-defeating self, Dorothy, she thought. *Give it the old college try.* Despite her inclination to give up, she dug her icicle-cold fingers under the lid and tried to lift it once again—or it would be never again. To her surprise it lifted easily this time and locked open at a ninety-degree angle. She sat back on her haunches but leaned her head over the opening and warmed herself on the rush of room-temperature air that flowed up at her.

The glow of the light illuminated the figure of a person next to her.

"Mr. Benchley!" she cried in surprise. "So you helped me open that lid."

"At your service, Mrs. Parker."

"I didn't even see you there. Where did you come from all of a sudden?"

"Once you disappeared around the corner, I couldn't bear to think of you out here in the cold. I followed after you. But let's talk inside. Here, give me your hands. I'll lower you down." He grabbed her hands. "My gracious, they're cold as ice. Come on, there's no time to lose."

He wasn't a particularly strong man—far from it. But she was petite. So he didn't have too much difficulty in lifting her off her feet and lowering her into the small room below. As before, she breathed in the warm air deeply. In a moment Benchley had dropped down next to her; flakes of snow fell along with him.

They were in a small room stocked with linens on wooden shelves—a linen closet. Against the wall was a chain that led up to the roof hatch. Benchley pulled the chain, and the hatch dropped shut with a bang.

"Hmm," she said. "We'll have to get one of those chains installed on Woollcott. It'd be nice to shut his trap so easily."

Benchley laughed and reached to hug her. His body was cold, Dorothy thought, but his embrace was—

Just then the door opened, and Douglas Fairbanks poked his head in. "What was that bang?" Then, suddenly realizing the situation, he asked, "What are you two doing in here?"

"Nothing," they said quickly moving apart.

We have to stop being caught in these tight spots, Dorothy thought. Then she said, "Just a minute, Douglas. What are *you* doing in here?"

"I was on my way back to my room when I heard a bang. I came to investigate."

"There's certainly no banging going on in here," Benchley said with a chuckle, but he stopped when he realized what he had said.

"But I heard—"

Dorothy considered something. "Douglas, do you come to this room often?"

"Well, no. Not often. Hardly ever."

"But you clearly have been here before."

"Certainly. As I said, it's just around the corner from my apart—"

"Have you been in here earlier tonight?"

"Whatever do you mean?"

She stepped toward him. "I mean, did you climb out your bathroom window like a cat, scurry along the roof and then drop down into this room? An athletic fellow such as yourself could do it easily."

"Dottie, if you're suggesting what I think you're suggesting—"

"That's exactly what I'm suggesting."

The door opened wider, and now Woollcott stood next to Fairbanks. "Aha, Mrs. Parker, you've converted to my point of view."

"Aleck, for heaven's sake, stop saying, 'Aha!'—and while you're at it, fetch me one of those hot coffee drinks. And make it snappy!"

Woollcott looked wounded. "Snappy?" he muttered sheepishly. "You're the one being snappy."

Back in Fairbanks' penthouse, they sat in the living room and waited for Woollcott to come up with the coffee. Several times Fairbanks—now joined by his wife, Mary—tried

123

to ask Dorothy what she was thinking, but Dorothy shushed him and told him to wait for "Detective Woollcott" to return.

Finally Woollcott came back. He was followed by Luigi the waiter, who pushed a room service cart laden with a silver coffee pot on a silver tray, as well as a glass carafe of cream and a silver sugar bowl.

"Café Alexander is served," Woollcott pronounced pompously, and sat down with the expectation of being waited upon, as though he were some royal dignitary. Luigi silently poured the coffee, added a splash of brandy and cream to each, grated some nutmeg on top and handed out the cups. Woollcott took a sip, nodded his approval and sat the cup on the saucer in his lap. This being done, he gazed steadily at Mary Pickford. "Now, Mary, tell us why you decided to kill Bibi in your own bathtub during your own party?"

Mary nearly dropped the cup in her hands. "Kill Bibi?"

"That is what I said."

"I did no such thing. You must be joking, Aleck."

"Aleck, really!" Fairbanks said angrily, standing up. "You don't talk to my wife that way in our own home."

"Very well. I'll talk to you that way," Woollcott said. "Why did you cover it up for her?"

"C-cover what up?" Fairbanks sputtered, his glossy veneer of Hollywood sophistication temporarily disappearing.

"Come clean, Douglas. Your wife had it in for Bibi. She suspected you of having an affair with the girl. Not to mention Mary was annoyed with Bibi for stealing the limelight at her party and making a spectacle of herself. So when everyone went downstairs for the countdown to midnight, Mary somehow murdered Bibi."

"Stop it, Aleck—" Fairbanks said.

But Woollcott didn't stop. "Then you, the loyal husband, tried to cover your wife's tracks by mysteriously locking the door from the inside and clambering like a monkey out

124

the window, only to climb back in through the roof hatch in the linen closet down the hall. Ah, but you didn't count on Mrs. Parker opening the bathroom window, allowing us to take notice of the tracks you left behind in the snow. Isn't that right?"

"No, not a lick of it—"

"Oh please, Douglas! Who else has the dexterity to get out of that window and back in the trapdoor so easily? And who else had such a motive to kill Bibi—?"

"Only almost everyone," Fairbanks protested, more calmly now, reclaiming some of his movie star savoir faire.

Mary said, "I did not like Bibi Bibelot, that's no secret. But neither Douglas nor I had anything to do with her death. It's horrifying to me that she died in our apartment."

"But weren't you the last one to see her alive?" Dorothy asked quietly.

Mary's mouth hung open; she didn't dare to answer.

"And"—Woollcott turned to Fairbanks—"didn't you try to cover for your wife by saying *you* were the last one to see Bibi alive?"

"Well, that—that was before . . ." Fairbanks trailed off.

"Before what?" Dorothy asked.

Fairbanks sat back down and clasped his wife's hand. "That was before Mary and I had a good, honest talk. That's what we were doing just now, before I found you two in the linen closet. We took a stroll around the hotel and talked."

"Talked?" Woollcott sputtered, as though it was the most absurd idea he'd ever heard. "What did you have to talk about?"

Fairbanks took a deep breath. "You're right that when I said that I was the last one to see Bibi alive, I was trying to cover for Mary—"

"Aha!" Woollcott said.

Dorothy kicked his shin.

"Ow!"

"Go on, Douglas," Dorothy said.

125

"I was trying to cover for Mary because I didn't know for sure what had happened. I knew she would never do such a thing, but . . . but . . ."

"But I was guilty of something," Mary said. "Douglas knew it."

"Ah—!" Woollcott began, but stopped himself after a quick warning glance from Dorothy.

"It's like this," Mary said. "I didn't know why Bibi would be wearing that locket that I had seen on my dresser. I certainly didn't like to see a beautiful young woman parade naked through my apartment. I'm no killjoy, but that's more than I can stand. So I somehow put two and two together, and figured—quite wrongly, I now know—" And she squeezed Fairbanks' hand and looked kindly into his beautiful eyes. "I foolishly jumped to the conclusion that Douglas was having an affair with her. So, while everyone was downstairs in the lobby, I took the locket from Bibi's neck, out of sheer jealousy."

Dorothy stood up. "You did what?"

Mary looked anxious and guilt stricken. "I know. It was silly. But I took the locket."

Dorothy had a million questions, but the only thing that came out was, "I nearly froze my ass off to prove you two are innocent, and this is how you repay me? Give me that damn lousy locket. I want it."

Mary looked even more anxious now. "But I can't," she said helplessly. "It's gone missing."

Chapter 18

"Gone?" Woollcott cried in disbelief. "Gone where?"

"I don't know," Mary said. "After I took it from Bibi, I put it in my top drawer. I couldn't very well put it on—I *didn't want* to put it on. And I don't have any pockets in this dress. But later, when I went to look for it, it was gone."

"Are you sure it's missing and not mixed up in your lacy underthings?" Woollcott asked condescendingly.

Mary shook her head.

"Just one minute," Dorothy said. "Was Bibi alive when you took it?"

"Yes. I saw that she was breathing, like she was asleep. I'm quite sure of that. I just assumed she had passed out."

"What time was this?" said a deep voice from the door.

They all turned to look. It was Arthur Conan Doyle.

"What time," he repeated, "did you last see Miss Bibelot alive and breathing?"

"After eleven thirty. Maybe around a quarter to midnight."

"Tell me, if you will," he said, striding into the room, "did she have that pinkish marking around her mouth at that time?"

"I-I think so," Mary said.

"Be sure now," Doyle said. "Close your eyes, and remember your exact movements. Start with when you entered the room."

Woollcott stood up. "Just a minute here. I'm running this investigation. And I won't have it interrupted by some washed-up old sawbones—"

"I wouldn't think of it," Doyle said calmly to Woollcott. "You're doing a bang-up job, my good fellow. I thought perhaps you might like to let the amateurs have a go. Meanwhile you can rest your weary brain cells for the more salient points of the investigation."

Woollcott reluctantly sat down, eyeing Doyle warily. He clearly wasn't sure whether Doyle was mocking him or simply being a polite old gentleman—or perhaps a little of both.

"Let's try again, my dear," Doyle said reassuringly. "Close your eyes, and tell us what happened when you entered the room."

Mary's eyes fluttered shut. "No one else was in the apartment. The door to the bathroom was shut but not locked. I pushed open the door and looked at Bibi. She didn't move. I had thought I would have it out with her, so I was at first very disappointed that she had passed out."

"Passed out?" Doyle asked.

"That's what I assumed," Mary said. "Her eyes were closed, and her head was tilted to the side. In one hand, she still held a champagne glass."

"She was holding a champagne glass?"

"Just barely. I took it from her hand, and I placed it on the radiator next to the tub."

"Next to the ice bucket?" Dorothy asked.

Mary's eyes opened. "Ice bucket? I don't remember any ice bucket."

"Close your eyes," Doyle said with a curious glance at

128

Dorothy. "Think again. What happened exactly when you set down the glass?"

"I put it down on the very center of the radiator, so that it wouldn't fall. It was from a set of glasses we were given at our wedding, and I didn't want to see it broken. There was no ice bucket."

"You see?" he said. "You *can* remember if we take it step-by-step. Now what did you do?"

"I leaned over Bibi's head. I remember looking down at her—her chest. Yes, it was definitely rising and falling, couldn't miss that. Then I gently turned her head even farther to the side so I could get to the clasp of the necklace, which was at the back of her neck, of course."

"And do you recall seeing her face as you did this?"

"I do," Mary said with a note of surprise. "I remember the pink around her mouth now. I guess I must have thought it was smeared lipstick. Then I probably didn't think too much about it at all because I just wanted to get that stinking necklace off her before she woke up or before someone came strolling in."

"And you did? You were able to remove the necklace?"

"Yes, I unhooked it. I left Bibi where she was, and I went out of the bathroom. I stood for a moment in the parlor, not knowing what to do. Then I went to my bedroom and dropped the locket in the top drawer of my dresser."

"And then?"

"Then I left. I took the elevator down, and that's when I encountered Lydia Trumbull. We went back to her room to talk."

"And did you say anything to her about Bibi?"

"Or the locket?" Woollcott interjected.

"No, I didn't mention the locket. But we talked about Bibi, of course, and how she was acting like such a . . . such a . . . ."

"Yes, I think we quite understand," Doyle said genteelly.

"But you did *not* tell your friend Lydia that you had just left Bibi in the bathtub?"

"No, I didn't." Mary cast her eyes downward.

Dorothy felt anxious just then. She hadn't had a chance to get back to Lydia to ask her some questions. Such as, what had gotten Lydia so upset that she needed to talk to Mary? And what would make her faint like a Victorian dowager from just one question from Woollcott?

Woollcott stood up again. "That was quite a lot of questions from someone who refused to even play the game of Murder, Artie. You seem to have picked up the game quite well, my good fellow." His voice dripped with sarcasm. "But as I've said already, this is no parlor game — "

"Indeed it's not," Doyle said, frowning. "I'm afraid there's something deeply wrong going on here, much more than it even appears just from the body of a dead woman in the bathtub." He turned to Dorothy and Benchley. "Mrs. Parker, Mr. Benchley, would you accompany me, please?"

Dorothy set her empty coffee cup on the side table and stood up. "Where to?"

"My friend Quentin's room. I could use your excellent help in looking for a particular item."

Doyle turned and went out the door. Dorothy and Benchley followed him.

"You're leaving? Now?" Woollcott sputtered indignantly, jumping up. "But we're just getting some answers here. What about Fairbanks going out the window like a circus monkey?"

"I think that's also where your theory went, Aleck," Dorothy said over her shoulder. "Feel free to chase after it."

Chapter 19

Doyle didn't say a word as they took the elevator down to the ninth floor. Now, as he strode along the corridor, he slowed and turned to Dorothy and Benchley. He spoke in a whisper. "I need to find something in Quentin's room. A brown bottle. Will you help me?"

"We didn't come down here to play tiddledywinks," she said. "Of course we'll help. We'll turn his room upside down if we have to." She moved forward.

Doyle raised a big hand. "One moment, if you please. There is an obstacle in our path: Mr. Jordan."

Benchley seemed to bristle.

"Dr. Hurst's attendant is an obstacle?" she asked. "Just tell him to step aside. Better yet, he can help us look."

Doyle's forehead wrinkled in thought. He removed a briar pipe from his jacket pocket and leaned his broad back against the hallway wall. "That is much easier said than done."

Benchley took this as a cue to get out his own pipe. Not wanting to be left out, Dorothy searched in her little purse for her pack of Chesterfields. Soon the three of them were filling the hallway with smoke and plotting quietly.

"I don't understand," she said. "What's the matter with Jordan all of a sudden?"

Doyle nodded. "He seems quite agreeable, doesn't he?"

Dorothy, sensing Benchley wouldn't like her answer, didn't respond.

Doyle continued, "He and I were getting along famously well, I thought. All laughs and slaps on the back and what-have-you. Indeed, after we brought Quentin to his room and put the old boy to bed, Mr. Jordan and I sat down in two armchairs and proceeded to talk and pass the time just like two school chums. Peas in a pod, we were."

"So, again, what's the matter with Jordan?"

"I'm getting to that," Doyle said, annoyed, yanking his pipe from beneath his bushy mustache. "Before long, our genial conversation naturally turned back to the murder, and the peculiar circumstances in which the body of Miss Bibelot was found—in particular, the pink, rash-like quality of the skin surrounding her mouth."

"You mentioned that upstairs," she said. "Do you know what it is?"

"I was a volunteer field surgeon during the Boer War, and on occasion we'd see that condition of the perioral skin. It was not uncommon back in those days, although I dare-say surgeons don't see as much of it now."

"Boer War? What does that have to do with Bibi? Are you saying she had some rare, foreign-born disease?"

"Oh, hardly," he chuckled. "Back then we saw it from poor administration of chloroform, which was sometimes used to anesthetize a soldier for surgery. It was used when better, safer anesthetics were in short supply—which happened far too often. The medics we had didn't know chloroform from chamomile tea. They were just boys, of course."

A melancholy look came into Doyle's eyes, and his thoughts seemed to drift back to that time—or perhaps to another, similar sadness, Dorothy thought.

"Chloroform burns the skin?" she asked.

Doyle snapped back to the present. "Yes, if it is applied sloppily or with improper equipment, or left on the epidermis for too long, chloroform will cause exactly the same rash-like appearance that Miss Bibelot had around her mouth."

"So someone gave Bibi chloroform?" she asked.

"Someone who didn't know what he was doing?" Benchley added.

"Or," Doyle said thoughtfully, "perhaps someone who hasn't done it in a long, long time. . . . Perhaps someone who had a great deal to drink and didn't take the proper precautions."

Now Dorothy understood. "Dr. Hurst, you mean?"

Doyle didn't answer. He stood silently in the cloud of smoke. She couldn't make out his expression.

Suddenly she remembered something and snapped her fingers. "You recognized it right away! When you and Dr. Hurst came up to see Bibi's body in the bathtub, you acted a trifle strange at first. It was because you noticed the rash immediately, didn't you? Why didn't you say something then?"

Doyle's face clouded over. "Well, honestly, the notion of it took me by surprise at the time. I can't admit to being as cool and as calculating as my famous detective. When I saw the irritation of the skin and realized that it most likely came from chloroform, I naturally jumped to the same conclusion you did—my friend Quentin."

"But you had doubts that he was the one who did it?"

"Most certainly," Doyle said. "So I held my tongue. Although, upon consideration, I must say the circumstantial evidence seems rather against him. She was wearing that necklace of his. And he did go into the bathroom and have it out with her, and he acted very ungentlemanly, I must admit. And, most damning, he's probably the only one in this hotel with a bottle of chloroform in his possession."

"His medical bag!"

133

"Precisely. If you recall, I searched through his medical bag after he had the stroke. I was looking for the blood pressure cuff—but I also had the chloroform in mind."

"And?"

"It wasn't in there."

"So he didn't have any chloroform after all?"

Doyle shook his head. "There was an empty spot for it, along with a strap to hold the bottle in place. And the strap was clearly marked 'chloroform.'"

"So if it was missing from his bag, you think it might be in his room?"

He nodded. "If we can get a look at the bottle itself, it might provide some confirmation of Quentin's innocence."

"How so?"

Doyle was less certain about this point. "Hmm, perhaps the cap will be stuck, indicating it hasn't been opened in a long while? Or perhaps the bottle will be full, suggesting it hasn't been used at all?"

They all knew that Doyle was grasping at straws, but no one had the heart to say it.

"Well, I know a full bottle when I see one," Dorothy said, moving along the corridor to Dr. Hurst's door. "Let me at it."

"Just a moment," Doyle said. "Remember Mr. Jordan?"

"Oh yes," she said. "He's some kind of obstacle, you said? I doubt that very much."

"Don't doubt it at all. It's very true. He would not let me search the room. We almost came to fisticuffs over it."

"There didn't seem to be any love lost between Jordan and Dr. Hurst," she said. "I got the feeling he was downright unhappy about his assignment with Dr. Hurst, even."

"That may be so. Indeed, I have it from his own lips that he's not terribly fond of my friend Quentin, his employer. I know full well that Quentin can sometimes be difficult to get along with. Be that as it may, Mr. Jordan is a very studious employee and fiercely loyal, no matter his personal feelings. He stoutly refused to let me look through Quentin's things."

"Did you explain to Jordan that it could confirm Dr. Hurst's guilt?" Benchley said. Then, after a concerned look from Doyle, he added, "Or confirm his innocence, I mean, of course."

"Not quite," Doyle said. "I thought it best not to discuss the matter of the chloroform with Mr. Jordan. I want to see the bottle with my own eyes before I bring him into my confidence."

"But you let us in on it?" Dorothy said, smiling. "We're honored."

Doyle spoke jovially. "Foxholes make fast friends. Now we're in this together, for good or for ill."

She wasn't sure whether to take this as a compliment. "So what do you want us to do with Jordan? We distract him while you search for the bottle of chloroform?"

"Something like that," Doyle said, blowing the last puff of smoke from his pipe. "Actually, Mrs. Parker, I was hoping *you* could distract him, while Mr. Benchley and I look for the chloroform."

She raised her eyebrows. "Well, call me Mata Hari. I'll do it."

Benchley folded his arms. "No, Mata dear, you most certainly won't. I'll do it."

They argued for a minute. Dorothy insisted that she was fully capable of leading Jordan astray. But Benchley wouldn't hear of it. He explained how he regretted that he had let her go out onto the snowy roof by herself, and it was now his turn.

She batted her eyes at him. "Well, who's Hari now?"

Chapter 20

$\mathcal{D}$oyle knocked on Dr. Hurst's door. When Jordan answered, he cast a suspicious eye on Doyle but appeared to be genuinely happy to see Dorothy and Benchley.

"Well, if it isn't our little amateur detectives!" he said cheerfully.

She was taken aback until she realized that Jordan was referring to the guessing game they had played with him in the dining room. "Oh, our detective skills have vastly improved since we first met. I now detect . . . you'd like a cup of coffee."

This was no mystery. Jordan was stifling a yawn at that very moment. Nevertheless, he seemed pleasantly surprised. "Yeah, I sure would. But where can you get coffee at this hour? It's nearly two o'clock in the morning. Room service must have ended."

"Not if you go to the right room," she said.

Benchley jumped in. "Mrs. Parker is right. There's a whole sea of coffee up in Mr. Fairbanks' penthouse."

Jordan looked back at Dr. Hurst lying immobile in the bed. "I can't leave him"—he eyed Doyle suspiciously—"by himself."

Dorothy had an idea and changed the plan on the spot.

"Nonsense. Mr. Benchley and I will stay and keep an eye on the doctor. You two go up for a cup of coffee."

Now Jordan looked at Dorothy and Benchley with suspicion but spoke to Doyle. "If this is some kind of ploy—"

Doyle shook his big, shaggy head and lied very convincingly. "Not at all, my good man. I haven't said a word to them about our disagreement—nor should you, I'll warrant. They suggested, out of the goodness of their hearts, that you might benefit from some of the hotel's fine coffee. Now, come, come, let's you and I let bygones be bygones. I daresay you'll need some refreshment to get through this night."

Jordan allowed Doyle to lead him out. But he turned before closing the door. "Don't touch a thing. I'll know if you do. And if Dr. Hurst makes the slightest move, you come get me right away. Understand?"

"Completely," Benchley said. "Scout's honor."

"Absolutely," Dorothy added. "Girl Scout's honor."

When the door was closed, they turned and looked at Dr. Hurst. He lay faceup in the bed and was now wearing a set of navy-blue pajamas. Dorothy realized that Jordan, perhaps with the assistance of Doyle, must have dressed the paralyzed old man, and she shuddered to think of it.

They moved closer. One of Dr. Hurst's eyes was open a crack. Dorothy froze, clutching Benchley's arm.

"Ouch," he said, prying her fingernails out of his arm. He saw what alarmed her. "Don't worry. That's the immobilized side, remember? Poor fellow. His eyelid must be unable to close all the way."

Dorothy looked closer. The eye wasn't looking at them. It gazed forward at nothing. She moved nearer. Still the eye didn't detect her. Now she stood by the side of his bed. The eye, peeking from beneath the half-lowered lid, continued to stare dead ahead. She waved a hand in front of Dr. Hurst's face. The eye didn't move. She sighed with relief.

"He must be out of it, thank heaven," she said. "Come on, let's look for that bottle of chloroform."

Benchley put his hands on his hips and looked around. "Where might it be?"

The corners of the large room and every other surface were stacked with suitcases, books or equipment. Dorothy approached the most interesting of these: a portable desk that had been unfolded from the interior of an upright trunk. "Get a load of this. Have desk, will travel."

Benchley was inspecting a similar large piece of luggage, only this one was like a lab bench that was compartmentalized into an even larger traveling trunk. It was complete with a Bunsen burner (now unlit) and microscope. Benchley peeked into the microscope. "Looks like I found something. Perhaps a new species of fungi."

"There's no fun guy in this room," she said, glancing again at Dr. Hurst in the bed. "Keep looking."

"What exactly does a bottle of chloroform look like?" Benchley asked, turning to a crate full of beakers and books.

"According to Doyle, it's a stout brown medicine bottle. Holds about ten ounces. Smells like sweet dreams—if you smell it, that is."

Benchley peeked into a small suitcase. "And what exactly do sweet dreams smell like?"

"Damned if I know," Dorothy muttered as much to herself as to him.

He gagged. "Doesn't smell like this," he sputtered, and slammed closed a small valise. "And I thought the fungus smelled rotten."

"What?" she asked, alarmed. "What is it?"

"His dirty underwear." Benchley dropped the valise onto the floor.

She shook her head and turned to a pile of books on an armchair. They were about all kinds of subjects. Butterfly hunting. Stamp collecting. Orthopedic surgery. Model trains. Fly fishing. And several more. Then Dorothy noticed they all had something in common.

"Bless me, look at this!" She read a few titles aloud.

"British Philately of the Nineteenth and Twentieth Centuries ... Surgery of Knee and Elbow Joints ... The Best Salmon Streams of the Scottish Highlands ..."

"So Dr. Hurst enjoys a little light but dry reading. So what?"

"He didn't read them. He wrote them!"

"Imagine that." Benchley came and peered over her shoulder. All the books were authored by Quentin Hurst, MD, FRCS. "Our good doctor must be quite a Renaissance man—that is, if the Renaissance had been about beekeeping, model trains and paper clip collecting, instead of the more mundane subjects of painting, sculpting and architecture." He stole a guilty glance at the man in the bed. "Enough of the world's driest literature. Let's find that little brown jug before Artie and Jordan get back."

He started whistling the jazz tune "Little Brown Jug," and resumed his search.

She put down the books and looked around. She noticed Dr. Hurst's tweed suit hanging on a hook on the back of the hotel room door. She went over to it. It smelled of whiskey and body odor. Something weighed down the jacket pocket. Reluctantly she put her hand inside. She pulled out a stethoscope, then a pocketknife, a few coins and a balled-up piece of paper. But no brown bottle of chloroform.

"Anything in there?" Benchley asked. He was leaning against the bureau and sorting through an old leather toiletry case.

"No." She put the items back in the jacket pocket. But she held on to the yellow ball of paper. Something about it was familiar. Yes, that was it—it was the color of a telegram! Could it be ... ?

She carefully unfolded it. It was indeed a telegram! She recalled the telegram envelope that Frank Case had handed to Dr. Hurst in the lobby much earlier in the evening. She looked at the time and date stamped at the top of the page: SAT DEC 31. 7:41 PM.

139

Yes, this must be that telegram. Now, what had made Dr. Hurst so anxious when he saw it?

"What do you have there, Mrs. Parker?" Benchley asked. He had given up on the toiletry case.

She explained about the telegram. Benchley hadn't yet arrived at the hotel when it had been delivered.

"Well, for heaven's sake, what does it say?" he asked.

She looked again at the immobile old man lying in the bed. His thin white hair was splayed out on his pillow. His one eye was still open slightly, staring straight ahead at nothing like a dead fish. She shuddered and turned away.

It was wrong, she knew, to read this man's personal correspondence. Still, if it had anything, anything remotely, to do with Bibi's death, then she had an obligation to read it. After all, the moment he received this telegram, Dr. Hurst had suddenly asked for a safe place to store that locket— the one that had been around Bibi's neck, the one that was now missing.

"Please, Mrs. Parker, just read it!" Benchley was nearly hopping up and down like an impatient child.

She read aloud:

DOCTOR, AUTHORITIES IN ENGLAND KNOW YOU TOOK VALUABLE ITEM. BRING IT TO CHICAGO AT ONCE OR DEAL IS OFF. LLOYDS HIRED PINKS. BERLEY BROTHERS ON YOUR TRAIL TOO. LOSE THEM ALL. IF YOU BRING THEM TO CHICAGO, DEAL IS OFF. KEEP ITEM SAFE AND IN GOOD CONDITION OR DEAL IS OFF.

"That's it?" Benchley asked.

"That's it. No signature."

"What does it mean?"

"A valuable item. That must be the locket, right?"

"Do you think he stole it? And who's in Chicago? And what sort of deal—?"

140

She interrupted. "And what's this, Lloyds hired Pinks? Who is Lloyds and who is Pinks? Are those first names or last names?"

"Or nicknames?"

"And—"

Then the old man moaned. They turned. The one dead eye still stared dully ahead at nothing, but the other eye was now open wide and fixed directly on them. This eye was hard, clear and undeniably angry. Without moving his arm, the old man gestured to them with his one functional hand to come toward the bed. He moaned again—a low, throaty, unnatural sound. His mouth barely opened.

Dorothy and Benchley didn't move. *Should we make a run for it?* she thought.

Again the old man made that unnatural groan through gritted teeth. The eye on them was on fire. He stretched out his hand and beckoned them to come to him.

Unable to run away, Dorothy and Benchley slowly approached the bed. She wanted to hide the telegram behind her dress, but clearly Dr. Hurst had already seen that they were reading it. Now they stood by the side of the bed. His hand reached out again, motioning to them to lean toward him. He groaned, plaintively now.

Was he even lucid? she wondered. But the eye was so keen and clear—and so filled with furious intent—that she knew his mind was perfectly aware inside his nearly paralyzed old body.

Reluctantly, she leaned closer. She could see the fine wrinkles and folds in his pale, elderly skin. She could smell his fetid, whiskey-soaked breath between his clenched yellow teeth.

Suddenly his bony hand seized her wrist. He pulled her so close that she looked directly into his one good eye. She was nearly on top of him. Then he spoke in an urgent, creaking voice . . . but she didn't understand. . . .

141

He said it again. . . . Was it a word? A place? A name?

Then his clawlike grip released her. Quickly she pushed herself away — away from the old man.

"What is it?" Benchley asked. "What did he say?"

She was still facing the bed. Hurst's eye was still on her and still sharp, but it seemed desperate now. Not angry. She noticed his hand pointing at something. At himself? At the door? Then he moaned the sound again. It was a low, otherworldly sound. . . .

That was quite enough! She grabbed Benchley's arm and pulled him with her. Dragging Benchley behind her, she yanked open the door and ran into the hallway. Benchley had only a moment to tug the door closed behind them as she hurried frantically to the end of the corridor and toward the elevator — toward safety.

Still several steps away from the elevator call button, she had her finger pointed out, ready to press it. But before she actually reached the button, the elevator door opened. She ran toward the open door, but the large figure of Doyle stepped out, followed by Jordan, Frank Case and Alexander Woollcott. Dorothy and Benchley nearly collided with them.

"Mrs. Parker!" Doyle said, catching her with his big, bearlike hands. "By Jove, you're trembling like a leaf. What's put the fear of God into you?"

"It's not God I'm afraid of," she said breathlessly. "It's that devil Dr. Hurst!"

Chapter 21

Dorothy slouched on her couch in her own little second-floor apartment. Her Boston terrier, Woodrow Wilson, was curled warmly in her lap. She lazily stroked his brindle-colored head with one hand while she sipped from a glass of brandy with the other.

"Well?" asked Doyle impatiently, standing directly in front of her. His thick arms were folded over his barrel chest, and his droopy eyes looked disapprovingly at her. "We're waiting."

Also standing in front of her and equally impatient were Frank Case and Alexander Woollcott. Benchley sat a cautious distance away on the opposite end of the couch from her.

Her nerves had *almost* settled down to her usual indifferent, affable and sarcastic state—almost but not quite.

Woollcott checked his watch for the third time. "Hang it all, Dottie! It's nearly four in the morning, and there's still a lot to be done. I haven't questioned Lydia Trumbull yet. I haven't quite proven to my satisfaction that Fairbanks made those footprints in the snow on the roof. Furthermore, assuming we can take the word of Mary Pickford at face value, who took the locket from her dresser? And, most

143

importantly, we haven't even begun to search for the lost body of Bibi, which is certainly still somewhere in this hotel. Now, please, just tell us what Dr. Hurst said to you!"

She sighed and took another sip of the brandy. She hated to make Doyle and Case impatient—but she positively loved any excuse to annoy Woollcott.

Just then her front door opened, and Jordan hobbled in. Poor handsome devil. She perked up at seeing him. Benchley seemed to fidget in his seat.

Doyle turned to the newcomer. "Did you learn anything?"

Jordan shook his head. "He's out like a light. Whether he's unconscious or sleeping, I can't tell."

"See?" Woollcott said to Dorothy, flapping his hands against his chubby sides. "The man himself can no longer tell us. So it's up to you. What did Hurst say?"

She stifled a yawn. She couldn't help it if she was now tired.

Woollcott's pudgy round face turned red as a tomato. "Speak, you infernal woman! What did he say?"

Benchley said, "I heard him as we ran out—uh, as we hastily departed. Not clearly, mind you. His voice was very . . . hoarse, grunting."

They all turned to face him.

"Well?" Doyle asked. "What did he say?"

"A name, I think. Ned Besh."

"Ned Besh?" Woollcott said slowly, doubtfully.

"No, wasn't Ned," Dorothy finally said. "It was Ted. Ted Besh. I'm sure of it. I heard him say it twice right in my ear, then the once as we were leaving—Ted Besh." For once she wasn't joking or making up a silly name. She was even a little proud of herself for showing restraint, though she knew it wouldn't last.

"Ted Besh? Ned Besh?" Doyle repeated. He turned to Jordan. "Who is it? Whatever does it mean?"

Jordan shrugged. "Never heard the doctor mention either name before."

Case tapped his lips with a slender finger. "Give me a moment to go down to the front desk and check the hotel's register book. Perhaps another guest signed in with such a name." He turned to leave.

Doyle said, "If you find such a fellow, Mr. Case, don't knock on his door alone. Come get us, and we'll go as a party."

"Yes, that's just what this long night needs," Dorothy muttered, placing her empty brandy glass on the side table. "Another exciting party."

Case went out the door. Doyle turned back to Dorothy. He shifted from foot to foot. He looked at her meaningfully. "Well?" he asked expectantly. "Was there anything . . . more?"

She was puzzled by this, because she had told them right from the start that Dr. Hurst had said only one thing, although he said it three times. Then she remembered the chloroform. *That* was what Doyle wanted to know about— but Jordan was standing right beside him.

"Uh, no. That's it. Nothing else," she said.

She had been about to mention the telegram—but then she remembered Jordan's warning. He had warned her not to touch anything in Dr. Hurst's room, so he certainly wouldn't approve of her taking the telegram. She had left it under her purse on the little mail table by her front door when they had first entered her apartment. She decided not to mention it right now. Maybe she'd bring it up with Doyle later . . . maybe. . . .

Doyle seemed to take her response as a good sign. They hadn't found the chloroform—which indicated that Dr. Hurst might not be implicated. Doyle brightened. "Well, as Mr. Woollcott here said, there's still much to do. Let's get to it, shall we?"

"Indeed we shall," Woollcott said to him. "Why don't you—"

Doyle didn't seem to hear him. Instead he started throwing out orders like a commander on a battlefield or a surgeon in an operating room. "Mr. Woollcott, you go downstairs to the switchboard office and call the police. Notify them of our progress and request that they research both the city records and their criminal files for the name Ted or Ned Besh."

"It was Ted," Dorothy muttered. "I'm sure of it."

Woollcott stood with his mouth hanging open. He was not used to being ordered around.

Doyle continued. "Mr. Benchley, you begin the search for the missing body of Miss Bibelot. Start in the cellar, where you last saw her."

Benchley looked aghast at this command. *Go down to the subbasement by himself to look for Bibi's missing body?* Dorothy almost chuckled. Even if she hadn't seen his expression of sheer abhorrence at that moment, she would have known he would never go looking for a corpse by himself in a dark cellar.

Doyle continued giving orders. "Mr. Jordan, it would be wise if you returned immediately to Quentin's rooms in case he revives."

Jordan nodded in agreement and turned to go.

"Mrs. Parker, perhaps you'd better have a good talk with Lydia Trumbull," Doyle said, now ordering her around. "Confirm that she and Mary Pickford were holed up together in her room just before midnight having a . . . a ladies' talk."

Dorothy smiled. *What on God's green earth does he imagine "a ladies' talk" consists of?*

"For my part," Doyle said, "I'll return to Mr. Fairbanks' penthouse to pick up the threads of this murder investigation."

Back in the corridor they parted ways. Doyle and Jordan took the elevator up, while Benchley, Woollcott and Dorothy paused in the hallway.

"That Artie!" Woollcott spat. He was literally huffing mad. "Who in the world does he think he is?"

Dorothy was about to respond, *He probably thinks he's the world's best-selling author,* but Woollcott continued to sputter angrily.

"Ordering me around like his maidservant! I'll be damned if I follow his orders."

Benchley nodded. "That makes two of us, Aleck. I'm not about to go down to that horrible dark subbasement again—and by myself! Want to trade assignments?"

Woollcott brightened immediately. "By all means, my dear Robert. I'll search high and low in said subbasement—spiders, spooks and bogeymen be damned. And if I don't turn up the body of Bibi Bibelot, my name's not Alexander Woollcott! That'll show that Artie smarty-pants who's the real detective around here."

Dorothy and Benchley exchanged a knowing look. But Woollcott was already heading toward the stairs to the lobby. When he was out of earshot, she turned to Benchley.

"Before going to the operator's office to call the police, would you care to escort me to Lydia's room?"

"Escort you, Mrs. Parker? Are you afraid you'll get into a rumble with Miss Trumbull?"

"No, I'd just like some company."

A moment later they reached Lydia's door. Dorothy knocked. There was no answer.

"Sleeping, perhaps?"

Benchley knocked, harder this time. Still no answer.

Dorothy remembered all the varieties of sleeping pills and sedatives on the table next to Lydia's bed. Benchley banged on the door again.

"She's sleeping like the dead." Dorothy had said it innocently enough—but thinking over what she had said, she became alarmed.

"Lot of that going around tonight," Benchley said, equally alarmed.

He banged on the door even harder. "Miss Trumbull! Are you all right?"

Dorothy hit her fists against it, too. This hurt her hands, which prompted her to try something simpler. She grasped the knob—and turned it.

Surprisingly, the door was unlocked.

"Well, sure," Benchley said to her, "if you want to do things the easy way."

They shoved the door open. The bed, where Dorothy had left Lydia, was empty. But the bedsheets were turned down and rumpled.

She stepped inside. "Lydia? Are you in here?"

The room was silent. Dorothy went to the bathroom and turned on the light. It was empty, too.

When she stepped back into the bedroom, Benchley was standing beside the bedside table and looking at all the bottles. "My oh my! She has enough sleeping pills here to knock out an army for a week. And what, pray tell, is this—?"

He was looking at something behind the bed stand. He bent down and picked up a brown bottle. Dorothy hadn't seen that when she had been here before. He read the label. "Found it!"

He turned the bottle so Dorothy could see it.

"Chloroform!" She grabbed the bottle. "And look who the prescriber is . . . Quentin Hurst, MD!"

"But how did Lydia get her hands on it?" he asked. "Would Dr. Hurst have simply given it to her?"

"Hurst? That old skinflint? Obviously not. Lydia must have stolen it from his medical bag."

"When? How? And why?"

"The why is obvious," she said. "To put Bibi's lights out."

She hefted the bottle in her hand. For such a small bottle it was rather heavy—almost full.

"Lucky you found this," she said. "Imagine if we'd carried on thinking Dr. Hurst had somehow used it on Bibi—

at least, that's what Arthur Conan Doyle seems to think. We'll have to disabuse him of that notion since Lydia used this potion."

"Well, it's a natural assumption," he said. "Dr. Hurst had the chloroform in his bag. Bibi had the chloroform marks around her mouth. And for at least part of the party Dr. Hurst was visibly angry at Bibi. Doyle just added them all together."

"And he came up with the wrong conclusion. The creator of Sherlock Holmes isn't quite up to the detective skills of his creation. Then again all the road signs did seem to point to Dr. Hurst, almost as if—"

But she paused. Something seemed amiss.

"Almost as if . . ." Benchley finished her thought for her. "He was framed?"

"Exactly." Dorothy began to grow alarmed. "Why isn't Lydia here? Where is she? And what is she doing?"

"You don't think—"

"Dr. Hurst! First she killed Bibi and framed him in the bargain. Now he's up there lying helpless—vulnerable as a cream puff."

Together they ran out the door and down the corridor.

"Dr. Hurst is not entirely helpless," Benchley said as they hurried along. "After all, he didn't seem anything like a cream puff when we were up there in his room a quarter of an hour ago. He seemed positively atrocious. A skeleton come to life. We ran out of there like frightened rabbits."

"He's nearly paralyzed, Fred. A child could enter his room and smother him with a pillow."

"Why would a child smother him with a—"

"It's a figure of speech. You know what I meant."

They reached the elevator, and she punched the call button. Then, impatiently, she punched it again. "Lydia could be up there right now. She could be murdering Dr. Hurst as we speak."

The elevator arrived, the door opened and they stepped

inside. Maurice, the elevator operator, was nearly asleep on his feet.

"Ninth floor, and step on it," she said.

Maurice hardly seemed to stir, but he got the elevator going just the same.

"But explain this," Benchley said to her. "Why would Lydia even bother to smother him with a pillow? What's the point? Dr. Hurst can barely speak."

"Put yourself in Lydia's shoes. You've already killed once tonight, probably on the spur of the moment with hardly any planning. Luckily for you, almost everyone seems to suspect that someone else did it. After all, Dr. Hurst was the one with the chloroform, and he also had a beef with Bibi. Even his friend Sir Arthur suspects he did it. Now, if you're Lydia, how much easier would it be to completely cover up your guilt by simply smothering an incapacitated old man? No one would ever suspect you. Everyone would think Dr. Hurst had simply died of his stroke—and that he was guilty as charged. You'd get off scot-free."

"Just a moment," Benchley said. "Dr. Hurst won't need to defend himself. Your marvelous Mr. Jordan is up there guarding him."

That's true, she thought. *Jordan seems terribly protective of his employer. And certainly capable of handling any trouble little Lydia could dish out.*

The elevator stopped, and Maurice automatically opened the door. His ancient eyes were just about closed.

They hurried to Dr. Hurst's room. They were surprised to see the door open a crack. Through the slit, the room looked like a mess.

Benchley pushed open the door. The room was a disaster—clothes, books, papers, medical instruments and suitcases were tossed everywhere.

"Looks like a monsoon hit this place," Dorothy said.

"It did more than hit it," Benchley said, wide-eyed. "It knocked it into next Tuesday."

Despite whatever cataclysm had occurred, Dr. Hurst still lay in the bed, immobile and undisturbed.

They stepped in carefully, trying not to trip or slip on the debris that covered the floor. Dorothy noticed that there was an open door to an adjacent room. That door hadn't been open when they had been here before. And there was a body lying in the threshold.

"Look," she said. "It's Jordan!"

The man lay on the cluttered floor in the open doorway. His body was twisted and limp like a wrung-out washrag. They hurried to him.

"Is he dead?" she asked.

Benchley bent down and gingerly rolled the body faceup. "Good news. He's breathing."

"Oh, thank God!"

Benchley gave her a curious look.

"Don't look at me in that tone of voice," she said. "I simply can't stand to see another dead body tonight—unless it's Woollcott's, of course."

"Of corpse," Benchley agreed. "But now that we know that Mr. Jordan is alive, what exactly do we do with him?"

Dorothy raised an eyebrow. "I know what I'd like to do with him."

"Please, Mrs. Parker," Benchley said, disgusted. "Just a moment ago you thought he was dead."

She smiled. She merely wanted to get Benchley's goat. "Very well, then. Let's wake him up."

Benchley reached out and slapped Jordan's cheek a few times, gently at first but then with increasing firmness.

Jordan's face wrinkled. "Ow . . ."

"That's enough, Fred," she said. "You'll slap the boy silly."

"No, he's not hurting me," Jordan groaned. His eyes fluttered open. Propping himself up on one elbow, he felt the back of his head and winced. "It's my head. Somebody clocked me but good."

"Who attacked you?" Dorothy asked, taking in the room with a sweep of her hand. "What happened in here?"

"Don't know." Jordan jerked his thumb at the adjoining room. "I was lying in my bed when I heard a ruckus in here. I came running. As soon as I opened the door and stepped inside—*wham!* Somebody must have hit me from behind. Next thing I knew, I woke up to see your pretty face."

"You're too kind," Benchley said, batting his eyelashes. "Now let's get you up off this messy floor before you embarrass yourself."

They helped Jordan to his feet. The man wore a tight-fitting undershirt, loose striped pajama bottoms and moccasin-like slippers. "Wait a minute," he said, looking around at the clutter on the floor. He leaned down and snatched up his black leather orthopedic shoe. "Can't forget this. Thought I might be able to use it as a weapon."

"How ironic," Benchley observed wryly. "You were armed with footwear."

Jordan shrugged. "You could say that. Didn't do much good, though." He shuffled toward Dr. Hurst's bed, sat down on the edge of the mattress and took a close look at the old man. "Not a scratch on him. Didn't even wake him up. Whoever it was, he didn't want anything to do with Dr. Hurst."

"Then what did the intruder want?" she asked.

"He wanted something the doctor has—or had."

With a guilty pang, she thought of Dr. Hurst's telegram in her purse. She had picked it up again when they had left her apartment. Was the intruder looking for the telegram?

Jordan jumped up and ran into the adjacent room. He picked up his other shoe and looked inside. "Gone! It's gone! Damn it!" He threw the shoe to the floor. "Whoever it was, he took it!"

"He?" she asked. "He who? Took what?"

Benchley spoke ominously. "Maybe it was you-know-who."

152

Dorothy remembered the names from the telegram. *Lloyds or Pinks? Or the Berley brothers? Or even . . . Lydia?*

But Benchley remained silent.

"Who?" she and Jordan asked simultaneously.

"Ted Besh, of course!"

At that, Dr. Hurst's eye fluttered open. It rolled in its socket to look over the disaster in the room. Then the eye silently closed again, and there was a pained look on Dr. Hurst's distorted old face.

"You'd better go," Jordan said angrily, his arms crossed over his chest. "Now."

Chapter 22

"I need a drink," Dorothy said as she hurried down the hallway. "Come on, let's go back to my room and sort this through." Benchley followed her quickly.

On the elevator, she pried open one of Maurice's eyes. "Do you remember someone getting on at this floor recently? Maybe someone carrying a locket?"

Maurice grunted. "Hmmmphh . . ."

She let go of his eyelid. It snapped closed like a mousetrap.

"I think we can take that as a no," Benchley said.

Back in Dorothy's room, her dog trotted around their feet as she poured each of them a small glass of cheap scotch.

"Make it last," she said, handing it to Benchley. "That's the last of my emergency stash."

Benchley raised his glass. "Here's to emergency stashes."

"And to my gent's mustaches."

They clinked their glasses and sipped.

"So," he began, "we've learned that your Mr. Jordan is certainly not one to be trifled with."

"First of all, Fred, he's not *my* Mr. Jordan," she said

firmly. "Secondly, I was not trifling with him. And thirdly, what in heaven's name was he talking about? What went missing?"

"I think you already guessed it," he said. "The necklace— Dr. Hurst's locket. The one around Bibi's swan-like neck. The one that Mary Pickford stealthily took from said neck. The one that subsequently went missing from Mary's dresser."

"And the one that's mentioned in this telegram?" She held up the slip of yellow paper. "The 'valuable item'?"

Benchley took the telegram from her hand and read it over again. "'Keep item safe and in good condition or deal is off.' So Dr. Hurst was going to take the necklace to Chicago for some deal?"

"But the quarantine likely changed his plans," she said. "So Dr. Hurst gave it to Fairbanks for safekeeping."

"But then Bibi took it from Fairbanks' lousy hiding spot, where Mary had seen it. So later on Mary took it from Bibi."

"Then Jordan took it from Mary's dresser," she said.

"Then someone took it from Jordan's shoe. And knocked him into next week and demolished Dr. Hurst's room in the process."

"But who?" she asked.

"Not only who, but why?"

"The why is because it's a valuable item," she said, and drained her glass of scotch. She sat down on her couch, and Woody jumped into her lap.

"As for the who . . ." Benchley glanced at the telegram. "Perhaps it's the colorfully named Lloyds or Pinks? Or the mysterious Berley brothers, whoever they may be."

She sighed. "We can't forget about Lydia. Remember, she's the reason why we went tearing up to Dr. Hurst's room in the first place? We feared she might harm him."

"Little Lydia Trumbull." Benchley almost laughed. "She

155

can barely hit a high note anymore, much less hit a strapping young adventurer like your Mr. Jordan. I can't imagine her knocking him senseless."

"Again, he's not my Mr. Jor—" she said. "Never mind. But we still don't know where Lydia went off to, and she certainly has a strike against her by hiding this chloroform."

She removed the little brown bottle from her purse and set it on her side table.

"My money's still on the infamous Ted Besh," Benchley said. "What if Ted Besh is some longtime rival from Dr. Hurst's younger days?"

"Well . . ." Dorothy said uncertainly.

"There was certainly something foreboding in the old man's voice when he said that name," Benchley continued, his face animated. "Perhaps this Besh fellow has returned from days gone by with the sole purpose of avenging some past injustice given at the hands of Dr. Hurst. A botched tonsillectomy, perhaps?"

She frowned. "Sounds far-fetched. And I bet Frank Case has found no such name in the guest register."

Benchley raised his merry eyebrows. "Perhaps this mysterious Mr. Besh is registered under an assumed name?"

She was skeptical. "A John Doe?"

"Or a Johnnie Walker?" he asked playfully.

"Jack Daniels?"

"Jim Beam!"

She chuckled at him. "What kind of name is Besh, anyhow?"

He laughed. "Nothing but the besh for you, my dear."

She laughed and looked into his eyes. She laid her hand on his. "I'm so very glad you're here, Fred. I don't know how I'd get along without you."

He rested his head against the couch and returned her gaze. "Certainly, Mrs. Parker." He spoke softly. "I felt a little, well, a little rotten for leaving Gertrude and the boys at home on such a snowy, cold night. But to tell you the truth, I'm glad I'm here, too."

She felt a little pang of jealousy (and, to be honest, guilt) at the mention of his wife and children. But she quickly got over it. He was here with her, after all, wasn't he?

"Truly, Fred," she said gratefully. "If you hadn't shown up tonight, I would have been at my wit's end."

He smiled that warm, comforting smile. "Nonsense, Mrs. Parker. There is no end to your wit." He spoke in a whisper as intimate as the rustle of sheets.

"Flattery will get you everywhere," she whispered back. She moved closer to him.

"And where exactly is that?"

Then Woodrow Wilson stood up, pressing his wet muzzle in between them. Both Dorothy and Benchley reared back in surprise. She had nearly forgotten about the little dog. He turned around once or twice in her lap, then sat down on his haunches. His big, dark bulging eyes looked forlornly at her.

She cupped the dog's bat-eared head in her hands. "Oh, my little man, you need to go outside, don't you? It's been hours since you've been out. You poor thing."

Benchley reached out and scratched the dog behind the ears. "Poor little pooch." Then he spoke to her. "But what can you do? You can't take him outside. You can't leave the building because of the quarantine."

She had an idea. "But I can go outside. I already have."

He looked at her curiously.

"Up on the roof. I can take him up there."

With mixed feelings, she pushed herself away from Benchley and got up from the couch. The dog jumped down to the threadbare imitation Persian carpet. Part of her regretted that the dog had literally stuck his nose into her affairs. . . .

But, she realized, another, smaller part of her was relieved. *Where were things heading on the couch just now?*

157

She couldn't lead a married man astray, could she? Or was he leading her astray?

She shook her head to clear it. She picked up the bottle of chloroform—she'd need to show it to Doyle—then she went to her front closet to get her coat and Woody's leash. She clipped the leash onto the little dog's collar, then stood and addressed Benchley.

"Perhaps while I'm taking him for his walk, you could go down to the switchboard and call Captain Church, as Woollcott had suggested."

Benchley was standing now, absentmindedly searching his jacket pockets for something. He pulled out his pipe and clamped it in his teeth. She suspected he didn't need to smoke. He just needed to busy himself, distract himself with some movement.

"Yes," he stammered, with the pipe in his clenched teeth. "Switchboard. Yes, indeed. Good thought, Mrs. Parker. Good thought indeed. I'll go this instant."

Without another word, he followed her and the dog out her door and into the hallway.

"Come up to Doug and Mary's penthouse," she said, "when you're through."

He raised his pipe in acknowledgement, then turned and went toward the flight of stairs.

She gently tugged the little dog's leash and walked toward the elevator. "Well, Woody, I guess you've taught me a lesson just now. Always look out for number one."

Then she heard an unusual, surprising sound.

Chapter 23

The strange noise came from inside Mrs. Volney's apartment. It was the sound of laughter and chatter. And not just one voice but several voices. The sounds of conversation and merriment weren't unusual in the Algonquin—the surprising part was that they were coming from behind Mrs. Volney's door in the wee hours in the morning. But it would have taken Dorothy by surprise at any time of the day.

She and Woody slowly approached the door, and the noise of talk and laughter became louder, more distinct. No men could be heard. It was only women laughing.

Jeez, is there a tea party going on? she wondered, growing annoyed. *Isn't that just like a bunch of useless women— sitting around having a quilting bee while a murder investigation is under way.*

They laughed again as a group, and Woody yipped at the noise.

Shaking her head, tugging Woody to follow, Dorothy moved past Mrs. Volney's door.

Behind her, the door opened.

"Dorothy, wait," called Jane Grant. Ruth Hale was standing behind her in the open doorway.

159

Woody spun around, pulling to go back. Dorothy followed him.

"Jane? Ruth? What are you two doing in there?" she asked them. "Is old Mrs. Volney leading a coven of witches? Is Alexander Woollcott boiling in a big cauldron in there, by any chance?" But what she really meant was, *What are you two intelligent young women doing in that rotten old shrew's apartment?*

"We're discussing Bibi. Come on in. Join us."

Dorothy peeked past them to see at least a dozen other women inside. She was surprised to see that her guess was correct: It was a tea party. Mrs. Volney was actually serving them tea. Woody strained at his leash, trying to get in.

"No," she said to him firmly. She spoke less harshly but still firmly to the two women. "No, thank you. I have to take this little fellow out for a leak, and I'm busy helping Dr. Doyle." But what she really meant was, *I'd rather go look for Bibi's body and find out who killed her than sit and gossip about the sad, dead girl behind her back.*

Jane and Ruth somehow understood this as a reprimand. "Good luck, then," Jane said quietly. "Come back if you change your mind." They began to close the door again.

Before the door shut, Dorothy spotted Lydia Trumbull sitting among the group of women. Dorothy was about to call out—to catch Lydia's attention. But then the door was closed. And Dorothy stood there, angry at herself for taking an arbitrary stand on chitchat and gossip. She didn't mind a little gossip now and again.

No, the real reason she was angry was because they were all gathered inside thick as thieves while she was outside by herself as usual. Outside the group. Outside the invited circle of women. Outside, looking in. Woody stood facing the door, waiting to be let in.

She was about to yank on his leash to drag him along. But she stopped herself. Rather than taking her anger out on the little dog, she leaned down and picked him up, held him tight and carried him like a baby to the elevator.

On his way to the telephone operator's office, Benchley strolled across the lobby, which was mostly quiet now. Harpo Marx was curled up on one of the couches and sleeping serenely. Benchley, whose mind was a jumble of thoughts, envied Harpo's peace and quiet.

So when he saw Frank Case and Luigi the waiter hurry toward him, Benchley was glad for the distraction. Both Case and Luigi carried armfuls of pillows and bundles of blankets.

"The staff need somewhere to sleep," Case explained. "The spare maids' quarters on the top floor are not big enough for them all. So they'll have to take turns between napping in the staff lounge in the basement and roughing it on the floor of the Pergola Room."

Spare maids' quarters on the top floor? Staff lounge in the basement? Benchley wasn't aware of either area.

He began to ask Case about this, but the hotel manager interrupted him. "Before you ask, I checked the hotel register. But we have no guest with the name Ted Besh or anything like it. No Ted or Theodore. No Besh, Bosh, Bush, or any similar surname."

"How about Beam? Jim Beam?"

Case looked puzzled.

"Never mind," Benchley said. He clapped his extinguished pipe over a potted palm to shake out the ash. "I'm so confused, I don't know what I'm saying."

"Or what you're doing." Case frowned at the discarded ash in the planter.

"Oh. Right." Benchley sheepishly slid the pipe into his pocket.

Case and Luigi hurried off.

Still in a fog, Benchley made his way to the operator's

161

office. Unlike Mrs. Parker, who was a resident in the hotel, he did not know the switchboard operator very well. He knocked softly, reluctantly, then hesitantly opened the door.

The fog in his head, blown aside by a horrified sense of alarm, cleared instantly.

Mavis was slumped face forward, with her head lying awkwardly on the switchboard. Her arms were splayed haphazardly across the rows of switches and plugs.

She was as still and as silent as a fallen gravestone.

Following in the tiny paw prints of Woodrow Wilson, Dorothy and Doyle wandered together along the snowy roof. The dog meandered from here to there, his small snout sniffing in the snow as he tried to pick up a scent.

This time, instead of going out through a window, Dorothy used the regular door to the roof, which, she learned, was just down the hallway from Fairbanks' apartment. Now she looked out over the lights of the silent, white-covered city. The snow had finally stopped. A soft but frigid wind blew the tatters of moonlight-tinged clouds across the dark sky. Above the clouds, the night was velvet black, spotted with silvery-blue stars. She took in deep breaths of the crisp, cold night air. For once it didn't smell like soot.

She had found Doyle in the penthouse. He had gotten nowhere with Mary Pickford and Douglas Fairbanks, he told her. Their explanations went in circles. The couple teeter-tottered back and forth, arguing angrily with each other one minute, then passionately reconciling the next. When Dorothy had invited him to join her to take the dog for a walk, Doyle almost literally jumped at the chance.

Once on the roof, she broke the news to Doyle that someone had recently ransacked Dr. Hurst's room. She quickly reassured him that Dr. Hurst was unharmed—not even awakened by the ruckus. But Jordan had been knocked out.

"Knocking a man from behind!" Doyle huffed, shaking

162

his big old head. "It's perfectly reprehensible. Who would do such a thuggish, ungentlemanly thing?"

"An ungentlemanly thug, perhaps?" she said, perhaps a bit too flippantly. She was merely trying to put Doyle at ease. In any case, the only serious injury Jordan seemed to have suffered was to his pride.

"I should go down and examine him myself," Doyle said.

"Of course you should. Make sure he and Dr. Hurst are all right. But a word to the wise . . . don't ask Jordan about the locket."

She explained about how Jordan had admitted to hiding the stolen locket in his shoe. But it had gone missing in the attack.

Doyle was angry with Jordan now. Moving in long strides, he began pacing in the snow. Woody scuttled out of the way. "That brigand! Stealing a locket from a lady's bureau. But not only that, it was Quentin's possession in the first place. In essence, he pickpocketed his own employer! I would not have suspected this from Mr. Jordan. He seemed a perfect gentleman and a worthy employee."

Dorothy thought of something that she hadn't fully considered before. "What if Jordan hadn't stolen it from Dr. Hurst but stolen it *for* Dr. Hurst?"

Doyle stopped short. "What's that you say? What sort of rubbish is that?"

"What if Jordan somehow knew it was in Mary's dresser? What if, as a loyal employee, he snatched it back on behalf of his disabled boss, who could no longer do so on his own?"

Doyle grunted. She had clearly planted a doubt in his mind. "Perhaps I should go talk to Mr. Jordan myself." He strode toward the door to go back inside.

"You do that," she said. "By the way, do you happen to recall the room number for the family with chicken pox?"

Doyle turned. "Chicken pox? Smallpox, you mean."

"Oh, right . . . smallpox."

"No, I don't recall the room number. I didn't visit the family myself. It was Quentin who diagnosed them."

"So it was. Never mind. I'll ask Frank Case. He'll know which room they're in."

Doyle paused in the doorway. "I hear the skepticism in your voice, Dorothy. It's rather distinct from your usual sarcastic tone. You think Quentin misdiagnosed that family."

"I do," she said flatly. "And I think he did it on purpose."

Doyle considered this. "Perhaps. But to what end?"

"To try to escape somebody who's after him. He thought he could use the quarantine to shut his pursuer out of the hotel. But he was too late. Whoever's after him is already inside."

Benchley stared at the motionless body of the switchboard operator.

"Not another one," he groaned miserably to himself. A cold, sinister feeling crept up his legs and crawled along his spine.

He glanced around the little office. Was he alone? Could there be anyone else in the room? He hadn't forgotten that *someone* had recently tried to lock him and Mrs. Parker in the subbasement freezer. And that someone was still somewhere in this hotel.

The single table lamp on top of the switchboard left narrow shadows in the corners. Even so, Benchley could see that no one else was here. He was alone with the body. All alone.

He forced himself to do more than stand there. Slowly he moved closer to get a better look at her.

Mavis was facedown on the switchboard. Her headset circled the top of her head like a tiara. Her dark hair covered her face like a veil.

Poor woman. Who did this to you?

One arm was curved awkwardly next to her head. The other arm stretched out along the edge of the switchboard desk. This arm looked as if it was in danger of slipping off the desk. Benchley could imagine what might happen if it did. If her arm dropped to her side, her whole body might tumble over with the weight of it and crumple into a heap onto the hardwood floor.

He couldn't bear to witness that. So he reached out and gently grasped the arm with both hands. He gingerly moved it forward on the switchboard and away from the edge.

But as he did so, her body slumped down and backward. Her head lifted off the switchboard and tilted back against her chair. Benchley looked at her pale face: A few stray hairs crossed it like slash marks.

Then her eyes popped open.

Benchley yelled and jumped back.

The woman sat bolt upright and faced him. The headset went flying and landed with a clatter at Benchley's feet. He leaped away from it as though it were a giant spider.

"What the hell is the matter with you?" she screamed at him. "You trying to scare me to death?"

"Scare *you* to death?" he gasped. "I thought you were already dead. You nearly scared *me* to death."

"I was getting some much-deserved shut-eye," she snapped, and picked up her headset. "What's the idea, waking up a girl from her beauty sleep?"

"What's the idea of pretending to be a corpse?" he asked. "Isn't there enough of that going around?"

She ignored him. She was busy rummaging through a large purse. She pulled out a compact and flipped it open. Looking in the mirror, she smoothed down her hair.

After a long moment Benchley got his breathing and his racing heart almost under control. "Listen," he told her, "Mr. Case is arranging sleeping...arrangements for the staff. In the Pergola Room. You'd be more comfortable there instead of by yourself in here."

"Well, since I'm not getting any beauty sleep in here..." She stood up to go.

Then he remembered what he had come for. "Wait a moment. I need to make a call to the police."

She stopped and frowned. "Isn't there enough of that going around?"

He thought she might connect the call for him. Instead she mumbled some instructions and then staggered out the door.

Benchley faced the switchboard with trepidation—the thing was nearly as big as an upright piano. He was not on friendly terms with mechanical equipment and instruments. As a matter of fact, he secretly feared that technology was out to get him. Electric alarm clocks, typewriters, subway turnstiles, automobiles—they all held an element of danger. He sometimes told the story of a can opener that had once nearly decapitated him—or at least that's the way he told it.

But except for the intimidating array of lights, plugs, cords and switches, perhaps this contraption didn't look so dangerous after all. He finally sat down in Mavis' chair and managed to put on the headset and microphone without too much difficulty. Just for fun, he flipped one of the switches at random—and it pinched his finger. He stuck the finger in his mouth and sucked on it.

"Very well, switchboard," he said with narrowed eyes. He pushed up his sleeves. "Let the battle begin."

Chapter 24

Dorothy stood outside Mrs. Volney's door. Alexander Woollcott was by her side. She didn't want him there. She didn't want to be here at Mrs. Volney's apartment, either. But she had run into Woollcott outside the Fairbanks' penthouse as she was bringing Woody in from the roof. And Woollcott had attached himself to her like a leech. Dorothy had dropped off her coat and let the dog back into her apartment. Then she allowed Woollcott to drag her along to Mrs. Volney's.

"So," he said, "you're sure you saw her in there?"

"For the umpteenth time, yes, I saw Lydia in there. Yes, I'll go in and get her out. Yes, you can grill her all you want. Grill her like a hamburger, for all I care."

"Splendid," Woollcott said, grinning from ear to ear. He was still as excited, perhaps more so, as when their silly game of Murder had started hours before. He was still playing detective.

She had seen him get worked up like this many times before. Every few months he'd pick up a new passion. Cribbage, croquet, crosswords—it didn't matter. Woollcott had spent one entire winter planning Jane Grant's wedding to Harold Ross. No detail was too small to consider. In the end it had become more Woollcott's soiree than Jane and Ross'. Now he wouldn't let go playing detective until he solved this murder—or until someone beat him to it.

She sighed. "You don't need me for this. Go in there yourself and get Lydia."

"A roomful of women? Not on your life. They'll eat me alive."

"Are you kidding? You're twice the barracuda that any of those women are."

He glowed at this, because he considered it a high compliment. "You may be right. But I had a disagreement recently with Madam Volney, the cranky old eavesdropper, and I swore I'd never speak with her again. I stoutly refuse to set foot into her lair."

She looked at his paunch. "You do everything stoutly. No need to advertise it."

He automatically sucked in his gut but then quickly exhaled with the effort and let it out. "Be that as it may, this is an important mission that you—and you alone—can carry out, my dear Dorothy. Now go into the lioness' den and get Lydia out of there!"

"Just a minute," she said sharply, remembering what Woollcott was supposed to be doing. "What about Bibi? Did you even look for her in the subbasement? What did you find?"

He glanced down at his shoes; perhaps he was staring through them and visualizing the basement far below. He spoke softly. "I found that it's quite dark and dank down there."

"You colossal coward! What was it you said? 'Spiders, spooks and bogeymen be damned. And if I don't turn up Bibi's body, my name's not Alexander Woollcott'? So if your name is not Alexander Woollcott, what is it?"

"I have not given up the search!" he said defensively. "I'm merely taking a break for a small stretch."

"You're stretching credibility, I think."

"And you're stalling for time!" he snapped. "Now, are you going to knock on this door, or shall I do it for you?"

After several wrong numbers and even more numerous pinched fingertips, Benchley finally connected to the Sixteenth Precinct and eventually got Captain Church on the line.

"Mr. Benchley, how are affairs at the Algonquin?"

"Affairs?" He gulped, unavoidably thinking of Dorothy. "Affairs are . . . very perplexing."

"Events will likely become clear soon," Church said reassuringly. "I have good news. I was able to get through to the commissioner of the Health Department. Woke him up from his sleep. I have hopes that we will obtain permission to breach the quarantine—at least temporarily—in the morning."

Benchley said, "I hope you practice what you breach, Captain."

Church didn't respond to this. "Have you chilled the body?"

"Chilled the body?"

"Miss Bibelot. Is her body on ice, as Dr. Norris instructed?"

"Oh yes, of course. Mrs. Parker and I took her down to the freezer room," Benchley said, not telling the entire truth—not telling Church that it was really anyone's guess where her body was now.

"And Dr. Hurst? The elderly man with apoplexy. Is he resting comfortably?"

Benchley thought of Dr. Hurst lying calmly amid the chaos and destruction of his hotel room. "Quite comfortably. Like a pig in a sty. Like an eye in a storm. Speaking of Dr. Hurst, that's why I called. He woke up for a short while and uttered a name. Can you look it up in your files or records?"

"A name? By all means. What is it?"

"Ted Besh."

Church repeated it. Through the earphones Benchley could hear the scratching of his pencil. "If he lives in New York, or committed any crime in the city, or worked and paid taxes in the city, we will find a record of him right away," Church said. "Interestingly enough, I have some surprising information to tell you about Dr. Hurst."

Benchley sat up. This did sound interesting. "Go on."

"We received a wire from England. Dr. Hurst is a wanted man."

"Wanted? That's hard to believe."

"Because he is elderly and respectable?"

"No, because no one wanted him here in the first place," Benchley said. "What's he wanted for?"

"Theft and exportation of stolen goods." There was a rustle of paper on the other end. "He is the prime suspect in the theft of a rare item from the London Museum. He is believed to have taken the item and replaced it with a fake."

"A rare item? What was it?"

"Unfortunately the wire message does not provide that crucial detail."

"A silver locket, perhaps?"

"Does Dr. Hurst have a silver locket in his possession?"

"Well, no. Not anymore. But he did when he arrived."

There was silence on the other end. An angry, irritated silence. When Church finally spoke, his voice was a deep growl. "Mr. Benchley, if you or Mrs. Parker somehow damaged or lost an item of great value stolen from a friendly nation, you are in extremely serious trouble."

Benchley was so relieved that he laughed. "Not to worry, Captain. Mrs. Parker and I didn't damage it or lose it."

"I am very pleased to hear that."

"Benedict Jordan lost it."

"Lost it?" Church's voice exploded. "Who the devil is Benedict Jordan?"

Whoops . . .

*   *   *

Dorothy remembered that she had the bottle of chloroform in her purse. She had forgotten to mention it to Doyle when they were up on the roof. It occurred to her now that she could pull the stopper out and lob the bottle like a grenade into Mrs. Volney's apartment. It would put all those women to sleep for a week. Wouldn't that be fun?

"Go on," Woollcott urged once again. "Go in and get Lydia out of there. I'll wait right here in the hallway."

He nudged her forward. Dorothy felt spiteful, as she always did when ordered to do something. She rapped hard on the door. Woollcott began to move away, but she linked her arm through his and pulled him to her.

"What? No—!" he sputtered.

The door opened, and Mrs. Volney's wrinkled face stared blankly at them. She held a plate of cookies in her hand.

Dorothy smiled broadly. "We heard you're having a party in here. May we join you?"

Mrs. Volney opened her mouth to speak. "Well, cer—"

"Cookies!" Woollcott stepped forward and grabbed the plate from her hand. "Here, let me distribute those for you, my dear."

"—tainly," Mrs. Volney said uncertainly.

Woollcott gobbled down three macaroons before Dorothy had even entered the apartment and closed the door behind her.

"Mr. Benchley, I shall ask you again," Captain Church snarled through the headphones. "Who is Benedict Jordan?"

"A very good man," Benchley said, then thought of Dorothy. "Some people even think he's a rather dashing and handsome man—"

"Mr. Benchley, I will have none of your nonsense—"

Benchley spoke quickly. "Mr. Jordan is Dr. Hurst's manservant. His aide-de-camp. His captaindomo, Major—I mean, his majordomo, Captain."

171

"His manservant?" The captain digested this. "And you say that this Benedict Jordan took the locket from Dr. Hurst?"

"No, I didn't say that."

"Did Dr. Hurst entrust it to him?"

"No, I don't believe so."

Church was impatient again. "Mr. Benchley, I will not play twenty questions with you."

"Fine with me. I don't like parlor games." Then he tried to explain. "Jordan had the locket in his shoe, you see. Then it went missing."

"His shoe went missing?"

"No, the locket. He was armed with his shoe, which I thought was quite amusing."

"Why was he armed—?" Church began; then he gave up and switched gears. "Never mind. Why was the locket in Jordan's shoe?"

"For safekeeping."

"So Dr. Hurst *did* entrust the locket to him?"

"No, no! Jordan took it."

"Jordan took it," Church said slowly. "He took the locket from Dr. Hurst?"

"No, he wouldn't do that. Jordan's as loyal as a Labrador."

"Then how did Jordan get the locket?"

"He stole it."

"He *stole* it? From the London Museum? So you mean to say that Dr. Hurst is not the thief?"

"I don't mean to say that at all. As you know, Dr. Hurst is British. Meanwhile Jordan is as American as a sawed-off shotgun. And Dr. Hurst hired him here in America. So if Jordan wasn't even in England, how could he take the locket from the London Museum? No, it must have been Dr. Hurst."

Church thought about this. "Very well. Then how did Jordan obtain it?"

"From Mary Pickford. Well, from her dresser, that is."

"Mary Pickford?" Church asked skeptically. "The Hollywood movie star?"

"That's the one."

"How did Mary Pickford come into possession of it?"

"She stole it," Benchley said. "From Bibi Bibelot."

"Bibi Bibelot? The dead girl?"

"That's the one."

Benchley heard what sounded like the grinding of teeth on the other end. "Mr. Benchley—!"

"Shall I walk you through it again?" he said helpfully. "It's very simple. Before Mr. Jordan used his shoe as a weapon, he used it as a safe—which, come to think of it, is just as ironic as being armed with a shoe. A safe weapon, if you see—"

"Mr. Benchley!"

But Benchley had gone quiet. He had realized something. Then he spoke more to himself than to Church. "Jordan ran into his room to look into his shoe. . . ."

"Yes. But the question is, who took it from his shoe?"

"I don't know. But that's not the question on my mind right now," Benchley said quickly. "I'll have to call you back later. You can let me know what you find out about Ted Besh. 'Bye!"

"No, Mr. Bench—!"

But Benchley yanked the cord out of the socket. The cord snapped back into place. The line went dead.

I must find Mrs. Parker. He was about to pull off the headset and go looking for her, but then he stared at the switchboard's array of lights and plugs. Each darkened light and each plug represented a telephone in each room in the hotel. Each had a tiny number—its room number—printed beneath it. *In which room is Mrs. Parker right now?* He realized that instead of running around the hotel, he could simply place a call or two to find her—

Grrrzzzz!

Benchley jumped in his seat as a loud mechanical buzz sounded in his ears. One of the little bulbs lit up. The light was bright red, and the buzz was insistent. He felt flustered. Who was calling? Then again, perhaps it was Mrs. Parker trying to reach him?

Benchley flipped the corresponding switch, once again pinching his finger. "Hello. Operator speaking!" he said, a phrase he'd heard a thousand times before.

There was no response. Then the buzz sounded, and the light flashed again.

Oh, right. Connect the cord! Benchley grabbed the metal tip of the cord nearest to him and rammed it home into the socket beneath the red light. The light went out. The line was connected. "Operator speaking!" Benchley said merrily.

It wasn't Dorothy's voice that answered. It was a man's voice. A gruff voice. "Give me Klondike-5, 5482."

"J-just one moment," Benchley stammered. He was so surprised that it wasn't Dorothy on the line and so flustered by the gravelly voice that he flipped the switch again and promptly disconnected the call.

Chapter 25

"So glad you could finally join us, Dorothy," said Jane Grant. Dorothy's other friend, Ruth Hale, sat next to Jane and looked equally pleased. *What are these two young, intelligent women doing in this old hag's den?* Dorothy wondered again.

About ten other women, one of whom was Lydia Trumbull, were also crowded into Mrs. Volney's living room. The actress wouldn't meet Dorothy's eyes.

Woollcott had apparently forgotten all about Lydia. He continued to help himself to the plate of cookies and was now happily accepting a cup of tea from Mrs. Volney, who still looked surprised at his appearance.

The women were gathered in a close circle. Some were squeezed into the little armchairs and the small, uncomfortable couch. Mrs. Volney had evidently brought out a few rickety folding chairs, and the rest of the women sat precariously on these. Her cats had disappeared somewhere.

"Dorothy, come sit here," Jane said, sliding aside on the couch. Ruth slid the other way to make room and beckoned her over. Dorothy saw that if she sat there, she would be directly facing Lydia Trumbull. She hurried over and squeezed in between Jane and Ruth.

175

She realized this was actually a pleasant little treat to be among only women—not counting Woollcott. She was often the only woman among a group of men. Most days, she was the only woman seated at the Algonquin Round Table. She was also the only woman in the editor's bullpen at the *New Yorker*. And she was one of the few women invited to the men's Saturday night poker game, though she never played.

She loved the company of men. She was proud to hold her own against them. Many of them had degrees from Ivy League colleges. But there she was among them, not even a high school graduate and hardly more than five feet tall—yet she could cut them to ribbons or leave them in stitches. Or sometimes both.

So being among a big group of women for the first time in a long time was like visiting a foreign country. She hadn't quite decided whether she found it comforting or distressing. How did they speak here? What were their customs like? Dorothy had nearly forgotten.

"So," she asked, "what are you gals chatting about so late in the night—or so early in the morning, as the case may be?"

"Still talking about Bibi, of course," Jane said.

"Jane was in the middle of telling us more about that article she wrote in the *Times* last fall," Ruth offered.

"Ah." Dorothy remembered, turning to Jane. "The one that put Bibi on the map. You had mentioned it earlier. . . ."

"We were just speculating about the identity of Bibi's rich benefactor," Jane said. "Bibi wouldn't tell me when I interviewed her."

"And? Any ideas of this mysterious patron?"

Jane shrugged. "Some Wall Street sugar daddy, most likely. Probably has a wife, so that's why Bibi had to keep his name a secret."

Ruth raised an eyebrow. "What about that Dr. Hurst? He seems like he might be the sugar daddy type."

Dorothy thought of the spindly old man lying in his bed and perhaps paralyzed. And she felt sorry for him. "Then again, maybe Bibi had no rich benefactor," she said. "Maybe it was just a lie. Maybe she simply wanted to fool everyone into thinking someone actually cared about her."

Lydia finally spoke up. "It was no lie," she said spitefully. "*Someone* paid Bibi's way. It's impossible for a girl like that to come from nowhere. Someone paid for her to have the best dance lessons. The best voice lessons. The latest clothes. Memberships in nightclubs. Introductions to Broadway agents, publicists and producers. Trust me, a penniless girl doesn't hop off the bus one day and become the toast of Broadway the next day. She needs help."

Dorothy looked at Lydia, a prominent stage actress whose star would likely soon be fading. Lydia knew it. Everyone in the room knew it.

"So who helped her?" Dorothy asked.

Lydia's face soured and she looked away. "Who knows? Does it even matter?"

Dorothy wondered. Did it matter?

She turned to Jane. "Someone will have to contact her family. You said she had family in New York?"

"A brother, I think? Or was it a cousin?" she said. "She didn't talk about a mother or a father, that's for sure."

"Embarrassing thing to have to explain," Dorothy said, putting her hand to her ear like a telephone. "'Your sister died naked in a bathtub on New Year's Eve, apparently murdered.' No family member wants to hear that, no matter how estranged."

"Well, it won't come as too much of a surprise to them," Lydia said bitterly. "You can't walk naked through a party in a famous actor's penthouse and expect to wake up without a scratch the next morning."

"What are you saying?" Dorothy asked her. "Bibi was asking for it?"

"Yes," Lydia said. "She most certainly was."

Ruth shook her head. "No woman deserves that."

"Certainly not," Dorothy agreed.

"But I don't condone what she did," Ruth quickly added. "That kind of behavior sets back women's equality by years. Will prancing around naked make men think we're their equals? Is that why we fought for the right to vote—so a cheap dumb blonde could act like a sexpot and make everyone forget that most women are smarter than that?"

Equals? The right to vote? Dorothy wondered. *What does that have to do with anything?*

"It's not all about smarts, Ruth," Jane argued. "And it's not about sex, either."

"Finally," Dorothy said, "someone in this room is making sense."

Jane nodded. "It's about power. Sex was probably the last thing on Bibi's mind, except to use it to her own ends. Let's be honest. With her clothes on, she could beguile men. But with them off, she could positively rule them."

"What . . . ?" Dorothy asked, bewildered.

"She wasn't just showing off her skin," Jane explained. "She was demonstrating her power. And someone— someone who either envied that power or was afraid of that power—killed her for it."

All the other women in the room—even Mrs. Volney and also Woollcott—nodded at the sense in this.

All except Dorothy. She stood up. "Are all of you nuts?"

Openmouthed, they looked at her.

Grrrzzzz! The noise buzzed again through the headphones. Even though Benchley had been expecting it, the sound still made him jump in Mavis' chair. Now the red light flashed again as though annoyed at him. It was like an eye—an ogre's angry eye—blinking at him.

Grrrzzzz!

Benchley plugged a cord into the socket below the angry red light. Blessedly, the light went out.

178

"Operator . . ." he said meekly.

"Why'd you hang up on me?" the man's gruff voice said, but didn't wait for an answer. "Just get me Klondike-5, 5482."

"Certainly, sir," Benchley said. But he had no idea how to connect to Klondike-5 something something something. . . .

Below the socket and darkened light—below every socket and light—was that three-digit number. Must be the hotel room number, Benchley figured. He'd better find out for sure.

"Sir," he said politely, "you're in room five-twenty?"

"Yeah. So what?"

Benchley was surprised how easily he came up with the half truth, half lie. "It may take awhile to connect the call. The snowstorm is playing havoc with the lines. Can I try to place your call and then ring your room when it's connected?"

The man exhaled impatiently. "It ain't long-distance. It's only Brooklyn."

"The snowstorm, sir . . ."

"Fine. Just don't take all night."

"Certainly not, sir."

The man hung up. The line went dead. Benchley unplugged the cord and sighed with relief. He'd bought himself a few minutes, but that was all. . . .

Wait a second! he realized. *I don't have to sit here and connect telephone calls in the middle of the night. This is not my job.* Of course it wasn't! He could get up and leave at any time. *Oh, what a goose I am!*

But first he should try to reach Dorothy. Let her know that Dr. Hurst was wanted by the authorities—and tell her of his newfound suspicion of Jordan.

"Let's see. . . ." He could try calling her room. He might be able to do that without pinching his finger again. He plugged the main cord into the socket above number 213—

Dorothy's room number. He flipped the switch and rang her room. Not one pinch!

The phone buzzed once ... twice ... three times. ... He could imagine Woodrow Wilson lying on the hairy couch and not even looking up at the sound of the telephone.

"Oh well, she must not be in her room." He disconnected the line.

Then he rang the penthouse, with only one pinch. Douglas Fairbanks answered—Benchley felt he was getting the hang of being a switchboard operator—but told him Dorothy wasn't there.

Now what? Where could she be? Lydia Trumbull's room, perhaps? But Benchley couldn't remember the actress' room number. It was just down the hall from Dorothy's room, though, so it must be two hundred something. ...

Grrrzzzz!

Oh no! The ogre's angry red eye was back, and with its evil buzzing in his ear. It was the man in room 520!

Do something! Benchley told himself. He ripped the headset off his head. But the red eye still flashed, even angrier somehow now that it flashed silently.

He couldn't take it. He wanted to turn and run, but the red flashing held him transfixed. He grabbed the cord and plugged it into the socket below the light. Reluctantly he picked up the headset.

"Operator," he said wearily, beaten. The switchboard had dished out its worst and had won.

"Buddy, where's my phone call? It's important!"

"I'm sorry, sir. Perhaps I took down the wrong number. Could you give it to me again?" Benchley picked up a notepad and pencil by the side of the switchboard.

"Yeah, fine. Klondike-5, 5482." The gruff man rattled off the numbers even more quickly than before. But one thing Benchley could do was write quickly.

"Got it, sir. One moment, please."

Benchley saw a number of sockets neatly labeled with

the names of different boroughs. One label said BROOKL. EXCH.

Brooklyn Exchange! Benchley plugged the cord into that socket and flipped the switch below it. Its light glowed, and it buzzed the operator.

"Your number?" the woman's voice answered in a tough Brooklyn accent: *Yah numbah?*

Benchley quickly repeated the phone number the man had given to him.

"Hold," the Brooklyn operator said.

Benchley held on for dear life. He gripped the edges of the switchboard with both hands. He knew he shouldn't care. He should have gotten right up from this seat. But he couldn't help himself. When someone asked for his help or told him to do something, he felt compelled to comply. And that angry red light and the gruff man's voice were plenty compelling.

"Your call," the operator said. "Go ahead."

There was a click and a man's voice said. "Yeah, who is it?"

It took Benchley half a second to answer. Not only were the telephone lines apparently working again, but he had done it! He had actually completed a call!

"It—it's the Algonquin Hotel," Benchley stammered, half-amazed and half-triumphant. "A party in room five-twenty has been trying to reach you."

"Yeah? Well, put him through, why don'tcha," the man's voice said.

Don't blow it now, Bob, old boy, he told himself. *Don't disconnect it!*

He crossed the plugs and flipped one switch, then the other. He held his breath. "Go ahead, caller."

The gruff man's voice said, "Mr. Caesar, you there?"

"Yeah, you nitwit," the other man said. He had a quiet, commanding voice. "No names."

Benchley nearly bit his tongue. He wanted to scream in

J. J. Murphy

exultation. *I did it! I did it!* He had taken on the switchboard and had won!

"Forget it," the gruff man said. "The operator's an idiot. Took me five minutes to get through."

An idiot? Benchley's joy turned to disappointment. *Five minutes? Certainly not!*

"Shut your trap," the authoritative man said, his quiet voice rising. "Operator, you still there? Operator!"

Benchley didn't speak.

"Forget it," the gruff man said. "He's off the line."

"What took you so long to call?" said the quiet man. "Do you have the piece?"

"Phone lines were down. And, yeah, we got it. Like taking candy from a baby."

The quiet man's voice dropped lower. "I ain't talking candy. I'm talking priceless artifacts."

"We got your priceless artifact," said the gruff man. "We got your tête-bêche."

Your tête-bêche? Now Benchley actually did bite his tongue. . . .

Ted Besh?

182

Chapter 26

Dorothy felt a change in the atmosphere, a coldness creeping into the room. The women had gathered in a warm, collegial circle, both literally and in agreement of mind. But Dorothy was about to break that circle. She couldn't help herself. She had to speak.

"Bibi wasn't murdered because she showed her power," she said sarcastically to Jane. Then she turned to Ruth. "And she wasn't killed because she was a threat to men."

They all looked at her skeptically, even angrily. Just a few moments ago, they had all been chatting happily, a group of women bonding through conversation. No longer. Dorothy had wrecked it simply by disagreeing with them.

She continued, "I don't know why she was murdered, but I know it wasn't for any of those reasons. It wasn't because she was a woman or because she was a sex symbol—or any kind of symbol. She was murdered because she was Bibi, pure and simple. She was murdered because of something she did or something she didn't do."

Jane folded her arms. "What makes you so sure?"

Dorothy threw up her hands. "Women's intuition."

She said it as an offhanded joke. But they didn't take it as a joke. They thought she was making fun of them;

she could tell. They thought she was being superior to them.

But she wasn't! She didn't feel superior at all. As a matter of fact she felt lousy. She didn't want to alienate these women. She liked their warm camaraderie. She liked being one of them for once, a part of them—but not at the expense of agreeing like a sheep.

Perhaps if she could help them see it her way . . .

"Look," she said, "if a man walked naked through the room and was later found murdered, would we all be asking ourselves if he was murdered because he wanted to demonstrate his . . . power?" She smiled, and some of the women smiled. "Would we wonder if he was killed because of something he represented? Of course not. We'd think, jeez, he must have made an enemy of someone. Or, gosh, what kind of trouble was he in? Who did he owe money to? Whose wife did he sleep with? So if we would think that of a man, why should we think any differently of a woman?"

"Because," Lydia snapped, "Bibi *was* a woman. That makes all the difference."

They nodded in agreement with Lydia, even the ones who had just chuckled a moment before. They looked at Dorothy as though challenging her to prove them all wrong.

Well, of course she was a woman, Dorothy thought. *But what does that have to do with it?*

As though reading her mind, Lydia responded, spitting out her words like poison. "Bibi wasn't just a dumb blond vamp. She *did* represent things. She was sex. She was power. She was fame. She was success. You look me in the eye, Dorothy, and you just try to tell me different."

Dorothy looked Lydia in the eye—and she found she couldn't disagree.

Benchley sat stupefied. *So Ted Besh isn't a person? He's a stolen priceless artifact.*

It, he corrected himself. *It is a stolen priceless artifact!*

Now he had two important things to tell Mrs. Parker. He had to find her right away.

But the quiet man—Mr. Caesar—was speaking. "What are you waiting for? Get it over here. The client wants it, and how."

"No can do," the gruff man said. "This joint is quarantined. Closed up tighter than a nun's knees."

"Quarantined? So what? Just slip out the back door. Who's gonna stop you? The bellhop? Just get the goods over here."

"Hold your horses," the gruff man said. "Snow's pretty heavy. Won't be any cabs now. At first light we'll leave. Good enough?"

There was silence on the other end. A threatening, uncomfortable silence, Benchley thought.

To fill the silence, the gruff man spoke again, his voice tentative now. "Mr. Caesar—?"

Mr. Caesar's quiet voice exploded. "You don't tell me to hold my horses, you two-cent crook! If you don't have the goods here by nine in the morning, it won't be a couple flakes of snow you gotta worry about. It'll be lead . . . in your head!"

"No problem, Mr. Caesar, no problem!" The gruff man spoke quickly, apologetically. "We'll be there by nine. Maybe earlier. Soon as we can, I promise."

We? The gruff-voiced man had said "we" before, hadn't he? *So there's at least a pair of two-cent crooks in the hotel,* Benchley thought. *They must be the ones who ransacked Dr. Hurst's room and took the locket from Mr. Jordan's shoe!*

"Oh, I must tell Mrs. Parker," he said to himself.

There was another silence—a shorter one this time.

"Who's there?" Mr. Caesar asked. "Who said that?"

"Operator!" the gruff man barked. "You still on this line?"

Whoops . . .

*   *   *

185

"Just what I thought," Lydia said when Dorothy didn't answer her. "You can't argue with the truth, Dorothy. Bibi represented all those things, and that's why she's dead now. It happens to everyone who tries to tame the monster of fame. It eats you up alive."

Dorothy shook her head.

"So true," Mrs. Volney said. "So sad and so true. I've been in this city more than eighty years, and it's only getting worse. Crime. Drinking. Fornication. Jazz music. These people who put themselves in harm's way, such as this Bibi girl, they get hurt. That's what this city does to people— especially the immoral and the proud," she said scornfully. "If you play with fire, you get burned—that's what my dear Donald always said. Nowadays I often think it's better to hide your head in the sand like an ostrich."

"I often think that, too," Lydia sighed, looking off to nowhere. Some of the other women nodded.

Dorothy was still standing, although they had been ignoring her. "Just a minute! The city didn't chew Bibi up and spit her out. It wasn't some grand scheme or moral reprisal delivered by the gods of fate." Now they were no longer ignoring her. But they, especially Lydia and Mrs. Volney, looked at her skeptically. "It was a mere mortal who killed Bibi. Just a person—one person, most likely. Someone who had it in for her." Dorothy stared at Lydia. "You had it in for her."

Lydia's frost-blue eyes went wide. She jumped to her feet. "How can you accuse me of such a thing? I hated Bibi, it's true. But I would never—"

Her eyes fluttered, and Dorothy worried that she might faint again.

"You would never kill her?" Dorothy said. "Maybe not on purpose—maybe. But how about by accident?"

All the women in the room became alarmed, angered, shocked or surprised. They gasped with hands over their mouths, drew a sharp intake of breath or muttered denials to one another.

Worried now, Lydia dropped back into her chair. "What's that supposed to mean?"

Dorothy pulled the bottle of chloroform out of her purse. "What were you doing with this?"

Lydia's eyes went wide again when she saw the bottle; then she glared malevolently at Dorothy. She stammered, "I've never seen that before in my life."

"I took it from your room. Mr. Benchley was there. He can attest to it."

Jane craned her neck to see. "What is it?"

"Chloroform," Dorothy said. "Dr. Doyle thinks Bibi was chloroformed. Knocked out."

With a loud clatter, Woollcott dropped his empty plate onto the tray in Mrs. Volney's hands. The little old lady was nearly pushed back from the force of it. Woollcott charged by her without noticing. "Dorothy! Where did you get that? This is my investigation! I make the accusations!"

"*Your* investigation? You're too chicken to look for Bibi's body in the basement."

"Bibi's body is in the basement?" Ruth said, aghast. The other women gasped and muttered in surprise.

"She's missing," Dorothy said to Lydia. "Know anything about that?"

Lydia's eyes fluttered again and closed. She slumped into her chair in a dead faint.

The women on either side of Lydia quickly tended to her by resting her head on a pillow and stroking her cheek. Everyone else turned to Dorothy as though she had forced Lydia into unconsciousness.

"What do you mean, she's missing?" Mrs. Volney asked in her shrill, brittle voice.

Dorothy felt all their demanding, expectant eyes on her. "Well, we sort of lost her," she answered weakly. "Mr. Benchley and I, that is."

"You *lost* her?" Mrs. Volney asked accusingly. She bared her ancient gray teeth, which seemed suddenly ferocious and frightening. Dorothy had never heard the nasty old woman speak so sharply, so viciously.

Then Dorothy noticed that Woollcott was glaring at her. Not only had she alienated every woman in the room, but she hadn't even accomplished her task of getting Lydia out. Far from it. Lydia, especially now that she lay unconscious, was ensconced tightly in their women's circle and was the strongest link in their chain. Dorothy was standing far outside of it.

She was once again severely tempted to rip the stopper out of the chloroform bottle, smash it on the ground and put them all quickly to sleep.

Instead she silently turned on her heel and made for the door.

"Operator, speak up!" the gruff man shouted. "We just heard you. We know you're there!"

"Sorry, wrong number," Benchley said hurriedly. He quickly yanked the cord out of the socket to disconnect the call.

Just for good measure, he grabbed a different cord and plugged it into the socket below room 520. Then he crossed another cord over it and plugged it into the socket for the Brooklyn Exchange. He grabbed another cord, then another and another, and plugged them into random sockets. He plugged cords into socket after socket—

Grrrzzzz!

It was the angry red ogre's eye blinking at him again. Benchley imagined that the gruff-voiced man in room 520 had identical angry red eyes. But Benchley couldn't get on the line even if he wanted to, because the wires were crossed all over the switchboard like a thick spiderweb.

Grrrzzzz!

He couldn't stand to see that red light one more time! He pulled off the headset and flung it down onto the switchboard. He was about to turn and leave when he noticed that the headset had accidentally flipped a couple of the switches, lighting up two more bright red bulbs.

Out of desperation or deviltry, Benchley set to work on the switchboard and flipped switch after switch. The panel lit up like wildfire. The buzzer sounded like a furious swarm of giant mechanical insects.

Grrrzzzz! GrrrZZZZ! GRRRZZ—!

All of a sudden, the panel went dark. The whole room went dark.

Benchley found himself in silent, inky blackness.

"Whoops . . ."

As Dorothy rushed along the hallway away from Mrs. Volney's apartment, she suddenly heard the sound of telephones ringing. The noise was coming from all over. Phones seemed to be ringing in every room.

She moved quickly to the stairwell and shoved open the heavy door. Up and down the stairs, the sound of telephones chimed from every floor in the hotel.

Suddenly the two heavyset nuns—the ones who had kept vigil by Bibi in the bathtub during the party—came charging down the stairs. Seeing Dorothy, they hurried past her with barely a polite nod. Then down the steps they went.

As quickly as the phones had begun ringing, they abruptly stopped. What was going on? Had the nuns somehow set off the telephones? It seemed a funny coincidence . . . ringing telephones and running nuns.

Then Dorothy realized there could be only one answer: Benchley!

She hurried down the stairs to the lobby to find him.

Chapter 27

B enchley stood alone in the darkened telephone operator's office.

"This is what happens when you lose your temper," he chided himself. "You blow a fuse."

He inched his way toward the door with his hands stretched out in front of him in the darkness. He found the door, felt around for the knob and opened it. He was surprised to see that the lights in the lobby were still on.

I'll have to commend Mr. Case on his hotel's smart electrical plan, he thought. *The switchboard must be on its own electrical circuit.*

He wasn't exactly sure what an electrical circuit actually was, but he knew it meant that some rooms might have electricity while others might not. He also knew it meant that the elevator might very well still be in operation.

He hurried around the unmanned front desk and toward the elevator. He pushed the call button and was pleased to hear the crank of the elevator somewhere up the shaft. In a moment the elevator arrived—Benchley could see its light through the tiny circular window. But the door didn't open as it usually did.

Benchley waited just a moment; then he gave up and opened the door himself.

Inside, Maurice the elevator operator stood leaning in the corner and snoring loudly. Benchley pulled aside the interior brass accordion gate and stepped in. He took one look at Maurice, then looked at the elevator controls. He shrugged his shoulders and closed the outer door and the inner gate. Then, still confident from conquering the switchboard, he pushed the lever to take him up to the penthouse.

Instead the elevator went down. Alarmed but hardly surprised, Benchley realized that he was descending to the basement.

At the bottom of the stairwell, Dorothy pushed open the door to the lobby. It was even quieter than before—except for Harpo Marx loudly snoring on a nearby sofa. She walked by him on her way to the switchboard operator's office. But she could see as she approached that the door was partially open, and it was dark inside.

Then, to her surprise, the two nuns came rushing out of the room. Lifting their black habits a few inches off the floor to avoid tripping, they ran right up to her.

"Excuse us, daughter," the larger one said breathlessly. "Have you seen the switchboard operator?"

"No. But perhaps she took a break for a catnap somewhere."

"She?" The nuns looked confused. "The switchboard operator is a woman?"

"Yes. Mavis has been a woman for quite some time. All her life, I think."

The nuns exchanged a glance. At that moment Frank Case came hurrying from the dining room.

"Ah, Frank," Dorothy said with a wave. "These saintly ladies are looking for Mavis. Do you know where she went off to?"

191

Case, as unflappable as always, answered politely, "In the Pergola Room. Just through there." He pointed back the way he had come. "But she's sleeping at the moment."

The nuns again slightly lifted their skirts and moved quickly in that direction. "Thank you, my son," the second nun said to Case as they went past him. He nodded to them and then to Dorothy as he moved toward the front desk.

"Frank," she called after him. "Since you seem to know everyone's whereabouts, have you seen Mr. Benchley?"

Case turned. "Yes, Mrs. Parker, I have. I saw him here in the lobby about fifteen or twenty minutes ago. But if you'll excuse me, please," he said in his unruffled, even tone, "I have an emergency to deal with."

"An emergency? Do you mean the ringing of telephones all over the hotel?" She glanced at the lobby's big old grandfather clock—it was almost five o'clock in the morning. "Quite a wake-up call."

"Yes, indeed." Case nodded. "But also the electricity has gone out in certain rooms."

He rounded the front desk and went behind it. He bent down and pulled something out. He dropped it—a small wooden cigar box—on the desk's blotter and began to look through it. Dorothy went up to the counter to see. Case was searching through an assortment of electrical fuses.

"Ah!" he said with a note of triumph in his voice. "Here's the one." He clutched it in his hand. Then he put the box away inside the desk and emerged from behind it. When he came face-to-face with Dorothy, he slowed his hurried pace. "Is there something else I can do for you, Mrs. Parker?"

Where was Benchley? A minute ago he was most certainly in the switchboard room. Now where did he wander to?

"No, thank you, Frank," she said. "But if you see Mr. Benchley, would you please tell him I'm looking for him?"

Benchley poked his head out of the door of the elevator. This was simply the basement, not the subbasement below.

It was better lit and not at all as dusty and dirty as the sub-basement, and appeared more frequently used.

The elevator had him stumped. He didn't want to press his luck with machinery anymore. And he couldn't bring himself to wake up Maurice. So he decided to venture forth and find the stairs to go back up to the lobby. He closed the elevator door, and it went upward almost immediately.

He smacked his forehead. *Now, why didn't I just wait for someone to call the elevator upward?* He shook his head at his poor decision but quickly shrugged it off and moved forward along the concrete corridor. Unlike in the subbasement, the walls on this floor were painted an industrial gray. It wasn't much cheerier, but at least it was more modern, less medieval.

Up ahead a brightened doorway spilled light across the corridor floor. Odd sounds came from the room—footsteps and a muttering voice. Benchley cautiously looked through the open door.

It was a large, brightly lit room—apparently a combination lunchroom and lounge for the staff. The first thing Benchley saw was a tall young man in coveralls who was walking back and forth. The man was grumbling to himself. "Can't take this anymore. Got to get out of here, or I'm going to go nuts. Nuts, I tell you!"

The man was pacing between two long, bare banquet tables, which took up the middle of the room. Surrounding each table were a number of cheap metal chairs. In the corner was an old, heavily worn sofa next to an ashtray stand, which was overflowing with cigarette butts. Hunched on the sofa was Luigi the waiter. His head rested heavily in his hands, and his elbows were planted firmly on his knees. He sat with a forlorn, desperate expression, as though he'd been sitting there for a million years. When he noticed Benchley in the doorway, he jumped excitedly to his feet with a broad smile on his face.

"Mr. Benchley!" Luigi said in his heavy Italian accent

and came forward to greet him. "So good to see you. Come in, come in. What brings you down here?"

"Got a little turned around, I'm afraid. Actually, I was looking for Mrs. Parker. Have you seen her?"

Luigi's eyes went even wider. "Mrs. Parker? No, sir. She's not here. No." He cast a glance over his shoulder at the pacing, grumbling man. "But you let me help you look for Mrs. Parker, all right? I help you look for her. We go."

The man in coveralls shot them an angry look. It took a moment for Benchley to recognize him. Ah yes, he was the man who spilled the tub of ice when Bibi had first appeared naked in Fairbanks' penthouse.

"This way," Luigi said, pushing Benchley out the door. "Stairs over here. We go up to the kitchen, then to the lobby. Come this way!"

Benchley followed the waiter, who still wore his black waistcoat, black bow tie and white apron from earlier in the night.

Luigi whispered over his shoulder. "That man's driving me crazy. Everyone in this hotel is going crazy, you know?"

"Must be cabin fever," Benchley said helpfully.

Luigi exhaled in frustration. "First the smallpox. Now the cabin fever. People dropping like flies around here. No wonder they going crazy also."

Benchley followed him to a set of concrete stairs with a metal pipe railing. Luigi climbed the stairs, and Benchley followed. At the top they found themselves in the kitchen— at least Benchley assumed it was the kitchen. The lights were off, and the room was nearly pitch-black.

There was a clacking sound.

"I flip the switches," Luigi said, confused. "But no lights go on. Something's wrong here."

Benchley knew exactly what was wrong but couldn't bring himself to explain that it was his fault the fuse was blown. Instead he said, "Just like everyone else, the hotel itself is going crazy."

* * *

Dorothy waited in the lobby for the elevator. She was on her way up to Fairbanks' apartment. She didn't know whether Benchley would be up there, but she didn't know where else to look for him.

Had she scared him off? When they had been sitting on the couch in her room, where had things been going? Would she have kissed him? More importantly, would *he* have kissed *her*?

Oh, nonsense! He's a married man! Just leave him be. Accept his friendship and leave it at that!

But she knew she couldn't quite leave it at that. Nor was she sure whether Benchley could, either.

The elevator door suddenly opened—she had been so caught up in her thoughts that she hadn't even heard it arrive. Inside was Ben Jordan. He smiled when he saw her, his face lighting up. He had changed out of his pajamas and back into his street clothes.

She was struck again by his rugged, handsome looks. *Benchley one minute. Jordan the next.* Her head felt dizzy from the mental leap from the one to the other.

"Mrs. Parker, are you all right?" he asked warmly, assuredly taking her arm. "You look faint."

"I'm delightful, Mr. Jordan. But call me Dorothy," she heard herself say. *What am I doing?*

He smiled. "All right, Dorothy."

He led her back into the lobby. Despite his limp, he moved smoothly. Jeez, he could lead her around like she was a trained lapdog.

She rallied her good sense. "So, Mr. Jordan, how is Dr. Hurst?"

"The doctor is sleeping soundly. And call me Benedict."

Benedict? There was no way she would call him that!

"Okay, Ben," she said. "What brings you down here?"

"Looking for Dr. Doyle. Have you seen him?"

"No, but I know where he is," she said, gently freeing her

arm from his hand. "He went to check on the family with smallpox."

"What a good man he is. True blue, that's him. Too bad he's a little cracked."

"Cracked?" Was he joking?

"You know, all the ghosts and spirits and such." He spoke with pity, as though he was saying that Doyle suffered from some unwholesome affliction. "He actually believes in all that mumbo-jumbo."

"Oh, right . . ."

Before she could offer any further response, he asked, "So what are you doing down here?"

"Looking for Mr. Benchley. Have you seen him?"

"No, but perhaps we can look together. Me for Dr. Doyle, and you for Mr. Benchley." He took her arm again and led her back to the elevator. She couldn't help herself. She felt a little thrill when he touched her arm. He was so tough, yet so gentle. And because of his clubfoot, she couldn't help but feel a certain tenderness toward him. Not pity, but sympathy. A desire to take care of him as he seemed to take care of others . . .

He opened the elevator door and escorted her inside.

Chapter 28

Luigi flipped the switches one last time, but the hotel kitchen remained dark.

"Forget it!" he said, adding a curse or two in Italian.

Behind Luigi and Benchley, the stairway down to the basement opened like a darkened void. Ahead of them the kitchen was shrouded in shadow. Only indistinct shadows and outlines of cooking equipment broke the blackness.

Then, on the other side of the room, the kitchen doors suddenly swung open. Someone stepped into the room. Then the doors closed just as quickly.

"Who that there?" Luigi said in alarm; his grasp of English broke down along with his nerve. "Who is it?"

"Luigi?" the stranger said in a cool voice. "Dear me, is that you? What are you doing here in the dark? You gave me quite a start."

"Mr. Case?" Luigi asked.

"Frank?" Benchley added.

"Ah, Mr. Benchley," Case said with a chuckle. "Of course you're here, too. So what are you two doing in my kitchen in the wee hours?"

"Quaking in our boots, that's what," Benchley said.

They heard Case move forward. "Mr. Woollcott already

stole the secret stash of brandy, if that's what you're looking for."

"Certainly not," Benchley said. "But perhaps you have an additional stash of something you might offer as a token of apology for that rude accusation?"

Case chuckled. "Unfortunately I don't. But speaking of apologies, the phones went crazy and a fuse blew a few minutes ago. You wouldn't know anything about that, would you, Mr. Benchley?"

Benchley snorted. "Again you've offended me by your unfounded allegation!" Then his voice softened. "But I'm willing to bury the hatchet over a nice glass of secretly hidden scotch."

Case sighed. "Oh, very well."

They heard the clack of a cabinet door opening and closing, and the clank of a bottle on the enamel preparation table. Then there was the squeak of a cork, and a glug and a splash into a glass.

"Ah, music to my ears," Benchley said, moving toward the sound. He smelled the sharp, smoky scent of good old scotch.

Case put a small, heavy glass into his hand. "Happy New Year, Mr. Benchley. One for you, Luigi?"

"Not while working, sir, thank you."

"Nor I," Case said. "Never touch the stuff."

"My feelings exactly," Benchley said, glad that they couldn't see him lying to their faces. "But I hate to see it go to waste. So bottoms up!"

He took a healthy sip and felt that familiar, soothing warmth.

"Oh, Mr. Benchley, I nearly forgot," Case said apologetically. "Mrs. Parker is looking for you. I just ran into her in the lobby."

Benchley put the glass down half-finished. "Is she? Well, let's go see what she wants."

"This way," Case said, turning away. "Follow my voice. I

would know my way around this hotel blindfolded. You, too, Luigi?"

"Of course, sir," the waiter said. But Benchley felt Luigi grasp his shirtsleeve.

Case led them forward. He pushed through the double swinging doors and into the service corridor. Light from the lobby filtered in, so Luigi let go of Benchley's sleeve with an appreciative wink. Benchley nodded in return.

A moment later they were back in the low-lit lobby. But Dorothy was nowhere to be seen.

"Darn the luck!" Benchley said. "Where did she go? I really must speak with her."

Case had already turned to go, undoubtedly on his way to replace the fuse. But he hesitated. "Something related to tonight's mystery, I presume?"

"Very perceptive, Mr. Case," Benchley said. "Lack of alcohol hasn't dulled your wits one bit. Specifically, it's something related to Dr. Hurst — and Mr. Jordan."

Case was intrigued. Even Luigi listened closely.

"Mr. Benchley," Case said after a moment's pause, "you can't just drop a hint like that and expect us to walk blithely away."

"Walk however you please." But Benchley considered this. "Can you keep a secret?"

They agreed that they could keep a secret.

Benchley whispered, "Dr. Hurst isn't exactly all he's cracked up to be. And, I suspect, neither is Mr. Jordan."

Once inside the elevator, Dorothy and Jordan made a quick inspection of elderly Maurice, who still stood leaning in the corner like an old broom and snoring quietly.

Jordan closed the elevator door and reached for the controls. The elevator ascended smoothly. He turned to Dorothy and gave her a look so warm it would melt ice, she thought.

"Listen," he said softly, "I want to apologize to you about

how I acted earlier in Dr. Hurst's room. I'm sorry I became so upset."

"I-it's all right," she said, trying to be nonchalant. She had handsome, rugged men breaking down and apologizing to her in elevators all the time, right? Happened every day.

"It's just—I take my job very seriously. But I failed twice tonight. Two tremendous failures. Dr. Hurst went into an apoplexy, and I wasn't there to help. Then one of his prized possessions was stolen from my own protection." He took a step closer to her. She could see the suntanned lines at the corners of his eyes and the five o'clock shadow of whiskers on his jaw. "You see, I'm afraid—afraid I might make another mistake."

"You?" she asked. "You don't look like you'd be afraid of anything."

He smiled, moving closer now. "Usually I'm not."

She gently put her hand on his chest. She didn't want him any nearer—yet she didn't want him to move away either. His chest felt hard, muscular. *Oh brother...* She should take her hand away, but she didn't. She stared into his dark, confident, serene eyes.

"So," he said, his voice in a whisper, "can I ask you something, Dorothy?"

"Of course," she whispered back. "Anything."

"The name that Dr. Hurst said. What was it again?"

The elevator jolted to a stop—and so did her interest in him. She was this close to him, and he wanted to know about some crazy thing his boss had said?

She dropped her hand from his chest and took a step back. She noticed that his hand was on the elevator controls. He had stopped the elevator. But he hadn't yet opened the door.

"What was the name?" he asked, no longer whispering.

Should she tell him again? He'd heard it once already.

He smiled and gave her that direct look again. But while it had been entrancing and charming a moment ago, it now seemed artificial and contrived, she thought. Who was this guy?

"Ted Besh," she said. "Dr. Hurst said Ted Besh."

Jordan nodded and thought about this. "I don't know any Ted Besh, and I've never heard Dr. Hurst mention him before. Who is he?"

How the hell should I know?

But she only shrugged. She wanted out of this elevator.

"Maybe he's the one who ransacked Dr. Hurst's room," he said. "Maybe he stole the valuables. Maybe Dr. Hurst wasn't asleep through it all. Maybe he saw who it was and was trying to tell us."

Growing animated at this idea, Jordan took a step closer again. Dorothy couldn't move away any farther. Her back was against the elevator wall.

"But," she said, "Dr. Hurst said the name *before* his room was turned upside down, remember?"

Now Jordan was standing right over her. His eyes were no longer serene—they now seemed cunning and cruel. "Then perhaps Dr. Hurst said it as a warning. Perhaps he knew that this Ted Besh would attack. Perhaps the man is even closer than you think."

She looked at him. *Is he trying to tell me* he's *Ted Besh?*

"Closer than I think?" she said, folding her arms over her chest. "Ha, I'm not thinking about that guy at all."

Frank Case was skeptical. "Dr. Hurst is not who he's cracked up to be?" He put his fists on his hips. "Then who is he?"

Benchley smiled. "He's still himself. But he's not. Not what you think."

"Who is he, then?" Case asked impatiently.

"He's a thief. He stole a very precious item in England and smuggled it here. The locket."

"The locket that he asked me to put into the safe? The locket that wound up around Bibi's neck? You're saying that he stole it?"

"That's the one!"

"Absurd," Case said drolly. "Dr. Hurst is here for a medical conference. He's a wealthy man who is widely published in the medical field and many others. Why would he steal a simple locket? It's quite absurd."

Benchley pursed his lips. He went to the elevator and pushed the call button. "Well, I didn't say I could explain it. But that's what the police told me. Dr. Hurst is a wanted man."

Frank Case and Luigi stood a few paces behind him. Case was still skeptical. "And Mr. Jordan?"

Benchley's eyes widened. "Guess what? He's not a cripple."

Case's expression soured. "Oh, now, really, Mr. Benchley! Mr. Jordan has a clubfoot. You've seen it yourself."

"But I also saw him run from one room to another, Frank. I was on the telephone with Captain Church when I realized that I'd seen Jordan run. Not hobble quickly—he ran! How do you explain that?"

"Perhaps you misremember."

"No, no," Benchley said. "I saw it. Mrs. Parker was with me. I must ask her if she remembers too."

Case frowned and looked around. "I swear she was here a moment ago. . . ."

"Perhaps you misremember," Benchley taunted. Then he punched the elevator button again. "And you know what else? There are robbers in the hotel. They have the locket. They're taking it to a man in Brooklyn. I overhead it when I was on the switchboard."

Case smiled slyly. "So it was you who caused the telephones to ring all over the hotel? And I gather you were also the one who caused the fuse to blow?"

Benchley froze a moment. Then he turned back to the elevator and pushed the call button again and again. "I'd love to stay and talk, but I really need to find Mrs. Parker! I

202

must tell her about these things. Where is this blessed eleva-tor?!"

Case softened. His voice lost its edge. "Dear old Maurice must be asleep. Come with me, Mr. Benchley. I'll put you on the service elevator. It's faster anyway."

Benchley was reluctant to leave the passenger elevator. He felt that it might arrive at any moment, and Dorothy would step out. But then again, if Maurice was asleep and the passenger elevator was not running, Dorothy wouldn't be on it. So he might as well use the service elevator. He followed after Case and Luigi toward the darkened kitchen.

Chapter 29

Jordan finally opened the elevator door, and Dorothy gladly and hurriedly stepped out into the ninth-floor corridor. She led the way back to Dr. Hurst's room. The door was halfway open. She pushed it open all the way and saw Doyle sitting in an armchair at Dr. Hurst's bedside and reading a book. When Doyle saw them, he stood up and took off his half-moon reading glasses.

"I was wondering where you scampered off to," he said.

Dorothy and Jordan spoke at the same time.

"I was looking for Mr. Benchley," she said.

"I was looking for you," Jordan said.

Doyle eyed them curiously. "Mr. Jordan, I was addressing Mrs. Parker. Are you wont to scamper?"

Dorothy looked down at Jordan's clubfooted shoe and wondered, *Is he wont to scamper?*

Jordan spoke quickly to Doyle like a schoolboy trying to explain to a stern teacher why he lost his homework. "I left Dr. Hurst by himself for only a few minutes while I went to look for you. Honestly, it was only a few minutes. I-I ran into Mrs. Parker—"

"Well, I daresay you've found me." Doyle spoke softly,

and his droopy eyes were gentle, but Dorothy could hear the challenge in his voice. "What is it you want of me?"

"The necklace," Jordan stammered and glanced at Dorothy. He didn't want to talk about this in front of her, she could tell. "It's missing. That is—"

"I am well aware that the necklace is missing," Doyle said. "But I don't have it in my possession."

"I know. That's not why I was looking for you. I mean, that's exactly why I was looking for you—"

"Make up your mind, young man."

Jordan was getting more flustered. "No, you see, I found the necklace—"

"Oh, did you now? That's wonderful news. But if you found it, then how can it be missing?"

"It was stolen!" Jordan said. "I was hoping you could use your . . . your abilities to help me recover it."

Doyle's face clouded over. "My abilities? What abilities?"

"Because . . ." Jordan stammered. "Because . . ."

"Because of Sherlock Holmes?" Doyle said wearily. "As I've said many a time before, the doll and its maker are never identical."

Jordan floundered. "No, no, of course not. It's just—"

Dorothy sat on the side of Dr. Hurst's bed. "Before he solves your mystery for you, perhaps you could do something first?"

Jordan nodded enthusiastically. "Of course."

"Go down to the kitchen and bring back a glass of milk."

He was perplexed. "Milk? For you?"

Dorothy scoffed. "Not for me. For Artie here."

Doyle raised his sagging eyes. "For me?"

She turned to him. "Your stomach is bothering you, isn't it?"

"Yes, as a matter of fact, it is," he said in surprise. "Indigestion and dyspepsia, very likely from that rich lobster dinner earlier in the evening."

"There you have it," she said to Jordan. "Off you go. Fetch milk for the master."

Slowly, still flustered and confused, Jordan backed out of the room.

She called after him. "And take the service elevator at the far end of the hall. It's faster."

Once he was gone, Doyle turned to Dorothy. "How did you know I was not feeling well?"

"Elementary!" She looked at him haughtily. "It's obvious to a trained observer. The dust on the cuff of your sleeve and the smell of your cologne give you away, of course."

"Oh, do they?"

She nodded. "The dust is clearly pollen from Ethiopian honeybees, which is a known irritant of the stomach lining. And that cologne you're wearing smells of spearmint, which, as anyone knows, all British gentlemen use to mask the scent of bad breath, a common symptom of indigestion."

His mustache drooped as he frowned. "Very interesting observations, Mrs. Parker. But entirely incorrect. For instance, how do you account for the facts that I do not have pollen on my sleeve, that there is no such thing as an Ethiopian honeybee, that I am not wearing cologne of any sort and, to the best of my knowledge, I am not emitting bad breath?"

She spoke airily as though teaching him a lesson. "When you have eliminated the digestible, whatever remains, however indigestible, must be the food."

He smiled knowingly. "What Sherlock Holmes actually said was, 'When you have eliminated the impossible, whatever remains, however improbable, must be the truth.' Now you tell the truth. How did you know my stomach was bothering me?"

She shrugged and winked. "I heard your stomach gurgling, and I took a wild guess." She leaned closer. "And I just

206

had to get rid of that Ben Jordan. He's turning into a real creep."

"Do you think Mr. Jordan was speaking the truth—that he found the locket and then it was stolen?"

She nodded. "The part about it being stolen, yes. Mr. Benchley and I were in his room over there when he discovered that it was missing. His surprise was as real as the cry of a baby. And he did have a big bump on the back of his head. I don't think he did that to himself just for effect. Somebody clocked him one."

Doyle considered this. "So how did he recover the locket in the first place?"

"I don't know. Perhaps Jordan snatched it from Mary's dresser."

"I suppose it's possible. Assuming that's true, who took it from Mr. Jordan?"

She shrugged. "Your guess is as good as mine, Artie."

He sat back down in the chair. He gazed at the unconscious face of Dr. Hurst. "Well, Dorothy, your suspicions were quite correct about Quentin's questionable diagnosis. I went to see the family who seemingly caused this quarantine. Poor blighters. They were all still awake and all very miserable. Two despondent parents of approximately your age, with a rather unhappy four-year-old daughter and a very itchy two-year-old son. I could tell on first glance that they did not have smallpox. They had chicken pox. Not as devastating to one's health but still very unpleasant. Especially when the whole family is stricken at the same time."

"How can you tell one from the other?"

"Several ways. Smallpox develops from deep in the dermis and generally appears rather evenly scattered across the skin. Chicken pox appear more on the surface of the skin and often occur in clusters," he said. "But the most telling thing in this case was that no one in the family reported illness, fever or vomiting a few days before the rash appeared. That's a classic sign for smallpox. Chicken pox, on the other hand, usually has no preceding illness."

"So Dr. Hurst was deliberately wrong. And there's no point to this quarantine?"

"Apparently not. But, then again, it is keeping the murderer contained in the hotel with us."

"You always see the sunny side, don't you?"

Doyle stood up. "It's unconscionable to let that family, and the other guests, go on thinking there must be a quarantine. We'll have to open the doors by morning."

"Since it's the quarantine that's keeping the murderer inside the hotel, we'll have to have this mystery solved by morning?" she asked doubtfully.

Doyle didn't answer her. He stared angrily at Dr. Hurst. "What would have made Quentin do such a thing? He's an eminent physician. He certainly must have known that unfortunate family had chicken pox, not smallpox. What can explain his reason for instituting a quarantine?"

She picked up her purse, which she had put on the floor. "I have a telegram to Dr. Hurst that may explain exactly that. Remember he received one last night, just before announcing the quarantine?"

"You're quite right, Mrs. Parker. He did. I had forgotten all about it. Come to think of it, he was rather secretive about the contents of that telegram."

When she opened up her purse, she saw the chloroform.

"Oh, but first, take a gander at this." She tossed the brown bottle to him. He caught it handily. "It's that missing bottle of chloroform you were looking for."

Doyle put back on his reading glasses and examined the label. "So it is." He went to a corner and pulled out Dr. Hurst's black leather medical bag. He placed the bottle into its appropriate niche in the bag. "Yes, this is most certainly it. Oh dear . . ."

He sank back into the chair.

"What's the matter?" she asked. "I thought you'd be pleased."

He shook his big head. "The bottle's been opened. Some of it appears to be missing." Once again he looked forlornly at Dr. Hurst. "Quentin, you old fool, what have you done?"

"I don't think he did anything," she said. "At least not with the chloroform. I found it in Lydia Trumbull's room. Remember seeing her at the party? Jet-black hair, ice-blue eyes? Another Broadway actress, but not quite so young as Bibi?"

He nodded. "Not quite so young, eh?"

"Actresses and vintage wines have something in common," she said. "A few years make all the difference."

"So I gather that you think it was this Lydia, not Quentin, who used the chloroform on Miss Bibelot?" he asked.

"Lydia already told me as much. I heard it from her own lips not half an hour ago in Mrs. Volney's room."

"Who is Mrs.—?"

"She's the bitter old biddy who was bothering you with medical questions at Fairbanks' party. But never mind Mrs. Volney." She waved her hand. "Apparently Lydia killed Bibi with the chloroform."

"But did you not just say she's an actress? How would she know anything about administering chloroform?"

"Women can do all sorts of things, Artie old boy. For example, Lydia was also a nurse during the war."

"She was? How do you know that?"

"She told me—in between fainting spells. Aleck Woollcott was grilling her."

"I see. So she picked up a trick or two as a nurse in a field hospital, eh? That's quite possible. Nurses doing doctors' duties and vice versa. I've seen with my own eyes that surgical protocol frequently falls by the wayside in the aftermath of battle."

"And few battle more fiercely than actresses," Dorothy

said. "So when everyone went down to the lobby before midnight, Lydia must have given Bibi the chloroform, which killed her."

He held the bottle up to the light. "Just one moment, Mrs. Parker. The dark glass obscured my observation. Examining it now, I see that there's only a small amount missing—not even an ounce, I'll wager. If administered correctly, that might be just enough to render a small or slender person unconscious—a woman of Miss Bibelot's size and stature, for instance—but it's hardly enough to cause cardiac arrest and death."

"It's not?"

"Not unless she drank it."

She snapped her fingers. "That's it. Lydia put it in Bibi's drink!"

Doyle shook his head. "No. I didn't mean to suggest that she actually drank it. I was being facetious."

"Skip the facetious and get on with the factual."

He smirked. "My suspicions were first aroused when I saw the reddish inflammation of the skin around Miss Bibelot's mouth—those markings were perfectly characteristic of the old method of chloroform administration. The substance irritates the skin. The better, more modern method is to place a sort of breathing mask on the patient, and drip the liquid onto the mask. But in Miss Bibelot's case, the chloroform was likely applied to a dry towel or washcloth, which was held over her mouth."

"And the chloroform gave her skin a sort of burn. Okay, so she didn't swallow it."

"No. But if this Lydia—the former army nurse—had used less than an ounce of chloroform, it suggests the victim was merely anesthetized. I can't fathom that she'd die from such a small amount."

"Merely anesthetized? So my theory, and the murderer, went right out the window." Dorothy slumped in her seat. "Ah, who was I trying to kid? Only myself, I guess. Nurse or not, I suppose Lydia would have fainted before she could bring herself to murder anyone. Even Bibi."

"Don't be discouraged," Doyle said warmly. "Motives and murder aren't as straightforward as they are in detective stories. Now, what about that telegram?"

"Right, I almost forgot." She reached again for her purse and handed him the message. "Take a quick look before Jordan runs back up here with your milk."

"Oh, I doubt that. With that clubfoot of his, the one thing Mr. Jordan cannot do is run."

Suddenly remembering, she jumped to her feet. "Yes, he can! I just realized I've seen him do it—in this very room!"

Chapter 30

Luigi and Frank Case crossed the dining room and disappeared through the swinging doors into the darkened kitchen. Benchley followed slowly after them. But just as he reached the doors, he heard Case call out.

"Who's there? What do you think you're doing?"

Benchley quickly shoved open one of the doors. In the darkness he heard a grunt. Then something heavy and metallic was rolling toward them. There was a bang and then the clatter of things crashing to the floor and breaking. Luigi yelled, and Benchley heard him fall down.

"Frank!" Benchley shouted. "What is it? What's happening?"

Case didn't answer him. Instead the hotel manager yelled, "Stop right there, whoever you are. You cannot come into my hotel and wreck my kitchen—"

Something whooshed through the air and knocked into Case. He was thrown backward and collided with Benchley, who caught him in his arms.

Case wheezed, hardly able to speak. "Ow, I think that was our soup pot. Knocked me right in the chest."

Benchley lowered Case to a sitting position on the

floor. He called out to whoever was across the room. "All right, sir. No hurling crockery, please. I mean you no harm."

From somewhere on the floor, Luigi groaned. "Hit me with my own tea cart, right in the *coglioni*."

"That's hitting below the belt," Benchley said sympathetically. He realized he was the only one of the three still unharmed and standing, which made him quite nervous. Still he managed to gather his courage and call out. "Let's declare a truce, shall we? The truce, the whole truce, and nothing but the tru—"

Something whizzed by Benchley's ear, clanged against the door behind him, hit the floor with a metallic clunk and skidded to a stop at his feet. He crouched down and picked it up. It was a butcher's cleaver.

"So you want to bury the hatchet, too?" he called out shakily. "Just not in my skull, if you please."

Something else zipped overhead in the dark. It was another knife. Benchley could tell because he heard it dig into one of the swinging doors with a thunk. Good thing he had hunkered down, or it probably would have plunged into his head.

Something grabbed on to his leg. Ready to strike, Benchley raised the cleaver. But then Frank Case spoke, his usually smooth voice still a wheeze. "We caught him trying to unlock the back door to the alley. But it's bolted shut. Then he attacked us."

Benchley raised his voice. "Do you hear that, whoever you are? The back door is locked. There's no escape. We have you cornered."

Case gasped, "Mr. Benchley, what are you doing?"

A sudden flurry of knives, platters, serving utensils and metal pots began flying toward them. *Oh dear, what am I doing?* Benchley thought. Then he remembered: the tea cart! He dropped the cleaver and reached out. Something hard hit his arm, and he yelped. But he didn't stop. He found the tea cart and wheeled it toward him for protection.

"Frank! Luigi! Move over here!"

He grabbed Case's arm and dragged him near, then reached out and pulled Luigi toward him. They huddled behind the cart as trays and plates crashed all around them.

"You saved us," Case wheezed. "Very selfless of you."

"Hardly," Benchley said. "If something happened to you and Luigi, there's no lunch. If there's no lunch, there's no Round Table. Then what would our little group do each day? Gather on the sidewalk around a hot dog cart?"

"Very sensible, Mr. Benchley," Case said wearily. "But now what do we do?"

Benchley imagined the kitchen when lit—when he had been there earlier with Dorothy and Woollcott. The stove was ahead and to his right. The doorway to the cellar stairs was just beyond that. Somewhere between him and their attacker was the long, wide enamel prep table. (He had left his half-finished glass of scotch on it—probably a casualty of the fray by now, he thought morosely.) A few paces to his left was the big double sink and the drying rack next to it. And near that—

Benchley suddenly had an idea. He jumped to his feet. Just then something hit him in the head. But it wasn't hard. He even managed to catch it. A cloth pot holder! That meant two things to Benchley. For one, the intruder was running out of things to hurl at them. For another, once the intruder ran out of objects to throw, he'd likely come charging across the room and start throwing his fists instead.

Benchley couldn't hesitate a moment longer. He rushed in the direction of the sink. But he slipped on a tray or something on the floor and went down, and his head hit against the edge of the counter.

"Ow!" he yelled.

There was just a moment's pause—a half second of silence—from the attacker across the room. Benchley sensed that the man was listening for him and lying in wait. The attacker was the well-armed hunter in the dark forest, and Benchley was the poor, defenseless deer.

"Oh dear," Benchley mumbled as he stood on wobbly legs.

That was enough. The attacker grunted in grim satisfaction, and then he was on the move.

Benchley could hear the man's quick footsteps—coming his way.

He reached out and felt the edge of the sink. Then he stretched to the right and searched for the large enamel tub next to the sink.

The attacker's footsteps pounded closer—almost here.

With the pot holder in his hand to protect him from the acidic blue liquid, Benchley flung the drum to the ground. It landed with a deafening crash, spilling its contents of liquid cleanser, forks, knives, spoons and ball bearings all across the kitchen floor.

Doyle rocked back on his heels. "What balderdash are you saying, Mrs. Parker? You saw Mr. Jordan run? Impossible! The poor man is a cripple."

Dorothy explained how Jordan had slippers on his feet when she and Benchley had found him unconscious on the floor. And when he hurried to look for the locket, he ran from Dr. Hurst's room to his own, only to find that the necklace was missing from its hiding place in his shoe.

Doyle rubbed his chin. "So you think his clubfoot is a fake? That's monstrously absurd."

She paced the floor. "But what if it is? That brings Jordan in as a suspect. He seems to be an adventurous and athletic man—except for the clubfoot. Perhaps athletic and adventurous enough to crawl out the bathroom window, after killing Bibi, that is."

"But why? Why would any grown man pretend to have such an infirmity?"

"Why does any grown man do anything?" she asked wearily. "Usually it has something to do with sex or money."

"That's a womanly point of view," he said dismissively.

She stopped in her tracks. "Is it? Didn't Antony start an entire war just to hop in bed with Cleopatra?"

"Not exactly. You're trivializing history, I think."

"Am I? That's a manly point of view. It's just like a man to take a triviality and start a war over it."

He frowned at her. "Now who's starting a trivial war, Mrs. Parker? Can we please get back to the question of Mr. Jordan's foot?"

She hung her head. "I'm sorry, Artie. I was on the receiving end of a browbeating a little while ago, and I'm still sore from it. I didn't mean to take it out on you."

He smiled kindly. "And I'm sorry I said yours was a womanly point of view. So let's forget it. Now are you sure you saw Mr. Jordan run? Perhaps he just hobbled quickly, and you mistook it?"

"Nope. Not a hobble. Not by a mile."

"Then why didn't you realize this before?"

She considered it. "I think Mr. Benchley and I were so taken aback when Jordan got all worked up over losing the necklace that it completely slipped by us."

"Very well, then," Doyle said. "Let's take it as a given that Mr. Jordan really is able to walk normally. And for some unknown reason he's wearing an orthopedic shoe and pretending to have a clubfoot. Where does that leave us?"

Dorothy pointed to the yellow square of paper in his hand. "Right back there."

"Oh, quite right. The telegram!" He slipped on his reading glasses again. "Let's see what it says. Hmm ..." He scanned over the telegram and read bits aloud. "*Authorities in England ... Valuable item ... Bring to Chicago ... Lloyds*

216

hired Pinks... 'Lloyds hired Pinks'? What does that mean?"

"Pink elephants, for all I know. What does *any* of it mean?"

He continued reading. "*Berley brothers on your trail... Lose them all... If you bring them to Chicago, deal is off. Keep item safe and in good condition—*"

"—or deal is off," Dorothy said. "The deal is probably the sale of the locket to this guy in Chicago."

He nodded. "Quentin did say he was leaving the medical conference early to take a trip to another city. He may have said Chicago, I don't recall. But he told me he had to give a lecture. Another lie!"

Doyle practically spat the words at Dr. Hurst's unconscious body, and Dorothy turned to look at the elderly doctor lying immobile on the bed. She had nearly forgotten he was there.

"I find it utterly impossible to comprehend," Doyle said. "Quentin is not only a superb and innovative physician, he's been a true humanitarian. He has devoted his life to his hospital back in England. He's the lifeblood of it. You wouldn't know it to look at him now, but the man is a saint."

"The kind of saint who hits you over the head with his Bible?" she asked wryly.

"It's true. He's very rigid in his manner. The classic stiff-upper-lip British gentleman."

"His upper lip is so stiff, it's positively erect."

Doyle didn't take offense. "Yes, Mrs. Parker, I know his prickly personality only too well. And so do his residents and interns. They run like rabbits when they see him coming down the corridor. But believe me, under that thick rusty armor is a bleeding heart."

"So, if he's such a saint, what's he doing selling a cheap little necklace to some hoodlum in Chicago?"

"Perhaps it's not so cheap after all. If Mr. Jordan was in such a frenzied state when it was stolen from him, and if this

217

man in Chicago is so concerned about obtaining it, perhaps the locket actually has rather significant value—as the telegram indicates."

"And that's why all these other fellows are after Dr. Hurst? Such as Lloyds or Pinks or the Berley brothers?"

He nodded. "If it is a valuable item stolen in England, then the name Lloyds is obvious. It's Lloyd's of London, the famous insurance firm. Surely you've heard of them?"

"Oh, sure. Lloyd's of London. Big insurance firm. I insured my yacht with those boys," she said. "So, of course, a big insurance firm like that hired some little guy named 'Pinks' to follow Dr. Hurst? That doesn't make much sense."

"Perhaps 'Pinks' is not a name of a person or persons. Perhaps it is shorthand for something else. At any rate, while I can't explain 'Pinks,' I do feel confident—especially in regard to a valuable object—that 'Lloyds' does refer to Lloyd's of London."

She bit her lip. *I suppose that does make sense.* She had read something of Lloyd's of London in a newspaper article or a book. She associated the firm with insuring fancy things—rare diamonds, masterpiece paintings and winning racehorses. "But what about the rest of the message?"

Doyle gazed over the telegram to look at Dr. Hurst. "This is when the power of the spirit world would be of great service. If only we could commune with Quentin's spirit . . ."

Oh dear, Dorothy thought. *He's over the edge. Just like Jordan said he is.*

She spoke hesitantly. "His spirit? You mean like a séance?"

"Well, yes, that's one way to communicate with the spirit world. But not the only one."

"Wouldn't he have to be deceased for a séance? I mean, isn't that for 'communicating' with only, you know, the dead?"

He chuckled good-naturedly. "That's one of the misunderstandings of Spiritualism. The spirit world is not something that's *out there*. It's not up in the clouds or deep down in the earth. It's right here, all around us. Whether alive or dead, we all exist in the spirit world, just as fish live in the ocean. Only we can't see it or hear it — most of us can't, anyhow." His face grew melancholy; his eyes drooped lower. Then, just as quickly, he brightened again. "But if we could only lift the veil to the spirit world — oh, what joy that would be! Oh, what wisdom! Oh, what power!"

Oh, what baloney! she thought.

Chapter 31

With a splash and a crash, the enamel barrel of cutlery and cleansing liquid splattered to the ground. Then Benchley heard the hailstorm of innumerable pings as hundreds of ball bearings bounced and rolled on the hard kitchen floor.

The attacker yelled. Benchley could see only a tall, dark figure of a man suddenly disappear and crash to the floor. His landing sent knives, forks and ball bearings flying.

Benchley stood frozen, waiting. It took but a moment. The man began screaming. Shrieking. "*Ahhhhhh!* It's burning. *Burning my legs!*"

The man floundered on the floor and scrambled to get to his feet, but he was slipping and rolling in the ball bearings and acidic cleanser.

Benchley didn't recognize the man's voice, but he still felt sorry for him. He wondered whether there was anything he could do. So he reached toward the sinks. In one of them was a deep pot—the pot in which Woollcott had made the coffee. It was full of water—dirty water, most likely, but Benchley didn't think it mattered. He lifted the pot from the sink and upturned it where he thought the man might be.

"*Agghh!* What's that?" the man sputtered.

"Just water," Benchley said. "Maybe a teensy bit of cold coffee."

There was a skittering sound, like a crab scurrying across a hard surface. The man was back on his feet.

Benchley realized that Case and Luigi were now also on their feet.

"Stop him, Mr. Benchley!" the waiter yelled. "Don't let him outta here!"

With a miserable groan, the figure disappeared into the darkness.

"Where did he go?" Case asked. "Is he still here?"

Footsteps clattered down the stairway to the basement.

And good riddance, Benchley thought.

"Come! We go!" Luigi said, tugging on his sleeve. "We go after him. Right now!"

Case's voice was even-toned once again. "I think that's quite enough mayhem for now, Luigi. Let's not chase after the intruder in the basement—in the dark. We'll find him after we replace the fuse in the fuse box."

"I agree. Enough mayhem for now," Benchley said.

"All we need is a flashlight or a candle," Case said. "Shall we look for one, Luigi? Coming with us, Bob?"

"Count me out," Benchley said, still feeling a slight pang of guilt about crisscrossing the switchboard's wires and blowing the fuse. "Just lead me first to the service elevator. I need to find Mrs. Parker."

Dorothy felt the hotel coming to life. People were starting to wake up and move about. It was not yet dawn, though. She guessed that the ringing of just about every telephone in the whole building had roused the guests and residents.

Doyle silently walked alongside her as they left Dr. Hurst's room and strolled to the elevator. She wondered about him. *What would make such a smart man—the man who invented the logical Sherlock Holmes, no less—become*

221

so obsessed with the questionable, dubious concept of Spiritualism? He actually believed in talking to the dead? Had the old man lost it, as Jordan seemed to think? Or was there some other, deeper reason Doyle had become such a firm believer?

"So," she said to him gamely, "you say a person doesn't have to be dead to be able to communicate through the spirit world? Are you talking mind reading?"

Doyle looked at her quizzically, perhaps skeptically, even. "Sometimes the living can communicate with one another mentally—a language between minds, so to speak. It's called telepathy. It's not truly mind reading. More of a sensation between two spirits, or souls."

"Not mind reading?" she said, disappointed. She was thinking of Benchley. "There's a mind or two I'd like to read."

Doyle chuckled knowingly. "It would be fantastic, wouldn't it? Perhaps scientists one day soon will invent such a machine to allow us to do just that."

"Nah, forget it. I have a big stack of books by my bedside, and I don't have time to read them. How would I find time to read a stack of minds as well? A lady has to know her limits."

They came to the elevator door, and Dorothy pressed the call button. The door opened almost immediately. And there stood Alexander Woollcott.

Dorothy frowned. "Speaking of limits, I think I just reached mine."

Woollcott stepped out of the elevator and was followed hesitantly by Lydia Trumbull. The actress' eyes were red and full of tears.

"Hello to you, too, Mrs. Parker," Woollcott said. "I'm an unwelcome sight to you, am I?"

"No more so than usual," Dorothy muttered. "Forget I said anything."

"Indeed I will," he said, beaming. "Because I have something important to announce: I've solved it! I've solved the murder of Bibi Bibelot!"

"Have you, now?"

"Indeed I have. And Lydia Trumbull here has proven to be the linchpin in the case, so to speak."

At this, Lydia released a sob and a fresh flood of tears.

"Don't worry, Lydia," Woollcott reassured her with an indifferent hand on her shoulder. "The courts have pity on women, especially pretty ones such as yourself. You won't be hanged—most likely."

Lydia wailed and cried more tears.

"Don't listen to this blowhard," Dorothy said to her. "You didn't kill Bibi."

Lydia shook her head and blew her nose into a handkerchief offered by Doyle. "Yes, I did. Oh, I'm afraid I did. I poisoned her—with chloroform."

"No," Dorothy said sternly. "You did not."

"Yes!" insisted Woollcott. "Yes, she did!"

"No, she didn't," Dorothy said, and turned to Doyle. "Artie, please explain it to them."

"Certainly," Doyle said. "Simply put, you could not have killed Miss Bibelot, because you did not use enough chloroform to do so."

Lydia's eyes glimmered with a slight hope and yet a fear of hoping. "I-I didn't?"

"Yes, you did!" Woollcott snapped. "Of course you did. You confessed it."

"But . . . but maybe . . ." Lydia stammered, hope seemingly growing in her.

"No maybes about it—!" Woollcott said with a stamp of his foot.

"Not a chance, Lydia," Dorothy said. "Artie's a doctor. He just explained to me that you couldn't have killed Bibi with less than an ounce of chloroform."

Lydia brightened. "Oh, what a relief! I hoped I hadn't— I found her passed out drunk. And I had only wanted to give her enough chloroform to make sure she would be sick. Truly, I did. You must believe me."

"Never!" Woollcott howled.

"Certainly we believe you," Doyle said with tender reassurance. Then he spoke evenly. "But you did give her enough to anesthetize her and render her unconscious. And that likely gave the real murderer a much easier opportunity to commit his villainous crime."

"Or *her* villainous crime!" Dorothy interjected. "Let's be fair."

Woollcott sputtered but said nothing.

"But why did you do it, Lydia?" Dorothy asked. "What good would it serve you to knock out Bibi?"

Lydia sniffed. "They're holding auditions for a new musical on January second." Her hand flew to her mouth. "Oh my, that's tomorrow already. Well, I'd be a shoo-in for the lead role—if only Bibi doesn't show up, that is."

"And thanks to you," Woollcott said, "she most certainly won't!"

Lydia cringed and burst out in more tears.

"Don't listen to him, dear," Dorothy said. "But tell us, where did you get the chloroform?"

She dabbed her eyes with the handkerchief. "From that mean old doctor. Well, from his case. He left it unattended at the Fairbanks' party. I recognized it as a medical bag and guessed there would be something useful inside—it was completely a spur-of-the-moment decision! I had no preconceived plan to harm Bibi. You must believe me."

Dorothy remembered the many sedatives and sleeping pills on Lydia's bedside table. Had Lydia actually planned ahead to knock out Bibi, she could have found a way to use any one of them.

"Of course we believe you," Dorothy said.

"*I* don't!" Woollcott bellowed.

They ignored him.

"Tell me," Dorothy asked, "after you gave Bibi the chloroform, did you lock the door behind you? Or somehow put a towel against it?"

Lydia looked confused. "No. I closed the door, but I didn't lock it. And I had used a washcloth to administer the chloroform. But I just dropped that in the tub so no one would be able to smell it later. I didn't put anything against the door."

There was *a washcloth left behind in the bathtub,* Dorothy thought. "Do you remember anything else unusual about the room? Did the champagne in the tub feel cold? Was the window open?"

Lydia shook her head. She was regaining her Broadway-star composure. "No, the champagne was . . . well, it was lukewarm, I suppose. And the window was closed. I would have noticed if it were open."

"Were there any other objects in the room?" Doyle asked. "Think carefully. Imagine yourself back in that bathroom."

Lydia appeared lost in thought. "I'm remembering now. . . . Bibi held a champagne glass in her hand. But I didn't want to touch it. I-I didn't want to get my fingerprints on it."

Doyle nodded. "Anything else?"

Imagining the moment when she found Bibi dead, Dorothy also pictured the bathroom. "How about an ice bucket? Do you remember an ice bucket on the radiator?"

"No, I don't think so. I don't remember any ice buck—"

Woollcott couldn't hold his tongue any longer. "Ice buckets! Who gives a buckety-buck about an ice bucket? Doesn't anyone care that this woman caused Bibi's death—directly or indirectly?"

Doyle knit his bushy eyebrows. "Lydia did not kill—"

"Oh ho! Here he goes again." Woollcott threw his hands in the air. "A doctor is speaking. Everyone pay attention! This old dodo went to medical school about a century ago, so he must be correct about absolutely everything." He narrowed his beady eyes at Doyle. "Who do you think you are, *Doctor*?"

Dorothy couldn't resist a sly smile. *How will Woollcott react when he finds out who he's really talking to?*

"Not only is he a doctor, Aleck," she said, "but he's also the best-selling author of detective fiction ever. All night you've been playing detective right under the nose of the creator of the most famous detective of all time, and you didn't even know it. Allow me to properly introduce you to him. This is Sir Arthur Conan—"

Woollcott spoke dismissively. "Arthur Conan Doyle. Yes, yes, I know exactly who he is, Mrs. Parker. What do you take me for? I was being sarcastic just now when I asked who he thinks he is. I know who he is, all right, and I'm not impressed in the least."

She glanced at Doyle, who looked troubled and hurt.

Woollcott added, "This man's just a loony old has-been, that's who he is!"

Chapter 32

B enchley stood alone in the darkened service corridor. He held a tiny lit match that cast just enough light to see the door to the service elevator in front of him. But the glow of the small flame was not enough to illuminate the rest of the corridor, which remained in darkness—a nearly solid darkness.

The flame flickered as the match burned to the tips of his fingers. He dropped it and immediately found himself—

Totally in the dark, he thought. *Story of my life.*

He quickly lit another match and realized that this one was his last. In the silence he listened for the service elevator but could not hear it moving. It could be stuck in the basement or on the top floor—there was no way to know. But he couldn't very well stand here in the dark much longer. It would drive him up the wall.

Moving cautiously to keep the match flame from going out, Benchley turned and went back the way he had come. Now he was again in the kitchen. He carefully stepped in between the puddles of blue liquid and ball bearings. He reached the swinging doors to the dining room just as the match sputtered and went out.

The dining room was dark, but light streaming from the

lobby lent enough illumination for him to weave his way through the tables and chairs.

In the lobby he paused by the door of the passenger elevator. But, like the service elevator, this one was not available either. He gave up and yanked open the door to the stairs.

He climbed the steps to the second floor, opened the door to the corridor and strolled down the hallway toward Mrs. Parker's room. He wished he could light his pipe. . . . *Funny how the moment you run out of matches, you want to have a smoke.*

He knocked on her door and waited a moment. He wasn't surprised that there was no answer. He tried the knob—it was unlocked—and peeked inside. Woodrow Wilson lifted his head from the couch. His little tail began wagging.

"Excuse me, young man," Benchley said. "Is the lady of the house at home?"

Woody yawned and dropped his head back on his paws. His tail stopped wagging.

Benchley closed the door and turned back around. Across the hall a door was ajar. In the crack of the open door, a little old lady's eye peeked at him.

"Hello there, Mrs. Volney," he said with a merry wave of his fingers. He approached the door. "Have you seen Mrs. Parker out and about?"

She pursed her prim, wrinkled mouth. "I can't say I have."

"You can't—or you won't?"

Abruptly the door opened wide from the inside. Mrs. Volney turned in surprise. Ruth Hale and Jane Grant emerged from the old woman's apartment.

"Oh, Mr. Benchley," Jane said, nearly running into him. "We're looking for Dorothy. Have you seen her?"

"As a matter of fact, I'm looking for her, too."

"We all owe her an apology," Ruth said, actually wringing her hands.

"Not all of us!" Mrs. Volney chimed in. "I don't owe her

a thing except a piece of my mind. That arrogant young lady is going to have heck to pay—"

Jane closed the door on the old woman.

Ruth smiled and squeezed Jane's arm, then turned to Benchley. "It's been a long, long night. Let's find Dorothy so we make our peace with her."

"And then we can get some much-needed rest!" Jane said. "Maybe that's what Dottie's doing. Lying in bed."

Benchley knew that Dorothy wasn't in her bed. Then he thought of Jordan. *No, of course she wouldn't climb into his bed . . . would she?*

"Bob, what's the matter?" Jane asked him suddenly. "You're white as a sheet."

He forced a smile and a chuckle. "Oh, don't mind me. Sometimes I'm just full of sheet. Come on, let's try the elevator."

"Aleck! Show some respect!" Dorothy yelled. Her small voice reverberated along the ninth floor corridor.

"Respect?" Woollcott said harshly. "I can no more show respect for this old bird than I can show respect for a carnival barker or a circus performer. I'll say it again, Dorothy: He's a loony old has-been. He *has been* a doctor, and he *has been* a detective writer. But those accomplishments were in the past. Now he's just an old crackpot who makes a buck on the lecture circuit ranting about spooks and spirits!"

Doyle pursed his lips but said nothing. There was a look of utter sadness and pain in his eyes. "If you only knew—" he mumbled with trembling lips. Then he turned abruptly and stalked back down the hallway toward his room.

Silently they watched him go.

Aghast and ashamed, Dorothy slapped Woollcott's chest. "What's the matter with you?"

He raised his chubby hands in defense, and the only harm she inflicted was to dislodge his small boutonniere of holly sprigs.

She slapped at him again anyway. "I thought you were supposed to be looking in the subbasement for Bibi's body! Instead all you're doing is accusing and insulting people."

Woollcott ignored her. Wordlessly he adjusted his boutonniere, then his glasses, and then smoothed down his hair.

She turned to Lydia. "Go back to your room for now. Stay there so we know where to find you in case we need you." Then, less severely, she added, "And get some rest, dear. God knows we all need some."

Lydia tried to open the elevator door, but the elevator was no longer there. She pressed the call button.

"As for you, Aleck, you're coming with me," Dorothy said. "We're going to the basement to finally find Bibi. And with a little luck we'll run into Benchley while we're at it."

The elevator arrived on the second floor. Benchley allowed himself a little hurrah of triumph. It seemed as though he'd been trying for hours to get on one of the elevators.

"What was that cheer for?" Jane asked him as they stepped inside.

"Oh, I just find elevators very uplifting," he said.

Maurice, snoozing quietly, still stood in the corner.

Benchley thought it best to let him sleep. "Can either of you operate this thing?" he asked.

Ruth seemed to know exactly what to do. She stepped on the release button on the floor and seized the control lever. "Easy as pie. Where to?"

He considered this. Doyle, Dr. Hurst and Jordan all had rooms on the ninth floor. But something was nagging at Benchley's brain. . . . He couldn't quite remember, though. . . . What was it?

"Fifth floor!" he said suddenly.

"Fifth floor it is," Ruth said and flipped the lever up. "What's Dorothy doing on the fifth floor?"

"Nothing," he said. "She's not on the fifth floor. Not that I know of, anyhow."

230

Jane and Ruth exchanged a puzzled glance.

"So," Jane asked, "why are we going to the fifth floor?"

"I nearly forgot about something." He had almost forgotten about the men in room 520. "It'll only take a minute. Just need to check on a pair of ruthless, thieving gangsters who have absolutely disgraceful telephone manners."

A minute later Benchley, Jane and Ruth walked quietly along the fifth-floor hallway and stopped in front of the door marked 520.

Jane looked askance at Benchley. "Did you say 'ruthless, thieving gangsters'?"

He nodded. "A pair of them, yes."

Ruth cocked an eyebrow. "And why do you want to check on them?"

"I want to get a good look at them. I believe they have the item at the center of this whole mystery."

"And what item is that?" Ruth asked.

"I call it Ted."

He knocked on the door. He had absolutely no intention of confronting the gruff-voiced man and his partner in crime, of course. He would merely get a look at them and then quickly mutter an apology: *Sorry, wrong room.* He would be careful to disguise his voice so they wouldn't recognize it from the telephone.

But there was no answer. Benchley knocked again, harder this time. Still no answer.

He bit his lip. Surely the thieves hadn't made their escape already? They had said they would leave at first light ... but, then again, that Mr. Caesar had been so demanding. Maybe they had left—before Benchley or anyone else could identify them!

He reached to knock again.

Jane said, "Just try the door." She reached out and turned the knob, but it was locked.

Ruth said, "Let me have a try." She was a tall, strong, forceful woman.

Jane gently pushed Benchley aside. Ruth gripped the knob with her large hand.

"You don't expect to break it down, do you?" he asked skeptically.

Ruth looked at him with a scowl. She withdrew a letter opener from her purse. "Certainly not. I'll use this." She put the pointy end of the letter opener into the keyhole and delicately manipulated it.

"Dare I ask why you carry a letter opener in your purse?"

"For protection," she said. "On the subway."

"Are you frequently attacked by envelopes on the subway?" he asked lightheartedly.

"Not since carrying this," she said coolly.

With a smile, she pulled the letter opener out of the keyhole and turned the knob. The door opened easily.

"Astounding," he said. "Do you use a house key to open your letters?"

Ruth smirked and entered the darkened room. She flicked on the lights.

It was an ordinary Algonquin hotel room. There were two twin beds, with a small washstand in between. The beds were still made, but someone had evidently sat on the nearest one. Against the opposite wall stood an identical pair of dressers. A framed print of a blue jay from Audubon's *Birds of America* hung on one wall.

Ruth went to the first dresser and opened the top drawer. She pulled out a large men's nightshirt.

"Don't do that," Benchley said anxiously. Out in the hallway he had been full of confidence. But entering the room was a different story.

She dropped the nightshirt back into the drawer. Then she pulled out a thick, well-worn leather wallet. "Who walks out of his hotel room without his wallet?"

Jane opened the top drawer of the next bureau. She, too, pulled out a wallet. She opened it. "Well, it is the wee hours of the morning in a quarantined hotel. Why would they need their wallets?" She pulled out a small photograph.

"Really," Benchley said, grabbing the wallets from them. "I think we should leave." He threw the wallets back into the drawers.

"Look at this. . . ." Jane said, scrutinizing the photo. Ruth leaned over her shoulder to see. "Do these two men look familiar to you?"

Ruth took the photo and extended her arm. "Too blurry for me without my reading glasses. Who are they?"

Benchley snatched the photo. "All right, ladies. You've had your fun. Now let's—"

"Just a minute," Jane said. "Look at it first. Then we'll go."

He glanced at the photo. It pictured two men standing on the bank of a river with fishing poles in their hands. One man was taller and of medium build, while the other was shorter and more heavyset. The taller man had a smile of success and held up a fish the length of his forearm.

"Well?" Jane asked.

"So what?" he said. "It's a big trout."

"Not that. Do you recognize those men?"

Benchley took another look at the men's faces. Jane was right. "Now that you mention it . . . But I can't remember where I've seen them."

Jane grabbed back the photo. "I think they were at Fairbanks' party last evening."

Ruth snickered. "Everyone in the whole hotel was there. What makes these men memorable?"

Just then the door flew open. A man wearing pajamas and a wild expression burst into the room.

Chapter 33

Dorothy and Woollcott stepped onto the elevator. She nudged the sleeping Maurice. "Second floor, please," she whispered to him.

Somehow, still snoring lightly, the elderly elevator operator reached out and flipped the lever. The elevator descended.

She nodded contentedly. Perhaps things were finally going her way for once. Even the air of the elevator smelled pleasant. . . . *Is that . . . ?*

She sniffed at the familiar smell. It was the scent of Mr. Benchley's hair tonic, wasn't it? Had Benchley just been on this elevator? She turned to Maurice. But the old man's eyes were shut tight.

She couldn't very well ask Woollcott for confirmation of the smell. Not after she just slapped and berated him. She felt suddenly sick at heart.

Fred, where are you? We were supposed to be spending this night in each other's company. Yet here she was with surly Woollcott.

The elevator stopped on the second floor, and they got out. The door closed behind them.

"Well?" Woollcott asked.

"Well, what?"

"What are we doing here? I thought we were going to the basement to look for Bibi."

"We need Woody," she said. "For protection."

He snorted. "That ugly little beast can't protect itself from the tiniest flea. What sort of protection can it provide for us?"

"For one thing, Woody isn't afraid to sniff around the basement — unlike some lowly creatures around here."

Woollcott lifted his nose in the air but responded only with an offended grunt.

She retrieved the dog from her room and carried him in her arms. They went down the stairs to the lobby. As she had sensed earlier, the hotel was waking up — but not altogether pleasantly. Two of the bellhops, grumbling as they worked, were halfheartedly straightening things up in the lobby. Most of the furniture was still pushed against the walls. The whole place had accumulated confetti, half-empty champagne glasses and plenty of cigarette butts from the revelry the night before. A few guests had wandered down and sat or stood about in an aimless, agitated mood. However, Harpo still slept soundly on one of the comfy couches.

Dorothy and Woollcott hurried through the lobby and into the dining room. They strolled past their famous Round Table and entered the double swinging doors of the kitchen. The room was brightly lit and a complete disaster.

"What the devil happened in here?" Woollcott said, aghast.

Their eyes scanned the room. The floor was covered with every kind of cooking item. Metal pots, pans and lids surrounded their feet. Their shoes crunched the shards of broken bowls and plates. In the middle of the room, a tea cart was turned on its side — and several feet away the teapot, saucers, cups and spoons were scattered in a wide arc across the floor. Below the sink was an array of forks, knives, spoons and innumerable ball bearings, all of them swimming in pools of the blue cleansing liquid.

Something glimmered in the corner of Dorothy's eye. She turned to see a long carving knife stuck into the back of one of the doors.

Benchley! He had been here; she knew it. He had been in danger. *Maybe he still is.*

"Don't just stand there," she snapped at Woollcott. "Let's go."

Clutching the dog to her chest, she carefully navigated through the debris while making sure not to step into one of the blue puddles. Woollcott huffed but followed after her.

She made it across the room to the stairway that led down to the basement, and suddenly found herself face-to-face with one of the waiters, who was trudging up the stairs. She recognized the man's face, but she couldn't remember his name.

"What happened in here?" she demanded.

The man shook his head and shrugged his shoulders; then he stepped past her.

No tip for him next time, she thought. Then she remembered somewhat guiltily that she rarely had a spare coin to tip any of the waiters. She made a mental note to carry more coins. No wonder they hardly gave her the time of day.

She scurried down the stairs to the basement and stopped at the bottom. *Now, where is Benchley?*

Woollcott arrived at her side. "If I were Bibi, dead and in a wheelchair, where would I be?"

Oh, right. They were here to find Bibi, not Benchley. But now she hoped she would find them both.

"The subbasement," she said grimly. Woollcott nodded equally dourly.

They turned down the corridor on the left, then turned another left, which led to a darker corridor. The stairs to the subbasement were here. The small dog wriggled slightly in

Dorothy's arms and nuzzled close to her. She clutched him more tightly.

Woollcott sneered at Woody. "Some guard dog."

She ignored him, gathered her courage and descended the concrete stairs to the subbasement.

It was darker down here. Colder, too. The corridor itself was narrower, making her feel closed in. The air seemed both humid and musty. It was eerily quiet, as though sound were swallowed in this place.

"Which way?" Woollcott asked hesitantly.

"You make it your business to know this hotel," she said archly. "So you can lead the way."

"You're the one with the guard dog. You lead the way."

She sucked in a breath of the stale, clammy air and moved cautiously forward. Within a few paces the corridor took a right. As she rounded the dark corner, Woody whined and squirmed in her arms. *Something's there!*

Instinctively she jumped back and bumped hard into Woollcott, who tumbled over with a yelp of fright.

"Mrs. Parker! Mr. Woollcott!" said Frank Case, emerging from the shadows. Luigi the waiter stood next to him. "Whatever are you doing down here?"

Woollcott rolled his pudgy body and scrambled to his feet. "Getting scared out of our wits by you two, that's what!"

The man in pajamas held a plunger over his head and appeared ready to strike with it. "Stop right there! Don't move a muscle."

Benchley, Jane and Ruth had no intention of moving. They were too stunned by the odd sight of the intruder to move any body part whatsoever.

The man appeared to be in his early thirties. His thinning sandy-colored hair was mussed, with parts of it sticking straight up, as though he'd spent a sleepless night. His powder blue pajamas hung loose on his thin frame. But his strangest feature, other than the plunger clutched in his hands, was the rash of pinpoint red dots all over his face and neck.

"You people don't belong in here," the man said. "This isn't your room!"

Benchley didn't think it wise to point out to the man that he didn't seem to belong in this room either. "How right you are," he said with a friendly smile. "I think we must have stumbled into the wrong room. We'll just be going, won't we, ladies?"

Jane and Ruth nodded agreeably. But the man blocked their way.

"Nothing doing," he said. "I saw you through my peep-hole from across the hall. You didn't stumble in by accident. You jimmied the door and broke in here."

Benchley wore a cheerful smile. "It's all right. Not to worry. This is my friend George's room—"

"No, it's not." The man narrowed his eyes. "There's no George in this room."

"Well, not now there isn't," Benchley said, looking around. "He must be down in the lobby, I suppose. So, if you don't mind, we'll just—"

"I do mind," the man said. "I'm calling the manager. There's no man staying in here. This room is taken by two nuns."

They stood for a moment just looking at the strange fellow in pajamas. Then, unable to control himself, Benchley burst out laughing. Jane and Ruth laughed, too. And not just a chuckle. A full, uproarious belly laugh.

The man kept the plunger over his head but didn't hold it so threateningly now. He was confused by their laughter, and that somehow made him seem even funnier, and they laughed all the louder. A moment ago he had appeared to be a dangerous, wild man. Now he was just a funny guy in pajamas, with a plunger in his hand and red pockmarks on his face. And he believed the room was occupied by nuns. He was perfectly ridiculous, the poor old boy!

Benchley, still giggling, reached out and patted him on the shoulder. "You can lower your weapon, my friend. The only thing clogging up the works is you."

Jane and Ruth laughed even harder at this.

The man was crestfallen. "What's so funny? I don't get it."

"You're mistaken. There aren't two nuns staying in this room," Benchley said. He opened the drawers and showed him the nightshirts and wallets. "It's occupied by two men."

The man narrowed his eyes at the nightshirts and the wallets. Mystified, he shook his head. "Nah, I don't believe it. I saw two nuns enter and leave this room. They even blessed me once when I passed them in the hallway."

Benchley shrugged. He couldn't think of anything to say that wouldn't embarrass the man even more.

The man seemed to make up his mind. "Well, there's only one sure way to find out. Let's go find them."

Now Benchley shook his head. "Not in your condition, my friend. You should be holed up in your room. We'll go find them."

The man spoke piteously. "Mister, I've been cooped up with an angry wife and two screaming kids for the past twelve hours. This was supposed to be our winter vacation. But what did I get? I wasted my entire Christmas bonus on this trip only to be locked up like an inmate in a loony bin." He looked at Benchley imploringly. "Can you understand why I want to go even just to the lobby?"

Benchley nodded. "Come along, then. Let's go find these men. And bring your plunger with you."

"We're looking for Bibi's body," Dorothy explained to the hotel manager.

"You won't find her down here," Case said with a glance around the dark, dank subbasement. Luigi the waiter, trying not to look fearful, stood close to him. "As a matter of fact, you won't find anyone."

"We found you, didn't we?" Woollcott said harshly, dusting himself off. "What do you think you're doing lurking down here and jumping out of the shadows?"

"Just looking for an attacker covered in acidic blue liquid," Case said. He quickly explained how they had been attacked in the darkened kitchen.

"Is Mr. Benchley all right?" Dorothy asked. She forced herself to speak calmly, as though inquiring about the weather. But she didn't feel calm whatsoever.

"You know him," Case said reassuringly. "He laughed it off as usual. Life's just a joke to our Mr. Benchley."

Is it? she wondered. *Is everything just a joke to our Mr. Benchley? Including . . . me?*

"He's been looking for you," Case said, interrupting her thoughts. "He has something important to tell you, he said."

"Well, isn't that odd? I've been looking all over for him, too. Woollcott can't find Bibi. You can't find your assailant. I can't find Mr. Benchley. And he can't find me. This is a large enough hotel, but it's certainly not that large!"

Case adopted his polite manager's voice, which he rarely used with her. "We do our best. We think of the Algonquin as intimate, yet comfortable."

She had unintentionally hurt his feelings and wounded his professional pride. "That's not what I meant, Frank. It's just—" Then a thought occurred to her. "You were attacked in the kitchen! A few minutes ago!"

"Yes, that's what I said."

"Jordan!" she said. "Doyle sent him down to the kitchen to fetch a glass of milk. That was only a short while ago. Do you think it was Jordan who attacked you?"

Both Case and Woollcott looked doubtful.

"Mr. Jordan?" Case asked. "You mean Dr. Hurst's attendant? The man with the clubfoot?"

"Preposterous!" Woollcott roared. "The man is not only a cripple but a sweetheart."

"He's not, as you put it, a cripple," she said, remembering how Jordan had sprinted across his room. "And he's not exactly a sweetheart either." She recalled how he had cornered her in the elevator. "Come on, let's go back up to Dr. Hurst's room! Jordan may have returned there."

She turned to go.

"Let's take the service elevator," Case said after her. "It's much—"

"Much faster," she said impatiently. "Yes, I know!"

Chapter 34

$\mathcal{B}$enchley, Jane, Ruth, and the man in pajamas all crowded together into the passenger elevator. Ruth manned the controls. She lowered the lever, and they began their descent to the lobby.

Benchley looked at the man's haggard, red-dotted face and felt sorry for him. Clearly it was his family who had been the cause of the quarantine. The man had had a rough night, and he likely had a few more ahead.

"Robert Benchley, at your service," he said amiably. "Forgive me for not shaking your hand in your condition."

"Don't mention it," the man said with a wave to his pockmarked face. "I wouldn't wish my condition on my worst enemy."

"Then you haven't met our friend Alexander Woollcott." Benchley smiled. "But never mind that. This is Jane Grant and Ruth Hale. What shall we call you? Not Ted Besh, is it?"

"No, it's John Simpson." The man was confused. "Who is Ted Besh?"

"Yes, who is Ted Besh?" Ruth asked. "One of your pseudonyms?"

"Oh, you don't want to know." Benchley chuckled. "I

was just talking nonsense as usual. Besides, it's not really Ted Besh anyhow. It's tête-bêche."

"Tête-bêche?" John Simpson looked surprised. *"Tu parles français?"*

Now it was Benchley's turn to look surprised. "What?"

Simpson said, "I just asked you if you speak French. Tête-bêche is French, so I assumed you speak it."

"No. Do you?"

"Yes, I was a translator in France during the war. I learned it from my mother. She's from Quebec."

"And tête-bêche means something in French?" Benchley asked.

"Yes, head to tail."

"Head to tail?" Jane asked with a smile. "Is that some kind of saucy French expression?"

Simpson shook his head. "It's just a way of saying head to foot." He searched for an example. "It's like shoes in a shoebox or sardines in a can. One points up, one points down. Head to tail. Tête-bêche."

Benchley considered this but could make nothing of it. Head to tail? Why would Dr. Hurst make such an effort to say that? And in French of all things. He asked Simpson, "I don't suppose you have a French book to tell us more?"

"No, I don't. It's not like I travel around with my own personal library, you know."

"Of course not. Who does?" Benchley said, disappointed. Then he thought a moment and snapped his fingers. "Dr. Hurst does!"

They looked at Benchley as though he was crazy. He didn't care. "Ruth, stop the elevator. Take us back up to the ninth floor."

Dorothy and Woollcott hurried to the door of Dr. Hurst's room. Frank Case and Luigi were right behind them. She knocked on the door, then tried the knob. It was locked.

"Frank." She turned to the hotel manager. "Have a skeleton key?"

Case nodded and stepped to the door. He rapped his knuckles on it first. "This is the manager. Is anyone in there?" Without waiting for an answer, he pulled out a key ring filled with keys. He quickly selected one and shoved it in the lock. In a moment he flung open the door.

Dr. Hurst still lay in the same position they had last seen him. The room remained in disarray from the ransacking earlier.

Dorothy pointed to the connecting door, which was slightly ajar. "In there. That's Jordan's room."

She scurried through the mess of equipment, books and clothes on the floor, and pushed open the door.

Jordan stood bare chested in the middle of the room. He was just getting dressed, Dorothy could see, and buttoning up his shirt. She could also see that he had a hard muscular chest and rippling, carved abdominal muscles. . . .

"Oh my," she said.

Then she noticed the red splotches that looked like burn marks on his body. Probably from that acidic blue cleanser!

Jordan looked up at Dorothy and the others who had suddenly appeared in his room. "How did you get in here?"

"Forget about that," she said. "How did you get those burns all over your . . . your big, muscular chest?"

Jordan finished buttoning up his shirt. "I slipped and fell into a puddle of something in the kitchen, thank you very much. I went on a fool's errand to get that glass of milk, and when I came back, you and Dr. Doyle were gone."

"Aha!" Woollcott cried. And at that moment Benchley, Ruth, Jane and John Simpson—the man in pajamas—entered Dr. Hurst's room behind them.

Dorothy's heart skipped a beat. She couldn't contain the smile on her face at seeing her best friend.

"Benchley, there you are!" Woollcott said. "Come over

244

here. Tell us, is this the man who attacked you in the kitchen?"

Benchley joined them at the connecting door. "Mr. Jordan? That was *you* in the kitchen?"

"What are you talking about?" Jordan said. "Yes, I was down in the kitchen a minute ago—"

"Aha!" Woollcott shouted again.

"Stop saying that," Dorothy muttered, then said to Jordan, "Did you assault Mr. Benchley, Mr. Case and Luigi in the kitchen?"

"No," he said, growing angry. "I just told you. I was in the kitchen getting a glass of milk for Dr. Doyle."

"Don't hand us a line," Woollcott said. "You just put your foot in your mouth."

"Your clubfoot," Dorothy and Benchley said in unison.

They turned to each other. She spoke first, unable to conceal the worry in her voice. "Fred, where have you been? I've been looking for you everywhere. When I saw that disaster in the kitchen and knew you had been there when it happened, I just . . . I just—"

Benchley smiled warmly, reassuringly. "Oh, that. Just a little squabble. Nothing for you to be concerned about, my dear Mrs. Parker."

"*Squabble?*" Luigi spat. Then he pointed at Jordan. "This man, he nearly kill us!"

Benchley ignored this. He took Dorothy's hand and patted it. "There, there. All is well."

"All is well?" She snatched her hand back. "You don't need to hide things from me to protect me. And you don't need to treat me like a child."

Benchley looked wounded. He spoke in a whisper. "Believe me, I don't think of you as a child, Mrs. Parker."

"Save your reunion for later, you two," Woollcott grumbled. "Now, Jordan. How did you get those burns on your chest?"

"As I was trying to explain to you," he said impatiently, "I was down in the kitchen, getting a glass of milk for Dr. Doyle. It was completely dark. The lights didn't work. So I had to feel my way to the icebox. I found it, and I got the milk. But then my orthopedic shoe slipped on something, and I found myself in a puddle of some corrosive liquid and tiny metal balls. I don't know what the liquid was, but it burned. The more I tried to get up, the more I slipped. By the time I got back on my feet, I was nearly covered in the stuff. I ran back up here and took a quick bath to rinse it off. Then all of you burst in—"

Woollcott eyed him narrowly. "How do we know it wasn't you who attacked these three gentlemen in the kitchen? Why should we believe you?"

"Because of that." Dorothy pointed to the dresser—on it was a glass of milk. "If he had attacked them, would he really have bothered to bring up the milk?"

Woollcott was momentarily stumped, then arched an eyebrow. "It's the perfect cover."

Jordan threw up his hands in disgust.

Dorothy said to him, "You just told us you ran back up here. I didn't think you could run. So tell us, do you really have a clubfoot?"

"When I said I *ran*, that was just a figure of speech." He limped forward. On his left foot was the large, ugly orthopedic shoe, much wider than a normal shoe, with a heel and sole as thick as a book. "Would I really wear this if I didn't have to? What do you think?"

Benchley made a satisfied hoot. "Did you also remember that, Mrs. Parker? Mr. Jordan seemed to run to look into his shoe earlier? It certainly looked like he could run, at least."

"That's right," she said, feeling not quite so angry with Benchley now. "You realized it, too?"

He nodded. "I found out a number of other things as well." He quickly explained to her and the others about his phone call with Captain Church: that Dr. Hurst was a wanted man for stealing the locket from the London Museum, and that somewhere in the hotel were two thugs who now had the locket—and who were going to deliver it to some underworld crook in Brooklyn as soon as they could leave the hotel.

He also explained that Ted Besh was very likely tête-bêche. "Poor Mr. Simpson here clarified it for us."

Case hadn't noticed him before. "Mr. Simpson? What are you doing out of your room? You must return at once. You're contagious!"

His red-dotted face turned redder. "I'm sorry. I just had to get out of that room. At least for a little while. I certainly hadn't forgotten that I'm contagious."

"Contagious? We knew you were sick—" Jane said, and Ruth now looked alarmed, too. "How contagious? We just rode up in a tight little elevator with you."

Dorothy intervened. "Don't worry. Dr. Doyle said it's not smallpox. It's chicken pox. You've all had that when you were kids, right?"

They all nodded.

"Then you've got nothing to worry about." She extended her hand to him. "Dorothy Parker. Nice to meet the man who caused all this trouble."

He hesitated a moment, then shook her hand gladly. "Are you joking? It's really not smallpox?"

She nodded. "For once in my life I'm not joking. I'm happy to tell you that you have chicken pox."

He grinned broadly, looking years younger. "My wife is going to be so relieved."

Jordan interrupted. "Excuse me. Can you tell me more about those 'thugs' who now have the locket?"

Benchley nodded. "Certainly. What would you like to know?"

"How can I find them—and the locket?"

"Uh," Benchley said. "I don't know. They might return to

room five-twenty. Or perhaps some nuns might return to that room. There seems to be some question about that."

"Some nuns?" Jordan said doubtfully.

"Speaking of questions," Benchley continued, "we have some about that locket. Did you know that Dr. Hurst had stolen it?"

Jordan tightened his lips but didn't say anything.

"Hmm, very well," Benchley said. "Do you know what a tête-bêche is?"

"A Ted what?" Jordan asked skeptically. He looked at Dorothy. "Didn't you say something about that earlier?"

She looked to Benchley. "Fred, what are you getting at?"

"Books!" he said. "Everyone search Dr. Hurst's room for books. We're looking for something like a French dictionary or phrase book."

They searched through Dr. Hurst's room for a quarter of an hour; as a result, they managed to straighten it up as they rummaged through the equipment and materials. Meanwhile Dr. Hurst, apparently asleep, lay motionless on the bed. But they found no French dictionaries or French books.

"Nothing!" Woollcott fumed. "How do you say 'nothing' in French?"

"Rien," Simpson said.

"That was a rhetorical question, you francophonic fool," Woollcott said.

"Aleck," Dorothy said. "Once again you're full of *merde*, because I just found something. Look at this."

They gathered around her, even Woollcott. She had put on her horn-rimmed glasses. In her hands she held a heavy, thick single-volume encyclopedic dictionary. "You'll never believe this."

"What is it?" Benchley asked.

She read aloud: " 'Tête-bêche. French. Head to foot, head

248

to tail or, literally, double headed. A term used in the printing of postage stamps.'"

"Postage stamps?" Benchley said.

"Here's the good part," she continued. " 'For more, see Hurst's *British Philately of the Nineteenth and Twentieth Centuries'*—a book written by our very own Dr. Quentin Hurst."

"Philately?" Simpson asked. "What's that?"

"Stamp collecting," she said. "Has anyone seen Dr. Hurst's big book on stamp collecting?"

"I just put that one away!" Jane said, and reached for a large volume in the traveling desk.

"I'm ready to put one away," Benchley mumbled. "Has anyone seen anything to drink around here?"

They ignored him. Jane handed Dr. Hurst's book to Dorothy, and they again gathered around her.

"Here it is. 'Tête-bêche—An error in the method of stamp production, with the careless placing of one printing plate of stamps upside down adjacent to another printing plate right side up. The stamps must be collected in a pair to show the error. Not to be confused with an invert stamp.' It has an example photo here."

She pointed to the small black-and-white image of a connected pair of stamps, which showed the profile of some nobleman, an earl or duke, perhaps. The first stamp was right side up, and the other stamp was upside down.

"That's it? That's all there is?" Woollcott asked. "So what's this invert stamp?"

Dorothy flipped the pages until she came to the entry. " 'Invert stamp—Stamps requiring two separate printings (such as stamps printed in two colors) have given rise to many curious errors in printing. A sheet passed through the press upside down after one color has been printed, for example, results in one portion of the design being inverted. In the 1869 issue of the stamps of the United States, no less than three of the values had the central portions of their designs printed upside down. Frequently the printer catches the error before the stamps are issued to the public and, consequently the sheets are destroyed. However, in several instances the mistake has been found only after the release of the stamps. The few invert stamps that remain from this printing often become quite valuable to the collector due to their unusual appearance and scarcity. Not to be confused with the tête-bêche.'"

"Is that all?" Woollcott said. "Sounds to me like the invert kind of stamp is worth more than the tête-bêche kind."

"No, that's not all," Dorothy said. "The last line is: 'See Appendix 19: The rare invert tête-bêche.'"

She turned to the back of the book and found the appendix. The first thing that caught her eye was a color photo—one of the few color photos in the book—of a strange pair of stamps.

She read aloud, "'An invert tête-bêche combines the printing error of the invert stamp with the striking upside-down juxtaposition of the tête-bêche. One of the most singular and rarest examples of the invert tête-bêche is the 1899 English two-pence stamp of Lady Cecily Shrewsbury— or, as collectors now call it, the "British Bearded Lady." It is so called because, due to the printing error, the tiara on her head of one printing plate was inverted, and this consequently gives the appearance of a beard on the lady's face on the adjacent tête-bêche stamp.'"

Benchley chuckled, "I'm sure the lady was not amused."

Dorothy continued reading, "'The error was caught before the stamps were sold to the public. Indeed, Lord Shrewsbury personally set a fiery torch to the sheet sets and engraved plates and burned them. However, it is believed that a postal clerk absconded with one sheet set beforehand and subsequently sold it to a wealthy French collector, who was quick to boast of it in his native land. Word of the existing stamps eventually reached Lord Shrewsbury, who challenged the collector to a duel. Both gentlemen were wounded in the challenge, and most of the stamp sheet was ruined in the fracas. The remainder of the stamps were recovered and returned to the Royal Mail. Lord and Lady Shrewsbury withdrew from society to reside quietly at their country estate. Today the only known example of the rare "Bearded Lady" invert tête-bêche stamps are now in the archives of the London Museum. Its value is beyond price.'"

Dorothy lowered the book and found herself looking at the old man in the bed. Both of his eyes were open, and he stared back at her. He raised a hand, which was curled tight like a claw. He moaned, "Tête-bêche . . . !"

His head dropped back to the pillow from the effort. His eyes closed, and once again he was still. Jordan went to the bed to check on the elderly man.

"Is he still alive?" she asked.

Jordan nodded.

"So," Woollcott said slowly, "the valuable stolen item is not the locket. It's a postage stamp."

"A pair of them, at least," she said.

"Which must be hidden inside the locket," Benchley said.

"But that brings us back to the same old question," Jordan said. "How do we find the locket?"

Woollcott snapped at him, "I'll ask the questions, if it's all the same to you." Then he turned to Dorothy. "Very well then, how *do* we find the locket?"

She frowned in reply. "We need a detective, Aleck. A *real* detective."

Chapter 35

Dorothy knocked on the door of Doyle's room.

There was no answer at first. Then from inside he called quietly, "Come in."

She opened the door and poked her head into the room. It was so dim that she could barely see anything. Only one tiny votive candle in a small glass placed on the dresser gave the room the faintest glow. Eventually she perceived Doyle sitting on the edge of the bed and facing away from her. He appeared to be staring at something on the wall—and mumbling to himself?

Then without turning around he said, "Good early morning, Dorothy."

"Good morning to you," she answered automatically. Then she realized that he couldn't see her and she hadn't even said anything. "Hold on, Artie, how did you know it's me?"

Only then did he turn to her. He spoke in a quiet but happy voice. "My son told me."

She had a cold feeling. "Your son?"

He nodded. "I was just speaking with him."

"You were?" She didn't see anyone else in the room. "So where is he?"

Again Doyle's voice sounded happy—delighted, even. "He's passed on."

"Come again?"

"He died during the Great War. He was injured in the battle of the Somme, and in his weakened state he caught influenza and died. On rare occasions his spirit now comes to visit me."

She involuntarily shuddered. Was Doyle really talking to the ghost of his son? Or, most likely, was he just plain crazy? Either way, she was unnerved by it. She was particularly disturbed by his happy, almost giddy mood as he talked of his own dead child.

"Oh yes?" she said as breezily as she could, as though speaking to the spirit of one's deceased son was a perfectly ordinary thing to do. "How's tricks with him?"

"Just heavenly, thank you for asking," Doyle said with a pleased smile.

Was he putting her on? Did he really believe in such nonsense?

Then another thought struck her. She hesitated to speak, but only for a moment. After all, what did she have to lose? "Listen, can your son give us any clue about how to find that missing locket? Or tell us who killed Bibi? Or where her body went?"

"Well," Doyle said, a little put off, "I suppose I can ask."

He turned away to face the wall again, then mumbled something. Dorothy stood and waited and felt the hairs on the back of her neck stand on end as she listened. She heard only Doyle's voice, but it was the complete ordinariness of his tone—so matter-of-fact that he might have been chatting with someone on the telephone—that spooked her.

At last his mumbling stopped, and he turned again to her. "He's gone."

Like father, like son, she thought. *He's gone, all right.*

"Switch the light on, please," he said. "I can hardly see you there."

She flipped the wall switch by the door, and suddenly the small room was bathed in bright light. Doyle rose and shielded his eyes. He went over to the candle and blew it out.

"So," Dorothy finally said, "where did he go?"

Doyle shrugged. "Well . . . everywhere and nowhere."

"What's your son's name?"

"Kingsley. A fine boy."

"How old was he?"

"Twenty-five."

"You really believe in it? In Spiritualism?" She blurted it out before she could think twice.

He smiled, not offended. "I abandoned my congenial and lucrative work, traveled long and far away from home and subjected myself to all sorts of inconveniences, losses and even insults to bring the truth to people. It's been my sole mission for some years now."

"Some years?" she asked. "How long have you been at it?"

"My interest started in middle age, I suppose. It's increased over the years. The older I get, the stronger my conviction grows."

"And your conviction has grown stronger . . . after your son died?"

He smiled again. "I had been searching for answers long before Kingsley died."

She thought about this. "Must be sad to lose a son. Must be heartbreaking."

He beamed with the face of the converted. "But that's the importance of Spiritualism! We're never alone. There isn't really an end to life."

She didn't know whether to pity him or to envy him. *We're never alone. . . . It'd be nice to feel such comfort,* she thought.

But she couldn't swallow the idea whole. Did Doyle really think he could talk to the spirit of his dead son? She looked at his beatific face, and she realized that it didn't matter. Whether he imagined it or not, the effect was the same. He was happy in his knowledge, and that was that. She couldn't argue facts against faith—not with such a pleasant, even jubilant old fellow, at any rate.

She took a deep breath. "What did your son say to you? Does he know who killed Bibi?"

"He did not say. He could not say."

"Oh . . ." She felt her skepticism rise higher.

"But he did propose two ideas."

"Yeah? Let's hear 'em."

"He told me: 'Put Toby on the scent. And set a trap.'"

She looked at Doyle for a further explanation, but he didn't offer one. Finally she asked, "Who the heck is Toby?"

Doyle bit his lip and chewed at his big walrus mustache. "Toby was a dog in a Sherlock Holmes story—a dog with an amazing power of smell. Holmes and Watson used Toby to track down a villain."

"I gather this pooch is purely fictional?"

He nodded. "It's my assumption that Kingsley was referring to your little dog, Woody."

"Woody? He's a chowhound, not a bloodhound."

He shrugged his big shoulders.

"All right," she said with a sigh. "I suppose it's a spirit's nature to be vague on the details. So what did he mean, 'set a trap'?"

"Kingsley was somewhat more specific about that. He said to take the top hat—Mr. Woollcott's hat, I presume—and play a new game. Like the game you played before."

She felt the hairs on her neck and scalp rise again. "Murder? Your son wants us to play Murder?"

Doyle nodded. "'Only use a different slip of paper this time,' he said. Does that make sense to you?"

255

She thought a moment; then she chuckled. "As a matter of fact, Artie, it does make sense to me. It's one hell of an idea! Come on, now. You're coming with me to the dining room—to the Round Table. Soon we'll point the finger at Bibi's killer."

Chapter 36

Darting between chairs and under tables, Woodrow Wilson tugged at his leash. The dog wasn't often allowed into the Algonquin dining room, and he was very excited. His stubby tail wagged rapidly. When he saw Benchley standing by the Round Table, the dog yanked Dorothy across the room. Doyle, bemused, followed behind them.

"Hello, my friendly little fellow," Benchley said, reaching down and scratching the dog on the head. "You're certainly wide-awake for such an early morning hour."

"That makes one of us," Dorothy said with a yawn.

All the chandeliers were fully lit. The dining room was as bright as day, though it wasn't yet dawn. Waiters and other members of the hotel staff were beginning to hustle in and out, getting ready for the breakfast service. Benchley grabbed one of them. "Excuse me, my good man. Can you please bring Mrs. Parker some coffee?"

Dorothy smiled. Good old Benchley. He was always there for her.

The waiter, a tall fellow, was the one who had hardly answered Dorothy on the stairs. The man gave Benchley a similarly unhelpful response—an indifferent nod—and moved toward the kitchen.

Doyle called after him. "And perhaps a cup of tea, my good man?"

The waiter didn't even turn around. He disappeared through the swinging kitchen doors. They caught a glimpse between the doors and saw the kitchen staff cleaning up the mess from earlier.

"I guess it might be awhile before the hot beverages arrive," Benchley said, and gave Woody another pat on the head. "We don't see this fellow down here too often. To what do we owe the delightful pleasure of his company?"

Dorothy pointed her thumb at Doyle. "Artie gave me the idea. He didn't come up with it himself—that's another story—but he gave it to me. We'll use Woody to track down Bibi or her murderer. Or both. We'll see how it goes."

Benchley looked amused and curious. "How exactly is Woody going to do that?"

She turned to Doyle. "Yes, how will he do that?"

"Typically the bloodhound already knows the quarry's scent. So in a fox hunt the dogs are set off in an area where they're likely to pick up the trail. But in instances in which the hounds are unfamiliar with the quarry, if they're being trained for the first time, the huntsman introduces an item that possesses the fox's scent—a scrap of something from the fox's den, for instance."

"His robe and slippers?" Benchley asked.

"Not quite," Doyle said. "Now, with human quarry—a fugitive prisoner or a missing child, for example—the hound is often given an article of the person's clothing. Do you have something of Bibi's? Where did her clothes go, after all?"

Dorothy thought about this but was interrupted by the presence of Frank Case, who carried a steaming silver carafe. "I thought I heard your voices out here. Care for coffee?"

She picked up a china cup and saucer from a nearby place setting. "Thanks, Frank. Just what the doctor ordered."

"Actually," Doyle said with a smile, "I ordered tea. But coffee would be lovely. Thank you."

He, too, held out a cup, and so did Benchley. Case filled all three with the hot black coffee. Just the rich, roasted smell perked Dorothy up. Woody sat on his haunches and looked at her imploringly.

Case turned to leave. "Is there anything else I can get for you?" he asked, almost as an afterthought.

"Yes," Dorothy said brightly. "Everyone."

The hotel manager stopped in his tracks with a puzzled expression. "I beg your pardon?"

"Get everyone, please. Thank you."

"Get *everyone*? What exactly do you mean, Mrs. Parker?"

"Bring everyone down here. We need to get this whole thing finally sorted out. And we need everyone to do so."

"Everyone? Every person in the entire hotel?"

She thought about this. "Is that a tall order? Okay then. Get everyone who was at Fairbanks' party last night. That should be good enough."

Case set the coffee carafe on the Round Table with a plunk. "Mrs. Parker, you know very well I can't do that. I can't go around the hotel waking up our guests at six o'clock in the morning."

"Not to worry," she said. "Mr. Benchley already woke them up by ringing all the telephones a short while ago. You just need to bring them down here."

Benchley grinned sheepishly.

"For what possible reason?" Case asked.

She sipped the hot coffee. It soothed her and roused her at the same time. "For breakfast, of course."

Case folded his arms.

She smiled. "I want to catch them unaware. We'll start with a grilling of bacon and eggs—followed by a grilling of the suspects."

He took a deep breath. "We are not prepared to provide breakfast service for so many guests all at once."

She smirked. "And are you really prepared to last out this quarantine? A quarantine may have seemed like an inconvenient yet jolly good idea last night, when we were all in a party mood. But I'm sure the reality of it is sinking in now, isn't it, Frank? How are you going to feed and entertain a hotel full of cranky guests for a week or more—especially with a skeleton crew of surly, overworked waiters and maids?"

Case thought about this. He rocked back on his heels. "You make a good point—"

She spoke quickly. "If we carry out a one-by-one interview of the suspects and a little sniffing by my canny canine here, we'll have Bibi's killer in our hands in no time—and we'll get the quarantine lifted, too. So what do you say?"

Case nodded. "I say that's an intriguing idea. But I've already called the Health Department to cancel the quarantine—to come down and remove the sign and the seal from the front doors."

Her eyes went wide. "Why did you do *that*?"

Case was confused. "Dr. Doyle confirmed that the Simpson family has chicken pox, not smallpox. There's no longer any need for the quarantine."

"Yes, there most certainly is!" she said. "It's the quarantine that's keeping the killer inside this hotel. If the quarantine is lifted, and the doors are unlocked, then it's bye-bye to Bibi's murderer."

He pursed his lips in thought.

She said, "How long until the authorities get here?"

"With all the snow out there, and it being New Year's Day, it could be as much as an hour until they arrive."

"Only an *hour*? They'll be here that soon?" Then she spoke as much to herself as to the others. "How can this city be so abysmally inefficient when you actually need something and yet miraculously on its toes when you don't?"

"Very well," Case said, resolved. "I certainly don't want to be the one who let a murderer go free from under my

260

own roof. I'll do my best to get everyone down here right away, and you can have your grilling." He turned and hurried off.

They watched him go. Woody, bored, stretched and lay down on the carpet.

"Oh no, my little man, you have work to do," she said to the dog. "You need to track down a dead body."

Doyle frowned. "But with what, I daresay? The last time anyone saw the woman, she was naked as a jaybird. Where can we find Miss Bibelot's clothes to give the dog her scent?"

Dorothy thought, trying to remember Bibi's movements and actions the night before. She snapped her fingers, and Woody jumped to his paws. "I think I have it. Remember how Bibi made her grand entrance into the lobby? She dropped her coat to the floor and flaunted herself in her little high-hemmed flapper's dress."

Benchley shook his head. "That must have been before I arrived."

"It doesn't matter," she said. "Follow me."

Tugging the dog on his leash, she led the way through the dining room and back into the lobby. She aimed at first toward the front door, but then she turned right toward the coat-check closet.

"Here," she said. "I think Bibi left her coat here."

The entrance to the coat closet was a Dutch door, the top of which was partially open. Dorothy reached in and unlatched the bottom half of the door. She yanked a cord to turn on the overhead light, and then she quickly ferreted through the many coats, wraps and jackets.

"Bibi came in wearing an ankle-length silver fur coat. I'd remember it anywhere—and here it is!"

She held out a long, fuzzy garment of silky silver fur. Woody sniffed at it curiously.

"Well done, Mrs. Parker," Benchley said.

Doyle reached out to feel it. "Dear me, is that—silver

fox? How extraordinary. I was just speaking of foxes, wasn't I? Perhaps her spirit is communicating to me . . . ?" He gently stroked the lustrous fur.

"Nonsense," Dorothy said, pulling the coat from his touch. "You must have seen her enter the building just like everyone else. That planted the seed of thought in your head, that's all."

Doyle looked doubtful but didn't argue with her.

"Well, now we have the fox," Benchley said. "Let's see what the hound can do."

They all looked at the little dog. He plopped down on his rear end and lazily scratched behind his ear with his hind paw.

"Woody," she said, presenting the fur to him. "Here, smell this. Smell Bibi. That's right. Smell that little vixen."

The dog sniffed at the fur indifferently at first; then he dug his nose deep into it and snorted up whatever it was that he smelled. He pulled his snout out and sneezed.

"Bless you," Dorothy said with motherly affection. Then she looked up at Doyle. "How do we get him to follow the scent?"

"How, you ask?" he said. Then he bellowed deep as a bassoon, "Release the hounds!"

She reached down and unclasped the leash from the dog's collar.

Woody didn't hesitate. Incited as much by his new freedom as by Doyle's thundering command, Woody sped off through the lobby. He darted between the lobby's cozy armchairs and coffee tables and zipped straight into the dining room.

They followed him.

When they entered the dining room, the dog was nowhere to be seen. But the swinging doors to the kitchen were just closing, indicating that the small creature had recently nosed its way in.

A FRIENDLY GAME OF MURDER

"The hound is on the scent, all right," Benchley said. "The scent of breakfast."

They went into the busy kitchen. The savory smells of bacon, eggs, toast and coffee, accompanied by the noisy sounds and sights of the waiters and kitchen staff hurrying to and fro, overwhelmed their senses.

Most of the mess from the scuffle in the night had now been cleaned up. Luigi the waiter stood amid the kitchen chaos with a mop in his hand, a metal bucket at his feet and a world-weary expression on his tired face. They looked down and saw a track of little dirty paw prints on the white tile floor.

"You are looking for your dog?" Luigi asked blearily. "It came through here and went into there." He pointed toward the service corridor.

Apologizing to Luigi as they tiptoed across his newly mopped floor, they hurried through the kitchen.

In the service corridor, they found the dog with his snout against the closed door of the pantry closet. His wet nose sniffed at the space where the door met the floor, and his little stub of a tail wiggled with excitement.

"Perhaps he's located his quarry?" Doyle said with equal excitement.

"He certainly has," Dorothy said, a little disappointed. "Unfortunately his quarry is a dog biscuit. Frank Case keeps a box for him in there."

"Oh," Doyle said, equally disappointed. His big mustache drooped. "Now what shall we do?"

"Elementary, my dear Doyle," Benchley said brightly. "Let's get the poor pooch his biscuit. Then let's all have some breakfast before we continue on with this caper. I'm famished!"

With that, he opened the pantry door—and yelped in surprise. Dorothy and Doyle crowded next to him and followed his gaze.

There in the center of the little room sat the body of Bibi in the wheelchair. She was fully clothed in her slinky flapper's dress and shoes. Her eyes were closed as though she was merely asleep, though her whitish skin confirmed that she was well beyond sleep.

Woody charged in, sniffed at her feet and gave her motionless leg an obligatory lick. Then he barked with a proud little yap.

"On second thought," Benchley said in a low voice, "I've just lost my appetite."

Chapter 37

Dorothy stepped into the small pantry and coaxed Woody away from Bibi's body. Benchley picked up the dog and stroked his fur.

The little room was claustrophobic. There was hardly enough floor space for the wheelchair and Dorothy together. The walls were lined with shelves, which were stocked almost to overflowing with cans, boxes, cartons and bags of food. A big burlap sack of potatoes squatted in the corner, giving the room a musty, earthy smell.

Dorothy found the carton of dog biscuits, opened it and took a treat for Woody. The dog crunched it down quickly. She then turned and moved closer to Bibi's body to inspect it. Bibi was not wearing the necklace, of course. Otherwise, she appeared exactly as she had when she arrived at the party. Well, *almost* exactly . . .

Doyle stood next to her to examine Bibi as well. "Hmm, what do you observe?"

Dorothy didn't like being put to the test. Still, this was the father of Sherlock Holmes. So, what the heck—she could try the Dr. Watson role if it meant that Doyle would put on Holmes' deerstalker hat, figuratively speaking. "She's fully dressed. Even her makeup has been reapplied."

"What do you make of that?"

"Someone who cared about her—or at least cared about her appearance—did this for her."

"And why would a person take such care of her, given that she is now deceased?"

"I can think of two reasons. One, it was someone who loved her and wished for her to not appear quite so . . . dead."

"And the second reason?"

"Perhaps whoever fixed her up wanted to get her out of the hotel. A nicely dressed woman in a wheelchair is certainly a more acceptable sight on Sixth Avenue than a naked corpse."

Doyle smiled. "You're rather good at this. But why take her out of the hotel?" He spoke as though he already knew the answer.

"No habeas corpus," she said. "If there's no body, there's no crime."

"Not exactly, from a legal point of view," he said. "But, still, that's probably the killer's general idea. So that would lead us to believe it was indeed our killer who spruced her up and put her in here. Correct?"

"Yes, indeedy. He was the one who hid her here, just waiting for an opportunity to wheel her out the front door when no one is looking."

"He?" Doyle asked archly. "Weren't you the one who suggested the killer might just as well be a woman?"

"I know it's a man."

Doyle was taken aback. Up to this point he seemed to be leading Dorothy to all the answers. "I agree with you that our culprit likely is a man. But, if one considers all the possibilities, certainly a woman with enough strength and determination could very well have dressed Miss Bibelot and positioned her so, don't you agree?"

"No," Dorothy said firmly. "At least, I don't agree that a woman did this."

He frowned skeptically. "And what makes you so sure?"

"Her makeup, my dear Doyle. It was applied by a man."

Doyle raised his eyebrows. Then he adjusted his glasses and looked closely at Bibi's face. "Good heavens, you're right!" he exclaimed. "I see it now. The powder is rather heavily caked on her cheeks, but there is hardly any on her nose."

"A woman abhors a shiny nose," she said.

"And the lipstick," he continued. "It is thickly and unevenly applied. There is a certain ... squareness to the shape of the lip coloring. Not very ladylike, I should say."

"You said it, all right. A woman always blots her lips after applying lipstick. If a woman had applied this makeup—even if she was in a hurry—she would have given Bibi's mouth at least some lip service, so to speak."

Doyle straightened up and looked down admiringly at Dorothy. "So we know that it was a man who dressed her and positioned her here—a man who apparently cared about her, perhaps even admired her. But where does that lead us?"

Benchley sighed. "Almost right back where we started. You can take your pick of men who admired her. There must be two dozen of them in this hotel alone."

Suddenly Woollcott appeared at the pantry door. "Aha! Here you all are! I've been waiting at the Round Table for—" He caught his breath when he spotted Bibi. He turned to Doyle. "You found her! My hat's off to you, sir. You truly are as great as your famous detect—"

Doyle interrupted as Woollcott was literally tipping his hat. "I cannot take the credit. It was Mrs. Parker's little 'bloodhound' that led us to the body. He's the one who deserves your praise."

"Oh." Woollcott turned to the dog in Benchley's arms. He gave the dog a perfunctory pat on the head. "Well done," he muttered. Then he turned back to Dorothy. "Now that we have the body, what do we do about it?"

"I guess we leave her here for now. It won't be long before the authorities arrive. In the meantime I suggest we continue with our little game as planned," she said with a scheming glint in her eye. Finding Bibi's body had boosted her confidence. "I see you've brought your top hat, which we'll soon require. Have the guests arrived in the dining room?"

"Most of them are there—Doug Fairbanks, Mary Pickford, Ruth Hale, Jane Grant, Ben Jordan, Lydia Trumbull, Mrs. Volney, and a few dozen others—with more and more arriving every minute. Come to think of it, I should wake Harpo. . . ."

"Get back in there, then. We're right behind you."

Woollcott hurried off. Woody squirmed in Benchley's arms.

"You can set him down now," she said. "I'll put his leash back on."

Benchley lowered the dog to the floor, and Woody scampered to Dorothy. But then he wiggled between her legs and back into the pantry. He sniffed a moment at Bibi's bare leg, then turned and smelled the cylindrical cartons of Quaker Oats. Before Dorothy could grab him, he had moved on to a large, empty cardboard box. He scratched at it with his paw, then leaped inside and sniffed it thoroughly while turning in circles.

"That'll do, my little man," she said, latching the leash onto his collar. But before she pulled him away, something in the box caught her eye. It was a stained gray piece of paper—a form of some sort. But it was the signature on the paper that had captured her attention. She snatched it up and looked at it more closely.

The paper was a packing slip. Or was it an invoice? She wasn't quite sure. It was a typewritten list that itemized a shipment of two dozen live lobsters and an assortment of seafood. The signature that had caught her eye was written neatly in bold blue ink. . . .

B. Bibelot.

*   *   *

In the kitchen, Dorothy grabbed Frank Case by the sleeve of his natty jacket and held the paper in front of his face. "Did Bibi buy these lobsters?"

Case was momentarily taken by surprise. But he quickly recovered and took the paper from her hands. "Certainly not," he said calmly.

"Then why is Bibi's signature on this invoice?"

Case scrutinized the sheet. "Ah, now I see. Here are Luigi's initials at the bottom. That means we took delivery, and the hotel paid for them out of its account with this particular fishmonger. See? It says it's paid in advance. We paid for this, not Bibi."

Dorothy looked at the paper, but all she saw was a list of lobsters and fish, and countless inscrutable numbers—and the signature *B. Bibelot.*

"But why does it have Bibi's name on it?"

"Well," he said, somewhat confused, "it says she *delivered* the order."

Dorothy put her hands on her hips. "How could a skinny little girl like Bibi have delivered two dozen lobsters and an assortment of seafood? *Why* would she deliver such a thing? Not to mention when."

Case pursed his lips. He handed the invoice back to Dorothy. "I can't explain it. It would indeed take a strong person to carry all that seafood—and some of it packed in dry ice to add to the weight. Or it could have easily been transported on a cart, of course. But, if it's all the same to you, we have to get breakfast ready for more than a hundred guests all at once, thanks to your suggestion. So if you'll excuse me, perhaps we can consider this later in the morning?"

He turned away with an apologetic smile and went back to work, directing the waiters and line cooks and handling their questions and problems.

Doyle and Benchley stood by the kitchen doors, ready to

enter the Algonquin dining room. She moved to join them. Then she stopped. Something occurred to her. She turned back and hurried again to Case.

"Frank."

"Yes, Mrs. Parker. Something else?" His calm demeanor was showing signs of strain.

"There's always something else," she said. "Did you say that seafood was packed in dry ice?"

He touched a finger to his lips. "Not the lobsters. They were alive upon arrival. But when we get seafood, especially certain fish imported from a great distance, it's packed in dry ice to keep it fresh."

"What happened to the dry ice?"

"The dry ice? What happened to it?"

"Have you suddenly become a parrot? Yes, the hotel was without ice of any kind last night, and yet the dry ice from this seafood was not to be found. What happened to it?"

Case finally let his frustration show. "We certainly didn't serve it, if that's what you mean. We usually unpack the fish, then throw the ice into the alley. It disappears in no time. On the other hand, perhaps someone left it around and it evaporated. We *were* rather busy last night. And we're quite busy right now, Mrs. Parker! So if you don't mind—" He gestured toward the twin doors to the dining room.

"Evaporated?"

"Yes, evaporated. Don't you know about dry ice?"

"Of course I know about dry ice," she answered quickly. Then after a moment's thought—and realizing she actually didn't know much about dry ice—she asked, "What about it?"

"It's incredibly cold. Much colder than regular ice. It's frozen gas. So when it warms up, it turns from a frozen solid directly to a gas, never a liquid, you know."

Incredibly cold. So cold that it burns? she wondered. She remembered that when she had fallen down in the service elevator, her hand had touched a shard of ice—an extremely nasty shard of ice.

"Well, of course it turns into a gas. *Everyone* knows that," she said, although she admitted to herself that she may have forgotten it.

"There you have it," Case continued. "Whether someone threw it out into the alley or whether it was left around last night, it's probably long gone now."

"Probably?" she asked.

"Yes, probably. That's the extent of my knowledge on the subject, Mrs. Parker," he said with finality. "If you have more questions about dry ice, try asking Douglas Fairbanks. But this is a kitchen, not a science laboratory, and we do have breakfast to serve. So, if you'll please excuse me—"

"Fairbanks? What would *he* know about it?"

Case started backing away. "Dry ice is used for effects in the theater. They drop a large chunk of it into a tub of water, and it makes fog—a swirling mist that rolls across the stage. Surely you've seen that?"

"Well, yes, I suppose—"

Then the kitchen doors swung open. The right door bumped into Doyle, and the left pushed Benchley aside. Alexander Woollcott strode in.

"Come, come, my dear Mrs. Parker! The stage is set. We have a packed house, and it's your cue. All await your grand entrance with bated breath."

"Aleck, it's only *your* breath that smells like bait," she said. "Have a mint or something."

Benchley chuckled. "That'll teach you to fish for a compliment, Aleck."

Woollcott turned to him. "Ah, the Benchley wit," he said. "As sharp and as cutting as a butter knife."

"Ahem," Doyle said, clearing his throat. "That's quite enough trading insults. Shall we get back to the matter at hand?"

"But," Benchley said, disappointed, "trading insults is our stock-in-trade."

"Sorry. Artie's right," Dorothy said. "Let's get this show on the road."

She grabbed the top hat from Woollcott's head, tugged on Woody's leash and pushed open the double doors.

She stopped short. At least a hundred people were crowded into the dining room. Many were packed around the tables, while the rest stood expectantly—and looked slightly annoyed at being summoned at such an early hour after such an uproarious night.

As one, they turned their bloodshot, bleary eyes toward Dorothy.

Oh dear, what did I get myself into?

Chapter 38

Dorothy merely stared at the friends and guests gathered before her in the crowded dining room.

Suddenly Woollcott snatched the top hat from her hands. "I'll handle this bunch," he said to her. Then, in an announcer's voice, he spoke. "Good morning, my good people! We're here to play a little game of Murder. Only this time it's no game. One of you gathered here murdered Bibi Bibelot. And I intend to point the finger at the one who 'done it.'"

Dorothy nearly smacked her forehead. She and Aleck had briefly discussed this plan earlier in Dr. Hurst's room. But clearly the discussion had been too brief, because this was not what she truly had in mind.

Then again, there was no time to lose. The Health Department would arrive before long. Woollcott might as well get things underway in his own inimitable—and insufferable—style.

"Douglas Fairbanks!" he said, his voice heavy with blame. "You, sir, had both the ability and the motive to attack Miss Bibelot. The young woman effectively took over your party and insulted your hospitality—and that of your wife, Mary. You possess the key to the bathroom, and you

273

had access to the locket. And you, above all, had the acrobatic ability to climb out the window and scamper across the roof—"

"Well, so did I," Dorothy said before she could think twice about it. "If I could get out the window and get across the snowy roof, just about anybody else could—anyone who could fit through the window, that is. It certainly wasn't Fairbanks who killed Bibi. That's preposterous, and you know it, Aleck."

Woollcott spun around and glared at her. But he quickly ignored her interruption and resumed his accusations.

"Mary Pickford!" he said, literally pointing the finger at her. "Bibi ruined your party. You yourself admitted that you entered the bathroom and took the locket from around the young girl's neck. If you are so bold to perform such a theft, is murder also out of the question?"

Mary opened her mouth to speak, but Dorothy spoke first.

"Of course it's out of the question, Aleck," she said. "We've gone over this. Why would Mary kill another woman and leave the body in her own tub? No woman would corrupt her own bathroom like that. She'd never want to use it again."

Woollcott again faced her with beady, angry eyes. "Whose side are you on? This was all your idea, remember?"

She bit her lip. She couldn't help interrupting, especially when Woollcott seemed so wrongheaded. But at the same time she didn't want to be involved in the accusations. "Fine, then. Go right ahead. You're the detective."

He turned away with a huff and leveled his irate gaze at Lydia Trumbull. "You!"

She froze. Woollcott continued, "You have a veritable storeroom of sleeping potions and narcotics, or so I have heard. And, as a former army nurse, you know how to use them. Indeed, you poisoned Bibi with a lethal dose of chloroform, which you stole from Dr. Hurst, did you not?"

Lydia's eyes had widened to the size of half-dollars. Then her pupils rolled upward, and her eyelids fluttered. She swayed sideways, and, to no one's surprise, she fainted.

"Very well, let's move on," Woollcott said matter-of-factly. "Benedict Jordan!"

Jordan folded his muscled arms over his broad chest and returned Woollcott's stare.

Woollcott, who stood safely across the room, was unperturbed. "You stole the locket from Mary Pickford's bureau with the aim of returning it to your employer, Dr. Hurst."

"It was his," Jordan said gruffly.

"Oh, was it?" Woollcott said archly. "Or was it stolen from a museum in England?"

By this point, Dorothy's curiosity had gotten the better of her. She picked up Woody and weaved her way through the crowd toward Doug Fairbanks and Mary Pickford. They smiled when they saw her approaching with the little dog.

"Happy New Year's Day, Dottie," Fairbanks said warmly. "Say, you don't have anything to do with this lousy third degree from Woollcott, do you?"

"Certainly not," she lied. "Now tell me what you know about dry ice."

"*Dry ice?*" Mary asked. "Why do you want to know about that?"

She didn't answer directly. "You theater folk use it for special effects?"

Fairbanks nodded. "We use it in the movies, too. Makes wonderful fog."

"Can it be harmful?"

"Yes, if you touch it in its frozen state," he said. "Its temperature is something like one hundred degrees below zero. It'd freeze your fingers right off your hand."

Again she thought of the shard of ice in the elevator.

On the other side of the room, Woollcott was now loudly

accusing Dr. Hurst in absentia. Jordan and Doyle—God bless them—were standing in to defend Dr. Hurst's innocence in Bibi's murder. Dorothy shook her head ruefully. Why did she get Woollcott involved? He only made things more difficult.

She turned back to Fairbanks. "Dry ice melts directly into a gas, right? What do they use the gas for?"

Fairbanks shrugged. "Other than stage effects, nothing that I know of. It's pure carbon dioxide. You can't use that for much."

She frowned. Perhaps her curiosity had led her down a blind alley after all.

Woollcott was now widely accusing many of the partygoers of egging on Bibi. He singled out some of the men who had poured the champagne into the tub. *Oh dear.* She had to stop him soon and get the Murder game underway—otherwise there would soon be another murder on her hands: Woollcott's.

"Oh, wait," Mary said to her husband. "Tell Dottie that story about the stagehand!"

"Stagehand?" she asked.

Fairbanks nodded, remembering. "Oh yes, that's right. This is a funny story—well, not *that* funny, I guess. The young man nearly died. But in the end we all had a good laugh about it." He smiled.

"What happened?"

"Well, this was a few years ago, before I had really hit it big. It was a small theater, a far cry from Broadway. One of the stagehands got stuck in an old basement broom closet or something with a carton full of dry ice. Of course the stage manager went looking for him. Everyone thought the fellow was out playing hooky, because he was a rambunctious young lad, and it was a lovely, warm day."

"But of course he wasn't," Mary said.

"No, he wasn't," Fairbanks agreed. "He nearly asphyxiated in that broom closet. When the stage manager finally

276

found him, his first thought was that the stagehand was falling-over drunk. Then he got a good look at the boy. His lips were blue, and so was the skin under his fingernails. He was nearly dead from lack of oxygen."

"Lack of oxygen?" Dorothy asked.

He nodded. "On such a warm day and in such a small space, the dry ice had quickly turned to carbon dioxide. The stagehand was overwhelmed in less than an hour. Fortunately that kind of thing doesn't happen every day, or stagehands would be dying off like . . ."

Then a funny look came into his eyes. At the very same time, a thought popped into Dorothy's head.

"Dying off . . . like spring flowers?" she asked. "Dying off . . . like *Bibi*?"

"You read my mind!" he said excitedly.

She picked up Woody from the floor. "We'll be right back," she said to Mary. Then she grabbed Fairbanks' hand. "Come with me."

She pulled him through the crowd. But there were so many people packed so tightly together that she progressed very slowly. Fairbanks halted her.

"Where are we going?" he asked.

"The pantry. It's through the kitchen."

"I'll lead the way." He stepped in front of her and zipped through the crowd like a speedboat cutting through calm waters. She quickly followed in his wake. Before they reached the kitchen, she had just enough time to consider how easy life must be if you're a wildly popular masculine movie star—as compared to a petite, little-known female poet.

But she pushed these thoughts aside as they emerged from the crowded dining room to the less congested but more frenetic kitchen.

Suddenly Jacques the chef was yelling, pointing a large carving knife at her. "You stop bringing that filthy dog into my kitchen, or else!"

J. J. Murphy

As Fairbanks pulled her in the direction of the pantry, she called over her shoulder to the chef. "Or else what? You'll turn him into tonight's special?"

Jacques' face went beet red. "Don't tempt me!"

Looking behind her, she saw that Doyle and Benchley were now coming through the swinging doors.

"What is this, Grand Central Station?" the chef yelled. "Stay out of my kitchen!"

Now she and Fairbanks were in the service corridor and standing in front of the pantry door.

"In here?" he asked.

She nodded. "Afraid so." She opened the door, and there was Bibi just as they had left her.

"She almost looks alive," Fairbanks said with a tinge of sorrow in his usually cheery voice.

Woody jumped out of Dorothy's arms and waddled up to the body. He took a quick sniff of Bibi's leg, then moved on to the empty seafood carton again.

"Something afoot?" Doyle asked as he and Benchley joined them.

"Do you have a hankie?" she asked him. Doyle quickly produced an ivory-colored silk handkerchief. She took it from him and leaned toward the body. "Remember we noticed her thick lipstick? Watch this."

She rubbed the lipstick away from Bibi's mouth—it required quite a few wipes—and stood back so they could see.

"By Jove," Doyle said. "Her lips are blue!"

"She was suffocated," Dorothy explained.

"Suffocated? But how? Not strangled, surely! I saw no handprints or ligature marks on her neck."

"Carbon dioxide," she said. "Someone filled the bathroom with carbon dioxide while Bibi was knocked out from the chloroform. So she asphyxiated. She ran out of oxygen and died. That's why the bathroom was closed and locked up. That's why the towel was placed at the bottom of the bathroom door, to keep the gas from escaping. If we

278

chipped the polish off her fingernails, I bet they'd be blue, too."

"Well done, Mrs. Parker," Benchley said admiringly. She smiled in return.

Doyle looked skeptical. "How could anyone fill a hotel bathroom with carbon dioxide? That's rather far-fetched."

"Not if it's in the form of dry ice," Fairbanks said. "It'd be easy as dropping a bucket of it into the tub. Half an hour or so later, and Bibi is dead."

As the cold-blooded horror of the murder dawned on him, Doyle understood. "Asphyxiate her with dry ice while she lay there naked and unconscious? But who could have done such a vile, monstrous thing?"

Dorothy stared at Bibi's porcelain countenance as if the answer could be found there. She studied her delicate, motionless features—her sensuous mouth, her high cheekbones, her slender pixie nose—

Suddenly Dorothy realized who *could* have done such a vile, monstrous thing. "The answer's as plain as the nose on her face!"

Chapter 39

"You know who did this?" Doyle asked heatedly. "Show me the brute, and I'll tear him limb from limb."

Dorothy wondered, *Now where did I see him last?* She couldn't be sure. Finally she said, "I don't know. I guess we'll have to organize a manhunt."

"Gladly!" Doyle said. Even Fairbanks seemed thrilled at hunting down the murderer. Again she wondered what it would be like to be one of these virile men. What hot-blooded, callous thoughts rushed through their single-minded brains? She felt a mix of envy and repulsion.

But Benchley didn't seem quite so full of bloodlust. Actually, he seemed rather deep in thought. "What if," he said slowly, "instead of a manhunt, we first try a dog hunt?"

"Benchley's right!" Fairbanks said. "We'll hunt this murderer down like a dog."

"No, no," Benchley said, amused. "That's not what I meant. I mean we use the dog to do the hunting." And he gazed down at the furry little figure of Woody, who had again hopped into the large, empty seafood carton and was busy sniffing about.

"That's it!" Dorothy cried. "Come with me."

She snatched up the dog and then grabbed the carton. She led the group out of the pantry and into the corridor. Then, to their surprise, she put the dog down again and shoved the carton to his nose. "Here, Woody, here." Then she tossed the carton back into the pantry and shut the door. "Now, go! Find!"

But the dog just stood there, looking up at her expectantly with his big, wet eyes.

"Go, Woody. Find the smell!" she urged.

The dog put his nose to the concrete floor and sniffed.

"Good boy. That's it!"

He sniffed his way back to the pantry door, then looked up at her and barked.

The men groaned.

"No, my little man. Find where it came from!" she said desperately to the dog. Then she turned to Doyle. "I thought Kingsley said this would work."

Doyle shrugged his shoulders.

When she looked back down again, the dog had trotted away. He was now sniffing along the corridor and moving away from the kitchen.

"Good boy!" she cheered.

"Follow that dog!" Benchley said. And they did.

Woody scampered toward the street entrance of the service corridor. But before he reached the heavy door to the street (which was now locked and barred), he made a quick right turn toward the door to the lobby. He was moving faster now. But then he had to stop at the leather-clad swinging door and wait to be let through.

Dorothy pushed open the door. Woody hurried into the lobby. They found themselves between the telephone operator's office on the left and the front desk on their right. The lobby was deserted, but they could hear Woollcott's nasal voice and the murmur of the crowd in the dining room at the upper end of the lobby.

The dog zipped forward, then darted to the right toward

281

the front foyer. He was momentarily out of sight, and they heard him give a quick bark. Then they heard a grunt, a thump and a plaintive yelp. Woody came sliding toward them across the tile floor, as though he had been given a hard kick.

Dorothy was the first to round the corner and see the tall man at the front entrance. He wore a waiter's clothes. He faced away from her and was shoving furiously and ineffectually at the locked doors. His clawlike hands ripped at the paper quarantine notice. He seemed to Dorothy to be both dangerously enraged and yet wretchedly pitiable.

Then he saw her out of the corner of his eye and turned his desperate gaze at her.

"You," he sneered at her. "You and your pampered, precious friends—!"

Benchley, Doyle and Fairbanks were behind her now.

"You don't even know me," she said. "But I know you."

She stared into his bright eyes and studied his thin face, his high cheekbones and his narrow, pointed nose.

"He's not a waiter," Benchley said. "He doesn't even work here."

"Why, that's the ice deliveryman!" Fairbanks said, perplexed. "The one who spilled that tub of ice at my party!"

"Oh, but he's much more than that. Aren't you?" she said to the man. "In fact, you're Bibi's brother."

Her statement took the men momentarily by surprise — it was just enough of a moment for the man to make his move. He lunged forward and grabbed Woody by the scruff of the neck. Fairbanks, a natural athlete, rushed forward to tackle him. But the tall man flung the poor dog toward Fairbanks' midsection.

Fairbanks deftly caught the dog as though catching a football and tucked Woody tightly into the crook of his arm — but doing so slowed him down. At the same instant, Dorothy instinctively reached forward to grab the dog. She suddenly found herself entangled with Fairbanks, which prevented him from chasing after the man.

Moving quickly, the man dodged around them and was now running full tilt toward the dining room.

"After the blackguard!" Doyle yelled, leading the chase. Although he was a big and virile man for his age, he was no match for the younger man's speed.

The man reached the threshold to the dining room, shoved his way into the crowd and quickly disappeared from their sight.

Fairbanks handed Woody over to Dorothy, then he sprinted forward and quickly caught up to Doyle. But the two of them stopped at the edge of the crowd and stood on tiptoes to see over everyone's heads to determine where the man went.

Fairbanks jumped straight up to get a better look. "I see him! He's almost halfway to Woollcott already. Come on!"

Fairbanks slipped into the crowd as though parting a curtain, and Doyle followed. But, like a curtain, the opening closed quickly. And Dorothy and Benchley found themselves against a seemingly impenetrable wall of people.

"We'll never get through this mob in time," Benchley said.

"We don't have to," Dorothy said. "We can go around."

She turned and hurried back through the lobby. Benchley followed. They rounded the front desk and pushed through the leather-clad door to the service corridor. They hurried past the pantry and back into the kitchen.

"I thought I told you not to bring that dog—!" the chef wailed.

She ignored him as they rushed through the busy kitchen.

They burst into the dining room and nearly bumped into Woollcott. He was facing the crowd and holding the upturned top hat over his head. He was in the middle of making some kind of announcement.

"And I have here the most valuable postage stamp in all the world—the invert tête-bêche, the 'Bearded Lady'—in this very hat!" he said in his most theatrical voice.

Dorothy tugged at his tuxedo. She hissed at him, "Never mind that game. It's too late. We've already found the killer."

Woollcott turned to her with incomprehension inscribed on his face. "You . . . *what*? But our plan—"

All of a sudden a tall figure leaped from the crowd toward Woollcott. Dorothy automatically clutched Woody closer to her and backed away, bumping against Benchley.

But the attacker wasn't the tall man in the waiter's outfit as she might have guessed. It was Jordan.

"Give it to me!" he yelled at Woollcott, and grasped for the top hat. But Woollcott's chubby arms clamped the hat to his belly as tightly as a vise.

Then, to Dorothy's surprise, the tall man in the waiter's uniform did jump into their midst. He shoved Woollcott and Jordan out of his way and raced toward the kitchen. Woollcott and Jordan fell down in a heap at Dorothy's feet. But before the man could get entirely past her and through the doors, Woody lunged forward and snapped. The man yowled in pain but didn't slow down. He shouldered his way through the swinging doors and into the kitchen.

Jordan was now on his feet, with the top hat in his hands and a victorious smile on his thin lips. He pushed through the crowd to get away. Woollcott lay on his back on the floor, twisting like a tortoise unable to get to its feet.

As soon as Jordan was safely out of their reach, he turned back around. He held aloft the hat, which was now crumpled into a tight ball in his hand. "Ha, I have it! Finally I have it back!"

But from behind Jordan, the taller of the two nuns appeared. "What do you have, mister?"

Jordan was slightly taken aback but not enough to quell his feeling of victory. "The tête-bêche! The 'Bearded Lady'! I have it!"

The taller nun, now joined by the other nun, said, "You sure about that? 'Cause then what do we have here?" and held up the silver locket.

Jordan's look of triumph disappeared. He reached for the locket to snatch it away, but the nun was too quick for him and pulled it out of his reach.

"Uh-uh," the second nun chided. "You can look, but you better not touch!"

Then, with a taunting look, the first nun popped the locket open for Jordan to see.

"But it's empty," Jordan said, and the victorious smile returned to his face. "Didn't you dimwits even look inside it first?"

The second nun grabbed the locket out of the other one's hands and looked inside. "Damn it! He's right. It's been empty all this time! Where the hell is that stamp?"

Jordan held up the balled top hat. "Right in here, sisters." Then he hobbled away through the crowd toward the lobby. "*Pax vobiscum*, suckers!"

The nuns followed him.

By this time Doyle and Fairbanks had joined Dorothy and Benchley. Woollcott had finally risen to his feet. "What's going on?" he yelled.

"Where's that damned deliveryman?" Fairbanks asked.

"He just went into the kitchen," Dorothy said.

"Dr. Hurst needs that stamp back," Doyle said. "We must split up—to divide and conquer."

"I'm going after that bastard who murdered Bibi," she said. "Who's with me?"

Both Benchley and Fairbanks stepped forward.

"No, Fred," she said to Benchley. "You go after Jordan. You never liked him anyway." She moved close and gave him a kiss on the cheek. "Take care of yourself."

To her surprise, Benchley blushed. He turned quickly, grabbed Woollcott by the sleeve and moved through the crowd after Jordan and the nuns.

She looked to Doyle and Fairbanks and gave Woody an affectionate squeeze. "Let's get him, boys!"

They once again entered the kitchen, and she braced herself for another of the chef's tirades. But although the room was crowded with waiters and kitchen staff, all was silent and still.

Jacques stood frozen at his preparation table. His head was bare, and his face was as white as his smock. On the cutting board in front of him, his tall white chef's hat was skewered through the middle with his long carving knife.

When he saw Dorothy, Jacques pointed at the opening to the basement stairs. He spoke in a hoarse whisper. "That man, he went down there."

With Doyle and Fairbanks right behind her, she hurried toward the stairwell.

"Mrs. Parker," the chef said. "I would not go down there if I were you."

She gathered her courage, held Woody tightly and descended the darkened stairs. Fairbanks and Doyle followed.

Chapter 40

Benchley and Woollcott threaded through the dining room's buzzing crowd and emerged into the quiet and nearly deserted lobby.

They arrived just in time to see Jordan, running full speed, suddenly stumble and fall hard to the floor.

Harpo Marx lay half-awake on a couch and with one leg extended out.

"Have a nice trip?" he asked Jordan. "See you next fall!"

In a moment the two nuns were almost on top of Jordan and ready to rip him to shreds.

But then Jordan did something unexpected—he slammed the heel of his big black orthopedic shoe against the floor. The heel and sole popped off, and a small snub-nosed pistol sprung up into the air. Jordan caught it with a practiced hand and quickly pointed the gun at the nuns. They couldn't stop in time. They skidded across the smooth hardwood floor and looked as though they would collide with him.

But in a flash Jordan was on his feet. He reached out and grabbed the shorter nun around the waist. He held the pistol to the nun's head.

"Stop right where you are!" Jordan commanded.

The other nun froze, hands in the air. Benchley, Woollcott and Harpo halted in their tracks as well.

"Jordan, what do you think you're doing?" Benchley asked. "You really don't have a clubfoot after all?"

Jordan still held the crushed top hat in the hand that encircled the nun's waist. "I'm returning the stamp to the rightful owner—the London Museum. I was assigned to do it, and I always finish the job."

"Assigned?" Benchley said. "By Dr. Hurst?"

Jordan snickered. "That crazy old fool? Hell no. I'm a Pink agent working undercover. I was hired by Lloyd's of London to bring the Bearded Lady safely back to England. It's insured for millions, and they don't want to pay up if they can avoid it."

"A Pink agent?" Benchley asked. Then he remembered Dr. Hurst's telegram. LLOYDS HIRED PINKS. . . .

"What the devil is a Pink agent?" Woollcott sneered.

"A Pinkerton!" Jordan said indignantly. "A detective. A private investigator. You know, 'The Eye That Never Sleeps'?"

"Well, what do you know, Aleck?" Benchley muttered. "We had a detective right here all this time. You didn't need to pretend to be one after all."

"Pretend!" Woollcott roared. "Who said anything about pretending?"

"The eye that never sleeps, huh?" said the tall nun, who had produced a large pistol and now aimed it directly at Jordan. "You certainly slept when we knocked you on the head and took the locket from your shoe. You slept like a baby. And now I'm going to put you to sleep for good."

"It's Bibi's brother?" Doyle asked Dorothy as they moved cautiously and quietly along yet another twisty, darkened subbasement corridor. "How did you know?"

"Yes, how did you know that?" Fairbanks asked.

"I should have known it sooner," she said. "They have exactly the same pixie nose."

"No one else recognized the similarity," Doyle said. "A beautiful Broadway starlet and a lowly ice deliveryman—who would guess they are siblings?"

"Well, I didn't," she said. "Not at first. Not until I saw that invoice with the name 'B. Bibelot' on the bottom. But the initial *B* is not for Bibi. It's for—I don't know—Bill or Bob or Barry. . . ."

"How did you even know Bibi had a brother?" Doyle asked.

"Jane Grant mentioned it in passing last night. She wrote a puff piece on Bibi a few months ago."

"Can you be sure that he was the one who murdered her—his very own sister?" Doyle asked with distaste.

"Once it was apparent that Bibi was killed by dry ice, then it just became a question of who had access to a bucketful of it. Frank Case told me they usually just throw it out into the alley to dispose of it. But because the whole hotel was locked up last night, it seemed likely that the dry ice was still somewhere inside. And the person who had access to it was the one who brought it to the hotel in the first place—"

She stopped. Up ahead in the darkness there was a sudden wail. Woody trembled in her arms.

Doyle cocked his head to hear. "That's someone in pain. Quick, we must go!"

"Hold on," she said. "That wasn't someone. That was some*thing*."

"What are you talking about?" Fairbanks asked. "That was an inhuman scream."

"It was inhuman, all right," she said. "That was the sound of the freezer door."

Very slowly and reluctantly, she continued forward. Doyle and Fairbanks followed right behind her.

"Let's be very cautious, my friends," Doyle said—quite unnecessarily, Dorothy thought.

They reached a corner, and she took a cautious peek around the bend. The tunnel was empty. She saw only the closed door of the walk-in freezer. Just the sight of it gave her chills.

"He must be inside," she whispered.

"I say we leave him in there, then," Fairbanks suggested. "Let him freeze to death for what he did."

"Certainly not," Doyle said in a low voice. "Freezing's too good for him. He should be brought to justice and his crimes paraded in the light of day. Dorothy, what do you think?"

She looked back and forth between their stern faces. She decided she wasn't too thrilled about either option.

"How about we split the difference?" she said after a moment's thought. "We'll let him cool his heels in there awhile, and when he's had enough—when he's nearly frozen stiff and harmless—then we'll drag him out. That's a kinder gesture than he gave to me and Mr. Benchley when he locked us in there."

Suddenly the door swung open with that deafening, rusty wail. Woody leaped out of Dorothy's arms and sped away around the corner, back from where they had come. Bibi's brother stepped halfway out of the freezer. Something glinted in his raised hand. He flung it hard at them.

Dorothy—already half-turned away to see where Woody had gone—managed to step aside. The object whirred past her head. It hit Fairbanks right between the eyes with a sickening thump and knocked him backward. His head smacked against the stone wall, and his body, limp as a rag doll, slid to the floor. Across the ground skittered the shattered chunks of the thrown object—a thick icicle.

The man disappeared back into the freezer but left the door wide open.

"Stay away!" His voice echoed from inside. "Just leave me alone!"

"You detestable coward," Doyle thundered, his big hands balled into fists. "Come out of there or—"

She put a hand on Doyle's arm to quiet him. Then she called out, "Tell us, what's your name? Is it Bill? Bob?"

"Blake."

"Blake"? Jeez, one kid named Bibi and the other one named Blake? What kind of oddball parents did these two have? No wonder both children turned out so wrong.

She spoke as patiently as she could. "Listen, Blake, you didn't mean to kill your sister, did you?"

"Yes. Yes, I *did* mean to do it." His quavering voice echoed. "But . . . I-I didn't want to. I *had* to. I couldn't take any more!"

The taller nun still had the big gun pointed at Jordan. "Now give me the stamp and let my partner go. Or else." Then the nun pulled off her—or rather *his*—veil, revealing a square, closely shaved head.

"Look!" sputtered Woollcott to Benchley. "That nun is a man. A man!"

"Why, certainly," said Benchley with a bored yawn. "Both nuns are men. Didn't you know? I've known that for ages."

"You have?" Woollcott asked. "What other secrets are you keeping from me?"

"Well, both nuns are gangsters, of course," Benchley said matter-of-factly. "Anyone around here who knows anything knows that. They're here to steal the stamp from Dr. Hurst. Then they're supposed to take it to their boss in Brooklyn, who's going to sell it to an even worse gangster in Chicago. . . . Aleck, why are you looking at me with such a surprised expression? You mean to tell me you don't know *any* of this? And you call yourself a detective? Tsk-tsk."

291

Benchley was rather enjoying himself by teasing Woollcott this way. Then he noticed that the gangsters were staring at him, too. But unlike Woollcott's surprised expression, theirs were extremely angry.

"You!" said the tall one to Benchley. "You're the telephone operator! We been looking for you for hours. Don't go nowhere, mister. Soon as we take care of this little cream puff"—he waved his gun at Jordan—"then we're going to take care of you, and how."

But while the tall one was talking to Benchley, Jordan swung his snub-nosed pistol, aimed and fired. The bullet caught the tall gangster in the upper arm.

"Ow! That hurt," the gangster yelled, and clapped his hand to his injured arm. Then he reached out to take Jordan's pistol. "What is that, a .22? Give me that little peashooter before—"

Jordan fired again. But as he did so, the smaller gangster wriggled free from his grasp and knocked away his gun hand. The shot went into the grandfather clock with a metallic clang.

The smaller gangster swung his fist into Jordan's face. Jordan came back with a hard left hook—but this fist held the crumpled top hat. The taller one stepped in and stopped the punch with both hands. Then he grabbed the top hat.

"I guess that hat's ruined," Woollcott muttered sourly. "Well, it was last year's style anyhow."

Benchley whispered, "What about the stamp?"

Woollcott chuckled to him, "There's no stamp in there. Heaven knows where that damned stamp is!"

The shorter gangster socked Jordan in the jaw and snatched away his little pistol. Then he punched Jordan again, just for good measure. Jordan fell down in a heap.

The taller gangster unfurled the crumpled hat and reached inside.

"Perhaps," Benchley whispered, "now would be the time to make a hasty retreat. . . ."

The gangster pulled a small slip of white paper out of the hat. "This ain't no stamp!" He held it out at arm's length to read it. His voice thundered. "*Detective—Woollcott!* Who the hell is Detective Woollcott?"

"Yes," Woollcott whispered to Benchley, "that *is* a swell idea." He took a small step backward.

"The fat one! He's trying to get away," the taller gangster yelled. "*He's* got the stamp! Get him!"

Chapter 41

Dorothy glanced over her shoulder. Fairbanks lay on the hard concrete floor with his head against the stone wall. He moved slightly, groggily. His eyes were half-lidded. He wouldn't be doing backflips anytime soon, she thought.

At her side Doyle, anxious to rush forward, puffed in frustration.

Should she peek inside the walk-in freezer? Would it be better to talk face-to-face with Blake Bibelot?

This man was truly deadly, she reminded herself. She glanced again at Fairbanks, who had been knocked down with one blow. And she knew that Blake had fought like a devil against Benchley, Case and Luigi in the darkened kitchen. Also, Blake was the one who had locked her and Benchley in this very same freezer.

So, on second thought, perhaps it was best to keep her distance.

"Listen, Blake," she called out. "I think I understand what you're going through."

"You don't know a damned thing—!"

"Hear me out," she interrupted. "Bibi was ashamed of you—of her background—and you accepted that. You wanted to help her to achieve superstardom, so you sacrificed everything. She even called you her 'guardian angel,' didn't she? She also referred to you as her 'mysterious benefactor'—as if you were some Wall Street tycoon or Arab sheik or British nobleman. And yet you were no less generous than a millionaire, even though you're only a regular working Joe. Am I right?"

He didn't answer. Doyle folded his arms over his big bear chest—he didn't want talk; he wanted action.

Dorothy continued, "You worked hard. You were the one who paid for her dance lessons, her voice lessons, her fancy clothes and anything—*everything*—that would make her a star, didn't you?"

Blake still didn't answer. She felt that his silence meant that she had guessed correctly so far.

"But," she said, "when Bibi did achieve stardom—when she became the toast of Broadway—what did she do? She forgot all about you and all your sacrifices. She was supposed to pay you back, wasn't she? What did you want for yourself? A college education? To open a restaurant? Start a family of your own in comfort? What?"

"A farm." Blake's voice came softly. "A quiet little farm. Away from the city. Away from the noise, the people, the smells. I had the land all picked out—"

"But Bibi reneged on the deal. You devoted years of your life to someone, only to be unrepaid. I think I know what that's like," she said, unable to keep the emotion out of her voice. "And then what happened? You came to deliver ice—"

"Fish!" he said. "I deliver fish. We deliver ice as a courtesy."

"All right. So you were delivering some ice to this posh penthouse party, and what do you find? Your very own sister prancing through the place naked for all to see. Was that what you had scrimped and saved and sacrificed everything for? So she could treat her life like a joke?"

295

"So you do understand?" His voice had lost its edge. The edge was replaced by something like hope. "So you know I had to do it. I had enough. I couldn't take any more. She saw me—that's when I spilled the ice all over the carpet—but she didn't care. She even winked at me! In her head she was laughing at me, I know. Seeing her act like that—it was the last straw."

"Certainly," she said sympathetically. "So you waited until Bibi was alone. Lucky for you, someone else doped her with chloroform. The rest was easy. All you had to do was dump the dry ice in the tub, lock the door so no one could come in and find her, and put a towel against the floor to keep the gas from escaping. Then you climbed out the window, closed it, went across the roof and climbed back inside. A piece of cake for a quick young man like yourself."

"You make it sound like a crime, like I'm some lousy thief or something. She had it coming. She was the criminal. *She* was the thief! She stole my life from me!"

Doyle couldn't be contained much longer. He was nearly shaking with anger. He muttered to Dorothy in a low whisper through gritted teeth, "The unmanly coward. Let me at him."

"What was that?" Blake called out.

"Nothing," she said. "Just come on out. Come with us. Bibi already took this much of your life. Don't sacrifice the rest of it. Come on out."

"And what?" he said desperately. "It's too late to try to bargain. They'll be after me. But as soon as I get out of this hotel, I'm going straight up to Canada. Open, empty spaces. A man can live free up there—"

"All right," she lied. "I'll get you out. I'll send you on your way. Just don't hurt anyone else. Come on out."

Doyle gaped at her with rage on his face. She put a calming hand on his arm.

Blake peeked halfway out of the freezer. His eyes looked haunted. "You'll let me go?"

"If you leave quietly, I'll—"

Suddenly Fairbanks was on his feet with a roar and lunged forward. "I'll throttle the cad!"

Blake didn't blink. His face was as hard as stone. He stepped forward menacingly and raised his hand to strike. He gripped a long, thick icicle, as hard and sharp as a steel spike.

"I don't have the stamp!" Woollcott screamed in a high-pitched voice. He turned to run, his hands up in the air.

The two gangsters charged forward. Benchley couldn't move. He expected to be knocked aside at best or trampled and pulverized at worst.

Then from across the room a puckish voice shouted, "Hey, you dumb, ugly goons!"

It was Harpo Marx! The Berley brothers turned toward him and slowed down.

Harpo put his thumb to his nose. "When you two were babies, your mother should have kept the dirty nappies and thrown *you* away."

It was only a moment's diversion, but it was enough. Benchley tiptoed quickly behind the gangsters' backs on his way to the front door. Benchley saw the first rays of daylight shining in through the ice-frosted plate windows ahead of him. And he detected the silhouettes of a few vehicles moving slowly on the snowy street.

"What kind of sisters are you, anyways?" Harpo jeered. "You sure got some lousy habits." He yanked one button after another off his vest and threw them at the gangsters.

The tall one, indifferent to the flying buttons, stalked toward Harpo. He raised his gun, but Harpo dodged behind one of the lobby's stately columns. He was safe for the moment. But now the shorter gangster, with Jordan's snub-nosed pistol in his hand, was moving toward the other side of the column.

Harpo wouldn't be safe much longer. So Benchley

sprinted to the twin glass doors of the front entrance. He banged on them as loudly as he could and shouted so that anyone on the sidewalk would hear him. "Help! Help!"

The two gangsters stopped in their tracks.

"It's the telephone operator!" the tall one yelled. "*He's* got the stamp! Get him!"

The tough brothers charged forward with their black habits flying behind them. Benchley banged on the door all the harder. He looked over his shoulder to see how quickly they approached him. The smaller one stopped abruptly and raised Jordan's little pistol. "Give us the stamp, or else!"

Benchley didn't have it. Readying himself, he took a deep breath. "Let's go with 'or else,' shall we?"

"You asked for it!" the short gangster said, and fired the gun.

But Benchley was ready—he dropped to the floor with his back to the door. Right behind him, the small-caliber bullet hit the door at chest height. The glass pane shattered into a million sparkling shards. Benchley tucked himself into a ball and launched himself backward through the jagged opening. He felt relieved as he landed safely on a thick layer of soft, fluffy snow.

This is heaven, he thought. *Although this heaven is rather chilly on the nape of one's neck.*

Suddenly the two gangsters burst one after the other through the opening. They were surprised to find Benchley on the snowy ground at their feet and jumped over him on instinct. The tall one landed awkwardly, and the shorter one crashed into him. Together they tumbled forward, their black habits swirling around them, sending up clouds of snow. They rolled to a stop directly at the feet of Captain Church. Behind the captain stood Detective O'Rannigan, as well as a pair of uniformed policemen and a five-man crew who wore coats marked *NYC Department of Health.* Parked at the curb were O'Rannigan's unmarked sedan, a police squad car, and a large panel van.

"Well, good morning, sisters!" O'Rannigan chuckled. "Or should I say 'brothers'? Thanks for coming out to greet us."

The tall gangster pounded his hand on the snow in frustration. He looked around for Benchley. "You don't really have the stamp after all, do you?"

Benchley shook his head.

The tall brother turned to the shorter one. "Well, this new year is starting off pretty crappy."

"Get used to it," O'Rannigan said with a grim smile. "Where you're going, you've got five to ten crappy years ahead of you."

With a roar, Douglas Fairbanks leaped past Dorothy and Doyle. He lunged forward and collided into Blake, ramming his head into Blake's abdomen. As they stumbled backward together, Blake brought the icicle down toward Fairbanks' head. But Blake's aim was thrown off by the struggle. The icicle glanced sideways against the back of Fairbanks' skull.

Dorothy and Doyle stepped closer to look inside. Blake twisted his body and spun Fairbanks to the ground—to the floor of the freezer. Fairbanks' body hit the hard, cold floor with a dull thump, and Blake landed on top of him. Then Blake was quickly on his feet again. Fairbanks was motionless on the floor.

Blake, with anger and resentment in his eyes, turned on Dorothy. He still held the stump of the icicle in his hand. His voice was a hoarse snarl. "You lied to me. You'll betray me, won't you? Well, I won't let you. I won't let anyone betray me again."

He charged forward.

"The door!" she yelled at Doyle.

Doyle grabbed the edge of the big door and tried to push it closed. It screamed on its rusty hinges. But Blake was too quick, and the door moved too slowly. Blake had his shoulder against the back of it. Then Doyle put all his weight against the front of the door. They struggled against each other, but Doyle—despite his size and strength—couldn't last. Dorothy saw the sweat break out on his old, grizzled forehead, and the desperate, wild look in Blake's eyes.

Then she reached for her little purse, which she had slung on her shoulder and nearly forgotten about.

"Just hold him a little longer," she yelled to Doyle.

"I'm—trying!" Doyle said. But Blake was pushing too hard. He'd be able to shove his way out any moment.

She dug her hand into her purse and searched around.

"No time for that!" Doyle grunted. "Help me!"

She agreed. She flung the purse—and all its contents—as hard as she could through the opening. She heard it hit the inside of the freezer with a shattering sound.

Blake turned his head. "What—?"

It was enough of a distraction for her to help Doyle to slam the door closed tightly.

"But there's no lock!" he wheezed. "He'll shove it open again in no time. And Fairbanks—he's trapped in there with that madman."

She shook her head. "Nope. Blake Bibelot won't bother us, or Fairbanks, anymore today."

Doyle leaned his weight against the door and looked at it expectantly. But it didn't move. After a moment he looked at her quizzically.

"The bottle of chloroform," she said. "Still had it in my purse. He's literally knocked out cold."

Chapter 42

Dorothy and Doyle stood by the side of Dr. Hurst's bed. The thin, white-haired old man opened his one good eye and slowly turned it to them. His stony expression seemed to grow alarmed when he saw them. He raised his arm. His hand, held like a claw, jabbed feebly toward them.

"Tête-bêche!" he moaned. "Tête-bêche!"

Doyle followed the motion with his eyes. He looked over his shoulder in the direction Dr. Hurst seemed to indicate with his hand.

"Does he mean the door?" Doyle asked. "Something coming in—or out—of the door?"

A tear, then another, streamed down the doctor's wrinkled face. He held his paralyzed hand out one last time, then dropped it to his side. He turned his face away.

"Oh dear me," Dorothy said softly. She suddenly understood.

She reached down, grasped the old man's fist and turned it over. She uncurled the tightly coiled fingers and opened up the nearly petrified hand.

And there in the center of Dr. Hurst's palm was a connected pair of postage stamps. But the markings were almost unidentifiable. The colored ink of the stamps had run

301

and had stained the skin of his hand, as a child's chalk drawing spreads across the sidewalk in a summer downpour. The "Bearded Lady"—the most valuable stamp in the world—was utterly ruined.

Dorothy looked at the old man's eyes and watched the tears stream down the side of his face and dampen his pillow. He clamped his eyes shut.

"Tête-bêche," he moaned almost silently, painfully.

Benchley stood in the lobby and looked out the plate glass windows. He watched O'Rannigan shove the handcuffed Berley brothers into the rear seat of his unmarked sedan. He saw Frank Case talk to the men from the Department of Health, and he watched them remove the seal from the door and scrape off what was left of the quarantine notice. A minute before, the two officers had dragged the unconscious Blake Bibelot into their squad car. And now an ambulance was arriving for Dr. Hurst, and a hearse had come for Bibi.

Benchley watched it all as though it were happening far away—as though he were seeing these things from a distance.

Then just behind him—so close that he almost flinched—he heard a giggle and a squeal. He turned and saw John Simpson—still red from chicken pox, still wearing his pajama bottoms—hugging two little children, one boy and one girl. A thin, lovely woman—lovely except for her chicken pox—wrapped her arms around her husband and their children.

Benchley checked his watch. Then he went to the coat room for his hat and topcoat.

Dorothy and Doyle got off the elevator and entered the bustling lobby.

"So Bibi's murder really had nothing to do with the missing stamp," she said, as much to herself as to Doyle.

302

"Evidently not," he said. "Except for Quentin using the locket as a hiding place. Poor choice, that. Still, he couldn't have foreseen that the stamp would wind up around the neck of a naked actress in a bath full of champagne."

"But why?" she asked plaintively. "Why would a wealthy, prominent physician take the risk to steal such a priceless item?"

Captain Church approached them. He looked very tired. He probably hadn't slept in the past two days, Dorothy thought. She wondered whether she herself looked as worn out.

"I may be able to answer some of that," Church said. "I have been in communication by telephone and telegraph with Scotland Yard. Apparently, the hospital to which Dr. Hurst devoted so much of his time was nearly bankrupt."

"St. Angus, bankrupt?" Doyle asked, bewildered.

Church nodded. "My counterpart at Scotland Yard believes that Dr. Hurst stole the stamp with the intention to sell it here in America in order to cover the hospital's financial losses back in England."

"So he did it to save his hospital?" she asked. The mean image that she had of Dr. Hurst didn't really match with such a noble—and reckless—deed. Still, she thought, devils sometimes look like saints, and vice versa. She turned to Doyle. "Isn't there a better way to finance a hospital?"

"Most certainly," he said. "Indeed, if it had been a matter of dire urgency, I certainly could have arranged to transfer a healthy injection of funds from my own personal assets. Then again, Quentin always was a stubborn one, as I've told you. Always had to do things his own way. But I'll wager he'd sooner die than let that hospital go under. Of course, now that I know—and given Quentin's feeble physical state—I shall see to it personally that St. Angus suffers no further insolvency."

"Very good of you," Church said. "Now if only we could find that priceless artifact ..."

"Show him," Dorothy said to Doyle.

Church's stony face registered surprise.

Doyle withdrew a neatly folded square handkerchief. Then he unfolded it and offered the police captain the withered remains of the postage stamps. "Take it. Send it back to Scotland Yard."

Church stared for a long moment at the faded, wrinkled bits of paper. Then he took the handkerchief, carefully folded it up and put it gently in his pocket. "I will be sure not to sneeze on this."

Dorothy watched him turn and walk away. And then she laughed. "I've *never* heard that guy make a joke before. Will wonders never cease!"

Doyle smiled warmly, expansively. "No, fortunately for all of us, they never will." He was looking in the direction Church had taken toward the front doors. There stood a very respectable-looking older woman—undoubtedly it was Lady Doyle. He took a step toward the woman, then quickly turned back to Dorothy. "Lovely to have made your acquaintance, my dear Dorothy. Keep writing." His hand, as big as a bear paw, gently shook her little hand. "Oh, and one more thing. Kingsley says 'snowdrop.' Does that mean anything to you?"

Snowdrop? She shook her head.

But Doyle had already turned away and hurried toward his wife. He greeted her with open arms and embraced her tightly for a long moment, and they eventually left the hotel arm in arm.

Seeing this embrace—so soon after the confrontation with Blake Bibelot—left Dorothy with mixed, bittersweet feelings. Relationships are so complicated that sometimes it's easier to simply stay aloof, she thought. Just look at the snarl and tangle of emotions between Bibi and Blake—devotion, jealousy, resentment, indebtedness, ingratitude—and they were simply brother and sister! How much more complicated it is when you're in love. . . .

304

But then again, Doyle and his wife didn't make it look so complicated. A kiss, a hug and then walking arm in arm ... how difficult is that? Perfectly natural. And now she noticed the others around her—greeting each other, hugging each other, so happy just to be together. A few steps away Jane Grant held the hands of her husband, Harold Ross. On one of the couches sat Ruth Hale side by side with her husband, Heywood Broun. She could see Mary Pickford away in the dining room, holding a very groggy Doug Fairbanks closely but tenderly.

Dorothy hugged her own arms to herself for warmth—the opening in the door had made the lobby chilly.

Then it occurred to her—where the hell was Benchley?

She figured that he would ... That is, he owed her ... She had at least expected ...

Well, damn it! He was supposed to *kiss her*! Where had he run off to now?

"Looking for someone?" Woollcott had suddenly and silently sidled up to her. "Robert left, if that's who you're looking for. Had to catch the train home. Had to gallop—huckety-huck—back to the bosom of his family."

Benchley left? But he ... He didn't even ... He left and he didn't even say good-bye? What ...?

She looked at Woollcott. He could be so cruel sometimes. And she hated that term, "the bosom" of his family—and she hated it all the more for the context that Woollcott now put it in.

"Ah," Woollcott sighed contentedly, gazing around at the loving couples and families. "I love a happy ending."

But she thought of the many sad endings she'd recently witnessed: Blake, Bibi, Dr. Hurst, Jordan.

She said, "I know this will come as a shock to you, Aleck. But in all history, which has held billions and billions of human beings, not a single one ever had a happy ending."

He turned to her with a superior look. "Happiness is where you find it. Apparently you have not found it."

She recalled, like a whisper in her ear, the word *snow-drop*.

She sauntered toward the front door, pushed it open slightly and reached down to scoop up a handful of snow. It was cold, yet delicate. She observed a few individual tiny flakes that lay on the skin of her fingers and outside of the lump of snow in her hand. As she moved back into the warm lobby, some of the flakes melted and yet some did not. Nature is truly a wonder to behold sometimes.

Then, while Woollcott had his back turned, she dropped the snow down his collar.

"AHH-haaa!" he shrieked. For a moment his body went perfectly straight, as though hit by a bolt of lightning. Then he hopped and danced and tried to reach around with both hands toward his back. "AHH-haaa!" He jerked and bounced his way out of the lobby.

"Ah," she sighed to herself, watching him go. "Sometimes you just have to make your own happy ending." Then she yelled after him, "And stop saying 'Aha!'"

She turned to go up to her room. She was thinking about cuddling up with Woody and perhaps another hot mug of that creamy coffee and brandy.

$\mathcal{H}$istorical $\mathcal{N}$ote

It may seem unlikely that Sir Arthur Conan Doyle, the creator of the world's foremost deductive detective, would become a convert to the illogical and downright odd Spiritualist movement. But that's history for you—it's sometimes more difficult to swallow than fiction.

Here I'll try to distinguish between history and fiction, at least in regard to this story.

The Game of Murder

The members of the Algonquin Round Table loved their games. (Robert Benchley was the exception—he didn't enjoy the ferocious competition involved.) In addition to the sparkling wordplay at their daily lunches, they played cribbage, croquet, poker and many other games—all with almost maniacal fervor.

One of their games was Murder, and it was played as described in this story (although they referred to the detective role as the "District Attorney"). Harpo Marx, in his book *Harpo Speaks!*, describes one particularly memorable game of Murder. In this game Harpo played the murderer, and Alexander Woollcott was the District Attorney. Harpo used an ingenious method to commit his crime—he sneaked into the bathroom, wrote the fatal message in lipstick on the roll of toilet paper and then rolled it back up.

Alice Duer Miller, an occasional member of the Vicious Circle, was the unfortunate recipient of the message. As required by the rules of the game, she remained at the scene of the crime—for five hours!—while the other players searched and sleuthed.

Harpo writes:

> Aleck put the finger on me without having to ask a single question. I had outsmarted myself. I had tipped my hand without knowing it. What I had written in lipstick on the roll of toilet paper was: YOU ARE DED. Little Acky had a terrible tantrum and went to bed without his supper. He refused to play with anybody who didn't obey the rules. The Murderer had to confront the Victim face-to-face or else there was no crime committed. . . . Alice herself, on the other hand, couldn't have been more delighted. A stroke of genius, she called my plot. Too bad it had to be an illiterate stroke of genius, she added.

Dorothy Parker

In the first chapter of this book, Dorothy acknowledges that she never went to college and didn't even finish high school. This is true. She left school at age fourteen to take odd jobs and to take care of her ailing father.

Also, Dorothy was instructed by the Sisters of Charity at a Roman Catholic elementary school—and she apparently gave the sisters a lot to pray about. Her Catholic school education reveals itself in this story, as she realizes that the Berley brothers (who are fictional) are certainly not nuns. While nuns may be mannish and a few may even have facial hair, Dorothy would have known full well that sisters of the early twentieth century would never pull up their skirts (even to their ankles) and run through a hotel lobby.

It also bears repeating that Dorothy and Benchley, although extremely close, were never known to have a romantic relationship.

Sir Arthur Conan Doyle

As a point of fact, and as all Sherlockians know, Sherlock Holmes never did say "Elementary, my dear Watson." (And while we're clearing up misconceptions, Doyle received his knighthood for writing a book on the battles of the Boer War, not for inventing the world's most famous detective.)

Doyle did tour through America with his wife and family in the midtwenties. He had become extremely devoted to Spiritualism and was out to convert the world. He attended and hosted séances, gave lectures, donated and raised money for Spiritualist causes, and wrote books about it. (While he was visiting New York, his lecture and slide show nearly filled Carnegie Hall.) He affirmed that he had communicated with his dead son, Kingsley, but on both occasions it was through a medium. Many people at the time thought that he had lost his senses.

In this story Woollcott describes Doyle as a has-been. Not true. Doyle published another slew of Sherlock Holmes stories, *The Casebook of Sherlock Holmes*, in 1927.

In real life, as in this story, Doyle acted as a sort of consulting detective in a few cases. For one, he came to the defense of a neighborhood collie named Roy, who had been accused of killing sheep, and proved Roy could not have committed the crime. More importantly, Doyle acted as a detective in the case of George Edalji, a young lawyer convicted of a series of cattle mutilations. One of the ways that Doyle helped to show Edalji's innocence (in the court of public opinion at least) was by demonstrating that the young man's poor eyesight would have made him incapable of such a crime. Last but not least, Doyle even stepped in to assist when mystery writer Agatha Christie went mysteriously missing for nearly a dozen days. (For his efforts, Christie repaid him by mocking Sherlock Holmes, through the words of Hercule Poirot, in one of her stories.)

Doyle's friend in this story, Dr. Quentin Hurst, is fictional. His stamp-collecting book is based on and uses excerpts from a 1902 book, *Stamp Collecting as a Pastime*, by Edward J. Nankivell, an avid British stamp collector.

There is no such thing as the British "bearded lady" invert tête-bêche stamp.

Douglas Fairbanks and Mary Pickford

While Doyle was on his tour of the United States in 1923, he did indeed meet Douglas Fairbanks and Mary Pickford while in Hollywood. (Doyle described Mary as "intensely psychic . . . with many gifts of the spirit," while Fairbanks "had a robust open mind which only asked for definite experience.")

It's difficult to adequately describe what a huge celebrity Douglas Fairbanks was and what a long-lasting impact he had on moviemaking. Furthermore his star status multiplied when he married his equally famous wife, Mary Pickford. He was just about the biggest star on Broadway, and together they were the biggest superstars in Hollywood. On one occasion during World War I, Fairbanks went out to promote war bonds—when he showed up at the corner of Broad and Wall Streets in New York, some twenty to thirty thousand people had gathered to see him.

Fairbanks was a friend to Frank Case, owner of the Algonquin, long before Fairbanks became such a celebrity. When the Fairbankses came East, they stayed at the Algonquin. (Fairbanks was a teetotaler, though, so if he had thrown such a New Year's Eve party, he would not have served alcohol. But that would take a lot of the fun out of this story.)

However, there was (and is) no fancy penthouse at the top of the Algonquin Hotel.

The Algonquin Hotel

Although there is no penthouse, there is something of a "hidden" thirteenth floor, as briefly described in this book. It's set back from the facade, so it's not visible from the street, and it's used mostly for housekeeping.

Also, it's entirely possible that Dorothy might have taken Woodrow Wilson up to the roof. Frank Case tells the story of how an Arctic explorer once came to stay at the hotel—along with his four big Alaskan malamute sled dogs. Case, unflappable as usual, simply ordered the dogs to be housed on the roof.

Over the many years since it opened in 1902, the venerable literary landmark has gone through many, many updates, changes and renovations. (As of 2012, the Algonquin Hotel has undergone yet another redo—and it's now more beautiful and appealing than ever.)

While this story takes some literary license with the hotel (such as the addition of the penthouse), every effort was made to provide an accurate description of the approximate state of the hotel as it stood in the 1920s. At that time and for a number of years afterward, it was in part a residence hotel, and Dorothy Parker did live in a small suite on the second floor.

Jane Grant and Ruth Hale

There was no Mrs. Volney. (The Volney, now a co-op apartment house, was a residence hotel on Manhattan's Upper

East Side—it was the last place Dorothy Parker lived. She died there in 1967.)

But Jane Grant and Ruth Hale were real. As described in this story, Jane Grant was a writer for the *New York Times*, and she helped to found the *New Yorker* magazine with Harold Ross, her husband and a member of the Round Table.

Ruth Hale was a freelance writer whose stories appeared in the *New York Times*, *Vogue* and *Vanity Fair*. She was an outspoken (even fanatical) crusader for women's rights and was the first president of the Lucy Stone League. (Jane Grant was also a member.) This organization lobbied for a woman's legal right to keep her maiden name after marriage, which was not permitted at the time.

The Properties of Dry Ice

There was no Bibi Bibelot, no Blake Bibelot and no Benedict Jordan. (The Pinkerton Detective Agency was very real, though. Pinkerton still exists today, though it mostly provides security services, as opposed to "private eye" work.)

In any case, it is certainly possible for someone to be killed by dry ice. Or, to be more specific, it's possible for someone to be suffocated and killed by carbon dioxide gas that's formed after dry ice "melts." (Again, to be specific, dry ice doesn't actually melt—it sublimates, turning directly from a solid to a gas with no liquid state in between.)

As a matter of fact, New York's chief medical examiner in the 1920s, Dr. Charles Norris, investigated the case of five longshoremen who were found dead in the cargo hold of a steamship. The men were bunking in a storage room containing fruit, which was chilled with dry ice. The dead men's blood was found to be saturated with CO_2, and they had "obviously died of asphyxia."

HISTORICAL NOTE

So in this story, when Dorothy entered the bathroom and found Bibi dead in the tub, it wasn't Dorothy's nerves that failed her and caused her to feel faint—it was the lack of oxygen.

Truth be told, it would have been extremely unlikely for someone to be killed this way in the 1920s—dry ice was less common than it is now, because it was much more difficult and expensive to manufacture back then.

$\mathcal{A}$cknowledgements

I owe considerable thanks and recognition to:

Dorothy Parker, who is still an inspiration (and also something of a cautionary tale) for writers, aspiring authors, poets and hopeful storytellers all around the world.

Robert Benchley, one of the great humorists of the twentieth century, who is all but forgotten.

Frank Case, for his dryly witty history of his days (and nights) as owner and manager of the Algonquin Hotel in *Tales of a Wayward Inn.*

Sir Arthur Conan Doyle, for thoughtfully chronicling his 1920s tours of the United States in *Our American Adventure* and *Our Second American Adventure.*

Daniel Stashower, for his informative and evenhanded biography, *Teller of Tales: The Life of Arthur Conan Doyle.*

Deborah Blum, for her book that provided the impetus for "death by dry ice," *The Poisoner's Handbook: Murder and the Birth of Forensic Medicine in Jazz Age New York.*

Ken Ackerman, the "Dry Ice Man" at dryiceInfo.com, for explaining the properties of dry ice—and its requirements for being used as a murder weapon.

Joseph Ditta, reference librarian at the New-York Historical Society, for assistance with blueprints and clips in the Algonquin Hotel file in the George B. Corsa Collection.

315

ACKNOWLEDGMENTS

Alice de Almeida at the Algonquin Hotel, for the exhaustive tour of the entire building—from subbasement to roof. Also, the Algonquin's Barbara McGurn, for her memories of the glory days of the hotel. And, of course, Matilda the Cat, for her understated encouragement.

Mrs. Mary Pierce, for her behind-the-scenes insights into hotel service (albeit at the Waldorf Astoria) of yesteryear.

Michael Gibbons, as well as Kathleen Barrett and the other members of the Between Books Critique Group (a division of the Delaware Valley Sisters in Crime), for their editorial advice with the first draft.

Vince McIndoe (www.vincemcindoe.net), for his wonderful, evocative cover paintings for this series. My apologies for not acknowledging him until this book.

Sandy "Hard as Nails" Harding, editor extraordinaire, for her patience and kind encouragement.

Karin, as always, for her enduring support and cheer.

Of course, any factual errors are mine, not theirs.

About the Author

J. J. Murphy, an award-winning health care writer in Pennsylvania, is a lifelong Dorothy Parker fan. J.J. started writing the Algonquin Round Table Mysteries after the birth of twin daughters, as an escape from toddler television. Please visit J.J. on any of the social media platforms below.

CONNECT ONLINE

www.RoundTableMysteries.com
www.facebook.com/RoundTableMysteries
twitter.com/#!/rnd_tbl_mystry